THE GREAT LOS ANGELES BLIZZARD

THE GREAT LOS ANGELES BLIZZARD

A NOVEL BY
THOM RACINA

G.P. PUTNAM'S SONS,
NEW YORK

Published simultaneously in Canada by Longman Canada
Limited, Toronto.
SBN: 399-12033-5
Library of Congress Cataloging in Publication Data

Racina, Thom, 1947-
The great Los Angeles blizzard.

I. Title.
PZ4.R122Gr [PS3568.A25] 813'.5'4 77-4156
PRINTED IN THE UNITED STATES OF AMERICA

The Great Los Angeles Blizzard is based on an
idea by Thom Racina and Les Rumsey.

For Drs. William Mudge, Myron Shapero,
John David Romm, and—especially—
Mitchell Karlan.
Without them I would never have lived
to write this book.

PREFACE

"THE BIG FREEZE" OF 1977 BROUGHT AMERICA TO ITS KNEES. IN the worst winter in more than 100 years, millions were driven from their jobs, tens of thousands were stranded in automobiles or snowed into their houses, and hundreds upon hundreds died. The arctic storm which relentlessly battered the country left behind it a wave of death and destruction to human lives, to shelter, to business and commerce, to livestock, and to crops. Raging blizzards buried bodies on street corners as people fought to get to their homes. The natural gas supply was quickly depleted, and huge oil tankers with precious fuel lay motionless, frozen in ice in all major waterways of the land. Many froze to death as heat gave out; others died in the rubble of buildings which had collapsed because of accumulated snow, or in raging fires which were unable to be fought in the below-zero temperatures. The United States Army was called into several areas in the last hope that lives could somehow be spared. And snow fell for the first time in recorded history on Miami and Palm Beach, Florida.

The winter was merciful to only one part of the country, the far Southwest. While 14 feet of snow piled up on the streets of

Buffalo, New York, the residents of Los Angeles frolicked on the beaches in 80° degree temperatures.

This, then, is the story of what happened just a few years later, when the same arctic winds swept down into the U.S., bringing a storm more devastating and powerful than anyone could have imagined possible. This is the story of how that spared section of the country, the Pacific Southwest, specifically the Los Angeles Basin, finally got its share.

This is the story of what would become known in history as the Great Los Angeles Blizzard.

IT SNOWED AND IT SNOWED. . . . OUR SNOW WAS NOT ONLY SHAKEN FROM WHITEWASH BUCKETS DOWN THE SKY, IT CAME SHAWLING OUT OF THE GROUND AND SWAM AND DRIFTED OUT OF THE ARMS AND HANDS AND BODIES OF THE TREES; SNOW GREW OVERNIGHT ON THE ROOFS OF THE HOUSES LIKE A PURE AND GRANDFATHER MOSS, MINUTELY WHITE-IVIED THE WALLS AND SETTLED ON THE POSTMAN, OPENING THE GATE, LIKE A DUMB, NUMB THUNDERSTORM OF WHITE, TORN CHRISTMAS CARDS.

DYLAN THOMAS,
–from *A Child's Christmas in Wales*

THE FIRST DAY

THURSDAY, JANUARY 15
HIGH TEMPERATURE 37°; LOW 22°

THE PEOPLE OF LOS ANGELES—IN THAT CURIOUS SOUTHERN California tradition—took it in stride, even enjoyed it. The general subject of discussion all over the city was the weather, on the telephone, in the supermarkets, on the sound stages of movie studios, at the drive-ins and car washes, at banquets in the finest hotels. The fact that it was the coldest January on record—or any month for that matter—fascinated some people; it was a phenomenon not unlike an earthquake. Certainly not unique, but captivating.

Others found it a chore. They waited it out patiently with suntan lotion in hand, wondering where that California sun was and what the hell was it doing there. Still others said oh, well, everything's crazy out here, why not the weather, too? And then there were those who loved it, like the Beverly Hills matrons who enjoyed parading around in their heaviest mink coats. And still others hated it—the tourist trade was down, and motel owners cursed the dark skies. And the rest? Well, the rest felt changing emotions ranging from love to hate. The thing that everyone agreed on was that it was *interesting.*

Carter DeSimone, professor of science and meteorology at the University of Southern California, was certainly more interested than most; some people liked to say he had created the situation. He was a meticulously precise man when it came to his field of study, and the changing weather over America had been his interest for years, especially the area of the country which was undergoing the greatest change from previous patterns: Southern California. Specifically, a vast area from San Diego in the south to Santa Barbara, 200 miles north or, to be exact, up to a few miles north of the Hearst Castle in San Simeon. For nearly a year the weather off the Pacific coast had defied reason—hurricanes, then perfect calm, warm breezes, and then gale winds which forced windows into living rooms in Malibu as if they were made of cellophane. The storms over the ocean itself were his reference point, and the effect of that weather on Los Angeles, or rather on the people living there, was his driving concern. Before his love for clouds and what made them drop rain and his interest in what pollution had done to upset the natural balance of weather conditions in the Los Angeles Basin, Carter DeSimone cared about people. His good friend Bob Sheppard had once called him "the weather machine with a heart."

The title was apt; Carter was brilliant, a walking computer filled with information on anything connected with meteorology. And yet he was a humanist. It was hard to figure him out if you didn't know him well. He loved people, adored children, and yet had never, in all his fifty-seven years, married. Bob Sheppard once asked him, "Why, Carter? Why'd you remain a bachelor all this time? You're the Henry Kissinger of weather. Where's your Nancy?"

"Isn't it obvious?" Carter had replied. "Look around." He pointed to the books, the maps, the instruments, the framed degrees hanging on the wall, and out the window to the clouds hanging in the sky. "I don't think a woman would get enough of me. She'd ask me a question about redecorating the house, and I'd answer with a barometric pressure reading." He smiled. "So I compensate by trying to help a lot of people or at least affect them in some way."

This cold spell had brought out the best in Carter. It was his big chance, his biggest challenge, this darkness which had settled over the city since Christmas Eve. The mayor of Los Angeles had appointed him to "oversee" the problem and "advise" the people of the city. And he was the logical choice for such a position. The President had commended him on his past performance—predicting a flood in Wyoming which, had he not warned the authorities to get the people out of the valley, would have killed hundreds more than the 86 lives it did take; forecasting, before anyone else, the treacherous winter of 1977; being instrumental in preparing New York City for the hottest and most humid December weather it had ever experienced, thereby avoiding major power blackouts and preparing people emotionally for a Palm Springs kind of Christmas; and, in general over the years, his predictions of all kinds of storms, which had been extremely accurate. The President, along with the governor and senators from California and surrounding states, urged him to see what could be done. A month of sporadic rain and darkness in Southern California meant millions of dollars lost in crops and a spectacular upset to the nation's economy. The importance of the chunk of land down in the southwest corner of the map of America was suddenly very visible to the world.

Carter DeSimone sat at his desk. The look on his face was grim. He leaned back and looked out the window as he tuned the radio to find a local weather report, looking at the bleak sky and listening to the same old crap. He wanted to hear some optimism for a change. Even the FM stations, the rock stations where the DJs who usually read the weather as though they were stand-up comics—even they were sounding depressed. He knew the people needed to be told it was going to get better.

But was it?

What was happening had everything to do with the top of the globe. Within the confines of the Arctic Circle is a factory, a great expansive factory that covers all land, sea, and ice. It is a major source in the production of that element of nature on which all living things must depend—the weather. Here is where molecules of gas and water heat and cool, rise and fall, and react with each other to create masses of energized air. As the earth spins like a child's twirling top, these air masses are thrown away from the axis and make their way south toward the equator, and in doing so react with other air masses which have formed at lower latitudes.

Normally, these air masses, the highs and lows weathermen on television mention all the time, follow certain paths and patterns, and because they so seldom vary from these patterns, their constant rhythms create the seasons and the localized atmospheric conditions we are used to living with. Within these patterns, the air masses are in constant motion, being created, dying, colliding, even avoiding each other. They play games, which makes weather prediction such a difficult science. Highs may glide over lows, lows cut off highs. Sometimes they smash into each other in such a way as to create violent thunderstorms. At other times they give little nudges to one another, and a subtle change in temperature and/or humidity may take place. But as long as the factory keeps producing these patterns without interference, the weather remains in a constant but moderate flux.

There are times, though, especially in winter, when for many subtle reasons the normal pattern of these systems is interrupted. The air masses from the Arctic regions become blocked, imprisoned in the frozen north by a belt of strong, stationary air systems, with no way of releasing the inevitable buildup of energy. The northern skies become angry. Masses of gas strain to break through, to break free of the encircling wall of larger masses that hold them in like the top of a pressure cooker.

Eventually something must give, and it is at this moment, with the proper circumstances, that all hell can break loose in the atmosphere. In the winter this polar outbreak, as it is called, can produce severe snowstorms and cause long weeks of bitter cold. Turbulence breeds turbulence. The energies released from the polar factory can be incomprehensible to the human mind because often they just do not make sense or what we think is sense.

The fact is few people have ever given the weather a second

thought except for the convenience or inconvenience it brings into their lives.

Which is the way it should be.

And lately the people of Los Angeles were certainly giving weather a second thought. Maybe even a third.

Carter switched off the radio and took off his glasses. The stack of satellite photos on his desk were now a blur. The map on which the phone sat looked like a place mat. Hell, how could he expect anyone to be optimistic? It had gone on long enough; everyone was sick of it. Maybe if he could give them some good news, something halfway substantial to go on, maybe then he'd hear a report that the sun was going to shine again in the land of sunshine. What bothered him was not so much the fact that he couldn't give them a prediction of the end of the cold weather. What got to him was what he was keeping secret, at least until he was dead sure, positive, or at least as positive as one could be about such a precarious science as weather prediction. What made him so mad was that what he wanted to say sounded like science fiction, perhaps like a madman talking. California, everyone knew, was full of kooks; was he just another one? But if he were, what of all the factual evidence that sat there on his desk?

Carter shook his head, chewed on his glasses, and picked up a fat book which had been published the year before. It seemed to represent all his fears and disbelief, yet it told him he could very well be right. He slammed the book down on his desk, picked up the phone and asked his secretary to bring him a cup of coffee, and then put his glasses back on. He could see clearly again. The title of the book, stamped in gold letters on the red cloth cover, seemed to jump out at him. *The Coming Ice Age–Fact or Fiction?* Carter crossed his arms and seemed puzzled.

Two men sat looking out the window of a plane coming into Los Angeles. "You ever seen anything so goddamn lifeless?" one asked.

Bob Sheppard shook his head. "Looks like we're coming in

over Nova Scotia. I thought maybe it would have changed while I was gone. I *hoped* it would change."

The man sitting next to him on the DC-10 stared out at the bleak sight of a drizzly, depressing expanse of land. "Strangest thing I've ever seen. Goddamn lifeless, that's what it is. You married?"

"Yes," Bob said, "wife and two kids."

"Then you know. She don't even want to go to the hairdresser, right? Who wants to go out in this? Nobody goes out in this. The whole goddamn city's been sitting home on their asses for almost a month now. It's a horror movie on the late show, that's what it is."

Bob only nodded. Not a horror movie, he thought, but one of those mood pictures where it's always drizzling and cold and some love affair is going to pot on the beach as the waves crash in the background. And the guy next to him was right. Julie hadn't wanted to go to the grocery store the day before he left for Washington. She simply didn't want to fight the wetness, drive down the hill in it, deal with it. It was easier and much more comfortable to sit inside, in front of the fire, and read, or knit, or listen to Susan play the piano.

As the plane taxied down the slick runway, Bob wondered how Susan was feeling. He'd talked to Julie on Tuesday night, and Susan had been doing better. Deciding whether or not to put her in the hospital again was a hard decision, one that had been faced so many times in the twelve years she'd been their bittersweet joy. That was it, exactly. Julie had said it one evening when they were together alone, after their son, Michael, had left, and Susan had gone to bed. Their only daughter was a joy, the delight of their lives, pretty and smart and talented and so very much alive, filled with a zest for living. And to have been born with a chronic illness—well, maybe that was the reason she lived the days when she was out of pain so fully, even desperately. The sweetness of a young girl to complete the family, then the bitter trick they'd been played, she'd been played. They'd wallowed in it at first, but over the years they had come to understand it. Not the *why* of the pancreatitis, no one would ever understand that–Julie and Bob had come to accept it as what it was, as God's will. What they understood was the illness itself, inside and out; they knew how to deal with it, how to handle it, how to comfort Susan when she was in pain, how to make the healthy days better for her, and how to prevent or at least to ward off the next attack.

Susan was an unusual case. Pancreatitis was usually associated with alcoholism, but in Susan it seemed to be the result of her premature birth, the cells inside the pancreas not having quite formed to do what they were supposed to do. And that was to supply the insulin to the body and secrete all the enzymes to digest food properly. Her insulin was fine, but the enzymes were a problem–she had to take supplementary enzymes by mouth. The worst part of the disease was the fact that it caused acute attacks of intense pain whenever the pancreas malfunctioned, and it often did in Susan's case. The enzyme level would be upset, the pancreas itself would become swollen and inflamed, and that inflammation would spread to the surrounding organs and tissues and cause severe pain and tenderness in the stomach and back. Nothing could be tolerated by mouth for several days, and the administering of strong painkillers was necessary, as well as drugs to shock the pancreas back into a normal state, to dry it up, to lessen the inflammation. Usually she had to be hospitalized, but if the attack were not bad enough to warrant constant supervision and if she were strong enough not to need continuous intravenous feeding, if she could take a little water by mouth to keep from becoming dehydrated, then she could remain at home through the duration of the attack.

So they hadn't put her in the hospital this last time. "Century City is dismal enough as it is," Julie had said, referring to the hospital where Susan had spent so much time that Julie felt as though the waiting room near the intensive care unit were an extension of her living room. "With this weather it's got to be suicidal in there." Bob had agreed. Susan could get through the attack at home; they would take her for daily blood tests at a nearby hospital on Sunset Boulevard, just south of their Los Feliz home. They would administer the hypos of Demerol and atropine every four hours. They would let her rest. It was the same care she'd get in the hospital—certainly quieter—and should something happen, the ambulance would be there in a matter of seconds. . . .

Bob said good-bye to the man who'd been sitting next to him and walked down the long corridor at L.A. International. In his head he saw the red light flashing on the ambulance in their driveway, then Julie and him standing at the door as they lifted Susan into it. Then the rush to their own car, to follow in the night. Following their daughter with fear and hope and prayers mixing in their heads.

Bob found a phone and dropped in a dime. He'd dialed three of the numbers when he heard a familiar voice. "Bob! Bob!" He turned to see his brother's wife, Dolores, rushing toward him in her high heels and fur coat. She looked like Elizabeth Taylor in the film *The V.I.P.'s,* running around the busy airport in bad weather, dressed to the teeth. The fact was, airport or no, she always looked like Elizabeth Taylor. The resemblance was uncanny, or it had been. Now the years, the lonely nights, and the worry and the drinking were taking their toll. She was now a high-strung shadow of what had once been a radiantly beautiful woman.

"Dolores, I thought Harry was meeting me." Bob dropped the receiver to the cradle and stepped out of the booth.

"He was in a meeting. I'm going up near the office anyhow. Julie's—"

"I was just calling her."

"She's home with Susan. I guess she had a rough night. Julie sounded worried. At least I detected some worry. I could tell."

"Maybe I should call and check?"

"Listen, do it from the office. I'm double-parked out there, and the congestion's awful. I think we'd better get out of here before rush hour. I talked to her about an hour ago, and Susan's asleep."

Bob picked up his briefcase. "Yeah, you're right. Let's go."

They started to walk away, but Dolores stopped, reached into the phone booth, and pulled out the dime in the coin return slot. "Finders keepers," Dolores said with a grin.

"You can have it." Bob laughed. "Harry cut your allowance?"

They walked outside. The drizzle was fanned into their faces by the wind. Dolores tied her rain bonnet over her dark hair. At the curb sat a white Lincoln Continental, parked nearly sideways, creating a backup of cars, limousines, and airport buses as far as the eye could see. Bob felt momentarily embarrassed to get into the car. "Want me to drive?" he asked as he saw the cop coming toward them.

"Nope, I can handle this," Dolores said decisively. She walked around to the driver's door and put her hand on the handle. Angry drivers behind her blew their horns, and a few shouted obscenities. Bob heard one guy yell, "Move that goddamn boat!" and he smiled. He'd always called his brother's car, when talking to Julie, the Great White Boat.

"Hey, lady!" the police officer said loudly.

Dolores yanked open the door and stared him down. Then, in a shrill and piercing tone, she screamed, "Jesus Christ! Can't you see it's *raining?*"

The cop looked perplexed, probably trying to understand what she meant. And as he stood there, his mouth open, Dolores jumped into the Great White Boat and spun the wheels as she took off into traffic.

Dolores muttered about the cop all the way to the San Diego Freeway, how the airport is for the people and she was parked there for only five minutes at the most, and anyway, did he really expect *anyone* to park in the lot and *walk* through this crappy weather?

"I was hoping it would be warm and sunny when I got back," Bob said. "Washington's as warm as New York. Odd for this time of year, but certainly comfortable."

"What the hell were you doing in Washington anyway? Harry doesn't tell me a thing. I didn't know you were gone till I called Julie this morning. Nobody tells me anything. I turn on the news, and *they* don't even tell me anything. . . ." Dolores lit a cigarette and clicked on the radio. "You're listening to the music of sunshine on KIIS, on this dreary Thursday in Los Angeles." She punched the button, and the car filled with soft music. "So was it business for the firm or another government thing?"

"Energy problems, relating to the weather. Government stuff." Bob paused for a moment. "You know what? Just yesterday in a meeting I was making the point of L.A.'s dependence on the automobile, and look. Look at all these cars, even in this weather. Fuel shortages, the chance of accidents, it doesn't matter. You need a car to survive in this town."

"To *survive* this town," Dolores corrected him. "I wish we were living in Arizona."

"It's raining there, too."

"Shit. Maybe I can get Harry to pack it in and build a little villa on the edge of the Sahara."

"The only Sahara Harry'd go to is the one in Vegas," Bob said; he knew his brother well.

Dolores nodded, flicking her ashes on the floor. "Hah. He won't even take me there. Maybe if someone were selling a Degas there ... oh, never mind." She was silent for a few moments and then muttered again.

"What's wrong?"

"Look."

Bob could see the string of red taillights up ahead. The Santa Monica Freeway was barely moving. "Let's try the streets. I can't deal with this," Dolores said, and she cut across two lanes and a patch of grass.

Bob breathed again when they slid to a stop. She asked him if he thought it was going to get any better soon. He shook his head and said, "I just don't know. I think we're in for a long siege."

"You know what some bastard said on the TV the other day?"

"What?"

Dolores stepped on the gas and pressed a button and then tossed the cigarette out the window. A spray of water hit her forehead. "Damn," she moaned, pressing the button to raise the window again. "Some jerk said he wouldn't be surprised if it snowed! Isn't that hysterical?"

Bob didn't smile. "Yeah."

At that very moment Bob's friend and sometime-colleague Carter DeSimone was riding down a similar Los Angeles street, his thoughts similar to Bob's—even without the eight-lane freeways, the mobility of the city depends on the auto. As the limousine turned onto Wilshire Boulevard, he saw a crowd of people huddled together waiting for a bus. A strike had just been settled—this time the city had gone without the RTD service for only four days—and the people who didn't own cars could ride again, instead of having to walk in the rain or staying home and possibly losing their jobs. He thought about the need for a subway, a BART system like San Francisco's, but then so did everyone; talk of a subway for the City of the Angels came up every year, was postponed for a couple of months, and then finally dropped completely. The question of whether or not the city would experience an earthquake was always the first argument against it, but what, Carter wondered, about the threat of the elements, things no one thought of? The threat of rain, sleet, hail, even snow? How are all these cars to keep moving if it were to snow? The freeways died when the slightest rains came; take that one step farther. Carter was sure the temperature, already dropping, would sufficiently go below 32° that evening, meaning the rain that already had fallen would turn to ice. What then? That's what he wanted to talk to Bob about.

Carter picked up the telephone in the back of the car. He called the communications center and informed them he'd be in Bob Sheppard's office for the next hour or so. "What's that storm off the coast doing?" Carter asked.

He was told the low-pressure front was moving inland. Rain was already pounding on Catalina. It looked as though the drizzle would turn into a good rain by the evening rush hour.

Carter hung up and settled back in the car. "Damn," he muttered.

If the Arctic Circle is the factory for weather, the ocean is the source of its fuel. There—in that expanse of water—is the main source of moisture; it finds its way from the surface of the water into the atmosphere. The transfer process is simple and basic to nature. Without it, the great landmasses of earth would dry up into lifeless deserts.

Just as important as the process is the temperature of the water, in particular, the Pacific Ocean. In the equatorial regions the warm water produces warm air. The atmosphere is heated from below. Warmer air near the surface of the ocean rises up into the colder air that exists high in the stratosphere. In the northern latitudes the water is lower in temperature, thus heating the air above it less. Because the surface process is one of interchange, the atmosphere affects the water temperature and movement also. They complement each other with a process that has varied little in millions of years.

And just as the air has currents, so does the ocean. On the surface of the ocean are fast-moving rivers of water. The best known of these is the Gulf Stream in the Atlantic, which is responsible for the generally moderate climate of the East Coast.

On the West Coast there are similar streams which also keep the temperatures in California moderate to warm. If these currents were to lower in temperature as much as 5°, the consequences could be profound.

In this particular January just such a thing was happening. A phenomenon known as upwelling had occurred off the California coast. Simply speaking, cold water which ran in slow currents along the bottom of the ocean had boiled up to the surface. It was a rare occurrence, for it can take up to 100 years for water to cross the bottom of the Pacific Ocean. But for uncertain reasons—most scientists did think it was mainly due to a change in the salinity of the water—the bottom current grew less dense in the shallower coastal area, and it rose like hot air in the atmosphere.

The result in California was much cooler weather than normal for this time of year, and when the air masses moving down the winter storm tract with their colder air and moisture gathered from the sea, it remained cold upon arrival in Southern California.

What was most amazing was that the temperature of the sea had fallen 7°.

Dolores dropped Bob off in front of the big office building on Wilshire Boulevard. "We'll see you at the house later," Dolores said to him. "Oh, listen, tell Harry I'll be waiting for him at the gallery."

"Will do. Thanks, Dee."

Dolores smiled and gave him a wave, and then the Great White Boat sailed off up the street. Bob ran into the building, stepped into the elevator, said hello to two men he knew, and pressed the button marked 12.

He surprised himself by not pushing 7. He and Harry had only moved into the brand-new building on Wilshire, just across the street from the LaBrea Tar Pits and the Los Angeles County Museum of Art, at Thanksgiving. Before that they'd been in Beverly Hills, and 7 had been their floor. A successful one at that.

Robert and Harry Sheppard owned Sheppard Public Relations, a large agency with more fingers in more pies than just public relations. Bob, the younger of the brothers at forty-four, had graduated from college, brought up a family, started a business, and worked it into becoming one of the most successful in the city. He made money, gained a respected position as a member of his community, and his work—specializing in governmental communications, on both the local and the federal level—earned him national recognition.

Though devoted to his business, and damn good at it, Bob Sheppard was basically an outdoorsman, an adventurer. He balanced office work with trips with family to the mountains and the beaches. When weekend vacations were impossible, backyard barbecues were the norm. An avid hunter in his younger years on a Minnesota farm, he abandoned the interest in guns and killing right about the time the Vietnam War was beginning to get him in the gut, when he realized it could have been his own son, Michael, who was being shipped home in a wooden box at the age of nineteen from some nameless swamp on the other side of the world. Michael never had to join the Army, but the possibility had changed Bob's sensibility greatly. He took a different interest in nature, in wildlife and the glorious foliage in the mountains surrounding Los Angeles; his camera became his gun.

Bob Sheppard was good with a camera, always had been. His

grandfather in Mankato had taught him on his little black Kodak box, taught him the wonder in receiving a lasting impression of what he was seeing by just pressing a little button. He refined his knowledge of cameras and lenses while in school and financed most of his college career by selling photographs. It was that knowledge of photo technique, plus his natural talent for "seeing" what made a good picture, that got him into the public relations field. He worked as a photographer for a large agency for a year, shooting everything from cans of pork and beans to Paris fashions, and then urged his brother, who was already a success in real estate and investments, to come into business with him. It was a good marriage, the artist and the businessman, and some of each rubbed off onto the other. Harry, in the years they were together, had developed a good sense of what made the public buy a product or respond to a concept and had nurtured a sense of color and space and impact that had rubbed off into his personal life as well—he had become an avid collector of art.

And Bob had become a shrewd businessman, but it never meant anything near what it meant to Harry. He left the office at the office; Harry brought it home. And Bob knew it, but that was his brother's problem . . . and Dolores'. Bob felt sorry for her; he always had. He felt sorry because Harry's ruthlessness seemed to carry over right into his marriage, and Dolores, for all her outward flash and elegance and wit, was an unhappy, unfulfilled woman.

But he had vowed never to get involved. Even when Harry boasted of his extramarital affairs, Bob would merely listen and forget. Not that it was some kind of secret he'd reveal; everyone knew Harry played around. What Bob couldn't forgive was Harry's lack of any consideration for his wife; Dolores always seemed to be some kind of afterthought. Bob felt she deserved better, so did Julie. But the façade of a happy marriage continued, Harry taking it for granted, Dolores seemingly resigned to it for all the days of her life. Bob thought it was sad how his brother, a communications "expert," could not find a way of communicating with his own wife. Or maybe it was just that he didn't even try.

The elevator opened at 12, and Bob was greeted by the receptionist, a bright-eyed girl who reminded him of his own daughter. "Your brother's in conference with a client, and Professor DeSimone is on his way to see you."

"Good, I'm expecting him. Ethel in?"

"Yup. Came in about ten, drenched. Poor thing."

"Thanks," Bob said, and entered the door with the sign that read "Robert Sheppard." "Ethel," he said to his private secretary, an older woman who looked a lot like Rose Mary Woods but vowed she'd never touch a tape recording in her life, "I hear you floated in today."

"Mr. Sheppard, do you know what it's like to stand on the corner waiting for a bus and then have that bus come racing by at ninety miles per hour and splash a puddle of water clear over your head?"

Bob rubbed his chin, looking at the stack of messages on her desk. "Actually, yeah, Ethel, I do. Happened back in the Midwest three years ago, in front of the Conrad Hilton in Chicago. Had to change my suit."

"This disgusting weather!" Ethel exclaimed. "If you were smart, you'd have stayed in Washington."

"If I were smart, Ethel, I'd be living there. Let me know when Dr. DeSimone arrives."

"Professor, Dr., Mr.—just what is he? Everyone calls him something different."

Bob smiled as he entered his private office. "Actually, he's Carter. Just Carter. Call him that; it's less confusing."

"Yes, sir. And welcome back."

"Thanks," Bob said, looking out the glass wall behind his desk. At first he thought the curtains had been pulled, but then he realized they were gold, and the color he was looking at was gray. He walked to the glass and looked out on what usually was a stunning view, even with the smog—green trees rising above houses in the distance, the hills lush and alive, the other buildings shimmering in the sunlight, the thousands of cars moving like little toys on a miniature railroad set. Now he saw clouds and only the faint outline of buildings, and they certainly didn't shine. The cars were moving, but through the drops of precipitation on the glass, they looked like drops of colored water moving down the pane. Bob could have sworn he was standing on the boardwalk at Atlantic City in the midst of a winter rain.

He sat at his desk, clicked on the lights from the panel under the top drawer, and asked Ethel to dial Julie. He looked at the photograph of his wife and Susan and Michael, taken four years before on a trip to Oregon, everyone in lumberjack shirt and jeans, their faces sticking out from the bright yellow pup tent which had collapsed in the middle of the night, on their heads. He felt himself wishing Susan would be well enough to go camping during the coming summer, and maybe Michael and Lorna could bring Dawn along, even though she was so young. He looked at the photograph of Michael and Lorna, the wedding picture, on the wall of the office, and then at the recent one, the one next to it, Michael and Lorna and their daughter, his first grandchild, his precious Dawn. It was her birthday today, well, a birthday of sorts, six months old, and there was going to be a party. It would be, he thought, the only good thing about a rotten week.

Ethel buzzed him. "Your wife doesn't answer, Mr. Sheppard."

"That's strange. . . ."

"Would you like me to keep trying?"

"Yeah, do that. Tell Harry to come in as soon as he's done with his client, will you?"

"Surely, sir."

Bob loosened his tie and flipped through some of his mail. The intercom buzzed again. "Your son's on the line," Ethel said.

"Thanks." He punched the first button. "Michael?"

"Dad. Greetings on this turkey of a day!"

"Michael, how's your sister? I called home, and there's no answer—"

"Hold on, simmer down, calm down, and listen to news from heaven. Julie, your wife and my mother, is at this very moment probably driving home from the Mayfair with the station wagon filled to the brim with luscious goodies for the party tonight."

"What?"

"Mom went to the store, to translate, and she told me to tell you Susan's feeling a lot better and has been sleeping all day."

"Has she needed another shot?"

"Nope. Sis sleeps well, on her own time, not on the needles. So relax."

"Jesus, Michael, you've got that uncanny ability to sound as if you just don't give a shit about anything."

"That's why I'm a good actor, giving impressions like that. Wanna hear my Jimmy Carter, speaking of impressions?"

"No, I don't want to hear your Carter, Jimmy or DeSimone. How's my granddaughter?"

"Just pissed in her pants, but other than that, she's fine. No, actually, she's had a cold, but it's getting better."

"Still up to partying tonight?"

"She can fake it. I've taught her a lot in six months. You have a good trip?"

"Fair. No one in Washington believes this is a serious matter out here."

"No one anywhere believes *California's* a serious matter, except maybe on Oscar night. But, Jesus, what you hear on TV, you'd think we're the hit topic at tea at the White House. But that's show biz."

"Yeah," Bob muttered, remembering a certain meeting in the nation's capital at which concern for the welfare of Southern California was of minimal concern. "I think when it gets worse, there'll be a response."

"Sure," Michael said with a laugh, "when the place is a fuckin' disaster area, they'll say, hey, let's do something to help poor California."

"What can they do to help *then?*"

Michael had an answer. "Give me a job."

"Jesus, Michael, that soap didn't work out?"

"Dad, do I look like a reformed rapist who now is married to Kathryn Kuhlman's hairdresser and secretly desires to bang her seven-year-old daughter by her previous marriage?"

Bob laughed. "Come on, Mike, what is this, *Mary Hartman?*"

"I think they're calling it *Beyond Mary Hartman, Mary Hartman.*"

"You're all nuts. Actors. Jesus."

"But, Dad, it's such *fun,"* Michael said sarcastically.

"How's Lorna?"

"Saving the world as usual. Wonderful. The Joan Baez of the 1980s. A closet protest singer. Being married to a social worker has its benefits, though. You get put in the *Register* automatically. . . ."

Bob was chuckling as Ethel opened the door. "Excuse me, sir, but Dr. ... I mean *Mr.* DeSi–Carter, sir, is here." She looked flustered by the time she got it all out.

"Send him in."

Ethel turned and motioned to the man in the outer office.

Bob shook his head as he talked into the phone again. "No, not you, Michael. I've got Carter coming in, I have to go. Listen, we'll see you at the house later, right?"

"Right, Dad."

" 'Bye, Michael."

"Later."

Bob set the phone down and got up. He and Carter shook hands and stood looking out the window for a moment. Carter put his hand on his friend's shoulder and said, "Shall we call Bekins?"

"Take to the hills?"

Carter smiled. "I have to joke about it to keep from shaking."

"That bad?" Bob sat down.

"Worse, I'm afraid."

"That's what I tried to convince them in Washington, but I didn't have any real facts to back it up. Do you?"

Carter nodded, gravely.

"Hey, Carter, you're not kidding, are you?"

"You're going to say I'm crazy."

Bob looked into his eyes. "Try me."

Carter sat on the edge of his desk. "What would you say if I told you it is going to snow? That Los Angeles is going to be blanketed with snow?"

"I'd say you're crazy."

Carter smiled. "But you know I'm not."

"Yeah. I know you're not." Bob leaned back in his chair and

put his hands up behind his head. "Come on, Carter, are you kidding me?"

"Not at all. I firmly believe there's a fifty-fifty chance that it will snow. And I mean *snow,* the kind that sticks, not just some flurries in the air. They've had that before, over in the Pasadena area some years ago. Gorman gets it every year. Thousand Oaks had a major snowfall in 1908. But none of it lasts."

"You're talking about Minnesota kind of snow."

"Yes, that kind. I tell you, Bob, no one will have to go up to Tahoe this year. They can ski down Doheny Drive."

Bob rustled his hair. The idea was unthinkable, a fantasy. "Carter, come on!"

"The storm's going to hit us from the northwest, the full force missing San Francisco, hitting squarely on Los Angeles. You want it technically?"

"Just so I can understand it," Bob said.

Carter told him. "For a month, the turbulent air up there in the polar region was held at bay by several giant high-pressure systems over Canada. The Canadian highs were in turn held in place by the natural east-west movement of air farther south, which carried with it burst after burst of smaller systems of air that bounced against the highs as they moved cross country. Follow me?"

Bob nodded. "Not only cross country. The world's been—"

"On the other side of the globe, over Russia, for example, there have been similar conditions. An awful lot of turbulence built up there, causing a winter more severe than usual. But that energy finally stopped building up, and it broke up, a lot of it over Alaska, breaking open like an aerosol can, like a broken dam, carrying bitter cold into the atmosphere.

"It's happened many times before over the past centuries, most recently in '77, but now there's an added factor to the drama, the upwelling of the ocean. With the water near L.A. colder than the water farther north, the massive air system would pick up moisture from the north and carry it south. When it got there . . . when it got *here,* it wouldn't warm up. Right?"

"Right."

"Hope that it would veer into the Rockies was futile. Some meteorologists are still hoping that it'll do that, but it won't. That low-pressure area around San Francisco is diverting the great polar air mass south along the coast. Eventually, it's got to turn inland with the natural easterly air flow. Unfortunately for us, L.A. is the most likely spot."

"Jesus," Bob said, shaking his head. "A snowstorm?" He muttered, as if talking to himself. Then his eyes focused on Carter's and he said, "Have you told anyone this?"

"The President."

"You told him everything you just told me?"

Carter nodded. "And he listened."

"Then a long silence, right?"

"No. He was gracious. He believed me. That is to say, he felt I believed in what I was saying, that I hadn't gone off my rocker. He said he had to discuss it with other experts. I sent him the data I'd compiled."

"The reaction?"

"His advisers and experts say the data is not sufficient, and it probably isn't, but, Bob, I have a sense about this, I've got an intuition. A sweeping change in weather from one side of the globe to the other is coming—is happening—and as outrageous, as preposterous as it seems, it is very much a reality."

"How about the mayor?"

Carter laughed. "Him? Wonderful man. He won't even admit it's raining outside, much less concede we're in for a snowstorm."

"Next thing he'll be asking me to do is put up billboards on the Strip that say, 'You're in Sun City! Honest you are!' He's up for reelection this year, and people have a way of blaming anything, even bad weather, on the mayor. I guess I'm saying I understand his position."

Carter walked around the room. "I think he's weak. I think we should at least think about it, prepare in our minds and on paper what we would do if such a thing would happen. Nothing more than that. Can you imagine the consequences?"

"Hey, look," Bob said. Rain was beating against the windowpane, the giant expanse of glass that was the wall behind the desk.

"The storm that's been over the Pacific has moved inland," Carter said, explaining, "and by night we'll be freezing, and all that rain's going to turn to ice."

"My God," Bob whispered, looking at the squiggles of color which were cars moving along Wilshire.

"I'm going to–" Carter was interrupted by the buzzer on Bob's desk.

"Sir, Mr. Sheppard is finished with his client now. He'd like you to come in."

"Thanks, Ethel." Bob got up and looked at Carter. "That's Harry. I have to go to his office. I don't think he's ever been in here, to tell the truth." They walked into the outer office, Carter taking his briefcase. "You started to say something," Bob reminded him.

"Yes, I was going to say I'm going to see the mayor now, again, to try to make him realize the danger he's missing in his head and, I hope convince him that the good of the city demands he at least consider the possibility of snow."

They passed the client who'd just come from Harry's office. Bob recognized him and was about to greet him when the man said, blurting, "He's the toughest bastard in the business. If you guys didn't do such good work, I'd punch him in the jaw." And with that he left.

Bob turned to Carter and smirked, as his son, Michael, would have done, he thought. "That's my brother, folks," he said.

And they went into Harry's office.

It was a stark contrast with Bob's warm office; overly neat, chrome and glass, track lighting on the ceiling to illuminate the paintings, it looked more like an art gallery than an office. "What did you do to Robinson?" Bob asked, still a little stunned at the client's reaction.

"Aw, hell with him. Got him to sign a half-million contract with us, that's all."

"He sounded as though you'd tortured him."

"Fuck him. We got the contract, and we don't have to deal with him personally again for another year. He's a little shithead anyhow. Carter, how are you?"

"Fine, Harry."

"Working hard in this monsoon?"

"That's the word for it."

"Hey, Bob, Dolores pick you up?"

"Yeah."

"She smash up the car again?"

"No, we made it somehow," Bob said with a smile.

"Christ, I wish to hell she'd drive her Gremlin. I buy her a nice little car for four grand, and I say, here, little lady, here's your own toy and you can smash the hell out of it if you want, but don't drive the big one anymore, okay? And when does she use it? Never. Last week I had to use it. You ever see the look on the parking attendant's face at Chasen's when you drive up in a goddamn Gremlin?"

"I've got a Pinto at home," Carter said, "and I don't mind who sees me in it."

"It's just not my style." Harry lit a cigar. "And, hey, don't give me that shit. You're being driven around in a chauffeured limousine. You could put your Pinto in the trunk of that thing and still have room for suitcases."

"How's business?" Bob asked, to change the subject. "We still solvent?"

"Your big brother held down the fort just fine. I suppose you heard we've got a good lead from the National Transportation Board?"

"Yeah. Heard about it in D.C."

"First thing I'm going to suggest, we get a fleet of boats for the street around here."

"Better order some sleds, too," Carter chimed in.

"Huh?" Bob and Carter exchanged glances. Bob wasn't sure they should even breathe it to Harry, but now it was too late. "Come on, what the hell you mean, sleds?"

"I think we're in for a snowstorm. Possibly a major one."

"Come again."

"Just what I said. Rain isn't the end of it. I don't know what will be, to tell the truth. But I'm willing to bet we're going to have a major snowstorm in a matter of days."

Harry frowned and sat still for a moment, chewing on his cigar. Then he pressed his intercom and said to his secretary, "Hey, try to find Robinson and send him back up here. I'd rather fight with an asshole than these idiots."

"I'll see you tonight," Bob said, turning to leave with Carter.

"All weathermen are nuts!" Harry called after them, laughing. "They predicted a warm winter, remember that? Look what's happening outside. Nuts!"

Bob turned back. "Oh, yeah, Dolores is at the gallery."

Harry pulled the cigar out of his mouth and smashed it into the oversized ashtray on his desk. "Goddamn Robinson, making me late. Thanks, Bob. Carter, good seeing you again." He went into his closet to get his raincoat as the two other men went out the door.

In the outer office, they could hear him laughing, and the word "snow" echoed behind them.

There is a kind of building typical of Los Angeles, the stucco apartment house built around a swimming pool and a few palm trees. Usually the walls are thin, and the neighbors, like it or not, are forced into becoming one big family. However, such places are comfortable and affordable. And it was for those reasons that Bob Sheppard's son, Michael, and his wife and daughter lived in one.

It was called Genesee Gardens, mainly because it was on Genesee Street, since it had no gardens to speak of. Just a palm tree by the pool. They all had names like that, Laurel Towers (on Laurel, though only two stories high), Bali Hai, The Palms, Westerly Plaza, and most had red, blue, yellow, and green floodlights out front at night, giving the places a garish Christmas-tree quality. For Southern California and the type of weather which was the norm there, they were perfect—most had large windows for the breezes, and some had air-conditioners; for the winter months, when the night temperatures went down to the low forties, most apartments had gas space heaters which did the trick for the whole apartment. But what was happening in January this year was different from what had ever happened in any previous winter. The space heaters were working overtime and hard, and the result was just enough to keep reasonably warm. The city's gas supply was being drained in face of an already mounting gas shortage, which was a prime concern Bob Sheppard had taken with him to Washington. If he knew anything about public relations, it was his job to convince the powers that a grave situation was possible and they'd better be prepared to dish the news out to the people in a way they could not only understand, but accept.

People were understanding it already; accepting it was quite another thing. Word was being passed along via radio and TV that the city was using more electricity and natural gas at a rate far higher than the summer peak period and far in excess of that used the previous winter. Some concern was already evident around the city, and the mayor's office was besieged with calls from worried citizens asking if they were going to lose their heat. Some, not understanding the capabilities of the heaters in their homes and apartments, demanded more gas, thinking Southern California Gas Company was to blame for their chilly bedrooms. The people needed to be informed, educated in the midst of the problematic situation, but little was being done other than to point up the uniqueness of what was happening to Los Angeles and to worry about the future.

About the time Michael Sheppard was talking to his father, Marguerita Alvarez, the sixty-three-year-old manager of Genesee Gardens, was watching one of her favorite game shows on TV. They interrupted with yet another bulletin, and Marguerita was tired of them already. She listened, however, to find out there had been a "tragedy in East Los Angeles when a gas heater blew up in an apartment, killing two small children and injuring three others."

"Jesús María," Marguerita said, and made the sign of the cross. She got up and lit another little votive candle in front of the statue of Our Lady of Guadalupe. "Bless the niños," she said, and then knelt in silent prayer as a man from East Orange, New Jersey, won a new Toyota and a dining-room set. Marguerita turned back to the TV and wondered how the shows could go on, so happy and jolly, while they were being taped right there in Hollywood, as though nothing in the city had changed.

Marguerita was scared, for she had always feared the Lord would one day seek His revenge on a people who had forgotten Him, but she felt her mission was to make others feel good, even if it meant to the end. She did not believe this was the end of the world, but if it were, if it were the will of God, she would accept it. No one would know she was scared. Oh, no. She was a big woman, earthy, filled with strength of body and soul, and she was a leader. Everyone in the apartment house loved her and counted on her. She was mama to some, a whole family to others. To one man she had taken the place of his dead wife, and she relieved his loneliness. To others she was the person who sewed up rips in their pants, the lady you could always count on to have a cup of sugar if you needed it, or an entire meal for that matter. To Michael and Lorna Sheppard, she was Dawn's godmother, baby-sitter, and their dear friend. And she would go on being those things through this strange time because now, more than ever, these people would need her.

Marguerita switched off the TV and pulled out the little present she'd got for Dawn. It was a hand-knit sweater, sent from her sister in Mexico, a beautiful piece of work. She was proud of it and knew her little Dawn would look lovely in it. As she wrapped it in tissue paper and searched for a colorful bow, she thought again about the children she'd just heard about. Dying in a fire, she thought, there could be no worse way to die. She thought about yesterday's news. A baby, only a few weeks old, and his two older sisters had died from the toxic gases of a charcoal fire their father had set up in their bedroom to keep them warm. He was a poor man, an uneducated man who didn't even speak English. He was not to blame. No one was to blame. *But the children, oh, God, why do the children have to suffer?* Marguerita blessed herself again and worried about Lorna's taking Dawn out so soon after she'd had a chest cold. In her day she would have kept the baby in for a week. She'd seen two niños die of pneumonia before she was ten years old. But modern mothers, who could figure them out?

Marguerita taped a little blue bow onto the package and smiled. Then she noticed Lorna walk past the window and run up the outdoor steps to the second floor. Good. She was home. Now Marguerita would go upstairs and give little Dawn her present. But there was a knock on the door. The elderly man, Mr. Rosenberg, asked if he could talk to her for a minute. Marguerita asked him in and found out he had a broken window in his bathroom and it was getting too cold....

"Why did you not tell me sooner, silly old man?" Marguerita opened a drawer and pulled out a roll of thick tape and some cardboard. "You could catch the death in a cold bathroom, Mr. Rosenberg!"

"Mrs. Alvarez, I didn't want I should bother you—"

"Crazy old man. Come on, this will not be the best, but it will help."

And they went to his apartment. Marguerita noticed the level of the pool had risen. It was the first time she could ever remember not having had to turn the filler line to the pool on in any given week. She mentioned it to Mr. Rosenberg, and he said, "That is good, Mrs. Alvarez. Save on the water bill."

She smiled warmly and shook her head. "Oh, silly old man. Come, let's get that window closed up."

Upstairs, Lorna popped into the apartment. "Ugh! I'm chilled to the bone." She shook her short hair like a dog who'd just jumped out of water.

Michael went over to her and kissed her lightly on the lips. "Mrs. Sheppard, you're a mess."

"It's wet out there, Michael." She walked to the heater and rubbed her hands over her face in front of it.

"But you had the car."

"I had to go see a family ... oh, Michael, they're so bad off, there's no food and the roof leaks and—"

He looked into her exasperated eyes. "Lorna, please. Don't. I just can't take hearing it. It wouldn't be so bad if we were warm ourselves and everything were jolly happy zingo time. But everyone's got the miseries, honey. Let's not make it worse. And you promised."

"Promised what?" Lorna asked, flashing her huge green eyes at him.

"Not to bring work home with you. It's okay, I mean, I approve and understand and sympathize and all that stuff, like I understand you going over there in this lousy weather, but I don't want to hear about it. Okay?"

Lorna nodded.

"And don't, for God's sake, tell Marguerita or she'll be cooking them a pot of beans, and she doesn't have enough money to feed the whole city."

"How's Dawn?"

"Terrific. We took a dip in the pool at noon, and then I got her to her dancing lesson on time, and it went grandly, and we think she'll make the Olympic team."

"I take it, card, that she's not sniffling anymore?"

"No sniffles. My daughter is one healthy girl." And then Michael sneezed.

Lorna broke up laughing. "Healthier than you, I hope," she said, and went into the bedroom to see her daughter.

Dawn Sheppard was a very pretty baby, which wasn't surprising since both her parents were beautiful, but in opposite ways. Lorna was dark, with a mane of chestnut hair (which she used to iron until she cut it) and green saucer eyes. She had a stunning body, and although she was small, she was strong. She was more athletic than her husband, and before Dawn was born, she was always dragging him onto the tennis court or out to run around the block a few times after supper.

Michael bore a strong resemblance to another Michael, the actor Michael Sarrazin, which often worked to his disadvantage. For Michael Sheppard was an actor himself, or at least wanted to be, and all too often he heard he wasn't "right" for the part, which meant he looked too much like Michael Sarrazin. He'd been mistaken for him on the street, too—once a woman asked for his autograph in a drugstore, and he gave it to her and told her the best movie he thought he ever did was *The Gumball Rally*—but it didn't bother him. He felt it was a compliment because Michael Sarrazin was, after all, a handsome man. And a good actor, too, he admitted.

Michael looked a little like his father, too. Or maybe it was their presence, their aura, that was similar. Both men were good, loving, eager to make life simpler and happier for those they loved. You could tell just looking at them that they cared about people, that they could be counted on. They had eyes which could hold happiness and pain. Theirs were the bodies of strong men, masculine men, but you knew they could reach out tenderly and comfort; you knew they could cry. When people saw them together, the same height, Michael a good deal slimmer, but that same head of thick dark hair, the high cheekbones, the long, slender legs, they looked closer in age than father and son, and they looked as if they enjoyed each other's presence. And they did.

The one worry Bob had about his son was his aimlessness, meaning his desire to make it in the entertainment business. Most fathers of actors wish their offspring had chosen another occupation, but most find a secret delight in it, too, for what Dad wouldn't like to say to the neighbors, "My son's on *Kojak* tonight"? The problem with Michael was no one could be sure he'd stick to acting or that it was really the main thing he wanted to do with his life. He'd wanted, of all things, to be an undertaker when he was a boy, and that went on for years and finally ended—much to the delight of his mother—when he decided he was going to study law. That lasted a month. Then it was travel and see the world and lead the life of an aimless hippie. And then he was going to open a submarine sandwich shop in a new suburb of Los Angeles. Then it was teaching and, suddenly, acting. But he'd been with it now for two years. Even the responsibility of marriage a year and a few months before hadn't changed his mind; perhaps it enhanced it, because he had a wife who believed in his talent and urged him to pursue a career in which he would be happy. And he'd been doing better, a commercial now and then, which brought in good money, enough to spread over the months and live on, and when things weren't so good, he'd grab an odd job helping a buddy who owned a moving van, or he'd paint houses and work at gardening. The one thing he wouldn't do even if it were offered to him was live off his parents' money. He'd grown up in a comfortable and, finally, somewhat wealthy home. But it didn't make him the spoiled little rich kid. He was as commonly normal as the kid from the four-room house, getting into all the usual scrapes and troubles that kids growing up get into, never believing he was better than anyone else, never thinking he was above anyone.

Michael and Lorna were like two sides of a scale.

Michael was a product of the TV generation, and now he wanted to crawl into that tube and act on the screen for another generation. The boy who had not yet become a man, even with the responsibility of marriage and fatherhood on his shoulders—but then, Lorna didn't want anything less or more than what she married. Once, before the wedding, she'd told Julie, "If I wanted someone more mature, I'd marry my father. He's divorced." She explained she was too serious a person. "I want to marry a clown. Michael's the closest thing I can find." Julie had nodded, not quite sure she understood. But she agreed.

And Lorna was right—she *was* serious. She took her work too seriously, her marriage too seriously, the world too seriously—and Michael balanced her off and made her laugh. He lifted her up, sent her into the clouds. He called Dawn the joy of his life; Lorna felt Michael was her joy, Dawn was her blessing.

Lorna loved Michael. She loved him when he acted, when they fought about politics, when they stayed up late into the night, dreaming, when they made love. "You're the skinniest man I've ever gone to bed with," she once said, "and the best, too." He didn't work at proving he was a man; he simply was one. Lorna knew men hated ballbusting women, but women hated ballbusting men even more. Michael was, well, Michael. In bed she told him he was a mixture of Tarzan and a cuddly little monkey. He never knew quite what she meant, but it appealed to his sense of amusement. And ego.

Beyond the bedroom, Lorna respected him. When he got serious, which was seldom, he was wise. He treated her equally, sometimes even admitting to learning from her, and he let her depend on him where she needed it. She respected his work too, his desire, his ambition, which she realized still had to be nurtured. He was a new babe in that big playpen called Hollywood, but with both their energies she knew he'd succeed. He would seek and deserve and win recognition. What she deeply respected was his self-sufficiency; he had gone out on his own when his parents could have put him safely away in college for four or six years or given him a comfy job in the advertising world. "Michael would be a dream at public relations," Lorna once told Greg, a close friend of theirs who lived on the first floor of the apartment house. "I mean, he *is* a public relation!" Michael had charisma, always attracting people, cheering them up. The funny thing, Lorna thought, was that he never seemed to need much cheering up himself. He needed cheers, applause. But cheering up? Why? He was as happy as he felt he could be. After Dawn was born he said, "Give me more, and I'll OD on smiling." He had his down days. But even then his outlook was uplifting. People loved him. Because he loved himself.

Lorna had a different way of attracting people, of drawing them toward her. She was a listener, not a cheerer-upper. Being a social worker was something she'd dreamed about ever since she could remember, not something she'd decided to do on a whim, like so many rich girls who wanted to rebel. The fact was, she didn't come from a rich family. Her parents had barely enough to feed and clothe their seven children. She was the youngest, and she knew if she'd had younger brothers and sisters, she would never have left home. But her father was retired, and most of the family was near them in Florida, so she left St. Louis for the magic world of orange juice and sunshine, all-night taco stands and fresh, fresh fruit in the markets. Lorna passionately loved Los Angeles. "It doesn't pretend to be anything other than what it is. Plastic, big, sprawling, smoggy, and nuts. It's right there in the open, take it or leave it. Other cities pretend so much; they're so dishonest." She felt the center of the world would eventually center in Los Angeles. Communications, banking, the arts. It's all over, New York. "You'd think she was born here, for God's sake," Michael—who had been—said.

Lorna worked at the Los Angeles Free Clinic and did part-time social work for the City of Los Angeles, as well as helped out at various hospitals around the city. She was always strong, always eager to help the less fortunate, the ill, the needy, eager to see social change, eager to save the world, with the best of intentions. While possessing a certain amount of resentment toward people with a lot of money, she grew to like and admire Michael's parents, for they did good with their money, they bettered themselves and their friends with it, and they helped others. Had Michael been "the little rich boy," she never would have fallen in love with him. In fact, she had never really given it a thought, whether or not he came from an affluent family, until she went to his house for dinner one evening. It was an impressive house, so warm and tastefully furnished, so filled with the sense of family and living. Winding up the hill in Los Feliz, just under Griffith Park, she had stared at so many of the glorious old Spanish-style homes, finding them aesthetically beautiful but cold and oppressive. She was relieved when she walked into Michael's and felt at home.

Lorna had the ability to give people confidence just by offering a few words, a glance, a pat on the back. She was Michael's biggest fan and took delight in seeing him act, whether it be a play at one of the little theaters in town or a TV commercial. In fact, that's how she met him. He was doing a play called *Lemon Sky* at a little theater on Melrose Avenue, and she and a girlfriend thought he was excellent. After the performance she waited around to tell him so. "My first fan!" he kidded, and asked her to marry him.

She did. (But after seven months of getting to know what she was getting into.)

Lorna was glad she did. She liked being a wife, a mother, a woman with a career. Those roles suited her. She was on the bandwagon for women's liberation when Michael met her but since then had switched gears to being an exponent of liberation of any sort. Her animated, sparkling freethinking sometimes became unrealistic, and that's when she needed the calm common sense that Michael possessed to see her through.

The one subject which caused friction between them was Julie, Michael's mother. Lorna liked the woman immensely—almost everyone did—but said she could not respect her because she was too dependent on her husband. She accused her of lacking any kind of real strength. After many attempts to change her mind, Michael finally just said, "Lorna, we won't talk about it again, huh? It obviously won't get solved."

And she never mentioned it again, though Michael knew her thinking had not changed.

And it really didn't matter. *Everyone's entitled to his own opinion,* he thought, and he had his own value system which he applied to his mom, and she came out pretty high on the list. It was his perception of her which counted to him, not anyone else's.

Michael wondered if there was any of that thinking behind the words when Lorna called out from the bedroom, "Does Julie want us to pick anything up on the way to the house?" They all knew Julie hadn't wanted to leave the house for the past week or so because of the weather. Was Lorna getting in a dig or simply asking an honest question? He gave her the benefit of the doubt. He told her his mother had gone to the store herself and hadn't said anything about needing anything. She'd baked a cake for Dawn and even had the candles.

"How's my little pumpkin?" Lorna asked, carrying Dawn into the living room. Dawn cooed and giggled as Lorna nuzzled her with her cold nose.

"Want some tea?" Michael asked.

"Sure. Rose hips, okay?"

"Coming up. Hey, Lorna, Mom said Auntie Dee picked up Dad at the airport today. Can you imagine that?"

"Wow." Lorna played with little Dawn on the sofa, eliciting

gales of giggles from the little girl as she nuzzled and tickled her. "How's Dolores getting through this whole thing?"

"The weather?"

"Yup. She's depressed enough as it is. I would think she'd be afraid her hair would dissolve if it got rained on."

Michael turned the gas on under the teakettle. "That's not fair."

"Sure it is. Dolores is covered with plastic. I mean, it's all real, but it's plastic. Plastic dresses and plastic furs, plastic fingernails and plastic hair. She's so . . . so *perfect.*"

Michael suddenly started laughing, doubling over in the small kitchen.

"Look at Daddy, Dawn. See Daddy? Daddy's flipped his nut." She kissed Dawn and said, "Michael, what is it?"

"She's got . . . she's got a plastic nose, too!"

"You're kidding!"

"No, she had a nose job years ago. Oh, Jesus, we're rotten. We're really rotten. But isn't it fun?" He lifted himself up onto the counter and sat with half his ass hanging in the sink.

"Nothing rotten about it," Lorna said. "I think Dolores is a beautiful person. Inside, I mean. She's so vulnerable, so afraid of her own shadow. She should have told that bastard to get off a long time ago, and she'd be one hell of a gal today."

"Come on, Uncle Harry's not that bad."

"Right. He's worse. What I'm saying is I feel sorry for Dee. Trapped in there, under all that plastic, is a person."

"Lorna, don't analyze so much."

"Your relatives bring it out in me," she said with a glimmer in her eye. She lifted Dawn high into the air. "Isn't it silly, little pumpkin, having a birthday party for you and you're not even a year old yet?"

"Who knows?" Michael said, dropping a big spoonful of tea into the pot. "We all may freeze to death here. Let her have at least one blow-out-the-candles shebang."

"Michael, that's so morbid. Jesus." Lorna scowled. She hated talk like that.

"Only joking. What else is there to do, moan about it?"

"It isn't funny. Not one bit." She cuddled Dawn close to her breast.

Michael got up and went to her. "Hey, girl, I'm sorry. Hey, forgive me? Come on, huh?"

Lorna finally smiled and laid her head on his shoulder. "I'm too worried about it all, I guess."

"Everyone is. That's why I have to joke. I'm worried too." The teakettle started to whistle. Michael got up and shut off the gas, and then there was a knock at the door. "Come in," he shouted.

Marguerita opened the door. "An old woman to say happy birthday to her favorite godchild," she said, with a smile.

"Come in," Lorna said.

Marguerita handed the little present to Lorna, and Lorna handed Dawn to Marguerita. The big old woman hugged the little girl, swung her around, and sang a few bars of "Happy Birthday" to her. Lorna opened the tissue paper and marveled at the lovely little sweater. "Oh, Michael, look at this!"

"You like it?" Marguerita asked with pride.

"It's handwoven! Oh, it's beautiful. . . ."

"My sister in Mexico City, she make it special for Dawn." Marguerita sat in the big easy chair near the heater. "I have Father Guerca bless it for me."

"Thank you, it's just beautiful," Lorna said, blowing the woman a kiss.

Michael poured tea for both of them and then looked at the sweater. "Gee, thanks, Marguerita, but I thought I told you I wear a men's small, not a child's small. It'll look lovely in the show, but I don't think I can get my arms into it."

"Sit down, card," Lorna said, "and shut up."

He did, sit down that is, but he didn't shut up. All three of them talked, mainly about the weather, what they'd heard, what the rumors were, what their feelings were.

". . . and people are leaving town," Lorna said.

"People are leaving Genesee Gardens," Marguerita added sadly.

"Really?" Michael asked. "Who? The couple downstairs with the cockatoo, I hope?"

"No. Helen Chambers left this morning, said she has enough rain to last forever. The people in twelve went back east until it is over."

"Jimmy Clarke went up to San Francisco to be with his parents," Michael said.

"I didn't know," Marguerita said.

"I saw him this morning, before it started to drizzle. He said it was just as gloomy up there, but somehow in San Francisco you expect that and can handle it better. He kissed the place good-bye until the sun shines, Nellie."

"Listen," Lorna said, pointing to the roof. They could hear the wind. "It's really blowing." Strong winds always seemed to follow the rain.

It was true; wind usually followed a storm front. The worst thing about it was it made it seem colder than it actually was.

There was a tap at the window. They saw the familiar face of Harvard, the black postman who lived next door with his daughter. He opened the door and stepped inside. "What is it," he announced, "neither rain nor sleet nor snow . . .? I'm soaked to the bone. You got a sip of brandy, Mike?"

"Hi, Harvard. Got some–what do we have, honey?"

"Um, we've got honey, honey, for tea. I don't know if there's any liquor in there."

Harvard shook his head and smiled, pulling off his rain cap. "You folk, drinkin' tea all the time. Don't you know it's bad for the liver? I'm gonna buy you all a bottle of brandy for Christmas and–"

"Make it Easter," Lorna suggested. "Christmas was just three weeks ago."

"No, ma'am. It's come 'round again. With this weather they're gonna start sellin' Christmas trees again. The President and the Pope agreed. We're gonna have Christmas instead of Valentine's Day."

"Come on in, Harve," Michael said. "Sit on the floor and let your feet hang."

"Naw, I gotta get me a little somethin' warm and smooth to get my blood goin' again. Oh, Lorna, here's some magazines I had left over." He reached in his bag and pulled out three or four women's magazines.

"Harvard, how do you get these?" she asked. "I mean, do you just decide who's going to be lucky this month and get their *Journal* or *Cosmo,* and who's going to suffer with an empty mailbox?"

"I got it down to a system, ma'am," the postman said, bending forward to relieve some of the weight from his feet. "You know what they say about mailmen and dogs?"

Marguerita said, "What are you talking about?"

"Dogs bite. If the Johnsons don't lock up Fido, Johnson ain't gonna get his *Field & Stream* next month, that's all there is to it."

Lorna asked if that wasn't against the law.

"Ain't against my laws," the black man said with a laugh, and then he added, "No, they're from people who move and don't leave a signed card that they'll put out the bread for forwardin'. We just take them home. Nobody's stealin' from nobody."

A voice came through the wall of the living room. "Daddy, that you in there?"

"Ah, the sweet ring of innocence," he said softly. Then he shouted, "Not so loud, Flora, you'll crack the plaster!"

"Don't worry," Marguerita said, laughing. "It's all plasterboard anyhow. Plaster, we're not that fancy. And the roof is made of cardboard."

In a moment Flora, her hair in rollers, shivering in her jeans and skimpy blouse, popped in the door. "Daddy, what you doing over here?"

"Gettin' myself some Christmas cheer, what you think I'm doin'?"

"Hi, everybody. Gosh, isn't it just so boring? I mean, look, the same thing again, fog, rain. I hate it. You can't do anything in this weather."

"You sure's hell can deliver mail," her father said.

"They're predicting freezing temperatures tonight. That should put the roads in one hell of a condition." Michael offered Flora some tea, but she declined. "The radio said it would freeze in the Valley for sure."

"Anyone who lives in the Valley deserves to freeze," Harvard said with a chuckle. "Daughter, we got any brandy next door?"

"Yeah, but you gotta come home to get it. I also have some hot soup and a nice sandwich waiting for you." Flora turned to the rest of them and said, "You know what I just heard? It sounds wonderful, I think."

"What's that?" Lorna asked.

"Someone predicted it might snow."

"Where? Here?"

"Los Angeles, California?" Harvard asked. "Honey, let's get you on home. Excuse me, folks, but this is one nigger who's gonna need a rest. Flora, you crazy?"

"Well, Daddy, that's what I heard on the television right now before I heard you screamin' through the walls."

"Snow?" Marguerita asked. And then she said it again, this time softly, almost as if it were a pastoral thought. And it was—white, calm, gentle, beautiful even. "Snow." She made it sound welcome.

"Hey," Michael chimed in, "just think, we could all build a snowman out front."

Lorna added, "And turn the tacky spotlight on him and watch him melt!"

They were all amused, but under that amusement there was a kind of wishful thinking. Harvard and Flora had never seen snow, as many Los Angelenos had not. Marguerita couldn't remember it all that well. Michael and Lorna had just been to Big Bear Lake before Christmas and had played in it, skied on it, and admired it from their cabin window, the way it glistened and sparkled in the moonlight. "Wouldn't it be fun," Michael said seriously, "to have a little snow on the ground in L.A.?"

"Honey, that ain't never gonna happen, so get used to the rain, 'cause *that* ain't never gonna stop!" And with that, Flora took her daddy's arm and pulled him from the apartment.

Marguerita left, too, telling them to drive safely. Then

Michael changed Dawn's diaper and dressed her, while Lorna took a shower and dried her hair. Then Michael dressed, and together they put the new little sweater on Dawn, which fitted perfectly. Lorna wrapped three blankets up and laid the little girl down on them. "You think it's too early to leave?" she asked.

And so, bundled up, the baby hidden under a cloud of fluffy yellow, they descended the stairs on the way to the parking space.

Already, the steps were coated with ice.

The moisture was in a turbulent air mass which had been created above Siberia only three days before. But now it was being pushed toward the California coast by the first punch of the developing polar outbreak. As the air mass reached Southern California, it particularly threatened Los Angeles because it ran into an even colder mass of air already in the area. Because of its weakness, the warmer mass lifted above the other system and, in doing so, began to cool as it moved higher and higher. The moisture grew heavy in the colder air. It had to release. When it did, it would fall through the cold air at ground level. That air was already below freezing.

It was the ideal situation for sleet, snow, and—as Lorna and Michael had already discovered on their steps—ice.

Harry Sheppard entered the auction room and found Dolores already seated in the middle of the crowd. He slid in next to her. "How's the car?" he asked.

"The car's fine." Her tone was as icy as the wind outside.

"You buy anything?"

"A new bra at Bullock's. Why?"

"I mean here. You buy any painting?"

She turned to him. "Oh, come on, Harry, me? I couldn't give a damn about paintings. The only art I like is Garfunkel."

Harry snorted. He raised his hand and made a bid on a sculpture he liked. "Where would we put it?" Dolores asked.

"In the hall?"

"How about on the hood of the Mark IV?" She giggled.

"Not funny." He raised his hand, indicating a thousand-dollar bid.

"I don't like it."

"I thought you weren't interested in art."

"I'm not. I'm just thinking Lily won't like dusting it. Too many nooks and crannies. You see Bob?"

"Shh. Dolores, I'm trying to ... oh, hell, I'm not going above that. It's not worth more than a thousand."

"You see your brother?"

"Sure I saw him. How'd you think I got the message to meet you here?" He looked up at the painting that was being offered. He snorted. Not to his taste. "You could have come up; we could have come together."

"I needed a bra."

"I had to take a cab. The driver was stoned. Kept telling me man, this is like Tahiti, it rains every afternoon. A madman."

"I wish I were."

Harry looked at her. "What? In Tahiti?"

"No. Stoned."

Harry didn't respond. He bid on the next painting but dropped out when he felt it went over what he wanted to pay. He was a shrewd buyer, and he knew his art. It was the one true interest in his life, his one hobby. Everyone who knew him at first thought the interest was there purely to impress, to decorate and embellish their Bel Air home. But as time passed, even the most skeptical (his own brother) had to admit that he'd really found an interest, and a good one at that. But he never seemed to have enough; every week he could be found in a gallery, buying. He had an insatiable desire to own art.

"I've decided not to go to that opening at the museum," Dolores said, holding her purse on her lap with both hands. All the women sat like that. She wondered why, why she was sitting like that, so proper, why *they* were sitting like that? Because it was the correct thing to do at a gallery? Kind of like a wake, Dolores thought, everyone on straight-back chairs, serious as hell and staring at the corpse surrounded with flowers. Here he was, the auctioneer, surrounded with colorful paintings. Was he dead? Maybe they were all sitting that way so their hair wouldn't fall. Maybe they all had to pee. She didn't know.

Harry started to bid on another, but after checking the printed listing in his hand, he stopped. "Wrong one."

"What do you mean?"

"Wrong one. Right artist, wrong painting."

"You're supposed to go by how it looks to you, aren't you? What's this wrong artist, right painting thing?"

"You've got it backwards. I want the one with the grapes, not the peaches."

Dolores let out a laugh. "I am sorry," she said to the people around her, and pulled a Kleenex from her bag. "I'm sorry, Harry, but it was so funny. Did you ever hear anyone say, in all seriousness, *I want the one with the grapes, not the peaches.* Oh, God, it's a riot!"

"Dolores, shut up."

"Oh, this is a panic, I tell you," she said, rubbing her nose.

"Dolores, please."

"Harry, bid on that thing." They looked at the piece of art the man was holding up. "We could hang it in front of the house and save money by getting rid of the security patrol."

"Oh, Dolores, don't try to be funny. That painting is worth a great deal of money. It's a—"

"I don't care if Picasso himself did it. It's the kind of thing they have nerve making us look at. Besides, a hundred a month for some man to ride by the house twice a night, that's so silly. How's he going to know if I'm being raped or murdered? Should I flash the lights for him?"

Harry bent over and whispered, "Dolores, nobody wants to murder you, much less rape you. You're safe, darling."

"And you can go to hell." She pulled out a cigarette and started to light it. An usher came over in a rush and asked her not to smoke in the gallery. She grinned at him and dropped the cigarette on the floor. "This place is a goddamn church," she muttered. "Stop flicking your Bic, ma'am. Jesus Christ."

"Dolores, please! Oh, this is the one. This is. . . ." Harry strained his neck and listened. Yes, this was it. He made his offer. It was bettered. He went higher. It was bettered. He went higher still.

"I'll be having to wash floors next week to pay for that piece of crap," Dolores said loud enough for most of the room to hear.

And the offer was bettered again.

Harry sat back and let out a deep breath. He looked defeated, disappointed.

"Harry, what's–?"

"Never mind, that's all."

Dolores thought he'd stopped because of what she said. She jumped up and shouted, *"What's the bid?"*

The startled auctioneer informed her, and she topped it by $500. Harry looked at her in surprise and anger. The man who'd been bidding fiercely against Harry doubled the bid, with a look to Dolores that could have killed a woman less strong than she. Just as she was about to say something–Harry feared she was going to double *him*–he grabbed her and yanked her out of the room with much commotion.

In the front hall they had it out. "I felt sorry for you," Dolores said. "I knew you wanted it, so I thought I'd get it for you."

"I stopped where I felt I reached my limit. I don't need you to do my buying for me."

"But I would like to buy you something you want. The shirt every Christmas isn't my idea of gift giving."

"Dolores, let's not make a scene, huh?"

"Let's get the hell out of here."

Harry, red-faced, embarrassed, opened the front doors. He handed the parking attendant the stub, and they waited under the canopy for the car to be brought. "I'm not going to that opening," Dolores said. "I told you that in there, and you didn't answer me."

"I didn't hear you."

"I just can't take any more art galleries."

"My dear, I think the true statement is, they can't take you."

"What's this *my dear* shit? Why are you so proper the way

you talk when you're in a place like this? When we're at the Bistro? When we're up at the Polo Lounge? You get in the car and you're Al Capone. Here you're Laurence Olivier."

The car drove up. "Shut up and get in," Harry whispered.

The boy opened the door for Dolores, and she stepped in. Just as he was about to close it, she said, "Do me a favor."

"Ma'am?"

"Go open his door for him, too, and when he gets halfway in, shut the thing on his foot."

The kid gulped and looked at Harry. "Don't mind her. She's always kidding."

"Yes, sir." Harry handed him a $5 bill. "Thank you, sir."

He got into the car and pulled out into traffic. "That goddamn scene wasn't funny, you hear me? You want to embarrass me in there and more than you did? Well, you couldn't. You're damn right you're not going to the opening of the Van Gogh exhibit with me. I'd be embarrassed to have you there."

"Van Go to hell. I could give a shit."

"You should."

"*You* should."

There was a long silence. "Harry, for God's sake, let's be social at Bob and Julie's. I want to have fun tonight, I really do."

After another long silence, Harry said, "Dolores, we haven't had fun in thirty years."

Julie Sheppard sat in her den, reading a book on California history. One particular passage interested her:

> On a cold day in January, in 1541, a Spanish explorer named Juan Cabrillo was leading an expedition along the coast of California. His ship's log revealed the plight of his sailors who were caught in an unusually severe winter storm.
>
> Without warning, Cabrillo's small group of ships were forced to take refuge at an island 30 miles offshore near Santa Catalina. There they waited as ice-cold winds and driving rain and sleet attacked them for over a month. The

bitter cold was the worst part of the ordeal, and it was noted that ice—several inches thick—formed at times on the surface of their water barrels. The ship's rigging was coated with ice and was unusable. The men had to build extra fires belowdecks, thus endangering their boats. There was little wood to be found on the brush-covered islands, and the wild winds thwarted any attempt they made to sail away from the islands until March of that year.

To emphasize the magnitude of this severe polar weather, it should be noted that Cabrillo and his men were offshore where the sea usually warms the air. One can only imagine what it was like on the land, then, the land around Santa Monica Bay where the Indian village which eventually would become Los Angeles lay. . . .

She closed the book and shook her head. She remembered the big snowfall up in Newhall, just back in 1975. Highway 5 had been closed to traffic because of the huge drifts, and that was just 35 miles from the center of Los Angeles. It had snowed in the Silverlake district back in the 1950s, she'd read in the paper. So this cold weather and the rain they were having weren't unique. At least it wasn't snowing.

She got up and looked at her hands. They were dry, chapped. The heat in the house did terrible things to her skin. She went up to the master bedroom to rub her hands with lotion.

From the upstairs windows, Julie could usually see most of Los Angeles, but today the windows were covered with drops of water. Most of the drapes were closed to help keep the heat in; fires roared in all three fireplaces—in the living room, in the den just off it, and down in the family room. The furnaces were doing a good job of heating the bedrooms, but there was no need to use them for the other rooms when the fireplaces could do the work without wasting precious fuel. Julie was glad she'd finally talked Bob into cutting down the old trees at the back of the property; it was as if she'd had a premonition that they were going to need a lot of firewood that season. Julie curled up in front of the fire in the den and sipped her coffee. The house smelled of roast pork and potatoes. It would be like Christmas again, she thought. It would relieve some of the gloom.

Bob and Julie Sheppard owned one of the most beautiful homes in Los Feliz area, an older section of town where famous stars had built mansions—Cecil B. DeMille, W. C. Fields, Bob Cummings, the film actress Madge Bellamy—and where the real estate values rose greatly each year. The house was Spanish Colonial, built in 1936. It sat on a cul-de-sac at the top of a winding, steep drive, and the backyard bordered on the land that was Griffith Park. The famous observatory sat directly above it on the mountainside, and the house had a view nearly as fine as the big white domed building above, where people put dimes into telescopes to search out Catalina on a clear day.

The house was built on the hillside, three stories and a Spanish-style garage to match. The first level was one large family room with a fireplace, wet bar, bathroom, and the utility room for the gravity heat furnaces, the water heater, and an extra freezer, which Julie found was used more often when Michael had lived at home. For a boy who was always slim, he ate like a horse. She envied him; she was slim herself, petite, but not by chance. She had to watch her calories.

On the second level was a huge living room. Two deep cushioned flowered sofas sat on either side of the fireplace, and the grand piano in the corner dominated the room. It was Susan's pride and joy, the Yahama she'd been given for her tenth birthday. A few prints hung on the walls, and Bob's favorite wing chair and table sat in another corner, under one of his favorite accomplishments, a photograph of John and Robert Kennedy sitting in the sandy dunes of the Atlantic. Near the double stained-glass doors leading to the den was an antique secretary, imported from Spain, a beautiful oak piece that Julie loved more than anything in the house. The bottom housed Michael's Sony quadraphonic stereo equipment (with a speaker in every corner of the room), which was still there because, as he'd explained, "Ma, if I bring that thing to the Genesee Gardens, we'll be arrested for running a disco without a license."

The den was white wicker, couch, chair, rocker, the walls and fireplace all done in white, the cushions and curtains a pale green and yellow. Two walls were glass windows which opened out onto the pool area, and the other two were floor-to-ceiling bookshelves. The fireplace was in the corner, miniature, just the right size to take the bite out of a cold winter morning. Plants hung from the ceiling, sat on the mantel, cascaded from planters standing between the chairs. It was the freshest room in the house.

Across the vestibule, which sat at the foot of a circular staircase and upstairs balcony, was the formal dining room, filled with antique table, buffet, and china cabinet, which looked out over a red-brick patio, the fir trees and all the front yard. The window was imported leaded glass, an improvement Bob and Julie had made when they bought the place in 1955.

The kitchen had been redone, too, to Julie's specifications. It was an old country kitchen with red Spanish tile on the floor and counters, red appliances, and all dark oak shelves. No cabinets with doors, just open shelves, with little curtains to pull to keep dust out. Earthenware bowls sat on the counter; wooden spoons were grouped in an old butter bucket. The only appliance of the day out in the open was the Bunn coffeemaker, which was nearly always on.

The pantry was filled with all the necessary appliances, including Julie's new toy, the Cuisinart food processor. Food lined the shelves, although right now there wasn't as much as usual because she dreaded driving in the inclement weather. The laundry room was behind the pantry, and then the door to the lower level. Across from that, what used to be the maid's room—that's what it was built for—was Susan's room. It had been Michael's, but when he got married and moved out, the little girl claimed her big brother's room for her own. It, like the den, looked out over the pool area, and it had its own walk-in wardrobe and complete bathroom. It was convenient for Susan when she was ill, but it sometimes was the cause of Julie's not being able to sleep. The master bedroom was upstairs, away at the front of the house, over the dining room. Bob often awoke to find Julie walking into the room after having gone downstairs to listen at Susan's door, just to be sure.

The upstairs was spacious, filled with light, windows everywhere which framed the trees and the lights of the city like so many paintings. The master bedroom had a porch of its own, with two doors opening onto it. Bob and Julie found it to be the most relaxing spot in the house, and they often took coffee there after dinner and watched as the sky turned several shades of orange as the sun set over the city. The master bath, and the bathroom connecting the other two bedrooms, were done in Spanish tile, beautifully handcrafted, and both had little toothbrush sinks which Julie had never seen in any other house before. Bob had turned one of the bedrooms into his office, and now that Susan had vacated the other, it was the guest bedroom, where Michael and Lorna often spent the night.

Outside, the grounds were expansive. The pool was a large oval, surrounded by terraces of red brick. Geraniums and fuchsia abounded, as well as every type of green foliage imaginable. Giant fir trees dotted the property, which was surrounded on three sides by a high red-brick fence. It gave the house a fortress look—especially with the electric gate which closed off the driveway—but the wall had been there when they bought the place, and no one cared to tackle dismantling a six-foot-high brick fence that surrounded nearly an acre of land. So they let it be.

In a sense, they liked the privacy, and it did ensure safety. There was no fence in the back, but it was hardly likely that someone would try to come down the steep hill leading up to the Griffith Park Observatory. But Julie had always wished for a fence there when winter came, every single year. When it rained hard, mud ran down the side of the hill and filled the backyard with globs of earth. One year in a particular bad rainstorm, they'd awakened to find the pool the color of dirty dishwater. Mud had rolled down the hill, right into the swimming pool. It hadn't been so bad this year. But as she looked out the den window into the backyard, Julie worried that by the time the wet weather was over she was going to have a tree from Griffith Park sitting in her swimming pool.

Julie Sheppard was a small woman, not frail-looking but somewhat fragile. She liked to kid Michael that he'd gotten his dad's height and her body—slim. When Michael had once said, "But, Mom, your tits are bigger," Julie blushed. Of course, they were, but not by a long shot. In fact, the first words Bob had uttered to Julie when they first met were, "Hiya, skinny." He hadn't let her know until long afterward that he found her type to be exceptionally attractive and that he'd had his eye on her for a long time.

Everyone told Susan she had eyes like her mother, and she did, but they were not nearly as striking as Julie's. Julie's were blue like a robin's egg and kind, not the sad eyes which automatically evoked another person's pity, but rather the soft blue eyes of perception, of understanding. She was a smart but simple woman. She asked for nothing more than a good healthy, happy life for herself and her family. She enjoyed working several hours a week for her favorite charity, a local group formed to encourage research in children's diseases. But most of all, she loved being with her family, at home, baking and cooking, playing Scrabble with Susan, sitting in front of the TV with Bob into the late hours, picnicking in the mountains with Michael and Lorna, curling up in front of the fireplace in the cabin with the latest Harold Robbins paperback while the others tried the ski slope. Julie liked to swim, but that was the extent of her athletic prowess; every now and then Bob could drag her onto a tennis court, but she preferred watching Bjorn Borg and Jimmy Connors do the footwork on the TV in the kitchen, as she whipped up a soufflé.

Julie got up and went into the kitchen. She checked the timer and poured more beer over the roast. Then she held the cutting board piled with vegetables over the roasting pan and slid them in over the meat. She looked out the window curiously. The drizzle, which had been so steady, had stopped now. The cold wind seemed to be coming in around the glass panes. She tightened her sweater and rubbed her hands together. It wasn't cold in the house. But looking at the scene outside gave her the chills.

There was a buzz near the phone in the kitchen. Julie walked over to the little panel and pushed the lever. "Yes?" she said.

"Let the Walls of Jericho come tumbling down," the voice said.

Julie laughed and pressed the button which opened the electric gates at the front of the driveway. Michael had dubbed the brick fence which surrounded the house the Walls of Jericho after he had seen the movie *It Happened One Night* the first time. Once, while he was in high school, Bob and Julie awoke to the sound of a trumpet blaring in the night. They didn't understand it, and finally, Bob got up to investigate the ear-shattering sound (and so did several neighbors, much to Julie's chagrin). It turned out Michael had had a few beers and had borrowed a buddy's trumpet from the school band. He said, "If Clark Gable can do it, I can do it," when Bob finally reached the gate (and gave him a swift kick in the ass). Michael buzzed from that day on, but the name stuck.

Julie watched the lights of the car coming up the drive. Oh, she wished they'd let Bob and her buy them a new car; how they needed it. But no, Michael wouldn't hear of it, and she was sure Lorna would object even more violently than Michael had when Julie'd mentioned it to him. She gave them credit—they were making it on their own—but still, she worried about them, especially in an old Mustang in this kind of weather. She unlocked the front door and looked through the peephole until she saw Lorna come up the steps with a large bundle.

Julie opened the door wide and took her heavy little granddaughter in her arms, as Lorna shook the water off her head. "Is Bob home yet?" Lorna asked.

"No. . . ."

"Michael wanted to know if he should put the car in back." Lorna waved to Michael, a signal, and he put the car in gear and drove around the back way so his father would have room to get his own car into the garage.

"How are you, my little darling?" Julie whispered to Dawn as she unwrapped her. The baby was smiling, not knowing what to make of the cold and all the fuss. "Your little cheeks are rosy. Come sit with Grandma by the fire . . . come in the den, Lorna. Coffee?"

"No, thanks. But the fire sounds nice. So much more romantic than our gas wall heater."

"I think you two should move in here with us until this passes. It must be so damp in that apartment."

"So far, so good," Lorna said, taking off her coat and gloves as they entered the warm, cozy den. "But when the ceiling starts dripping, we'll be on your doorstep."

Julie sat down and held little Dawn in her arms. "Oh, she looks so much better. The cold all gone?"

Lorna nodded. "She's a strong kid. Like her crazy father."

"Some strong kid." Julie laughed. "He had every childhood disease before he was four, including pneumonia twice, and we used to strap a box of tissues to him because he had a perpetual cold."

"You weren't a mother; you were a nurse."

Julie looked relieved. "And now it's your job."

Lorna laughed. "Do you like Dawn's new sweater?"

"It's beautiful. Where did—?"

They both turned their heads when they heard Michael shout "Dammit!" in the backyard. They saw him through the windows, hopping on one foot toward the back door.

"Not only does he have a perpetual cold," Julie said, "but he's a perpetual klutz, too."

"Yesterday he lost his balance stepping into his jeans and he put his foot right through the knee."

His mother just shook her head. "Oh, my Michael."

"Someone call me?" He stood at the door of the den.

"Whatja do?" Lorna asked. "Stick your foot in the wash machine?" Michael's shoe and pant leg were soaked up to the knee. "Put your foot in the fire."

"Very funny. Hi, Mom. Jesus, that man-eating puddle down at the bottom of the steps hasn't dried up in a month."

"Oh, it's getting worse, I know." Julie looked concerned. "The water runs off the patio and down the steps, and it's just digging a hole there where we had the rosebushes."

"You should cement it in," Lorna said, curling up in front of the fireplace. The glow made her skin look golden tan.

"Bob's been meaning to do that. And put a big planter there, a pot of some kind."

"Speaking of pot," Michael said, with a flash of his eyes to Lorna, struggling to get his wet sock off, "is that a pot roast I detect filling the air?"

"It's not fish. A beautiful pork roast."

"You didn't forget extra mushrooms this time, did you, Ma?"

"No, I didn't. And I used Michelob instead of whatever it was I used last time."

Michael looked pleased. "Terrific. Michelob's the best beer in the world."

"The expert here," Lorna said, pointing over her shoulder to him. "Some expert. I don't think he's ever tasted anything but Michelob and Coors."

"I once had Blatz in Milwaukee. Here, put my shoe by the fire." Lorna took it and set it up against the screen. "I said by it, not in it!" She moved it back. Then she turned and stuck her tongue out at him. He laughed.

"How's the driving?" Julie asked, rocking Dawn in her arms. "It was awful when I went to the market."

"I hate to tell you this, Mother, but you drove in sunshine compared to what it's like now."

"That bad?"

Michael looked serious. "I hate to say this, but I think it's starting to freeze."

"Carter said it would."

"Who?" Lorna asked.

"You remember Bob's friend, Carter DeSimone. . . ."

"The weatherman?" Lorna said.

"Yes. Well, he's more than that. He's a respected meteorologist. He's quite worried about all this."

Michael noticed the grave look on his mother's face. He

countered by saying, "Hey, you know what Dr. George said last night on the air?"

"Now I'm at a loss," Julie said. "Who?"

"Dr. George Fischbeck. He's the weatherman on ABC, Channel Seven."

"We watch two."

"Oh. Anyhow, he says, 'Nobody wants to hear the weather report tonight 'cause it's just the same as last night and probably will be the same as tomorrow night. In its place, I'm going to sing you a little song. . . .' "

"Did he?" Julie asked.

"Yup. 'On the Sunny Side of the Street.' Fantastic!"

"I like his sense of humor." Julie looked out the window. Even though the drizzle had let up, the sky was still black. "I do hope your father gets home soon. Harry and Dee are coming for dinner also."

"I just thought of something," Lorna said. "How does Bob have his car if he was out of town? Didn't Dolores pick him up?"

Julie lifted her granddaughter to her knees and kissed her on the forehead. "It's been in the shop. It needed servicing—I think, new brakes, too—and Bob just left it there for the week. He was going to get a ride to the station from someone at the office. Here, Dawn, you want to go by your daddy? I need to check the roast."

Lorna turned around and said, "Here, I'll take her. Her daddy's all wet."

"Hey, Ma," Michael said as she handed Dawn to Lorna, "I got a call from my agent this morning, I forgot to tell you. Got another interview tomorrow. A callback."

"Michael, that's wonderful!"

"Well, the part's only three lines. Is that nuts? You go through three callbacks, about twenty hours of inquisition and waiting, for a scene that'll be shot in ten minutes or less. Basic training's easier."

"I'd rather see you onscreen for three lines than in the Army any day," Julie said, meaning it, as she left the room.

"Some soldier you'd make," Lorna said, smiling. "Hey, Michael, it's stopped. Look."

There wasn't even a drizzle.

On the way from the kitchen, Julie opened the door to Susan's room. The girl's eyes were open wide. "Is Michael here?" she asked.

Julie stepped in. "Yes. Lorna and Dawn are toasting in front of the fire, and your brother is barefoot—one leg, that is."

"Why?"

"You know him. He stepped in a very big puddle."

Susan smiled. But Julie could see the pain in her eyes, in her face. It had drawn them so close together, Susan's illness, that sometimes Julie felt they were one, she felt the same pain, shared the constant struggle to get well, and had an intuition about when it was going to happen next. More often than not she'd say, "Susan, you're not feeling well, are you?" And Susan would shake her head. Julie, as if with a special kind of sense, could tell when an attack was brewing. At first she allowed the gift to upset her. It wasn't easy knowing it was inevitable that in two days her daughter was going to be lying on the table in the emergency room, screaming in pain. But then she had learned to turn this gift of prediction into something constructive—they were better able to prepare for the attacks, to warn the doctor ahead of time, not in the middle of the night when the first pain struck in her back and her tummy, and at times even to ward them off.

Julie walked close to the bed and sat down on the floor. Susan had taken Michael's old bed, the one on the floor. When he was sixteen, he threw out the frame and headboard and set the box spring and mattress down on the carpeting. He called it growing up. Susan liked that, and when shè moved downstairs, she refused to take her frilly canopy bed along; Julie took the frills off and let it become the guest bed. (Michael, whenever he slept in it with Lorna, said he thought he was doing a production of *Oklahoma!,* sleeping in the surrey with the fringe on top.) "How are you feeling?" Julie asked.

Susan took her hand. "Okay."

"Hurt much?"

She shook her head. "I'm so sleepy."

"Well, you sleep. I'll tell you when we have the ice cream and cake, and if you feel up to making an appearance, I'm sure everyone will be pleased."

"I really do want to play for Dawn."

"I'll let you know. Now, I'll just tell everyone you're asleep."

"Daddy home yet?"

"In a few minutes. The roads are very bad tonight."

"It seems that he's been gone so very long. The days seem so long when it's so dark."

Julie took a deep breath. Wasn't it the truth? She looked up to see Michael peeking his head in the door. "This a private gossip hour, or can anyone join in?"

"Hi," Susan said with the biggest smile Julie'd seen on her face in days.

"I'm going to go," Julie said. "If you want a pill, Susan . . ."

"No, I don't think I will, Mom. Hi, star."

Julie left as Michael sat on the bed next to Susan. "You still pulling this tummyache act just to keep from going out in the rain? Come on, Susan, pretend you're living in Tahiti."

"That's *Mutiny on the Bounty.* I watched it yesterday."

"The original?" Michael asked, wide-eyed.

Susan nodded.

"Oh, terrific. It's so much better than the remake. Marlon Brando with marbles in his mouth. How's the song?"

"I didn't get to work on it much since I saw you. I will, though, I promise." He'd given her a poem he'd written and asked her to put it to music.

"That's okay, no hurry. It's just that Diana Ross called the other day, asking about it. And Elton John said something about wanting it for his next album."

Susan giggled. But, almost immediately, she cringed, and her hands went into fists and she gritted her teeth. Michael reached up and pulled her hair from her forehead. It was damp. "Hey, you okay?" In a moment she started to relax. "What's worse this time, back or front?" He'd always figured the best thing to do was to get her to talk, to force her to take her mind off it. "Come on, confess."

"More in my back. It usually is. Starts out in the front but moves around. It's more like it's in the middle." She took a deep breath at his insistence, and then she tried to smile again. "Did the rain stop?" she asked.

"Yeah. You want the window open?"

"The window?"

"No, I mean the drapes, silly. You think I want to freeze the pancreas right out of you?"

Susan giggled. "When are you going to be on *Sonny and Cher?*"

"Susan, I keep telling you," Michael said with mock pride, "they're darlings, but they just don't pay enough!"

Susan lifted her hand and offered her little finger. Michael put his little finger around it, and they shook. It had always been their secret, private handshake. "I think I should sleep some more," Susan said.

"Hang in there, huh?" He got up, blew her a kiss, and left the room quietly.

Michael walked into the den to find Lorna feeding Dawn on the floor in front of the fire. "She couldn't wait, the party pooper," Lorna said.

"Where'd Mom go?"

"Upstairs, I think."

Michael walked up the steps, pausing for a moment to look at the Peter Milton lithograph hanging there on the wall between the floors. It was his favorite thing in the house, a gift he'd given his mom and dad after they'd fallen in love with it when they'd seen it in a store window in Beverly Hills. Michael had bought it with his own money and given it to them for their wedding anniversary. Whenever he was in the house, he always stopped to reflect on it.

But he didn't stand there for long. His face seemed serious, even worried, which was unlike him. When he walked into the master bedroom, he found his mother looking out the front windows, through the branches of the gigantic fir trees. "Oh, Michael," Julie said, almost startled.

"Looking for anyone in particular?"

"Your father, for one."

"Listen, Ma. How is she–really?"

"Susan?"

"No, Mrs. Kupperman next door. Of course, Susan."

"Michael, don't make me sound so dumb. I'm worried about your father in this weather. He should have been home by now. My mind wasn't on what you were saying."

"It's just that she looks, well, worse. So pale. I think she's in a lot more pain than she says."

"Well, I'm not sure about that," Julie said, sitting down on the edge of the king-size bed, "but they're fairly positive now there's a cyst on the pancreas. It's small, but it's growing."

"And it'll have to be cut out, right?"

Julie winced at his choice of words. But he was right, no matter what pretty words you put it in, a surgeon would have to go inside her young tummy and, yes, cut it out. Julie just nodded and looked at the window again. "Oh, dear, it's drizzling again. The tree branches are flapping so strangely in the wind. I hate it when they strike the window."

"Ma, what's this cyst thing? How long has it been there? Where'd it come from?"

"Michael, we don't know. It was nearly impossible to discover in the first place. Thank God for John Sherman; he refused to give up after all those X rays. He knew there was something, something he wasn't finding. Do you remember Dr. Ellison, the man we went to shortly after Susan was born, when we first had a hint there was a deformity in the pancreas?"

"The guy in Milwaukee? The one who has the disease named after him?"

"Yes. The Zolinger-Ellison Syndrome. Well, he's dead now, but his associate remembered us, and when Dr. Sherman sent him the X rays and all the records from over the years, he was happy to give us his opinion. He said the test told him there was something definite, perhaps a growth, a tumor, a cyst, and urged John to keep looking for it."

"Why couldn't they see it?"

"I guess it was too small. Now they've seen it, with the help of a marvelous new test where they inject a dye right into the pancreas. It was terribly painful, but—"

"Oh, Jesus, that's that awful thing Dad told me about, how they strapped her to the table and pushed that garden hose down her throat." Michael looked disgusted, mad that anyone would cause his little sister more pain than she was already experiencing.

"Michael, without that test Susan could well have died. A cyst holds poison, and when it bursts, as it will someday, that poison will spread through her entire body. Unless they remove it first."

"Well, when?"

Julie got up again, pacing in front of the window. "Oh, we had hoped for this week or next. John Sherman says there is only one man to do the surgery. A Dr. Kaplan, and he's out of town for two weeks."

"Well, there's got to be someone else. I know Marcus Welby's canceled, but there should be some good guys hanging around UCLA."

"No, John says Tom Kaplan is the best surgeon in the world. He studied under Dr. Ellison, nothing but pancreas research, and he now, I'm told, has exceeded what Ellison accomplished. Even Ellison's associate suggested Dr. Kaplan and no one else do the surgery."

"It's such a big thing to remove a little cyst?"

Julie shook her head and folded her arms tightly, as though she were shivering. "No, no, no. Michael, it isn't a *little* cyst, first of all. It was years ago when they couldn't find it, but I understand it's a good size now. That's why they want to remove it soon. And there's more to it, something about the duct from the pancreas being stopped up and pressing on the portal vein.... Oh, I don't know exactly; I'm not a doctor. And Bob hasn't been here to hear all this, and I feel as if I'm going to be given my degree in medicine."

"Dad doesn't know?" Michael looked surprised.

"I just found out a few days ago, the urgency of it all. I thought it best to tell your father when he came back. Why ruin his trip for no. . . ." Julie's voice trailed off as automobile headlights outside caught her attention. "Oh, your father's home!"

Michael walked to the window and stood looking through the wet glass as the car made its way up the long driveway. Then, almost directly behind it, another car, a bigger, whiter car pulled into the drive and stopped at the gate. "Michael, run down and let them in."

Michael dashed down the stairs and laid his hand on the button which triggered the electric gates.

Bob maneuvered his car around Michael and Lorna's Mustang and parked it in the garage. He closed the garage door just as Harry and Dolores were getting out of their car. "The rain's stopped," Bob said.

"Not only that," Harry added, "but it's warmer. Can you feel it? It's not gonna freeze." He smiled.

"What a relief," Bob said, stopping to let Dolores climb the steps in front of him.

She took his hand and tried to step over the puddle Michael had put his whole leg into, and she made it—barely. Some of the water rolled down into her little plastic rain boot. "Dammit," she muttered, turning to look at the two brothers who had just extolled the virtues of the climate of the moment. "Lovely, absolutely lovely," she said with a bite, and then walked up the stairs and opened the gate to the patio. "Shoulda gone to Miami for the winter," she said disgustedly as she walked toward the back door.

"Women," Harry moaned, looking at Bob.

Bob Sheppard just laughed.

Weather had wreaked havoc on California before. In 1950 heavy rains caused flooding in the San Joaquin Valley, the vegetable center of the United States. About 669,000 acres were inundated, and the crop loss was placed at over $35 million. In recent years, it had snowed in Pasadena to a depth of six inches. Actually that was in 1949, but the residents still talked about it as though it were yesterday, and, in the scheme of things some thirty years is a relatively short period of time.

So much depended on the weather in California, and not only people's dispositions. The state produced the most chickens, sheep, peaches, lemons, almonds, artichokes, avocados—the list is endless—in the country. Its huge fruit and vegetable industry had receipts each year totaling more than $8 billion. It boasted of the country's largest fishing industry outside Alaska, and for industry alone, it was worth more than $31 billion a year, not counting the oil industry, which was hard to put into figures because it was so vast. The fact was everything about California was big and important. The rest of America depended on the state, and when nature came into play, it took only a slight tilt of the scale to throw the great state into unbalance, and with it the rest of the nation.

Ever since Bob and Harry had become involved in business with the United States government, Julie was used to Bob's frequent trips to Washington. This past one had been difficult, however, because Susan was sick and the weather so bleak. Bob had tried to get out of it but couldn't, and the fact that it had to do with helping the city in which he lived, a city he loved, made the trip important for him. People who knew both brothers often remarked that it was unusual that Bob did the fieldwork when it was Harry who seemed to have something to get away from—an obviously unhappy marriage. But Harry hated to travel, and that was that.

But now Bob was home, and he took Julie warmly in his arms, holding her tightly for a moment, and then kissed Lorna and his granddaughter. "Michael, cut your hair," Bob said jokingly. It was his usual greeting for his son, whose hair wasn't really long at all. It sprang from the post-Beatles Sixties, when all Bob seemed to be uttering to his son at the dinner table was: "Michael, cut your hair." Michael never did, and it went on for years. Now it was a standard expression of their happy father-son relationship.

"How's Susan?" Bob asked, walking up the staircase with Julie. She told him what she'd told Michael, about Susan's day, and her request that he come in and see her even if she was asleep. "If she's sleeping soundly, I'll just have a look. She been resting well?"

"Yes, fairly well. She's really unhappy she has to miss out on tonight. Remember, she was the one who planned a six-month birthday party for Dawn in the first place."

Bob opened the armoire and set his briefcase inside. "Yeah, that's right. Honey, grab me a sweat shirt."

"A sweat shirt?"

"I know you'll say I'm nuts, but we planned a barbecue, and we're going to have one." Bob slipped out of his suit pants and put on his blue corduroys.

"You're not going to do a charcoal–"

"Yes, I am. Rain or no rain. Cold or no cold. The patio's dry anyhow, where the table is. I can just roll the Weber over there."

"You are crazy," Julie said, handing him a hooded sweat shirt from one of the dresser drawers. "All we need is you catching a cold."

"I'm strong as an ox. Anyhow, what good are hamburgers if they're not cooked over the coals, huh?"

Julie leaned against the bedpost with a silly grin on her face.

Bob stopped and stared at her. "Hey, what's that look?"

"Smell."

Bob sniffed. "Um. You're wearing Aliage, right? I win."

"Good guess, considering that's all I ever wear. No, don't you smell anything? Something cooking perhaps?"

Bob walked into the hall. "Oh, Jesus, I didn't even–" Then he laughed. "Here I'm talking about hamburgers, and you've got something delicious in the oven!"

"Sorry to disappoint you, chef, but I'm doing the cooking tonight."

Bob saluted. "Yes, sir."

"Honey, I just figured a barbecue was out, so I went to the

market and got a beautiful rolled pork roast and vegetables cooked in beer, and hot buttered rolls and—"

"Stop," he said, putting his arm around her as they walked toward the stairs. "I'm starving now as it is. Funny, all the way here I was having this vision of me running through the living room with cold hamburgers, standing there in my old Army jacket trying to cook in the corner there by the table."

"You're going to sit in the dining room and relax."

Bob walked down a step and turned to his wife. He put his hands on her waist. "I've missed curling up in that big warm bed with you."

"Meet you for cocoa at midnight?"

"Cookies, too? In the sack?"

"If you don't mind sleeping with crumbs."

Bob winked. "I don't care if they're rocks. You've got yourself a date."

They joined hands and went downstairs.

"Oh, Daddy," Susan said, surprised, as she opened her eyes. "I felt something on my cheek. I thought it was Samantha." At the sound of hearing her name, Samantha, Susan's silver tabby kitten, raised her head and meowed.

Bob looked at the cat and said, "Sorry, false alarm," and the kitten stretched, yawned, and went back to sleep, all curled up at the foot of Susan's mattress.

"Samantha sleeps more than I do," Susan said.

"Have you been sleeping a lot?"

She nodded. "You know it makes me sleep. It's better, though. I don't feel it hurt so much when I sleep."

"I'm going to leave you to do that right now. I just wanted to see you."

She looked up at him with her big, innocent eyes. "I missed you a lot this time, Daddy. You were gone so long."

He stood up. "It just seems that way, sassy. When there's no sun, it seems like one long night."

"I hate this weather."

"But it's great weather to be sick in."

That made her smile. He was right; she wasn't missing much, except school, and that wasn't much either. "Mommy's dinner sounds great."

"It smells even better," Bob said, now acutely aware of the scent of the cooking meat. "Hungry?"

Susan shook her head. "Just sleepy."

"Okay, sassy, we're going to sit down to dinner now. I'll come talk to you after everyone's left, okay?"

"Okay." She closed her eyes and was back asleep even before he left the room.

Julie's dinner was a hit. Harry put it just right: "There's nothing like a delicious roast on a cold winter night." But the night wasn't as cold as expected. In fact, it was already warmer than it had been that afternoon. During the meal Carter DeSimone called Bob to tell him that his assistant, a brilliant young man named Rob Wynters, of all things, had finally come to the same conclusion–it would snow on Los Angeles before it would get warm again. Carter felt it was a breakthrough of sorts, because Rob had been the one person staunchly against his prediction, and the young man's opinion meant much to him. He told Bob he was fairly sure it wasn't going to get cold enough to freeze that night, and Bob was pleased as, in his mind, he saw Lorna and Michael getting the baby home safely without freezing rain to make things perilous.

After dinner Bob went out onto the patio. Michael joined him, and together they looked up into the dark sky. "Doesn't look a hell of a lot different from this afternoon, huh?" Bob said.

"Black pea soup."

"Carter was right. It's warmer. Warmer than this afternoon."

"That doesn't make sense."

"Does any of this?" Bob walked over to the pool and checked the skimmer, as he did periodically. It was filled with leaves. He reached in the icy water and scooped them out, then replaced the cover. "Julie said Mr. Carlos wasn't here at all this week."

"Who's Mr. Carlos?"

"The man who does the gardening. You know. . . ."

"Yeah, but it slipped. Thought it was a hairdresser with a name like that. You know, Mr. Philippe, Mr. Jon."

Bob folded up a lawn chair and put it under the eaves of the house, near Susan's window. Samantha stuck her head under the drape to see what was going on. "Carlos is the man's last name," Bob explained.

"I wondered what Ma was doing having a hairdresser come up to the house. How very chic."

"That'll be the day. We're lucky the pool man comes once a week. I want Mr. Carlos to cut some of these tree branches back. They hang so low when they're wet, and look at the water." Little droppings of sap were collected like a gigantic bathtub ring. And leaves floated everywhere.

"Who cares? You can't swim in it anyhow."

Bob opened a cabinet at the side of the patio and turned the pool switch to the on position. "It should go on automatically at midnight, but I think it needs to run more with all the rainwater in it."

"Dad, you really think it's gonna get worse?"

Bob listened for a moment, making sure the pool motor and pump were running all right. Then he looked up at the mushy dark sky again and said, "Yeah. Damn sure."

"The rain stopped. Look, not even a drizzle. Not a single drop."

"Wait." Bob opened the back door but turned to Michael before he stepped inside. "The calm before the storm."

After they got inside, Michael turned to lock the door. "You really listen to that scientist friend of yours, don't you?"

"It's not only that."

"What then?"

"Some kind of . . . I don't know, creepy intuition."

Michael had never heard his father say anything like that before.

The satellite pictures that had just arrived showed Carter a slight change in the pattern of the onrushing polar storm. By the time it had reached the northern border of the United States, off Vancouver, it had managed to pick up an unusually large amount of moisture from the ocean, more than ever expected. It was threatening to become a dangerous system that could cause much damage. But the low near San Francisco which seemed to be in the way was not turning out to be the weakling it appeared to be. Somehow it was nudging the massive onrush of air out to sea. Not very far, but enough to keep its major force away from at least a few hundred miles of California coastline.

At the National Weather Service in Los Angeles, weathermen, meteorologists, looked at the same photos, maps, and pondered the alternatives. After some thought they decided to study the situation further before releasing any prediction which could cause a stir. Maybe the storm would blow itself out over the ocean, or cut east into the Sierras. Either one would be the classic thing for it to do. And that was easiest for them to predict, because in the science of meteorology it was particularly easy to look back and see what had happened in the same situation the last time it was around. It was an easy way to judge, and a pretty accurate one at that.

So all the men agreed on one thing, a safe thing–L.A. would get heavy rain.

They relaxed in the living room, gathered around the fire, until Dawn woke up. Just as Julie went upstairs to change her diaper and fetch her to "blow out the candle," the doorbell rang.

"Did you open the gate?" Bob asked, wondering if perhaps Julie had pressed the button while she was in the kitchen. He was sure he hadn't heard anyone buzz.

"It . . . it must be Mrs. Kupperman. I did tell her to drop in, but I sure didn't think she'd go out in this weather." Julie got up and went toward the front door. The Kuppermans lived on one side of them, and there was a gate next to the garage which didn't require electrical assistance to get it open; it opened into the Kuppermans' backyard, which was as private as the Sheppards'.

"Minnie, Sam, come in. Hi, there, Billy. Come in." Julie took their coats, showed them into the living room, and introduced them to Harry and Dolores, who had never met them.

The Kuppermans were an elderly couple, and their grandson,

Billy, had come to visit them for a month from New York. He was only eight, and his parents were in the process of a divorce, and they agreed that it could be too painful for him. Thus, they shipped him to sunny California to stay with Grandma and Grandpa. Julie felt a little sorry for him because of the weather, that he was unable to go out and play and meet some other children down the street. And with Susan so ill, he didn't even have a playmate there. Julie had mentioned the little party for Dawn and welcomed them to drop in, and she was glad they decided to do it.

"We've been cooped up inside for so long, we just had to get out!" Sam Kupperman said, warming his frail old hands by the fire. Julie knew he had arthritis, and the weather must have been causing him a great deal of pain.

His wife seemed chipper, and that was the kind of woman she was, always optimistic, seeming so much younger than her sixty-eight years. "I said, the rain be damned, we're taking Billy out tonight! And then the rain stopped, just like that. We didn't even have to bring an umbrella."

Dolores set her drink down and said, "Oh, thank goodness I can go out for once without having to tie a rain bonnet over my head."

Mrs. Kupperman pointed a finger at Dolores. "You. You're the one."

"I'm the one what?"

"The one who sings. Julie told me what a pretty voice you have. Oh, yes, she did. I used to sing in the opera myself, back in Chicago."

"Really? That's delightful. But I don't sing anymore, not even in the bathtub." Dolores seemed to be blushing.

"That's not what I hear," Michael said. "In fact, Mrs. Kupperman, I think with a little coaxing you'll even get her to sing us a song. That is, if you'll sing one yourself."

Minnie Kupperman looked thrilled. "Damn right I will! But only if she will." She looked at Dolores.

"Well. . . ."

Then a voice said, "Come on, Aunt Dolores, I'll play for you," and everyone turned to the hall to see Susan standing there in her robe, holding her kitten in her arms. She looked pale, but she was smiling.

Around the room voices breathed, "Susan!" and Michael said, "Well, kid, you're a trouper. I woulda bet you wouldn't let a chance to show off those nimble fingers go by."

Susan walked into the room and sat on the chair next to her father. "Hi, Billy," she said to the little boy, who seemed frightened.

"Hi, Susan. I was going to come visit you yesterday, but Gram said I shouldn't."

Mrs. Kupperman piped up. "Now, Susie, don't you go blaming me. I heard from your mommy that you were not receiving gentlemen callers yesterday, that's all."

Susan laughed. She thought Mrs. Kupperman reminded her of a record her big brother used to play, "The Little Old Lady from Pasadena."

"I'd like to play a song for you too, Mrs. Kupperman."

"What's a party without song?" Minnie asked, and got up and walked to the piano.

Everyone gathered around. Susan took her place on the piano bench. Julie gave her a look which asked, "Are you feeling up to doing this?" And the answer in Susan's eyes was an unqualified yes. Minnie Kupperman found the song she wanted to sing—"April Showers"—but she was voted down by everyone. "How about 'Raindrops Keep Falling on My Head'?" she asked, giggling.

" 'Don't Rain on My Parade'!" Michael said.

Susan played a few notes and sang, in a near whisper, "Rain, rain, go away, come again another day." And everyone applauded.

Lorna came down with Dawn and joined the group around the piano. Minnie Kupperman sang "A Bicycle Built for Two," with a few bawdy lyrics of her own, at which her husband blushed and which everyone else loved. Then Dolores sat on the piano bench with Susan and sang a song she loved, Stephen Sondheim's "Send in the Clowns." It had become Dolores' favorite song in the world the minute she'd heard it, and after seeing Jean Simmons sing it in *A Little Night Music*—three times—she'd bought the sheet music for Susan. It had become the girl's biggest accomplishment, and her piano teacher told her some of her older pupils had still not mastered it; Susan was still a little shaky on it, but she followed Dolores perfectly.

It never ceased to amaze Bob. Dolores had a wonderful voice. She had the uncanny ability to make you laugh or cry with her, with her music. He lost sight of it, forgot about it, when she wasn't near the piano. She was just his sister-in-law, his brother's wife. Talent seemed to be something reserved only for his kids, they were brimming with it. But others being talented, too? It knocked him out, and he loved it.

Julie found it a little sad. Dolores had such a beautiful voice, and yet what had she done with it? Nothing. She felt talent was a God-given gift and was required to be shared. Secretly she blamed Harry for Dolores' concealment of her talent; he had made her give up a professional career when they married. Dolores sang the lyrics, "... losing my timing this late in my career ..." and Julie looked into her eyes. Dolores was singing, she thought, about herself, about her life.

When she finished, Susan played "Happy Birthday," and everyone sang along, and Michael, who'd sneaked out during the song, walked in with a birthday cake and the smallest candle anyone had ever seen.

"Make a wish!" Julie said to Dawn.

"Wish for the weather to change," Harry mumbled.

Dolores said, "She'll make her own secret wish, won't you, darling?"

"We have the moon," Michael said dramatically in the best Bette Davis voice he could muster up, which was pretty terrible. "Let's not ask for the stars."

"Oh, shut up!" Lorna said, laughing.

"What's that from?" Minnie Kupperman asked.

"Now, Voyager," Michael said, "you know, where Paul Henreid lights the two cigarettes in his mouth and gives her one."

Minnie nodded. "I liked *Jezebel* better."

"Come on, Dawn, blow out the candle," Lorna said, getting back to the point.

Everyone huffed and puffed and nearly blew the frosting off the cake. It was a happy time, as though the depressing weeks of darkness and rain had disappeared. Everyone went into the dining room for ice cream and cake, and Susan said good-night and went back to bed.

However, fifteen minutes later, she called out, and Julie and Bob had to give her a hypo for pain. Julie expressed her concern over Susan's having joined the party, but the girl looked up and said, "Mama, I had to. I just had to do it."

Julie bit her lip. She held back tears. "I understand. Rest now."

And they left her with Samantha in her arms.

The mayor's broadcast went on on schedule, and the big surprise was that he made it official; he informed all Los Angeles that Carter DeSimone had made a startling prediction. Snow. It wasn't a surprise to any of the people gathered around the TV set in the Sheppards' family room; they all knew about the prediction from Bob. But they greeted the thought with the same kind of reaction that most Angelenos responded with—amusement. In any other part of the country the broadcast wouldn't have been an event at all.

The mayor assured the people that there was nothing to worry about. However, because he valued DeSimone's expertise, he was putting "snow crews on alert" at the request of himself and the City Council. "More than likely," he stated with a grin, "we're in for some very heavy rainstorms and some freezing temperatures. We urge those people who can get around without taking their cars to do so."

When he finished, Bob clicked off the TV and said, "My, my, our snow crews will have their first alert in history."

"What snow crews?" Michael asked.

"This city doesn't even own a snow *plow,*" Harry chimed in. "All this bullshit."

Dolores stood up. "Snow. Rain. *Yecch.* We should have gone to Miami, told you so, Harry."

"It's raining there, too; yes, it is," Mr. Kupperman volunteered. "My brother Frank lives there, and he said it doesn't stop raining this winter."

Lorna said, "God, maybe we all should have gone to Mars for the winter. Someplace warm, maybe even the sun."

"More coffee anyone?" Julie asked.

Dawn was squirming. "Time for us to go," Lorna said. She stood up, lifted the baby, and handed her to Michael. "Daddy'll dress you."

"Why me?"

" 'Cause I'm gonna have more coffee," Lorna said with a smile, and went upstairs.

"She got ya that time," Minnie Kupperman said, as they all got up to leave.

After the neighbors had gone home and the two cars had driven out the gate, Bob checked on Susan—she was sleeping soundly—and put out some food for Samantha and turned out the lights in the living room and den. Julie told him she'd be right up, as he went to the bedroom, washed up, and slid, relaxing, into the big bed he'd missed. Then, right at the stroke of twelve, keeping her promise, Julie walked in with a tray of cookies—chocolate chip, his favorite—and mugs of steaming cocoa.

"Winter be damned," Bob said, "but it does have its good points," as Julie got into bed with him.

THE SECOND DAY

FRIDAY, JANUARY 16
HIGH TEMPERATURE 35°; LOW 22°

THE RESPITE FROM THE WET WEATHER DIDN'T LAST LONG. BY morning a steady drizzle was falling, and people cursed it as they left their homes and apartments to go to work. It meant, of course, that the freeway traffic would be worse than usual; all the street traffic would be moving at a snail's pace. Los Angeles often boasted of the world's best drivers, the reasoning being that you *had* to be a good driver to survive on the freeways; you were forced into it. But a curious thing happened when it rained. Those "perfect" drivers didn't know what to do, how really to drive in it. The arteries to and from the city became tangled with bumper-to-bumper traffic, small accidents tied up roads for hours, and the people living in the hills thought they'd suddenly relocated to San Francisco because the sound of squealing tires and grinding brakes filled the normally quiet air.

The city was not quiet this morning, not by any means. Car horns seemed to be blowing everywhere. Children on their way to school shouted and squealed as they jumped over puddles. The city had put every bus it owned into operation because so many people had wisely decided not to drive; the roar of the big engines and the smell of the exhaust fumes lay heavy on the inner part of the city. In Glendale, at Forest Lawn, a funeral procession was making its way up the winding drive in the drizzle, a backdrop that seemed almost ordered for mourning. All along the ocean, winds battered the houses, and the waves threatened moorings. An athlete in his early twenties who jogged along the center strip of San Vincente Boulevard each morning—rain or no rain—finally gave up; his shoes sank too deeply into the saturated turf. The ground was too slick.

By 10 A.M. most people were at their jobs, and some of the tension was being relieved. Everyone had a tendency to forget, to forgive the skies for playing such a lousy trick. Well, maybe they deserved it; the weather earlier in the year had been the best they'd had in a long time. Especially when the rest of the country was being torn apart by tornadoes, hurricanes, and slight earthquakes. California was still the blessed land.

Shortly after 10 A.M., a car pulled to a stop in front of the Los Angeles Free Clinic, and Michael Sheppard got out through the passenger door. "Hey, I appreciate the lift," he said, and slammed it shut. Crazy jerk, he thought to himself, how the hell did we make it alive down Sunset Boulevard? He opened the door and ducked in out of the rain.

He found Lorna sitting at her desk, talking on the phone. "Sure, Mrs. Quesana, we won't close, we'll be here. . . . You do that, as soon as the weather breaks. . . . Okay, now keep your spirits up." She looked up at Michael, who was sitting atop her desk, rubbing his fingers through his hair. "You look shook."

"Um. Hitched a ride, and it turns out to be a guy whose former job was driving a roller coaster at Coney Island."

"What are you doing here? I was going to leave at noon to pick you up."

"Audition's been moved up. Marguerita took Dawn, and I figured I'd hitch here and get the car, and you can work later if you want. Okay with you?"

Lorna smiled. "Sure. I wasn't happy about taking the afternoon off anyhow. You sure Marguerita doesn't mind?"

"Loving it. What else can she do? She can't go out, can't putter with the flowers, can't go walking to the movies. Just sits in, watching the candles burn under the Blessed Virgin. I figured Dawn wouldn't mind watching the candles burn with her."

"Do you know when you'll be finished?"

"You kidding?" he asked, pouring himself some tea from the machine in the corner. Hot tea, hot soup, coffee, and ice water—all from one gadget. He liked it. "You should bring this home one day," he said. "They'd never know who took it."

"Oh, Michael, come on."

"Honest, I love it."

"Love it here. Drop in more often, and you can play with it all you want."

He flashed his eyes, and a silly grin came to his face. "Can we play with it together?"

"If you lock the door."

Michael leered at her and turned to the door—no lock. "How are you feeling toward exhibitionism this morning?"

Lorna broke up in giggles. "Didn't you have enough last night?"

Michael shook his head. "Nope."

Lorna whispered, "Well, I did. Fulfillment, they call it." She went over and let him put his arms around her. "Now I've got work to do." She kissed his nose. "And you're preventing me from doing it."

"Two orgasms does not a fulfilled evening make. For me."

She kissed him. Then: "Hey, what does that mean, exactly?"

"Exactly, I'm not sure. Generally, I have a bad case of the hornies."

"Good, it'll make you more alert for your audition."

Michael slid his hands down over her buttocks. "Oh, God, why can't this be an audition for a porno film?"

"You make a porno film, and I'll divorce you," she said, lifting his hands from her body, warning him. Then she smirked and said, "After I see the film, that is."

Michael smiled. "Rain makes me horny."

"Sunshine makes you horny. Wind makes you horny. Rain makes you horny. Ever been to the North Pole?"

"Yup."

"How'd you feel up there?"

"Horny."

Lorna let him put his hands back where they'd been. They kissed for a long time, and then Michael pulled away. "Oh, Jesus, I've got a–"

"Go take a cold shower." Lorna walked back to her desk.

"All you gotta do is go outside."

"Hey, aren't you going to be late for your reading?"

He nodded.

"Don't you think you ought to get going?"

"Guess what happened when we left last night?"

"Huh? Michael, what are you talking about?"

"Mom and Dad were doing it."

"Oh, you're impossible," she groaned, and fell into her chair. She lifted her bag from the floor and searched for her car keys.

"Lorna, I can always tell, I know the look in Dad's eyes. I really think he's been faithful to her all these years; he doesn't mess around on those trips. He comes home horny as hell."

"Like father, like son," she said, holding up the car keys. "Here. Take the chariot and get thee to work." She tossed the keys, and he fumbled and missed.

"I can't catch a ball, Lorna," he muttered, picking them up from the floor, "so what makes you think I can catch these?"

A woman knocked at the door and then opened it. "Lorna, there are some people here to see you."

"Thanks, Mavis." The woman walked out. "I may be late, Michael, so don't worry about me. Can you get dinner on?"

"You want me to pick you up?"

"No. I'll hustle a ride from someone here or take the bus. Make dinner, and I'll be ever grateful."

"What we got?"

"Everything's there for stew; just stick it in the pot."

"Will do. See you later. Wish me luck."

She pecked him on the cheek and he left, twirling the key ring on his fingers.

Outside, Michael got serious. He'd seen the people in the waiting room, the looks on their tired and bewildered faces, the confusion, the discomfort. He wondered how Lorna put up with it, all the depressing stories and the problems. It was bad enough people brought their physical problems to the clinic, accidents, VD, assorted diseases they didn't understand and didn't have the money to take to a hospital. But it was something else again to hear the emotional problems, the potential suicides, the pleas of the hungry and downtrodden and defeated. And that's where Lorna shone, for she had some miraculous ability to give people hope. Michael knew he could never do it, never in a million years.

He turned the key in the lock and jumped into the Mustang. Again he ran his fingers through his hair, so the water wouldn't make it sit flat on his head, so the curls stayed as they were supposed to. He looked in the rearview mirror. Not much damage. Vanity. He hated it, but he was an actor, and it was part of the life. He started the car and pulled away from the curb, wondering, seriously, if rain actually made him horny.

There was confusion not only in the waiting room of the Free Clinic, but everywhere. And one place it seemed magnified was the communications center, where Carter DeSimone and Rob Wynters and several hundred others tried to work in a chaotic environment. There had been confusion and harsh words in the office for the past few months, but not until today had it reached its peak. Today it wasn't the idea of an impending snowstorm that was causing the worry and the friction; it was the same fear as the day before, a more immediate fear—this time everyone was positive it would happen: freezing temperatures. It was the storm in a high-pressure area over Baja California which had saved the city from freezing temperatures the night before. But today the storm had passed. And the air was moving in from the deserts. It had been a cold 18° in parts of the high deserts the night before.

Rob Wynters walked into Carter's office with a grim look on his face. "You want to hear more?"

Carter put his feet on his desk and chewed on his glasses. "Why not?"

"The mayor's office is besieged—that's the word they used—with calls, all about snow. *How could His Honor believe such a joke to the extent of putting snow crews on alert?* That's one side of it. The full range extends to how wonderful it would be if it did snow; L.A. has been without it for too long anyhow." Rob shook his head and smiled. "It's funny, out there I was just thinking . . . oh, never mind."

"No, I want to hear. Tell me."

"I was just sitting here thinking how it would be fun to build a snowman right in His Honor's front yard."

Carter snickered. "I think the work's getting to you."

"Yeah, well."

Carter put his glasses back on. "What else?"

"Traffic bureau is crabbing because the situation on the streets is such a mess, and they're blaming it on everyone being scared out of their wits because of you."

"Oh, come on. What bullshit!"

"The word is, 'Let's have something more substantial,' that from the top PR officer of the great city of Los—"

Carter cut him off. "Yeah, sure, substantial. I dragged in a lousy map, satellite photos, even showed the mayor a book on the possibility of an impending ice age."

"I saw that."

Carter looked over his specs. "You read it?"

"No."

He reached under some papers and handed his young aide the book. "Here. Do."

Rob looked at the title and cringed. "You saying you really believe this?"

"I'm not saying anything. Just read it."

They were interrupted by a woman assistant who looked upset. She burst into the room and stood there, shaking. Then she laughed out loud and said, "Oh, it has to be a joke. Tell me it's a joke."

Rob and Carter just stared at her. They'd never seen her acting this way before. She was holding a computer readout in her hand. "Let me see, Marie," Carter said, reaching up.

Marie walked to him and handed it to him. "It's a joke; someone up there is kidding."

"Up where?" Rob asked. Was she talking about heaven? "You mean the National Weather Service, don't you?"

Marie nodded. "And more. The National Center for Atmospheric Research phoned ten minutes ago, and this just came over the wire." She dropped the National Weather Service computer readout onto his desk:

. . . SNOW POSSIBLE—SANTA BARBARA SOUTH TO AND INCLUDING SAN DIEGO—WITHIN 48 HOURS . . .

Carter put his hands behind his head and leaned back in his chair. "Well, now maybe they'll believe me," he said, somewhat satisfied. "Now maybe they won't laugh. The biggies are behind the prediction now."

"Not only that," Marie continued. "The national center said they can tell the world what's *going* to happen—that it is almost doubtless that it will snow here—but they aren't at all sure *why.*"

Rob nodded. "When it comes to explaining how all this happened, much less predicting how bad it will be or when it will happen again, professional weathermen are scarcely more knowledgeable than the rest of the shivering, bone-chilled people on the streets."

"We're not dealing with an exact science, Robert," Carter said. "Which makes us a little mad. Music is an exact science. If we wanted exactness, we'd have all been musicians."

"They're mad, too," Rob said with a smirk.

"Any more, Marie?"

The girl said, "Yes, there's a wire from the National Weather

Service's long-range prediction group in Camp Springs, Maryland. It says just how long the arctic winds are going to continue is anybody's guess. They're sure the trend of polar air will bring snow along with forceful winds, creating blizzardlike conditions. *I just find it so hard to fathom!* I want someone to tell me it isn't so, you're all kidding."

Carter wished he were. But every weather bureau and reporting station in the country was now agreeing with him; most had seen it coming but had remained silent until the last minute, because it *is* that very unexact science and because the whole idea seemed totally ludicrous, and weathermen were often more embarrassed than any other group of people in the public eye and didn't want to risk more scorn when they weren't sure.

Carter knew even the most sophisticated attempts at long-range seasonal weather prediction had to rely heavily on experience and intuitive judgment. Sure, Los Angeles could have prepared for snow, had the city known long before, but what experience in the world could foretell such a disaster? It had never happened before. The three-man team at the Camp Springs base had done what they could without alarming anyone; they'd predicted, as early as the previous spring, that California's winter would be "severe" and quite possibly the state would receive the largest amount of precipitation it had known in over a hundred years. That news was greeted with high hopes by the people of the Golden State, for the disastrous drought of 1977 was still affecting the state years later. Water—in any form—was welcome. But no one ever dreamed of snow. In the mountains, sure. The ski resorts were ready for the biggest year ever, and the men who managed the reservoirs in the valleys awaited the spring runoff with great anticipation. No one dreamed of snow on the streets of Los Angeles and San Diego and Santa Barbara.

The silence was overwhelming. Marie didn't know if she should leave or if Carter still wanted to talk to her. Their minds were racing, hers, Rob's, Carter's, all filled with the same things, the same thoughts, all trying to comprehend what the experts were saying was to come.

Finally, Rob said, "You've got a friend over at the NCAR, Carter. What does he say?"

"Steve? Steve's probably the guy Marie talked to, the one who said he's not sure why." Carter motioned Marie out of the room. "Rob, I talked with Steve many times in the last few weeks, and he knew I was right, but he couldn't go out on a limb. There was always the chance it could reverse, change. There's always that chance."

Rob's eyes met his. "You think that option still exists?"

Carter took a long, hard breath. "No, not anymore. We're in for it." He glanced at the weather bureau printout in front of him again. "Rob, get me the mayor, right away, huh?"

"Yes, sir."

"But how—how could it possibly snow here in Los Angeles, in Southern California?" the mayor asked. "I don't care whether it sticks or not, I care about the fact that it just comes down. I want to know how, and I don't want weatherman mumbo jumbo. I want it straight so the people of this city can understand it."

And Carter gave it to him, as best he could.

"There's no doubt about it. The temperature of the ocean, and the position of air masses all around us, and the strength of the oncoming storms—"

"What oncoming storms?" the man bellowed.

"Actually, storm. Singular. One storm, the one bringing the snow."

"Jesus, I don't believe I'm hearing this from a grown man. From an expert yet."

Carter continued. "What it amounts to is a major snowstorm. And that could be *two* snowstorms if a pattern develops along the path of this first one. The heavy moisture in the air is going to condense in the cold as it reaches land and rises. On top of this, the ground temperature is not warm enough to melt the frozen crystals as they form and fall." There was no sound. "Sir? Are you there?" Carter thought maybe he had hung up on him.

"I'm here," the mayor said sullenly.

"This storm is something you would only find on an open prairie in the Midwest, for instance, but there are too many circumstances that make it inevitable here. On top of all this is a massive high-pressure area just sitting on the other side of the Rocky Mountains. It might stick around for a while. It's the Western version of 1977. Our turn. Sir, I'm certain of what I say. I stake my considerable reputation on it." There was no response. Then Carter added, "Consider too, strange things happen in life, in the history of the world, things which can't clearly be pinpointed as to why, things that can't be precisely defined and explained. You might say—what's the old saying—life is full of surprises? The weather has been changing all over the globe, drastically, in the past ten, even twenty years, and—"

The mayor cut him off. "You telling me it's gonna snow?"

"That is exactly what I'm saying."

"What are we going to do?"

"I think, sir, the first thing to do is to tell the people. Let them get out. Let them be prepared."

"You realize what kind of panic that'll cause? Can you see the airport and train stations? Good God, man, you're telling me to start a riot in my own city!"

Carter kept cool. "You *owe* it to the people to inform them," he said. "Put the blame on my shoulders. If it doesn't happen, I'll gladly take the chastisement."

Long pause. Then only, "Okay." And that was it.

Carter put the phone down and smiled a little. "I don't believe it, but I think the man's finally going to do the right thing." Then he put his feet on the desk and felt better that he'd begun to win one of the battles facing him.

Carter, Rob, and all the other people working on that floor of the building gathered around the Sony to hear the mayor's special broadcast. "... and I can assure you, my friends, the residents of Los Angeles and surrounding areas, that the rain will let up by nightfall. The finest experts are in touch with this office. Dr. Carter DeSimone has just informed me that the chance of snow which I brought up last night is diminishing . . ."

"What?" Carter snapped. Rob looked at him in astonishment. Everyone seemed stunned at the blatant lie.

". . . although the low temperatures are to continue for some time, I am told a warming front is ahead—"

Carter slammed his hand against the on-off button, and the mayor disappeared. "Robert, get me a press conference set up as fast as you can."

"Yes, sir."

"They won't believe me, they won't believe this machine," he said, kicking the computer printer next to him, "and the mayor lies to the people on television. Well, maybe they'll believe it when sleet hits their windows tonight." He walked into his office and slammed the door.

Bob Sheppard didn't hear the mayor's attempt at altering the elements. He was on the phone with Dr. John Sherman, who confirmed everything Julie had told him the night before and filled him in on the details. "John, I understand about the cyst. My mother was cystic. But Julie said something about a duct."

"The test we took, the surgical procedure we did at Cedars-Sinai?"

"Yes, I remember."

"Well, it surprised me, but clearly there's an obstruction there. Something is clogging it up, like a little dam. The area is enlarged, and the danger is we're pressing on the portal vein, the major vein leading to the lower part of the body."

"What's causing it?" Bob asked.

"Frankly, I don't know. Tom—Tom Kaplan, the surgeon I want to operate—thinks it must be scar tissue from the gallbladder surgery." Susan had had to have her gallbladder removed when she was seven, and there had been hope that the pancreas would function better with the diseased gallbladder nowhere around. It hadn't helped, however. In fact, it seemed to hurt, for as the years went by, scar tissue continued to form, and it was creating a kind of webbing in her upper abdominal cavity. "It could be just a malfunction of the pancreas; it could be carcinoma; we should be prepared for anything."

"You know, hearing that word," Bob said, "it doesn't strike as hard as you'd expect. Everyone says, thank God it isn't cancer. Julie and I realize there are worse things in the world than cancer."

"Cancer can be arrested. Bob, I'll tell you, though, I tend to agree with Tom. We had a case a few years ago, a young man who'd had chronic pancreatitis all his life, and he was on the verge of death. He'd had a pseudo-cyst removed when he was seventeen, and a history of painful attacks every six months since. Tom operated on him at twenty-eight and found the scar tissue from the first operation had just about cut off the duct; it was so swollen it had caused the portal vein to balloon. Tom put in a plastic duct and relieved the pressure on the vein, and we held our breath."

"How'd he do?"

"He's never been healthier in his life. I think we've got the same kind of thing with Susan. We're going to get her through this and get it behind her."

"When can you do it?" Bob asked.

"As soon as possible, obviously. But Tom is out of town, and with the situation outside, the hospitals are overcrowded, and half the nurses and staff are calling in sick or get tied up on the freeways most of the day."

"But, John, how long can we wait? There's got to be enough staff for something like–"

"There is. I want to wait about a week. Tom will be back in a few days, but I want a few more tests, and he may want to order some also. Besides, Susan's just come through an attack, and I want to build her up. We'll order some blood, and I think maybe she can get back to food early in the week. Can you bring her in for an IV today or tomorrow?"

"Sure."

"Bob, if she doesn't get better in the next few days, don't worry. Whatever the weather, we'll do everything there is to do.

If she doesn't respond well to food, or if the pain increases, we'll get her in the hospital and prepare her for surgery at once."

"Doc, we're out of hypos."

"I'll call the pharmacy. I'm going to lessen the Demerol to one hundred and leave the atropine at one/one-fifty. It'll be better to operate when the acute inflammation has died down anyway. I'm thinking now perhaps it won't be good to try anything by mouth but liquids. We can build her up in other ways."

"Whatever you say."

"Excuse me. . . ." There was a long pause. "I have to go. I'm at the hospital."

"As crazy there as the rest of the city?"

"Most of the nurses are sitting on the Pomona Freeway. Call me if you have any problems."

"Thanks, John." Bob hung up and walked into the den and told her what the doctor had to say. "He wants us to bring her in for an IV today or tomorrow."

"In this weather?" Julie said with apprehension.

"I think we should do it right now. He's at the hospital now anyhow."

"All the way to Century City?"

Bob thought about it. "No, we'll go down the hill. To Hollywood Presbyterian. They can call him if he hasn't already put in an order."

Julie looked outside. The water was hitting the pool in droplets. "But it will be terrible driving."

"Julie, it's not going to get any better. I want to go now. I don't want to chance it later in the day."

"All right. I guess it makes sense. I'll see if she's awake. She may welcome the adventure of it."

"I'll call Harry and tell him I'm not even going to drop in this afternoon. Oh, wait . . . he told me he wasn't going to go in today. What the hell, bosses' day off. I don't have to call anyone."

Julie helped Susan get dressed, and Bob pulled the station wagon around to the front of the house. Together they helped the weak girl into the car. Samantha perched on a windowsill in the living room as the car slowly made its way down the winding driveway and out the gates into the street.

"What're they expecting, the blitz, for Christ's sake?" Dolores asked as she stood there staring at the other shoppers in Ralph's Supermarket.

"Jesus, there's nothing left on the shelves," Harry added incredulously.

And it was nearly true. Some shelves were almost empty, most of the stock depleted. People were buying, stocking up. Carts were filled to the brim; husbands pushed one and the wife the other and the children one each. Lines of people waiting for the cashiers extended to the back of the store. "Takes you ten minutes to shop," Dolores said, "and a half hour to check out."

She and Harry found what they could. Most all canned items were gone, except for the expensive gourmet brands, which pleased them because they preferred them. There wasn't a box of Kleenex or a roll of toilet tissue left in the store. People hovered over a poor boy in a white apron and grabbed at the cans of dog food as he pried open the boxes; others took the whole cases.

Liquor wasn't going as fast, or else the store had a good supply. Dolores put two quarts of Ballantine scotch into their cart. They walked toward the back of the store, toward the end of one of the lines, and she said, "You get in line. I'll be just a minute." Harry didn't argue. In a few minutes she came back with a bottle of Ballantine in each hand.

"You're getting four of them?" Harry asked, almost embarrassed.

"If we're gonna get the blitz, I'm gonna be blitzed," she said, almost with a twinkle in her eye. It was an annoying look, one Harry had seen so often. He sometimes thought she drank partly just to irritate him.

He was partly right.

On the eleventh floor of the Federal Building on Wilshire Boulevard in Westwood, a young assistant in the weather bureau was being dressed down by his superiors for his poor observations; he'd been rejecting any notion of snow, calling the men who were tending to agree with DeSimone "idiots." And the "idiots" had almost fallen into the same trap as the young man—it was hard to believe a massive snowstorm could hit the L.A. Basin. But the possibility was very real, they knew that now, and they had to give warning. It was their duty whether they liked it or not. Nothing would be served by pretending—as the young man had been doing—that such a thing would not happen. It was a matter of pride to say the right thing, but they did not wish to bruise their egos by going out too far on a limb. Weathermen had been viewed over the years by the general public as hit-and-missers at best; a statement about impending snow could ruin their credibility forever if it didn't happen.

But they were agreed now that it was going to; even the young man had given in. And Carter DeSimone was going to make the formal announcement for all of them.

About fifteen minutes later reporters filled the room, and Carter DeSimone read the following statement:

"Gentlemen, it is my painful duty to inform you that a major snowstorm is likely—certain—to hit the Los Angeles area within forty-eight hours. I have looked over satellite and ground reports many times and picked the brains of all my colleagues to make sure this was actually valid, true. It cannot be denied; the National Weather Service officially agrees. A massive polar outbreak of proportions rarely seen anywhere on this continent is heading toward us from the north/northwest. It is skimming the coastline, being held off by low-pressure areas sitting below San Francisco.

"To add to this I have just seen the first evidence of a second storm coming out of the Alaskan gulf and following in the path of the first storm. At best we are going to get a few inches of snow; at worst, I cannot say what will happen. As you know, the temperature of the ocean is very low for this area, and the westerlies are feeding cold air into the Southland. I do not see the possibility of this storm system's being warmed easily or suddenly. I am sorry, deeply sorry, to have to report this. But it is my duty to the people of Southern California. My assistant will now give you details of what people can do to take initial steps to help themselves in this most unusual situation. . . ."

Rob took over and warned people about driving, being careful about walking, slipping, and sliding, generally telling them to stay in and watch TV. But no one listened to Rob much; the real news was Carter's report, and the newsmen were rushing to get it to the world.

Michael walked out the door of a building on the Twentieth Century-Fox Studios lot and wished he'd stayed inside. He ran to the Mustang in the parking lot and fumbled getting the key into the lock. "Hey, Mike, you did a swell job!"

He turned to see the casting director who'd just read him getting into his shining new BMW. "Thanks!" Michael yelled.

"Sometimes I wish I had your talent," the man shouted, and then closed the door with a wave.

Sometimes I wish I had your car, Michael thought as he closed the Mustang door. Everyone told him it was worth money, an old '67 Mustang. *If everyone tells me it's worth so much, why hasn't anyone made an offer?* "They're worth money," he said aloud, praying that the car would start. It didn't like rain. "This one, in particular, however, is not worth money." It didn't even like dampness. In fact, Michael was sure if you spit near it there was a good chance it wouldn't start.

Finally, it turned over, and he turned out of the lot. Casting directors. *They're so full of. . . .* Such nice guys. On the outside. Maybe they weren't so bad, really. What were they? Frustrated actors themselves, hopeful directors? Who ever invented them anyhow? Why didn't directors cast their own shows? *I'll be damned if anyone else will cast my pictures, when I'm directing. What a lousy reading.* Everyone seemed to be in a bitchy mood. People were late. Most of the day shot. The afternoon gone. *Shit. And I was supposed to be home cooking a stew.*

Michael talked to himself all the way down Pico to LaCienega. He'd never seen the traffic move so slowly. He looked at the floor on the passenger side. It was a puddle. Water seeped in somewhere at the bottom of the windshield on that side. Oh, well, he shouldn't complain, the thing was getting him home, wasn't it? He turned on the radio and got a loud crackling sound. So he switched it off and thought about how horny he was. That didn't help. *I'll be beating off and a bus will come by and forty women will look down and faint.* So he sang a song.

He came to a stoplight at Third Street and glanced at the people standing at the bus stop. He thought he recognized— Then the light changed. He took another glance and pressed the horn. He leaned over and cranked down the passenger window. "Greg! Hey, Greg!" The driver in the car behind him also laid on the horn, but no one was going anywhere. Michael called the guy again before he noticed him.

He ran to the car and dropped the newspaper he'd had over his head. "Michael," he said happily, and got in.

"Careful of the puddle!"

Greg lifted his feet and put them on the console. "I like riding with my knees in my mouth."

Michael put the car in gear, but the lights changed again. The guy behind him hit the horn again, and Michael threw him the finger. "I thought Tom picked you up," he said to the young man.

"He does. But he's stuck someplace in Brentwood. I said I'd get a bus. Wow, am I glad you came along. What are you doing down here?"

Michael told him. "You know what they're filming? I walked into the wrong sound stage first ... a picture about some little town in the California desert, all about a drought ... can you believe it? The whole stage looked like the Mojave. It was incredible."

"Sure. Hollywood? I'd believe it if you told me *this* is all fake, it's all for some new Irwin Allen picture. They say it's going to snow. It's probably the only way to get rid of the plastic snow Ross Hunter had left over from *Lost Horizon.*"

Michael laughed out loud. "Film fan that you are, did you see that piece of shit?"

"The dancing boys in the orange jockstraps weren't bad, but that was about all."

"I saw it after they cut that section."

"They should have cut the rest of the movie and left just that section in."

Michael laughed again. "Hey, how's the animal business during all this? Lorna and I haven't seen you guys in over a week."

"I know," the good-looking young man said. "It seems we get home and it takes 3 or 4 hours to unthaw, and we just cuddle up and fall asleep. I guess I know how Eskimos live, now."

"Are . . . well, are things okay between you and Tom? The last time I saw you–"

Greg remembered. He remembered the advice Michael had given him–allow his lover some privacy. Greg had done so, and the problem turned out not to be a problem at all; it was just that they'd been getting in each other's way, and Tom finally voiced the discomfort. Greg had read too much into it, and all Tom had needed was a little more room to breathe, time to think. It had worked out; it had brought them closer than ever.

Greg and Tom had been lovers for nearly 4 years, and they were Michael and Lorna's best friends. Greg Crespi was a veterinarian, and he was perfect for it–kind, gentle, loving animals as much as he loved people. Tom Jensen was 2 years younger than Greg, 25, but he didn't look a day over 18. He had the look of a rugged surf bum, the broad shoulders and muscles, the long blond hair; but his face was pretty–Lorna said it was beautiful, angelic–and the dichotomy between the almost-feminine features and the hard masculine body is what made him so compelling a person to look at. Besides that, he was interesting, and interested in everyone and everything. They both were. Michael and Lorna had met them the day they moved into Genesee Gardens. Marguerita had introduced them as "her boys." And they'd made Michael and Lorna feel welcome, as though they had lived there for years.

Tom was a chauffeur and often gave Michael a ride to auditions and acting classes in a Rolls or Mercedes 600. It was a trip, but Michael had been sure he lost a commercial once when a casting director saw him arrive in a Silver Cloud. Perhaps if he were Zsa Zsa, it wouldn't have mattered, it would even have been expected; but the fact that he was nobody and there were other nobodies out there who had arrived by bicycle meant he didn't get the job.

The thing about Greg and Tom, Michael had once explained to his parents, with whom he was pleased he could talk honestly and openly about homosexuality (although Julie mostly listened), was they didn't flaunt the fact that they were gay and in love. They didn't go to any great extent to hide it, either, or to try to pretend to the world that they were straight. They were just honest, and as private about their sex life as any heterosexual couple. They were good people, and Michael was honored that he was their friend.

It was late afternoon, near sunset, as Michael turned onto Genesee from Beverly Boulevard. Then they felt the back of the car slide out from under them. The rear tire hit the curb, and Michael stopped. The sound hadn't been a good one, and he wondered if he should take a look. "Let me," Greg said, "my feet are wet anyway."

Michael smiled and waited as Greg jumped out and looked at the back side of the car. He got back in and said, "Nothing, it was just the hubcap rubbing against the curb. But there's something I can't believe."

"What?"

"Ice."

"Ice?"

"Look in the curb."

Greg pointed, and Michael looked at the little puddle. On top of it was—yes, he could see it, he wasn't dreaming—a thin sheet of ice. And the rain, it wasn't really rain anymore; it was sleet. "Jesus Holy Christ," Michael muttered.

"I guess we didn't notice it because the blower warms the windshield," Greg said.

"I hope Lorna makes it home okay," Michael said. His voice had the sound of tension in it.

"And Tom's out driving in this," Greg added. He was equally worried. Then something caught his eye and took his mind off his lover. "Look at that!" Michael saw that the sprinklers were on on a lawn in front of a big house. "In the dry California climate the omnipresent sprinklers run, thanks to the curious people who live here, run even in the rain. . . ."

Greg laughed. "Man, some people just stick with tradition."

Michael smiled and turned the corner. They were almost home.

About the same time Michael and Greg were driving up Genesee Street, Carter DeSimone and Rob Wynters were up at the Griffith Park Observatory, directly above Bob Sheppard's house. There were many reasons for their being there. One was to avoid the reporters, to get away from the office and the feud with the mayor that had now become as newsworthy as the weather itself. Another, and more important, was to use the new meteorological facilities which had been set up. A third and more secret reason was Carter's personal contingency plan. Every city had contingency plans for disaster, wars, riots, food shortages. Los Angeles had them, too; that Carter knew. But some things are never planned for because they just don't enter your mind, there is no logical reason even to suppose such an occurrence would happen, such as snow falling in Los Angeles, snow of any magnitude which would present a problem.

When it came to plans for snow, Carter had always been alone, and he only thought about it as an exercise. He liked to discuss it with students in his classes at USC; it made a good lab experiment. The germ of the idea had really come to him after the Rand Corporation think tank came out with its earthquake disaster report. The city had paid a lot of money to pick the brains of a handful of men, and brilliant though they were, Carter saw room for improvement. So he'd made his own unofficial contingency plan, and that included turning the observatory—a building high above where the greatest problems would lie—into a command post in conjunction with the U.S. Army, which would take over dealing with the city in such an extreme disaster. In a major catastrophe the Griffith Observatory would become the major spot from which operations would be run.

It was in an enviable position. Sitting high above the city on a big promontory near the high Mount Hollywood, the view spanned the Greater Los Angeles Area. The building itself was solid, strong, old, but it had withstood all the earthquakes, some flooding, and brush fires. It had the capabilities of becoming, in a matter of hours, a powerful communications center, a weather prediction center, even a headquarters where operations could be directed in a disaster. The large parking lot would be a perfect landing pad for helicopters, Carter knew, and it would certainly be a safer spot from which to work than a building in the heart of the city.

Rob and Carter looked over charts and discussed the possibility—probability, inevitability?—of moving their headquarters up there. Then Carter abruptly went out onto the observation deck. He held his hands up. He turned his face to the dark sky. Sleet hit his palms, his forehead. Sleet. Freezing rain.

He looked out over the vast city and saw nothing but the gathering of the icy wetness on his glasses.

Lorna climbed aboard a bus in front of the Free Clinic. It was full of wet, unhappy people. She had to push and shove to get on, but once the bus had started to move, a man offered her his seat, much to her surprise. She started to refuse, but he insisted. "I'm getting off next stop." She thanked him and sat down. She watched the window. And watched. And watched. What was happening fascinated her—it was just like the steps of the apartment house the night before. Sure, she thought, it freezes first on overpasses on highways; that's why the steps froze last night—they're just slabs of concrete suspended on steel.

But it wasn't the steps she was looking at; it was glass. The glass of the bus window, which now reminded her of her childhood, when she stenciled snowflakes and wreaths on the window panes with Glass Wax. It reminded her of waking up with Michael in the cabin at Big Bear Lake and seeing frost on the window.

My God, it is snowing! But then she realized it wasn't. The air was filled with rain, but the rain was freezing. The temperature was dropping; it had been for hours. The sleet was gathering on the windows. Lorna listened as the other passengers talked about what was happening. None of them had ever seen it before, not in L.A. Many people were seeing it for the first time in their lives.

Lorna thought about getting home and she hoped Michael had made a delicious stew. She dreaded the walk from the bus stop to the apartment in this slippery cold.

Then she began to worry about the Quesana family, their little apartment which already was cold, the broken windows. . . . She closed her eyes and put her head back and wondered why nothing seemed fair.

"I told you we should have gone straight home from the goddamn market," Harry growled as he sat tight in the seat, maneuvering the Big White Boat north on the San Diego Freeway. For some reason—and the San Diego Freeway never seemed to make sense anyhow—the traffic was moving fairly well, except for the cars which were sliding onto the center strip or into the green ivy to the side.

"You're the one who wanted Greek olives. You're the one who suggested Italian sausage in the first place. You're the one who doesn't like Italian sausage from anyplace but the Italian deli in Santa Monica. You're the one who won't eat mostaccioli without fresh imported Parmesan. You're the one who has to have Perrier water with—"

"Will you shut your goddamn mouth already?"

Dolores lit a cigarette and dropped the crumpled empty pack on the floor. "Blame me for getting stuck on Lincoln Boulevard for an hour."

"Dammit, Dolores, you flick ashes on the floor, you throw trash on the floor; if we had a dog, you'd probably teach him to shit on the floor. There's an ashtray, you see?" Harry was shouting, irritated as much by the traffic, the sleet, and a terrible headache as by his wife's lack of respect for his car.

"I never liked this tank," she said.

"Then why do you drive it?"

" 'Cause you won't buy me a Jaguar."

"Oh, Jesus, that again. You've got a perfectly decent car."

"I like how a Jaguar looks. I'm not crazy over a Gremlin." She flicked an ash to the floor.

Harry saw it but didn't say anything. He tried reasoning. "I've told you before. I buy American. I'm a believer in supporting my own country and its products."

"Like you supported Nixon." The car jerked as Harry slammed on the brakes to avoid missing a small pickup truck which had swerved in front of him. "Some product he turned out to be."

"You realize almost fifty percent of the color televisions sold in this country are Japanese made? That's a disgrace."

She slumped in the seat. "Do you realize those same fifty percent are of better quality than the American ones?"

"Like hell."

"And I'll bet if we were to rip open that set that sits in the family room, that good old red, white, and blue set of yours, you'd find it full of foreign transistors and whatever other crap they put in there."

"Look out that side for me," Harry ordered, seeing the sign for Sunset Boulevard.

Dolores turned her head and said, "Well, I can barely see through this stuff." The window was coated with sleet.

"Then roll it down, or we'll be driving up over the mountains into the Valley."

Dolores rolled down the window, muttering. She felt the gust of wind and the freezing rain hit her face. She put her head out the window and flagged the car next to them to hold back. "All right, get over there," she told Harry.

Harry put on his blinkers and turned into the outside lane. Dolores rolled up the window. She ran her fingers over her hair, brushing off the wetness. "God, I hate this," she said, stubbing her cigarette out in the ashtray.

Harry put his blinkers on again and started onto the ramp. But then, suddenly, another car swerved in front of him, turning onto the exit ramp from the middle lane. Horns blared, and

Harry shouted an obscenity, and Dolores grabbed the dash. He hit the brakes, but the incline was too great. They swerved and slid—the motion felt smooth, as if they were spinning on a cloud—and made a complete circle. Then there was a loud thud. "Harry!" Dolores cried, reaching out to him, and as he braced himself behind the steering wheel, they were hit in the side by another car. And then it was over.

There was little damage, to the automobiles, to the people. But they were stuck. The car which had caused the accident in the first place had somehow made it through and was moving in traffic on Sunset. But behind it, on the off-ramp, was a jam that would tie up the San Diego Freeway for days. Harry's Continental was sitting half in dirt, half on the ramp. Another car was pushed up against the driver's door, blocking the rest of the ramp. Another car, a truck, a van, and several other vehicles were lined up in corkscrew fashion all the way onto the freeway, all touching each other in some way. Doors started being opened, and angry, irritable, nervous drivers and passengers bemoaned the situation, but there was little to do and no one to blame. The blame went to the skies.

Dolores held on to Harry. "Oh, Jesus, what happened?" Everything seemed still now, as though a carnival ride had come to an end. "Are we all right?"

"I'm all right," he said. "How about you?"

She nodded and sat up straight. "Oh, God, look," she moaned, turning her head to the back seat. "I said we should have put the stuff in the trunk." Bags of groceries had fallen. Links of Italian sausage were strewn all over the floor.

"The trunk's full of all the stuff you were taking to Goodwill." Harry looked out his door window. He didn't try to lower it because he was afraid it wouldn't go down. A car's bumper was resting inside the door.

"We forgot to drop the Goodwill stuff off. Oh, damn."

"The hell with Goodwill, get outta the car." He started to slide toward her.

She looked at him with an incredulous expression. "Out of the car?"

"Outta the car! Gotta see if we can get outta this mess."

She opened her door and stepped out into the mud. The foliage around them was already covered with white sleet. Her heels sunk into the earth, and she pulled the collar of her fur coat up around her neck. "You okay, lady?" a young man shouted to her.

Dolores nodded. "Yes, thank you." He was standing next to his automobile, the one that had plowed into their side. Harry got out the passenger door and walked over to the guy as Dolores stood shivering in the rain. They talked, and others joined them. Finally, she sat back down inside the car and tried to close the door, but the incline was too steep–she couldn't pull the door shut.

And then she smelled something familiar and turned to look in the back seat. One of the bottles of Ballantine had broken open in the crash; it was flooding the fabric of the seats. "Oh, no," Dolores moaned. She was not bemoaning the fact that the car's interior was damaged.

Harry finally came around her side. "Come on, we're going to hike it."

"What?"

"We've gotta walk. It's only about a mile; maybe we can get someone to pick us up on Sunset."

"I can't walk ... I can't do this...." She seemed on the verge of tears. How could she walk on ice in those shoes? How could they just leave the car there? How could he even think of walking a mile? She was shivering already; what would happen if they tried to walk in this horrible freezing wind?

"Dolores, there's nothing anyone can do. No cops are around. None of us can get our cars to move; there's no sense in even trying. We'll leave it here and come back in the morning when it warms up. It's that or stay here and freeze to death."

"I can't!" she screamed.

Harry grabbed her by the arm and pulled her up from the seat. "Dolores, come on. If I can do it, you can do it. I'm not leaving you here, and I'm not staying here. So we're going hiking." He slipped and fell backward into the muddy soil. "Goddammit!" he yelled.

It stunned her, seeing him lying there, his coat covered with mud and sleet. "Oh, Harry, forgive me . . . forgive me," she cried. She helped him up. "I hate it, oh, I hate it so much!" Then tears rolled down her face. He let her cry. He reached into the car, took some papers from the glove compartment, and then put the keys in his pocket. "Come on," he said as he slammed the heavy door.

"But . . . but the food," she said.

"Hell with the food. It'll keep. Like one big refrigerator." He started to walk around the car, to the asphalt. Then he stopped and froze for a moment—everyone in the area did. There was a loud, nearly ear-shattering crash. Then nothing; silence. Whatever the accident, it had been much worse than their little scrape. "Thank Jesus for small favors." Harry buttoned up his coat and turned to help Dolores up onto the pavement.

But she wasn't there.

She had opened the car door again and was kneeling on the front seat. "Dolores!" Harry shouted, looking through the windshield. "What the hell?" And then he figured it out. He didn't need to see. It wasn't the groceries she was worried about.

She was getting the booze.

Bob walked into the emergency room waiting area. His hair was covered with sleet. Julie looked up from her novel. "Oh, it isn't!"

"It is. We've got to get home before the road gets too slick." He'd left Julie there while Susan was getting the IV and gone to the pharmacy to get the vials of Demerol and atropine.

Julie looked up at the clock. "About fifteen minutes yet," she anticipated. "Is it bad out?"

"Rotten. Cars are skidding all over the place. An ambulance went down the street, and I thought it was going to take off and fly."

"You know something I never thought about before?"

Bob sat next to her. "What?"

"Well, yesterday, driving down the hill to the market, I thought about it freezing. I've never driven on ice before. I don't know what it would be like."

"You and most other Californians."

Julie clasped Bob's cold hand in her warm ones. "I hope it won't frighten Susan any," she said almost in a whisper.

"Julie, she'll be sleeping; you know that. Even if she were alert, she'd probably love it."

Julie nodded, but without conviction. How could anyone love it? It wasn't even an oddity anymore; there was nothing curious about it any longer. It had gone on long enough, and it was time for it to be over. Love it? She had been able to stand it, to live with it, but she'd never even got close to liking it.

Now—with the freezing rain being the frosting on the cake, the last straw, all the clichés she could think of—she hated it. She hated it, and she hated what her daughter was having to go through. It wasn't easy to cope with, seeing her little girl in pain, knowing the surgery she would be facing soon, knowing the outlook for the future was none too good, surgery or no surgery, and now the weather, which had seemed just an ugly backdrop at first, was really beginning to affect them. Would they get home safely on the icy streets? Would the house stay warm? Could they get an ambulance quickly if Susan needed it?

Julie put her head on Bob's shoulder and closed her eyes.

The accident Lorna was in was a great deal more serious than the minor mishap Harry and Dolores experienced. A car slammed into the side of the bus, both vehicles slid, the bus driver lost control, and the bus came to rest on its side on the front lawn of a house. Lorna felt the impact and knew what was happening, but then everything went around, as though she'd grown dizzy and nearly fainted. Colors twisted before her eyes, the colors of people's clothing, their bags and umbrellas and briefcases and raincoats. Then there was a strange silence for a moment, and finally cries of pain, of confusion, of shock.

Lorna was unhurt except for a little cut above her eye. She felt the blood running down her face as she knelt there on one of the broken windows. She grabbed a kerchief she saw lying near her and pressed it to her head. She curled up against the ceiling of the bus and waited as people stepped on each other in an effort to get to their feet, to get out. Lorna covered her head as a man braced his foot on her shoulder, trying desperately to push himself up through one of the windows. A woman passenger fell against her as she lost her footing trying to move toward the door, where people were already reaching down and pulling the passengers out.

Finally, Lorna got up. She felt dazed, but she knew she was all right. Three men—one, the bus driver—helped her up and out. She sat on the top—which was the side of the bus—for a moment in the rain and caught her breath. "You okay?" a man said.

"I'm fine. My head . . ."

"Let me look." He pulled her hand away and saw the cut was minor. "It isn't bleeding anymore. Just keep it cold; put pressure on it to be sure. Here." He rubbed the bloody kerchief in the ice that had formed on the bus and pressed it back against Lorna's head. "It'll be fine."

"Can I help?" Lorna asked him.

"Well. . . ." Before he could say anything more, she had jumped down to the ground and found many people lying on the wet ground, many in pain, many in shock. She saw a man bleeding profusely from his hand, where it had evidently gone through a window. She turned to a man next to her and said, "Give me your necktie!" He didn't question her. He handed it to her, and she went to the bleeding man and put a tourniquet on his arm. Then she realized blood was again moving down her cheek. She saw another man, a passerby standing on the sidewalk, in a business suit and raincoat. "Can I have your tie, please?" He took it off and handed it to her. She tied it around her head, to hold the kerchief to her own wound.

And then she helped take care of others. In the distance were the sounds of ambulances and rescue squads and police cars, but she knew they would be a long time coming. A woman screamed, "My purse, they're going to take my purse!" Lorna comforted her and assured her no one was going to take her purse; it was safe in the bus, and someone would get it for her. She helped a woman fix a temporary splint for her little boy from a few tree branches. She tried to calm a man who'd gotten hysterical. When the first ambulance arrived, she led the men to the most badly injured, and she helped direct things from there on. The rain soaked through her coat, through her clothes to her skin, and the sleet made her hair seem gray. She helped distribute the articles which were recovered from the bus, including her own shoulder bag. And by the time it was all over she felt she had been there for days.

Refusing any medical attention for herself and assuring the police officers she lived nearby, she sat down under the tree in the yard in which the overturned bus lay and started to cry.

It was over, and she was all right, and she had helped.

Michael and Greg had dashed from the car to Marguerita's apartment, where Tom, Greg's lover, was already waiting for them. "God, we nearly didn't make it!" Michael said, taking off his wet jacket.

Greg bent over and hugged Tom. "How'd you get here so soon?"

"Soon?" Tom asked. "Why'd it take you so long?"

"Hey, shhhh!" Marguerita told them. "Hush. Dawn is sleeping. Come, have some soup."

Michael and Greg each had a mug of soup as Tom told them how he'd driven over three lawns in Brentwood to get past one hell of an accident. "I was supposed to pick somebody up at the Beverly Hills Hotel, but I said screw that. He's probably still waiting there for me."

Greg nodded. "Expecting you, too. I'll bet in the Polo Lounge they don't even know it's cold outside."

Michael laughed. "Sure, they're all sitting around in their tennis outfits, waiting to be paged for a phone call."

Greg shook his head. "This is the freakiest thing I've ever seen. It honestly is."

"That's why I just drove here. Fuck the guy at the hotel. Fuck the limo. Fuck driving. I want to stay alive." Tom sipped his coffee and looked at the steaming soup in the hands of the others. "Hey, Marguerita, on second thought, I'll have some of that stuff. I don't think Greg's going to feel like cooking me dinner tonight."

Greg smiled. "Me? You're the chef in the family."

"Aw, neither of you guys can cook," Michael told them. "And I know. You've had us to dinner. Marguerita, you ever been invited to dinner at their apartment?"

The old woman nodded and then cackled. "Sure. But I bring the enchiladas, the chile relleno, and the beans."

Michael looked back at Greg and Tom. Tom shrugged and said, "We provide the wine."

"It's TV dinner city from now on," Greg said. "Who's going to have the energy to cook? It's going to be enough to get to and from work."

"You hear the fight the mayor has with the weatherman?" Marguerita asked. Michael asked if she meant Carter DeSimone. "The one who says it will snow?" Michael nodded. She told him the story of the news conference and the mayor's speech earlier in the day.

Tom smiled. "I don't care if it rains or snows, as long as it's enough to keep me home." Then he thought for a minute. "Hey, I wonder if I get paid even if I'm not driving?"

Marguerita handed him a mug of soup. "You, driving," she muttered. "You don't look old enough to ride a tricycle yet. And you drive other people around. *Sweet Mary and Joseph!"*

Tom blew her a kiss. "Hey, I hope you're still saying that to me when I'm thirty."

"Don't knock thirty," Michael warned. "I'm almost there."

"I thought you were twenty-four," Tom said.

"I'm twenty-two," Michael replied.

"Then how . . . why are you saying you're near thirty?"

"They wanted someone older for the part I auditioned for today, so I'm feeling closer to thirty this evening, that's all. Age is all in the mind."

"I'm feeling a hundred and ten," Greg said. "God, I ache all over."

"Shall we go . . ." Tom started to say, but the phone rang. Marguerita answered and handed the receiver to Michael.

"Yeah. . . . Hi, honey. No, I'm down here. It was hell getting home. . . . You're not still at work, are you? What?" A look of panic came over him. Tom and Greg and Marguerita stared at him. "Oh, God, honey, are you okay? Shall I come and get you? Where are you? I mean, are you all right, you're not hurt? Lorna, I. . . ." He stopped talking. They could hear that she was screaming at him. She was fine, she told him, and she was only five blocks away. She would be there in no time. She just wanted to tell him what happened, why she was so late, she just needed to hear his voice. "I . . . I didn't get to make the stew," Michael said.

She told him she loved him.

In his orchard outside Santa Ana, just south of L.A., Matthew Whelan had been up all night trying to save his orange crop. For weeks he had been tending the smoke pots and ground propellers to keep the air around the trees above the freezing point. Several times he thought it was all over, but somehow the temperature never quite dipped that low, and he thanked God. But now he just sat on the back porch of his little house and stared at the frozen orange sitting there in his hand. This night he had lost the fight. All the other victories were now meaningless.

Matthew was one of the few small independent growers left in Orange County. The country's namesake was a vanishing symbol. Housing sprawls had all but uprooted every last orchard. Irvine Ranch had been one of the great citrus orchards of the world; now it was stucco tract homes and hatchback automobiles. He looked into the future now, for the first time really looking at the hard reality of giving it all up himself. He had made a good living for his family over the years, even though he was by no means rich. But if he quit now, what would he do? He didn't want to think about that now; the sense of loss was too great.

It never crossed his mind that around him for hundreds of

miles to the north and south, it was happening to everyone. The nation's largest source of fruit and vegetables was being slowly and completely wiped out.

The mayor of the city of Los Angeles walked up to Carter DeSimone immediately as he entered the Griffith Observatory and offered his hand in apology. "I'm hardheaded, Carter, and the last thing I want is panic in the streets of this city. But I just talked to the President, and his advice was that I listen to you. To all of you," he said, looking at Rob Wynters and a few other scientists and professionals on Carter's staff who'd arrived. "I realize we're rapidly approaching a state of emergency—although I must say I still cannot believe that we will actually experience snow on the ground—and that something must be done. What shall we do? I suddenly feel . . . I feel. . . ." He took a deep breath. The words were hard for him, a man not used to being humble. "I feel unsure. Powerless, suddenly."

Carter told him he understood, but the man was far from being powerless. His friend, Bob Sheppard, whom the mayor knew well, would find the way of easing his position, of changing sides; it was a political trick, joining the opposing force while making the people think they'd come over to your way of thinking. Bob would come up with a plan, and the people would love him as much as they did yesterday.

But the important problem was just that: How *important* was this problem? Carter said he felt the only way to deal effectively with it was to believe it was a problem of *utmost* importance. They had to believe not only all the scientific data and predictions, but the "feelings and intuition" as well. And someone should be on call or, better yet, called in immediately, someone who was an expert in dealing with disaster on a large scale. The mayor flinched, and then he finally agreed. Carter was right—act on the situation as though it were snowing out there right at that very moment.

After half an hour of deliberation and discussion they both agreed on someone from the Army, namely, a general, Alex Granville, a man they both admired. "How do we find him?" Carter asked.

The mayor reached for the phone and asked that he be switched to his office. Then he said simply, "Get me the Pentagon."

Carter breathed a sigh of relief. *Finally,* he thought. *Finally, they're going to listen.*

Rob turned to him and winked. The gesture said, "Congratulations."

But Carter knew it could already be too late. Only a day or two in which to get a plan into effect. He was optimistic. But cautiously so.

Bob backed the station wagon as close to the back stairs as possible, with one wheel in a flower bed. The drive had been harrowing, Julie thought, sitting in the back seat with Susan cradled in her lap. The girl was sleeping soundly. Bob had driven in worse, much worse weather in all the years back in Minnesota, and instant recall was present as he maneuvered the car slowly up the icy hill to their house.

They lifted Susan and helped her up the steps and into the house. Little puddles of water around the patio were already covered with sheets of ice, and the swimming pool looked uninviting. Julie flashed on the fact that so many plants would die because of the frost, and that was a shame. Bob worried about Michael and Lorna and wondered if they were attempting to drive in the rush-hour traffic.

They got Susan safely into bed. "How's the tummy?" Julie asked.

"It doesn't hurt as much."

"You think you can sleep for a while?" Julie secretly hoped the girl would never need another shot of Demerol; the stuff frightened her. Years ago, when Susan was in the hospital for a particularly bad acute siege, Julie had gotten to know the mother of a twelve-year-old boy. Their children were in rooms next to each other, and Julie would see the woman in the hall, and they would chat. The boy had cancer, and the parents had accepted it well. What they could not accept, however, was the fact that all the painkillers had made him an addict, and at the time Susan was in the hospital with him, they'd found something to arrest the cancer and were therefore trying to get him off the drugs. Julie could still hear his screams. She could still see the mother collapsing in her arms, asking, "Oh, why can't they *do* something for him? Why did they let this happen?" And she remembered the boy—a beautiful, blond, bright-eyed child—and the look of terror on his face as he crawled into the hall ... he had realized they were stopping the shots, stopping the narcotics, and he had ripped the IV tubing from his arm and blood seemed to spurt everywhere ... he'd knocked a nurse's aide against the window, which had shattered, cutting her head ... he'd mustered up all the power and strength left in his small body to get to the nurse's station, to get another shot....

"Honey ... Julie!" Bob had his hand on her shoulder. She was trembling, looking not at Susan but rather nowhere. "Julie, are you okay?"

She shook her head. "Oh, yes, just wandering.... Susan, are you all—" Susan had her eyes closed; she was already in a peaceful sleep. Bob helped Julie up and they left the room. Samantha curled up at Susan's feet as the sleet hit the window.

Miles away, Dolores walked into the kitchen dressed in her long robe. Her hair was wrapped up in a towel. She'd taken a hot bath the minute they got home, which hadn't been easy. One of the heels on her shoes had broken off before they'd walked even two blocks. The water soaked through her shoes in a matter of minutes, and her toes felt frostbitten. She had a hard time walking because of the shoes, and the ice, and also because of the bag she was carrying. "Put the stuff down, the hell with it," Harry had said, but Dolores clutched it, for dear life it seemed. She knew there was practically nothing left at home.

About half a mile off the freeway ramp where they'd abandoned the car, a van came along, complete with decals on the side and a surfboard on top. A young couple offered them a ride, a slow one, but a safe ride. They accepted, of course, and found themselves sitting on the floor of a wall-to-wall, ceiling-to-floor carpeted room. There was a small bed, a clothes closet, and even an ice chest. Dolores loved it—she'd seen an article in *New West* magazine some years ago and had been enthralled with the photographs of the new life-style, the vans which people decorated as if they were mansions. Harry thought the whole thing asinine, but he was thankful for the ride. And the heat. It was warm in there.

The young couple didn't talk much except to say that they were beach people and wanted their sun back. They were on their way to the girl's parents' house. The apartment they shared on the ocean had gotten too cold. The wind had broken the windows, and the cardboard they'd put up didn't do any good. Everywhere they walked, salty sea spray seemed to hit them in the face. So they were going "inland" to wait it out.

"What if it doesn't let up?" Harry asked.

The boy gave him a look as if to say "Are you crazy?" The girl said, "We'll just pack up and go into the desert, maybe across country."

Harry nodded. Aimless kids, he thought. Dolores' opinion was different from his. She envied them their freedom. For a moment she thought, *What I wouldn't give to live in a van.* And then she looked at her mink—wet, but still a mink—and her diamond ring and thought about the house she was going to and closed her eyes.

She poured herself a cup of warm milk and added the last of the Ballantine they'd had in the liquor cabinet. Thank God she'd held on to the bottles from the car. She eased herself into the breakfast nook opposite Harry. "What about the car?" she asked.

"I'll go back early morning and try to get it."

"Leaving it there all night? Can't you call the auto club or something?"

"I did. While you were in the tub. They said I would be put on a priority listing, I was the six hundred and seventy-fifth call this evening."

"You think the traffic'll be moving in the morning."

"No. Well, certainly not till then. No chance it'll get towed away before then." He dunked his stale doughnut in his coffee. "Of all the goddamn things to happen."

"It's lucky we weren't killed."

Harry said, "If Bob's friend is right, I'll eat my shirt."

"What?"

"Snow."

"Oh." She stirred the warm milk with her finger and took a long gulp. She felt better.

"Hungry?"

She shook her head. The scotch was soothing.

"What am I asking? The food's in the goddamn car."

"There's soup. Frozen stuff. Make yourself a—"

He stopped her. "I'm not hungry."

"Then why'd you ask?"

"I asked about you. I like to see you eat sometimes, you know what I mean?"

Without a word she opened one of the new bottles of Ballantine and poured a shot into the milk, her eyes on Harry all the time, as if to spite him.

"I'm going to watch TV," he muttered, getting up from the table.

"Why should this be any different from any other night?"

Harry stopped and turned back to her. "Outside it's different, Dolores, different from any night of the year, of the past fifty years. But in here it's been the same for as long as I can remember."

She laughed. "Indoor matches outdoor. The same chill, right, Harry?"

"Right, Dolores."

"Cheers," she said sarcastically as he walked out of the room. Then she went to the cookie jar on top of the refrigerator and took out the last half of an Oreo. She bit down on it, sat back at the table, and uttered the one word which, she thought, summed up the whole damn thing. "Shit," she said.

Greg and Tom had gone back to their apartment after Lorna arrived home. "I'm a mess, I know, but I'm fine," she announced as she walked in the door.

"You look like Ava Gardner when she went down the sewer in the last reel of *Earthquake,"* Michael said, ever the clown, telling her in those words how much he loved her and how happy he was she was okay. He took her in his arms.

"I'll do anything for attention," Lorna said with a sarcastic laugh. Then she collapsed on the couch. "How's Dawn?"

"Slept through her mommy's big scene."

"She's fine," Marguerita said. "Here, let's get those clothes off you and warm you up. I've got soup."

They helped her out of her wet clothes and wrapped her in blankets. Then, as she sipped the hot broth, she told them what had happened. Their eyes were wide—it was a wonder people were not hurt more, that someone wasn't killed—and Marguerita made the sign of the cross several times. Michael's heart was pounding, even though he joked and smiled. Even Lorna, looking back at it now, was more upset than when it had happened. "Grace under pressure, that's what you've got." She remembered her father's words when she had had to deal with another traffic accident, one her mother had been in a few years back. Sure, grace under pressure, but when it's over, I feel as though I'm going to shatter into little pieces. "You sure you're okay?" Michael asked. "Sometimes things don't show up till later."

"I'm fine, I told you."

"Now I don't want to find out you're going to be some kind of cripple or something. I mean tell me now so I can get a lawyer and get it over with."

Lorna laughed and tried to kick him, but he got out of the way. "Will you stop already?" she said.

"Yes, stop and we eat." Marguerita had dinner on the table. A big pot of meat and vegetables, much like the stew Michael had planned to make.

"You two eat," Lorna said. "I'm not hungry, had a late lunch." Which was a lie; she hadn't eaten all day. After the bus incident she felt as though if she would eat anything it would all come back up.

"Okay, Marguerita, it looks like just you and me. We'd like our usual table, Maude, thank you!" Michael joked.

Marguerita seemed puzzled. "Maude?"

"Maude. Maude Chasen."

Lorna giggled. She could see Marguerita had no idea what he was talking about. "Maude Chasen? Findley is their name, no?" the old woman said, sitting down.

"Maude Chasen, the restaurant . . . Chasen's?" Michael wished he'd just sat down and dug in.

"Oh. Is it a nice place?" Marguerita asked.

"I hear they got great chili," Michael answered.

"We should go there sometime."

Michael looked at Lorna and smiled. "Yeah, when I win the Oscar."

And Lorna added, "That would be the only night he could afford it."

As Michael and the old woman ate, Lorna got up to check on Dawn. She bent over the sleeping baby and kissed her on the cheek. "I love you," she whispered. And then she heard a strange sound–a shout for help, a shout of pain–and a thud. She ran out of the bedroom. "Did you hear?"

But Michael was already out the door. "Oh, God!" he yelled, dashing around the pool in the sleet, nearly falling into it.

"Daddy!" Flora Reynauld yelled as she too ran out into the cold in just her jeans and blouse.

They both ran to aid her father. Harvard had slipped and fallen on the icy steps leading to the second floor. He'd let out a cry as he went backward, as he tried desperately to grab the metal railing, and then came the thud as his back hit the landing. Even then he slid down the last six stairs to the ground, and somehow his mailbag rested beneath his head, as if it were meant to cushion his fall.

"Quick, get him inside!" Michael said. Tom and Greg were there now, as well as Flora and a few other neighbors. Mr. Rosenberg looked out his window, looking as if he wanted to help, but it was too cold for him to go out.

"Bring him in here," Marguerita called out.

"No, let's get him up to his own bed," Flora said. "He's not gonna be happy unless he's restin' in his own bed."

And so Michael and Greg lifted the man gently. They started

up the stairs; but Greg slipped, and they nearly dropped him. Tom yelled, "Wait a second," as he saw Mr. Rosenberg standing in his open door, in his robe and slippers, holding a package of Morton salt. Tom ran and grabbed the salt from the old man. "Thanks!" he said, and hurried back. He opened it and poured it all over the steps as Michael and Greg carried the man up to his apartment.

They put him on the bed, and he groaned. Flora helped them get his coat and shoes off, and Tom came in with the mailbag. In a few minutes the man seemed all right. A bit dazed, but all right. Nothing was broken, and he could talk. Lorna came in with Marguerita. The old woman asked if there was anything she could do, and then she went back down to be with Dawn. Lorna checked Harve over as best she could, and so did Greg. He knew a lot about medicine and illness and symptoms, be it cats or dogs or men and women. He was pretty sure there wasn't a concussion; only a bump on the head and some bruises.

The man's spirits were good. "Neither rain, nor sleet ... we stop right there," he said, trying to smile. He looked up at Flora. He seemed to know what she was thinking. "I ain't had one drink, girl!"

"Michael," Lorna said, "that's our phone ringing."

Michael heard it through the wall. But the thought of going out into the sleet and then taking the chance that they'd hang up by the time he got there was too much for him to handle. "The hell with it," he said. "Let the service get it."

"Listen, you all stop making a fuss over me!" Harvard snapped at them. "You just leave this old government servant to die here in peace."

"The government's gonna die before you do, Daddy," Flora said. She patted him on the shoulder. "You rest while I throw these folk out into the cold."

They all left the bedroom. "Michael, thank you ... and Greg, you're Greg, aren't you? I get you two mixed up."

"That's okay," Tom said, "we're interchangeable." He had a goofy grin on his face. Greg wasn't sure what he meant by it. But it was understandable that Flora got them mixed up—they lived on the first floor and she on the second, and it wasn't often that they met.

Lorna said, "Flora, I really think you should get the doctor out to see him tomorrow, just to play safe."

"The way it's goin' out there, we're gonna need Sergeant Preston of the Yukon to deliver a doctor," the girl said. "Yeah, I'm gonna call him right now."

Tom and Greg left. Michael asked Lorna if she wanted to go back down to Marguerita's or if he should go finish dinner and get Dawn. She started to tell him she thought she'd go to the apartment and take a hot shower when Marguerita called out from her apartment door. "Michael! Michael! Telephone, down here! It's your papa!"

Michael's eyes met Lorna's. That's who was calling. It must be important if he called at Marguerita's. Michael and Lorna both rushed down the steps. "Careful, you two!" Flora called after them. "Don't need you fallin', too!"

Michael took the phone in his hand. "Yes, Dad, I'm all right. Well.... Oh, good, we thought something was wrong because you called here. No, I understand, we're fine, terrific. Listen, Lorna was in an accident. No, don't get upset, Mom." He paused and turned to Lorna. "Mom's on the extension.... No, Mom, listen, I said she's fine. The bus overturned.... Hey, did you two call to talk to each other or do you want to talk to me?" Lorna sat down and started to eat the stew Michael had left. Marguerita dished a hot ladleful onto the plate, and Lorna smiled. She was hungry after all. Michael was telling his parents about the bus overturning, and Harvard's fall, and he and his dad exchanged views on driving in the freezing rain—both Sheppards hated it. "No, we're staying here for now." Lorna perked her head up and nodded. "Dad, listen, if it gets bad, really Last Judgment time, then we'll come to the house. But there's no reason for it now, and to fight the traffic is insane. The safest thing to do is to sit on your ass at home.... What?" He listened for a moment. His eyes widened. Then he asked if anyone had been hurt, and Lorna and Marguerita turned to him, their eyes questioning, saying "Who now?" He held the receiver away for a moment. "Harry and Dee were in an accident." He put the receiver back to his ear. "You think maybe ... well, maybe it wasn't anything and she'd been drinking and ... well, whatever, they're both okay, too. Jesus, we all came through one hell of a day." He cupped the receiver. "The Big White Boat is sitting abandoned somewhere on the San Diego Freeway!" Then he went back to his parents and said good-night.

As soon as he hung up, there was the familiar sound of a little girl crying in the bedroom. When Marguerita brought Dawn out, it was as if all the troubles were gone. She was the focus, and getting her fed and changed and smiling again seemed the main concern of the hour. Lorna couldn't even feel the throbbing pain in her head.

But later, in their own apartment, watching the familiar ABC Eyewitness news team doing their duty—and looking slightly bewildered through it all—all the troubles of the day seemed too real again. Lorna held a compress on her head, praying the Tylenol would start working, but when she saw some of the other accidents on TV, she felt she'd done nothing more spectacular than fall down and scrape her knee. In the Los Angeles area alone fifty-three people had died in accidents related to the rain and the ice.

Michael put his arm around Lorna, and they watched interviews on the screen. Most people were bewildered by the ice, the change it was causing in their habits, and the prediction that it might be more than a one-night-only occurrence. They tried to make light of it, calling it a freak phenomenon. One man—Lorna was sure it was a wino who'd been into the clinic several times—went so far as to tell a reporter that it was "refreshing."

But he was wrong. What was happening around the city was startling. Thousands of people were stranded in their cars during the rush hours, many of them having to leave their autos far from home. Accidents had been reported on virtually every freeway and major street in the city. Puzzled folk found a whole new experience in walking on icy sidewalks and steps; hospital emergency rooms were filled with cases of sprained or broken arms, legs, wrists, of concussions and the like. There were huddles of people under the canopies of gas stations, inside hotel lobbies, under the eaves of buildings, waiting for the sleet to stop. People were shaken, dazed. And in an effort to help–help the people and help his image even more–the mayor had ordered trucks to salt the main streets and boulevards on which traffic still moved. It was one of the most unusual nights Los Angeles had ever had on record.

Michael turned off the TV and looked out the window. The pane was frosted. "You know what? I don't even feel horny anymore."

She just smiled. Her eyes were heavy.

Then he took Lorna's hand and helped her up. "Hey, you're half asleep. Come on, you need some sleep."

"Ch, but we were going to make love," she moaned, not quite knowing what she was actually saying.

"You're going to make love to the sandman," he said, his arm around her, leading her to their bedroom.

After his shower, he crawled into the warm bed, curled up against her soft smooth skin, and felt his penis become erect. It was a physiological reaction; his head was already asleep, as if pounded into a comatose state by all that had happened in one short–or was it really endlessly long?–day. He pressed his body against hers and put his hand on her breast. "Michael ... beautiful ..." she moaned, turning her head toward him, her lips resting on his cheek. He suddenly had a feeling as if they'd just made love, that kind of afterglow where the body goes numb but the mind seems to keep on climaxing. They were one together now, their bodies excited and yet still, their minds making love and yet slowing, resting, relaxing.

Michael's last thought before he drifted off was that her hair smelled of apricot.

At midnight Carter got up and put his coat on. "I give up. Look."

"Yeah, I see." Rob glanced at the satellite report that had come in. It was the same as the last. "Carter, what can we do?"

"Get some sleep."

"No, I mean, what are we going to do, in the long run? What *can* we do?"

Carter put his hat on his head. "Robert, we're going to sing a chorus of 'You Are My Sunshine' and hope to hell it keeps us alive."

Then he left, and Rob sat down with a blank expression on his face. Then—he was sure no one else was left in the building—he actually started to sing. "You are my sunshine, my only sunshine. You make me happy when skies . . ." He stopped and shook his head. No, it wasn't funny. He needed some sleep, too.

Maybe it would all be gone in the morning.

THE THIRD DAY

SATURDAY, JANUARY 17
HIGH TEMPERATURE 34°; LOW 18°

HARRY SHEPPARD STOOD NEXT TO THE GREAT WHITE BOAT. HE was seething. The back window had been knocked out, and all the groceries had been taken. Only a celery stalk lay on the scotch-stained back seat. The back wheel had sunk deeper into the mud, all the way up to the body of the car. And the freeway traffic was moving, almost as if nothing had happened. It made him mad as hell.

He tried to start the Continental; but the engine quickly flooded, and his nerves were jangled enough to keep it flooded. Each time he tried to turn it over, he made it worse. Finally, the battery weakened and quit, and he smashed his fist against the dashboard. It wasn't enough he'd had to hike home in a sleet storm and lay awake all night worrying about his car, it wasn't enough he had to get up at 7 A.M. and walk in the cold morning air back to where the car had been abandoned (and this time with no kids in a van to give him a lift). Now this. He got out and kicked the door shut.

A highway patrol car drove up and stopped. The officers were pleasant enough and told Harry he'd better make arrangements to have the car towed or they'd do it for him, with a ticket to boot for his troubles. All the other cars which had been left at the off-ramp had been either moved or towed; Harry's was the last. It wasn't stopping traffic from getting onto Sunset Boulevard—it was far enough to the side—but it wasn't exactly a legal parking place either. Harry grumbled that he'd take care of it, and then asked the men for a ride. They gave it to him. In the back seat of the police car he said, "I appreciate this. I was going to drive back with my wife, in her car. But the damn thing, it's never been in weather this cold and damp. It wouldn't turn over either."

"Better get yourself a full-time mechanic, mister," one of the cops said.

"Yeah." Harry said no more.

Michael and Lorna were just about to go out the door of the apartment as the phone rang. "My agent calling to tell me I'm gonna star in a segment of *Sleets of San Francisco,"* Michael kidded as he went to the phone. "Hi, Chilly Willy here. Oh, hi, Mom."

Lorna walked back inside and stood by the door and listened to him try to convince his mother it was best for them to stay on Genesee. "Listen," he said, "we pooled some money, and Lorna and I and Greg are going to the store to buy stuff, *provisions* as they call it in the disaster movies." He paused for a long time and made a gesture which told Lorna that Julie was trying to use her motherly, feminine, innocent influence to sweet-talk him. He didn't buy it. "Ma, we're staying put. That's that. I don't want to take Dawn out again anyhow, and Jesus, getting home wasn't easy. I don't want to drive again till it's 97°.... Yeah, we're taking the car to get groceries.... No, Ma, that's it."

Lorna crossed her fingers. How long is this going to go on? But then he smiled and licked his finger and chalked up one for their side. "Oh, what happened?" He listened and then told Lorna, "Uncle Harry's car's still on the freeway; they have to tow it. And Auntie Dee's won't run either. He's having a fit." He listened to his mother for a few more minutes and then said, "Well, that's their problem. Don't worry about them. Tell Dad to be careful. How's Susan? Good. Listen, we'll call you later, huh? 'Bye."

He walked to the door, kissed Lorna on the cheek, and said, "Mothers. Hope *you* don't turn into one someday."

"I can't promise."

They went out into the cold. But surprisingly, there was no ice on the ground, just water. "Well, I'll be damned," Michael said. Funny, but Marguerita hadn't mentioned it when she'd come up for Dawn. Maybe she thought they knew. It was warmer. The sleet—the rain—had stopped. Maybe things would even dry up. "There's hope yet," Michael said.

"My God, you're the optimistic one today. And you're not even joking!"

"This whole thing's a joke."

Rob Wynters' prayer of "maybe it'll be gone in the morning" might have been answered. Bob Sheppard looked out the window when he awakened and saw that the glass was no longer covered with sleet and frost; in fact, the rain had stopped completely. It even seemed lighter outside than it had been in weeks, not sunny, but brighter. Maybe, just maybe, the sun would poke its head through for an hour or so.

It wasn't as if it were a warm day; Bob looked out the kitchen window when he went down to get some coffee and saw the outdoor thermometer near the window. According to the reading, it was 32°, and that was quite a rise from the low the night before. Julie walked in behind him, turning the warmer on the coffee machine on, and giving her husband a good-morning kiss. "It's one of those days when you just want to curl up in bed with a pile of Jackie Susann books, lots of snacks, and let time go by."

"How about a companion?"

She gave him a sensual smile. "I don't know, considering I was ravished by a madman last night."

He hugged her. "And you loved every minute of it."

"Have some coffee," she said, deadpan.

"Great of you to change the subject, but you've gotta put grounds in the machine first."

"Oh. Well, you do it. I want to see how Susan is." She walked through the laundry room to Susan's door. Then Bob heard them talking, and he felt relieved; obviously she was feeling all right.

He poured the water through the top of the Bunn and watched the steaming, fresh-smelling coffee fill the carafe. He waited until the dripping had stopped, and then he pulled the carafe and the basket of grounds out at the same time, so nothing would drip on the floor—Julie had given him three lectures before he'd got the hang of it—and dumped the grounds into the disposal. Then he poured himself a mug of strong Colombian blend and sat down at the kitchen table.

He felt lost without the morning paper. He'd looked out the bedroom window to see if it was lying in its usual spot over the gate, but there was no sign of it. He didn't blame the kid who delivered it. Who'd want to attempt riding a bike up the hill at 5 A.M. with a bundle of papers? So he fingered through a copy of *Family Circle* which happened to be sitting there. He found an interesting recipe for fried eggplant you didn't fry; you put it in the oven. He wondered if it worked.

Julie came back into the room and poured herself some coffee. "She's feeling a lot of pain again. I think we should give her a shot."

Bob winced. "Can we maybe hold off awhile longer?"

Julie shrugged. "She said she didn't need it, but she's running a temp, and she's sweating, and her hands are clenched in pain—" She was interrupted by one starving kitten. "Oh, Samantha, no one's fed you?" And she got up and opened a can of Purina tuna, Samantha's favorite. "Bob, do you remember that wonderful scene in *Klute?*"

"In what?"

"Klute. The movie. Jane Fonda got the Oscar for it." She set the dish on the floor, and the cat attacked it. "Remember, when she dished out the cat food for her cat, she licked the spoon. It was so subtle. Brilliant."

"Who the hell could stand to smell that stuff, much less lick it?"

"It's just tuna fish," she replied, rinsing the spoon.

"Say, who were you talking to on the phone? I had the pillow over my head, and I was half asleep anyhow."

"First, Dee, then Michael." She sat across the table from him and took her vitamin pills. "They say this stuff goes right through you if you don't eat something with them."

"So why don't you?"

"What?"

"Eat something."

"All we have are doughnuts, and they're fattening. We're out of eggs. I used them all in the cake. We'd better go to the store as long as it isn't slippery out. I think we should load up, really take some money and buy up enough to last us awhile. That's what Michael and Lorna are doing."

"What else did they have to say?"

"Nothing. I tried to convince them to come here and stay, but he wouldn't hear of it. To tell the truth," she said, leaning toward him, "I really think he'd come if it weren't for her."

"Julie . . ." he warned her.

"Oh, I can't help thinking she's on her we-can-do-it-on-our-own kick again."

"So what's wrong with that? We were the same way when we first got married. My parents—"

"Your parents didn't have money. She simply resents the fact that we're well off."

"We're not the Rockefellers."

"I know what we are. We have enough to live a comfortable life. But why should that affect her? Why should that make her resent the fact that we simply want them here because we love them and we're worried about them?"

"You want to know what I'm worried about?" Bob asked. "I'm worried that the nights are going to get colder. Oh, I know it's warmer out today, and there's a sun up there somewhere trying to get a look at us; but Carter says the nights are the things to fear. I'm worried that crummy apartment house they live in won't withstand the cold. You think I want my granddaughter to freeze to death in West Hollywood?"

Julie almost smiled. "I'm sorry, but it's so absurd. Freeze to death in Anchorage, maybe, but West Hollywood?"

"You think I should check on sassy?"

Julie shook her head. "Give her a minute. You know how she resents us gawking at her, giving her sympathy." She turned and pushed aside the curtains on the kitchen window. You couldn't see much from there because the wall of the convent came up to four feet of their property, but Julie saw that the weather looked better. "I do think the worst is over. I really do. I wonder how the sisters are doing?"

The top of the hill, the cul-de-sac, was shared by two residences, the Sheppard house and the estate that once was the home of a Beverly Hills car dealer and real estate man, which he'd willed to a group of nuns upon his death. Thus, the thirty-five-room mansion and guest houses and swimming pools and landscaped gardens and fountains and towering oak trees had become the property of the Sisters of Saint Theresa. It was Motherhouse, Retreat House, Novitiate, and Retirement Home. In other words, it was a small order, and everything was compact in one beautiful estate on the edge of Griffith Park.

The Sisters of Saint Theresa had gained notoriety in the Sixties with their feud with the then Cardinal McIntyre. They'd come to be referred to as the Rebel Nuns, mainly because they were the first—or at least one of the first—orders to petition to change from the flowing white and black and brown robes of centuries gone by to normal, feminine street clothing. Nothing flamboyant, but human. Realistic. After the good cardinal threatened to excommunicate them and close down their schools if they didn't shut up, they petitioned the Pope, held a sit-in on the cardinal's mansion lawn, and caused a lot of bad press for the Catholic Church. One good sister even had called the cardinal a "senile old man" in an interview after he said her playing the guitar at mass was a sacrilege.

The sisters finally won, but the glory lasted not long; as with all orders, the decline came. Many nuns left, and few new women applied for the novitiate. Now only seventeen women lived at the beautiful Spanish castle next to the Sheppards, and they felt it was a shame that such a glorious place was going unappreciated and unused. Julie had often talked to the nuns when she happened to see them on the street, and every so often she and Bob and Susan would take a walk through the grounds, even attend chapel there. Julie and Bob both detected a certain sadness in the eyes and words of the sisters, a sadness that an era had come to an end. Julie had once suggested the property be used by various church groups from parishes in the Los Angeles area, for retreats, for outdoor devotions, for bazaars. But nothing had come of it.

"I'll bet they're praying for the whole city," Bob said, getting up from the table. He poured himself another mug of coffee. "Listen, what did Harry and Dee have to say?"

Julie told him about the situation with their cars. "Why don't you call them back and ask them to come stay here, at least for the weekend?"

"You really believe it's going to snow, don't you?" She knew it; she could read it all over him.

"I just think banding together in a crisis is advisable," he said, avoiding the issue of the white stuff.

"I think you're not telling me the truth."

Bob turned away. "Why won't the kids come? Dammit!"

"Bob, stop it!"

He leaned over the counter. "Oh, Christ, I'm sorry. I had a dream it really happened. Consider what snow could do to us. . . ."

"Bob," Julie said nervously, "I just can't entertain such a thought. It won't fit into my head." She got up and threw the rest of her coffee into the sink. "Harry and Dee can't come, even if they want to. There's that opening, that exhibit he's been looking forward to for the last year."

"The Van Gogh. I'd like to see that myself. Black-tie deal tonight, big stuff."

"Well, I don't know if she means it or not, but Dee says she's not going."

"Harry'll be there, no matter what. It's going to be quite an exhibit. It's rare that these paintings are here; they rarely make it to America."

"Oh, yes, that's the one on tour, like the time they brought the "Mona Lisa" over. I wouldn't mind seeing that myself."

"It'll be here for a month. Let's make it a point to get down over there. It's practically next door to the office." Bob opened a closet. "Where's that big heavy mackinaw I wore up in the mountains last winter?"

"Oh, isn't it a little warm for that thing? It's awfully warm, Bob."

"I know. That's what I want to be, awfully warm."

"I think it's in the downstairs storage space, probably wrapped in a plastic bag. I'll check. I have to run down and pick up the glasses from last night anyhow." And she went downstairs.

Bob looked in on Susan. She had her face turned to the wall. He could see she wasn't sleeping. Her legs were drawn up almost to her chin, and a pillow was pressing against her stomach. He didn't say anything and closed the door.

"Julie, you find it?" he called down the stairs.

"No. . . ." The voice was faint.

He went down and found her at the back of the closet. "Look at this!" She held a pair of shoes in her hands. "I thought I lost these, looked everywhere for them for months. And here they are. I wonder how they ended up down here?"

"Samantha carried them down." Bob looked through the plastic bags hanging on a pipe. "Susan's doubled over, staring at the wall."

"Did she ask for anything?"

"No. Here it is." He pulled the coat out, ripping the plastic off it.

"Bob, we can reuse that! Just open the twist thing at the top." She took the shoes with her as she went upstairs.

"I'm going to get dressed and get down to the store. You want a heavy coat out of here, your ski jacket maybe?"

"I'm not going anywhere," she said, calling down to him.

Bob was having visions of mountain climbing. He pulled out her ski parka and then a heavy winter coat which Susan had worn in New York two winters ago; he wasn't sure that it would even fit her, but he put it over his arm. He checked the pilot lights on the furnaces, and they were burning fine. Then he went back upstairs.

When he got to the kitchen, he found Minnie Kupperman sitting at the table, having coffee with Julie. "Sam says to tell you there's so many things we need, if you're going to the store, he wants to go along. He doesn't dare drive even though the ice is melted."

"Sure," Bob said. "Or, better yet, I'll get the list from him and bring it up. No sense in his having to go out again."

"What, he should sit home and be cranky to me? No, you take him along. It'll do him good. So how's Susan today?"

Julie told her as Bob went upstairs to change.

For the first time since they'd been to the mountains the previous year, he put on his one pair of long underwear.

Dolores could hear the sound of Harry's shower as she sat at the vanity in the dressing room. She rubbed the creme into her cheeks and then rinsed her hands in the water from the gold-plated fixtures and dried them with a soft, fluffy towel. The bedroom was her sanctuary, her retreat; the dressing room her own little theater. She turned the sunlamp on and propped her chin on her hands.

The sound of the running water stopped, and Harry opened the sliding glass doors and continued where he'd left off. "Did you want me to call a tow truck and stand there waiting for it all day, freezing my nuts off?"

"Oh, will you stop already? I just don't understand why you can't take the Gremlin yourself to the opening. Maybe if you'd have waited for the Mark IV, I wouldn't have to drive you."

"Dolores, goddammit, I can't drive up there in that car, and the Continental's in a garage. The whole back window's smashed out. How the hell—" He wrapped a towel around himself and put a comb through his hair. "Oh, shit, never mind."

"You could park it around the corner and sneak over there," she said with a laugh. She picked up her glass and twirled the ice cubes. Then she took a sip.

"At that rate your supply's gonna run out."

"Don't worry about it," she spat.

"Here." He reached in his pants pocket and pulled out two

crisp $20 bills. He tossed them on the dressing table near the sunlamp.

"What's that for?"

"For driving me to the exhibit. Figured you'll want to stop at *a store* on the way home."

She stared at the money and then looked at him with contempt. She picked up the glass, toasted herself in the mirror, and guzzled it all down.

Harry turned on the radio as he dressed. The news report said patches of sunlight had appeared in various spots over Los Angeles, and all the ice—even in the highest elevations in the city, the Santa Monica Mountains, the nearby San Gabriel Mountains—had melted. Freezing temperatures could again be expected for the night; however, there was no sign of any kind of precipitation. The sleet storm would not repeat itself. Government offices would be open as usual Monday, mail would be delivered, life would go on; there was no emergency, no reason to be alarmed.

However, Colorado and Utah were experiencing the biggest snowstorms of the last fifty years.

But Harry couldn't care less about Utah and Colorado. He changed the station and listened to classical music as he pulled his tux out of the closet.

Dolores reached under the vanity and pulled out a bottle of scotch from the cabinet. She filled the glass, added water, and took a sip, all while sitting under the sunlamp with her eyes closed.

Harry did his best to ignore her.

Julie and Minnie Kupperman were watching a tennis match on the television set in the family room. Every so often Julie would turn and look out the windows to see if a car was coming up the driveway. "Now, stop worrying," her neighbor said, patting her on the knee. "Your hubby's one hell of a driver, and it's not even icy out there!"

Julie smiled, but still she worried. He'd been gone four hours now. He hadn't said anything about going anyplace but the grocery store. "Say, Minnie, would you like a sandwich? I'm getting hungry, and we didn't have much of a lunch."

"No, I'd best be getting home and rustle up something for Billy. He's doin' just like us, watchin' TV. And that gets a person mighty—" She stopped as she heard the cry from upstairs.

Julie jumped to her feet, listening, making sure.

Susan cried again. "Mama!"

They rushed up the stairs and into her room. "Mama, I can't ... it's getting bad again. I can't sleep ... I can't. . . ." She shut her eyes as the pain enveloped her. She twisted into an almost grotesque position on the mattress and clenched her pillow with both hands. Even the little cat was frightened, hiding in the corner. Looking at her daughter in such misery, Julie understood why many doctors had told her that pancreatitis can be one of the most painful diseases known to medical science.

Julie acted fast; she was nearly expert at it already. She prepared the hypo, drawing the liquid Demerol and atropine from the vials with the syringe as Minnie put a cold cloth to the young girl's forehead. Julie held the syringe up in front of her eyes, pushing the plunger until all the air was out of it—until the liquid squirted into the air—and then she said, "Okay, Susan, on your side."

Minnie helped Susan hold steady on her side. They lifted her nightgown above her buttocks. Minnie saw the tender area, the fleshy part of the hip where other needles had been poked. Julie didn't hesitate. She rubbed the area with alcohol and then jabbed the needle full length into the skin and pushed the medication into the body. Then she pulled it out as quickly as it had gone in and held her fingers over the little wad of cotton, rubbing gently to help it disperse into the bloodstream. "This stuff is awfully thick," she said softly to Minnie.

"You'd make a good nurse," Minnie whispered back.

"I am," Julie said with a smile. She pulled her hand away, smoothed Susan's nightgown, and pulled the covers up over her. "Okay, darling, just a little while. It'll be gone in a little while."

Minnie and Julie sat there on the floor for about twenty minutes, keeping Susan company, waiting to see if the medication was going to take effect, helping Susan relax. It was important that she not fight the painkillers, that she rest even though the pain was severe; that was the only way the Demerol would work to help relieve the severe pain. "Can ... my lips are so dry," Susan moaned. Minnie put the cold cloth to her lips, and the girl sucked on it. "That feels better," she said, and then turned a little toward them. "Thank you." She grimaced in a flash of pain. "Thank you, Mrs. Kupper–"

"Shhh, child," Minnie said, patting her cheek.

Julie could see the drugs were starting to work. Susan's eyes were growing heavy; she was feeling languid and lethargic. And she became talkative–the most telltale sign, because Demerol had an effect not unlike truth serum. "Remember, Mommy, the time when Michael had this room, the time the cat jumped in the open window, that big cat that used to hang around the neighborhood..."

"That stray you and the sisters used to feed. I think it lived up in the park someplace." Julie reached over and petted Samantha, who started to purr.

"...and it dragged in a little lizard that was still half-alive and started fighting with it right on top of Michael in his bed? And Daddy came down with the shotgun, and Michael was screaming and yelling, and the cat just kept chasing the lizard."

Julie nodded and then looked at Mrs. Kupperman, who could tell the girl's pain was nearly gone now, and she was feeling mellow and peaceful. "That's when we had the screens fixed on these windows," Julie said, "and Michael never went to sleep with them open again."

"Oh, I feel so tired," Susan whispered. "Is ... is Samantha here?... Did you feed Samantha?"

"Yes, darling, she's been fed, and she's right here." Julie lifted the kitten to the bed and Susan put her arm around her. Samantha curled up into a ball and started giving herself a bath. Susan's eyes were closed now. She was asleep.

Julie and Minnie got up and went into the kitchen.

"My, but I admire you," Minnie said. "I could never stand to watch any of the kids in pain, not even with a cold. Sam always took care of them. But this, God help you. How do you do it?"

Julie leaned over the sink and took a deep breath. "I try to tell myself it's what has to be done, because it is what is. I just have to be stronger than Susan or I'd be letting her down. I guess I try to muster up that Rose Kennedy kind of faith, that it all must be for a reason." Her voice faltered. "But I don't believe it, Minnie, not for a minute. This strength is all a façade. I'm a big baby. I'm terrified. But I have to pretend because—" The tears in her eyes made her stop.

"There is great strength just in that." Minnie walked to her and put her arm around her shoulder. "The only thing worse in life than having your child predecease you is to be a parent and see the child in pain. It goes against the order of things. It is a violation."

"She needs to be in a hospital." Julie wiped her eyes.

"She will be; she will be. It's getting warmer. Come on, now; I'll make the sandwiches. You just tell Minnie where everything is."

Julie nodded and opened the refrigerator door.

Bob Sheppard encountered it. Michael and Lorna and Greg had to deal with it, too. In fact, anyone who went near a supermarket or grocery store that Saturday afternoon had to face it—chaos. If people had worried over "the Blitz" the day before when Dolores had been to the market, today they were fearing the end of the world. Police were called into many a supermarket in town, to keep order, after fights had broken out in the aisles. Obviously the warmer weather of the day didn't dispel doubts that it was going to get worse before better, and the silly threat of snow, even if it had been laughed off by most people, still lingered subconsciously in everyone's minds. They wanted to be prepared. For more rain. For ice, sleet. For snow. They needed the basics. They had shelter; no one was sleeping in the parks. They had clothing, although the department stores were doing a bang-up business in winter clothing (they'd scrapped plans for putting out the new spring wardrobes, as was traditionally done in January, and even canceled sales on winter clothes; in fact, they were ordering more cold-weather garments). And now they wanted to be sure to have enough food.

By early afternoon most stock was depleted. Clerks and box boys had worked through the night to replenish the shelves, but everything seemed to disappear in minutes. The fresh meat and produce went first, along with dairy products. Bread was cleaned out faster than the bakery delivery trucks could get it into the stores. Then the canned foods, the vegetables, the soups, the fruits. When they were gone, people turned to the frozen foods; they bought canned first because they were afraid the electricity could go out and ruin the food they'd stocked up. No one seemed to give a damn about deodorants and hair sprays; the essentials suddenly became very essential.

Michael's first words, in the Alpha-Beta market on Fairfax and Santa Monica were, "I don't believe it!" His father had uttered the same words at Vons, on Hollywood Boulevard. In fact, people were saying that all over town, no one believing it, but everyone doing it. It was as if no one wanted to admit to being frightened about the weather, the predictions; everyone *else* was crazy. "We're just here to buy some groceries, *these* people are all nuts!" But the fact was everyone was stocking up. Panic buying. Lorna said, "It's like the time Johnny Carson made a remark about toilet paper, about a shortage of toilet paper, and the stuff disappeared off the shelves in minutes."

The Hollywood Ranch Market, which had never closed its doors for even an hour in all the years of its famous existence, shut down at 3 P.M. The owner explained, "There's nothing left in there. I never seen anything like it. When the trucks come in and we get the shelves stocked, we'll reopen. What're you gonna do with empty shelves, sell them to people?" He paused a moment and smiled for the news cameras. "You know, they'd probably buy them."

At 5 P.M. the mayor of Los Angeles went on television again to speak to the people. "I'm proud to say that at this hour, some semblance of normalcy has returned to our great city. The roads have been cleared of stalled automobiles, the freeways running smoothly, the airports on schedule. There have been reports of food shortages in the L.A. Basin. Some overanxious buyers have caused unnecessary reductions of certain food supplies, but suppliers to all the food chains have assured me personally that above-average quantities of food products will be shipped into the stores immediately. Warehouses all over the city have sufficient supplies, I am told.

"I must ask your help in our getting back to normal life here in Los Angeles. Any abandoned cars must be removed by morning, or they will be towed away by the city trucks at the owner's expense. We must conserve energy, for the cold spell might still be with us for a time. I ask that you heat your homes only enough to remain moderately comfortable, a suggested 65°. Shut off warm-air vents to rooms which are not being used. This is a time for optimism. There is no need for panic, no need for great worry. Together in the past years we've survived earthquakes, the gasoline shortage, the bus strikes, the worldwide energy crisis, the Watergate scandal, and the time of political skepticism. We can survive this damage to our crops and vegetation that the cold has brought. We will survive ... I promise you. I will not let you, the good people of Los Angeles, down."

General Alex Granville stubbed out his cigar and turned off the TV set. He turned to Carter and said, "Sounds like the asshole's running for President."

"He is," Rob Wynters said. "Someday."

The general had arrived only an hour earlier from Washington, and after a fast introduction to key people at the communications center and a warm hello to Carter, a man he respected and had worked for before, he got down to work. He was in charge now. Carter was his adviser, Rob the assistant to both of them. The governor had appointed them. The mayor had given them full authority, with the hope that it wouldn't hurt his public image. The President had given him his blessing. His wife told him he was a fool to go to California, a grown man off to deal with something—some idea—out of a science-fiction novel.

But here he was, and he was serious. Carter had tried to describe him to Rob. If Carter were a weather machine with a heart, Alex Granville was bionic, and there was some question if he had a heart. He was an expert, having dealt with large-scale death and destruction in wars, uprisings, natural disasters—in fact, he could have created a few of them himself. He had led the National Guard in the aid of Buffalo, New York, a few years ago. He was a hard man to know, a stereotype, the cigar-chewing, order-spewing Patton type of man. He liked to think of everyone as a statistic. It made people respect him because he got things done, he saved lives. But it convinced anyone who had ever worked near him that he had no such thing as feelings, that he didn't have—or want—a heart.

But his personality wasn't of interest now, only his performance. He was there to help Los Angeles in case that huge snowstorm raging in the Rocky Mountains swooped down on the city. Carter and Rob already knew it was going to; even the mayor secretly confessed he believed it could happen. "I find such a notion hard to fathom," Alex Granville said, but he had to go by the word of his advisers; that's what he'd been sent there for. Los Angeles didn't need him to tell the people how to drive their Toyotas in a freezing rain. It needed him if something white dumped on the city. It needed him to stay alive.

Alex checked the oil reserve supplies. Low, extremely low. What kind of equipment did the city have for zero temperatures, for snow removal? Nothing. Did the airports have heaters built in the runways to melt snow? Of course not. Did anyone even own a snow shovel? Stores had never even stocked them. He got on the phone and barked orders to the National Guard, to be on the alert. Then he talked to the President, who assured him his immediate action in the form of getting snow removal equipment to the city should such a phenomenon happen. Then he read the latest computer readout:

LIGHT SNOW FALLING IN MERCED, FRESNO, MOST OF SAN JOAQUIN VALLEY . . .

He looked on the map and turned to Carter. "That's not too far away."

Carter just nodded. Not far at all. In fact, too close for comfort.

Rob rushed in with another paper in his hand. "General, the temperature's dropping. *Fast.*"

It finally began to happen. Water molecules floating in the air over L.A. had risen into a cold region of the atmosphere, cold enough to cause them to condense and freeze. The collected weight of each crystal could not be supported by the air under them. The result was they began to plunge toward earth. The lower they got, the warmer it got around them, and there was the possibility that some flakes would melt before they hit the ground. But the temperature of the air never rose above freezing, and the crystals made the journey of several miles—completely whole.

A yellow Gremlin pulled up in front of the Los Angeles County Museum of Art, and Harry got out. "Just buy whatever they got on the shelves," he said to his wife. "Go home and wait for me. It's gonna freeze again, and the best place to be is home." He gave her a smile and shut the door.

She drove away.

Harry entered the lobby and was surprised to find such a small number of people there. He hated them for it, the selfish bastards, afraid to go out and get rain on their good clothes, staying home to watch Carol Burnett instead of braving the cold to see perhaps the finest works of art in the world. But the people who did show up were quite the antithesis of the people in the supermarkets at that hour.

They wore diamonds. They smelled of Halston and Cardin. They talked of art and culture. They held glasses of champagne. They nibbled on canapés and little colored round things which tasted awful but looked good. They all seemed to smile. There was little talk about the weather and little talk about the exhibit itself. If they did mention the Van Goghs, it was to say how important they were to have been asked to be there; mainly they talked about the new acquisitions to their own collections. And if they talked about the weather, it was how fabulously the Mercedes made it through the sleet, how the ice hardly affected the performance of the Rolls. It was the gathering of the money people, the rich and powerful, the beautiful people. Not the Hollywood establishment, although there were a smattering of stars there. But rather the people who ran little things like banks, insurance companies, real estate offices, even suburbs. A few good and honest "beautiful people" arrived and looked at the priceless paintings, people like Dorothy Otis Chandler and the Ahmansons and the French ambassador and Truman Capote, who happened to be in town. Even the mayor stopped in after his news conference, but no one there had seen it. He was pleased, for he'd had enough questions about what he really thought of the possibility of snow. Snow. He was already sick of the damn word.

There was a feeling, an air about the people, that their money and jewels and position guaranteed them sanctuary, protection from any crisis. Much less the elements. No one bothered to think that a Mercedes would need tire chains just like a Volkswagen if snow were to fall on the streets. No one bothered to think that if the gas lines went out in the tacky apartment houses in the central area of the city, the same gas lines were connected to the homes in Bel Air and Beverly Hills. No one bothered to....

And who could blame them? Why should they even entertain such possibilities, such thoughts? They'd lived comfortably for a long time. Los Angeles was a comfortable place. Threats came and went, but the forest fires and mud slides and earth tremors never seemed to affect them. Things like that happened in Sylmar. In Thousand Oaks. Out there in Barstow. You paid more in taxes to have a Beverly Hills address, but then too it was an insurance policy of a sort. Insurance of insulation from the rest of the world.

Harry popped a canapé into his mouth and felt as secure as he'd ever felt in his life. A woman with a large diamond rolling around between her breasts came up to him. "Harry, how good to see you! Shall we look at the paintings? I've not seen them yet." He offered his arm and they walked into the gallery.

He was glad Dolores hadn't come. Damn glad.

Bob and Julie were eating supper. He'd told her the tale of terror at the market, and she'd told him about Susan, and together they were feeling down. There wasn't much to say. The radio was on, and they heard the temperature was down to 23° already. That in itself was incredible, unthinkable! Unreal. Bob wondered if he should turn the pool heater on to prevent the water from freezing and cracking the sides, but the waste of gas would have been sinful. Julie suggested they drain the pool, and he agreed. He said he would open the valve in the morning, when it wouldn't cause an ice-skating rink at the bottom of the hill.

As they finished up, drinking coffee and eating sugar wafers for dessert (the only bag of cookies left in the store), Julie again expressed her concern for Michael and Lorna and Dawn.

"Julie, he's a man now. He's got his own life. I want him here too, I want all of them here. But we have to respect their doing it on their own."

Just as she was about to answer, Susan entered the room. Her little cat followed her. She walked slowly, weakly, holding onto the counter for support. Julie began to ask what she was doing, but she stopped herself. Susan seemed determined about something. Her eyes looked past them, into the dining room, out the big front window overlooking the yard. Her eyes were filled with wonder.

"Susan, hey, sassy, what is it?" her father asked. She was in obvious pain—what had compelled her to get up?

She walked into the dining room, and they jumped up and followed. Julie turned on the light, but Susan said, "No, don't, Mommy." Julie turned the light off. Then Susan said, *"Look!"*

She was looking at something she'd never seen happen out that window before. She was seeing something that intrigued her, fascinated her, and required proof from her parents that she wasn't dreaming. Bob and Julie stood next to her at the window; their heavy silence was proof enough that it was real.

It was snowing.

Dolores Sheppard walked out of the liquor store and nearly dropped the bag she was carrying. All around her, above her, below her, in her hair and on her face ... white flakes! She got into the car and opened one of the bottles and put it to her lips. Then she turned on the windshield wipers and watched the white flakes slide over the glass. She drove home with her mouth open. It was the most incredible thing she'd ever seen.

Marguerita first ran to the window when she heard Tom Jensen shouting, "It's snowing! Everybody, it's snowing!" into the courtyard. Sure enough, she saw it coming down in the light of the spotlight that shone on the words GENESEE GARDENS. She grabbed her shawl and pulled it over her shoulders and went out into the courtyard. Tom and Greg were already out there, in their shirt sleeves, feeling it coming down on their faces and hands. Michael leaned over the railing on the second floor and said, "Welcome to an Ivory Flakes commercial!" Old Mr. Rosenberg came out in his pajamas, looking bewildered, but Marguerita shooed him back inside and told him to put on his overcoat.

The others in the building—those who hadn't left the city—came outside to see something most of them had never seen in their lives. Flora danced in it with glee. "I think it's a gas!" she sang.

Her father had a different opinion. He watched from the window above his bed, opening it just for a moment to yell, "Nothin's gonna get me to deliver the mail in *that!*"

It was cold outside, cold enough so the white flakes didn't melt the minute they hit the ground. It took them awhile, but the ground hadn't frozen enough to let it mount up....

What it was was perfect snowball weather. Tom and Greg and Michael and Lorna all put their jackets and gloves on and had a snowball fight. Then, beside the pool, they built a small snowman, using a leaf from the banana tree as a hat and two avocado pits Lorna had been trying to get to grow as the eyes. Greg snapped a picture of it, of them gathered around it. It was an experience; it was fun. But it wouldn't last long, that wet snow, the packing kind. With the temperature dropping so rapidly, soon it would freeze and become ice, and the new snow falling from the skies would be dry, the kind that piles up and doesn't melt.

And most people in the city responded in the same way as the Genesee group–utterly fascinated, no one even thinking of the dangers it could bring if it were to stay on the ground. It would be gone by morning, so they would enjoy it while they could. Something to tell their grandchildren. Something to write home about. Flashbulbs lit up the evening sky like fireworks on the Fourth of July.

Marguerita heard the bulletin on TV, as her tenants were playing like children out in the courtyard. "We interrupt this program to bring you a special news bulletin. It is snowing in Los Angeles, California. Repeat–*snowing* in the city of Los Angeles and surrounding areas. Information will be broadcast as soon as it is received." Marguerita looked out the front window again. People were out in the street, all along the block. No one could believe it. Parents were waking their little children up to come out and see it. Even though it was a little over 20° outside, people were out there in undershirts, in housedresses. They didn't care about freezing. Everyone wanted to see and touch the snow.

The feeling of elation lasted for hours. Lights blazed in every window in the city, and though few cars traveled the streets, there wasn't a city block where someone wasn't playing in it, rolling the wet stuff into snowballs, tasting it, tossing it into the air. It was coming down hard, just the way it rained in Los Angeles. When it rained, it *rained;* the same, it seemed, was true with snow.

Quite awhile after the flakes had begun to fall, someone near the big windows of the County Museum of Art said, "My goodness, but I believe it's snowing out there." And the men and women in their tuxedos and gowns rushed to the doors to look out on the quirk of nature. But no one went out to play in it.

The beautiful white flakes were being looked at in quite another fashion at the communications center, however. "Why'd it have to happen so goddamn fast after I got here?" Alex Granville muttered. He and Carter and several aides and a representative from the Red Cross and the mayor's office looked over maps. "Take us two weeks to get the plows in here," Granville said, chomping on his cigar. In the background the mayor was on TV again, saying, "The streets will be cleared, and the temperature should rise to above the thirty-two mark by morning ... remain calm...." But no one was listening this time.

"Quakes, flooding, fire—we're ready for all of them," a man at the table next to Carter said. "But snow—what do you do with snow?"

"My suggestion, Alex," Carter said, "is that we move the center up to the Griffith Observatory site." Carter had explained his plans for a disaster center at the top of Mount Hollywood, with the parking lot for the observatory a perfect helicopter landing pad just below and the observatory itself a useful building.

The general agreed and gave the order. Machines and people began the move to higher ground.

Already there was crisis in the highlands. The resort towns of Big Bear and Lake Arrowhead were buried. It had been snowing in the San Bernadino Mountains since late October, the earliest snowfall in that area on record, and although at first it was controlled, for the mountain resorts were prepared for snow—they welcomed it because it brought in most of their revenue—it soon became too difficult to handle. Residents abandoned their houses and attempted to get down the mountainside to Riverside and San Bernardino, even to Palm Springs. But the snow seemed to follow them down the slopes; indeed, it was snowing at elevations lower than anyone could ever remember. And then the roads had to be closed. Even tire chains did no good; cars twisted and turned and dropped off the cliffs like toys falling off a shelf in a store. Massive accidents and stalled vehicles—including several highway patrol cars and rescue trucks—blocked any passage from and up to the resort towns. The windchill factor brought the temperature down to -40°, and hundreds upon hundreds of residents froze to death or died of asphyxiation in their stalled autos, breathing the fumes which they hoped would keep them alive, the air of their heaters, their engines, the only warmth in existence. Others were able to gather at ski lodges and hotels and other large insulated buildings, where there were supplies of food and enough gas and firewood to keep warm. But how long those resources would last was anyone's guess, because how long the treacherous blizzard would last was just as much a guessing game.

Things were worse in the Palmdale/Lancaster area, just to the north and east of Los Angeles proper. The residents there were used to cold winters and some snow, but nothing like what was happening outside their doors these days. It seemed to come all at once, great chunks of white, layers almost, dropping to the ground to create another foot of snow where just before desert plants had been visible. And the winds. It wouldn't have been so bad if it hadn't been for the winds. The force blew the icy flakes into people's eyes, through their clothing, knocking them to the ground, against walls, and hands froze to the bone as they clutched trees and signposts in desperation.

All routes to the cities were cut off, almost within an hour of the first flakes. Trucks jackknifed and overturned, blocking entire freeways. Poorly constructed houses—built for the desert, after all, and certainly not for affluent families—literally blew away. Rickety buildings collapsed, their frames unable to support the weight of the mounting snow. The ice had been around longer than it had been in the city of L.A. For three weeks, nights in Palmdale had been in the twenties. Cars with the improper amount of antifreeze in their cooling systems were dead for the winter, making travel to safer areas—if that could be done—unrealistic, impossible. They would have to stay put—and deal with it.

But no one knew how to. For some odd reason, no one bound together. No leaders were to be found. It was every man for himself. Men killed other men for propane fuel. A woman broke into the church she'd attended faithfully her whole life long and stole the candles off the altars. All for warmth. Anything for warmth. The power was out, and there were no crews to repair it. Water mains burst as easily as home water pipes. The law said pipes had to be only sixteen inches under the ground, as opposed to six feet in places like the Midwest. The law had not planned for the Palmdale area to freeze so deeply, so rigidly, and so murderously.

In Palmdale, where almost five feet of snow dropped in a record-breaking twenty-four hours, 344 people committed suicide. It was another record, but one people were not sure even Guinness would want to record.

Almost everyone had left the exhibit. Van Gogh had been upstaged by snow; all those colors, Harry thought, being overshadowed by pure white. The limousines pulled up, and the people got in; the valets delivered the Jaguars and Lancias. Harry refused a ride from some friends, knowing it was out of their way, and he didn't especially care for the way the guy handled a car in the first place. He would take a cab; cabbies knew how to drive in anything. Unless, of course, he'd have the bad luck to get the madman talking about Tahiti again.

He asked the curator of the museum if he could use the phone in his office to call his wife. "Of course, Mr. Sheppard. Feel free to go on up." The man had been Harry's friend for years. The office was on the second floor, overlooking the gallery and lobby. "And have a glance at the book I'm working on; it's there on the desk."

Harry thanked him and started up the stairs.

"Oh, just close the door when you're done. I'm getting home before this gets worse. One of the guards will let you out."

"Fine, sure. Thanks a lot." He went up to the office and turned on the bright fluorescent light. He sat at the desk and dialed, but the line was busy. He put the phone down and looked at the pages of the manuscript. The title was printed on a thick sheet of blue paper: *Great Museum Thefts & Forgeries.* He read a few paragraphs and then picked up the photographs which lay in a pile alongside the manuscript, all numbered for insertion into the book. He became so engrossed he forgot to try calling Dolores again for nearly an hour.

Dolores had made it home all right, but the fascination had turned to concern. She poured herself a stiff drink and called Julie. "I don't want to stay here; I just don't," she said.

"But Harry will be back soon," Julie said in comfort.

"I've believed it all along, what DeSimone said. I'm on Bob's side. I don't think we should stay here. I'm coming up to the house."

"Yes, we want you to. As soon as Harry gets there—"

Dolores interrupted, "No, he's at the museum, and he doesn't have a car. It will be easier for him to take a cab to Los Feliz than to come all the way home here. I'll start out right now. I don't want to stay in this house another minute. It's so cold—"

"Dee, you sound frightened."

"Oh, well, sure. I'll get in touch with Harry. I'll call him at the museum. I'll tell him to meet me at your house."

"All right, we'll expect you. And, Dee, please be careful driving. Bob says it isn't easy."

"I just did it, Julie. I just drove in it."

"But it's coming down harder now, and he says the streets will get very slippery as the car tires pack it down."

"I can do it. Is there anything I can bring?"

Julie thought for a moment. "Food. We'll always need food."

"I'm leaving now after I talk to Harry. Wish me luck."

"I'll say a prayer," Julie said. "And I'm going to get Michael and Lorna up here, too."

" 'Bye."

Dolores hung up and dialed the museum. At first she got a busy signal, but she knew that was impossible, so she dialed again. There was no answer. The switchboard was closed. She dialed again and again. Nothing. She put on her mink and started opening the cabinets, loading everything edible into grocery bags and laundry baskets and carrying them to the garage, setting them into the back of the Gremlin. She listened for the phone to ring, but it didn't. Then she cleared out the liquor cabinet and set the bottles in a box on the front seat of the car. Finally–hesitantly–she opened her drawers in her bedroom, spilled the jewelry into an overnight case, and then unlocked the wall safe and took out the papers and the few pieces of very expensive jewelry she had there. Perhaps it was an overreaction, a silly thing to do, but she did it nonetheless; she knew she could always put it back. But houses were going to be empty and burglars were going to know it. She doubted the damn security patrol was going to drive around in a snowmobile to guard the rich houses.

Finally, the car loaded, she sat down and contemplated one more drink before she set out, but she didn't want to be loaded as well. But she just sat there anyway, staring at the phone. Should she leave? Or should she wait just awhile longer, to see if Harry showed up or if he'd call? She wandered around the house, looking out the window to see the front yard turning white.

It still was hard to believe.

Bob brought the TV up from the family room. He told Julie it was silly to heat rooms that didn't have to be used. The furnaces were working at capacity now, and to overtax them would be risking disaster. And the house, though solid and well built, did not have the insulation for sub-zero weather. It was 18° now, and if the rate continued, it might go below zero before it got up to 80° again.

Bob built a roaring fire in the living-room fireplace and closed the heating duct a little; that would help keep Susan's room toasty warm. The house had three furnaces. The largest one handled the family room downstairs and the entire first floor, the living room, den, dining room, kitchen and Susan's bedroom. The second handled the guest bedroom and bathroom and Bob's office upstairs. The third took care of the master bedroom and bathroom.

Bob and Julie planned to put Harry and Dolores in the guest room. Bob closed the vent to his office and shut the door; there was no need to waste the heat, and this way he could put the second furnace on low, and it would be enough to keep Harry and Dee comfortable.

If Michael arrived, he and Lorna and Dawn could have the master bedroom; Julie would sleep with Susan, and Bob could sack out on the couch in the living room or in a chair in the den.

Julie was upstairs putting an extra blanket on the bed for Harry and Dolores when all the lights in the house flickered. "Oh, what's that?" she screamed.

Bob ran to her and held her. "Hey, it's nothing. Don't be afraid. Probably some idiot hit the wrong switch or something. The electricity only goes out in big rainstorms, not in this." He walked her over to the window and they looked out over the backyard. It was an astonishingly beautiful sight. The branches of the trees—in the yard and up the side of the mountain—were coated with a frosty layer of white.

Harry finished reading the manuscript. He had a faraway look in his eyes. Something seemed to have caught hold of him, taken him away from the world. He leaned back in the chair. If anyone had seen him at that moment, he'd have asked if he were ill, if something were wrong. Harry rubbed his hands together and bit his lip. Then he heard the faraway sound of a door closing, the echo of steel, of locking. It brought him back to the real world.

He picked up the phone again and dialed. Dolores answered on the first ring. "I'm worried sick!" she screamed. "I've tried the goddamn museum, the office, even a cocktail lounge."

"I'm in the curator's office in the museum."

"How? The switchboard isn't working."

"Honey, I'm on a private line, there's no one left in the whole building. I tried calling, and the line was busy."

"Don't blame me!" she shouted. "I had to call somebody. I'm all alone while you're living it up at some stinking party with all your goddamn artsy-fartsy art-loving friends."

He got mad. "Goddammit, Dolores, listen to me. I tried calling you when I found out it was snowing outside."

"What do you mean was? Is. Look out a window."

"I see it. I know what's happening. Look, don't blame me, I didn't desert you tonight on purpose because I knew it was going to snow and you'd be afraid. Remember you're the one who decided not to come to this."

"Harry, what are we going to do?"

"Just sit tight. I'll get a taxi and be there as soon as I can."

"Are you crazy? I've had the TV on, cars are sliding all over the streets. How are you going to find a cab, you're not even dressed for this. Anyway, I'm not staying in this house."

He listened for more. There was none. "What do you mean you're not staying in the house?"

"I'm going to your brother's. We both are. I want to be with them. Julie needs us, Susan isn't well—"

"Julie needs us? Since when does Julie *need* us?"

Dolores screamed at him again. "I'm going to Bob's. I'm not going to sit here worrying and waiting until you get here, if you ever do! I don't want to sit here while the snow piles up around the windows!"

He heard her glass rattle against the receiver. "Dee, for God's sake, take it easy, all right? Now, listen, you're right, we'll go to Bob's. It's much easier for me to get there than to come all the way home. Now. . . ." He thought for a minute. "Now listen to me. If the streets are that bad, call Chip next door. We've got tire chains in the garage. . . ."

"Where?"

"I don't know where. It's been two years since we used them up in the mountains. They're in a box someplace. Chip can find them. Have him put them on the car and give him five bucks. Then drive safely. Take only the big streets. Stay on Sunset all the way to Vermont and then up."

"I already loaded the car with things."

"Things? What things?"

"Food and clothing. You can't expect them to feed us; we can't wear their clothes. Jesus, Harry, you're so inconsiderate!" She was shouting again.

"Dolores, you're getting hysterical."

"I'm not getting hysterical!"

He had to hold the phone away from his ear, she shouted so loud. "Dolores, honey, relax. Promise me you'll have some coffee. Not another drink until you get to Bob's. It's rough enough to drive in snow, much less–"

"I'm not drunk." She said it softly, soberly. But he knew the truth. "I said I'm not drunk, Harry."

"Honey, have coffee anyhow, warm you up. You need some caffeine to stay alert anyway. Just don't drink any more. Promise?" No reply. "Promise? Dolores, please!"

Finally she said, "Promise."

He paused for a moment as he looked out the window. It was incredible, but it was reality. He could barely see the street, and what he could see of it looked white. "I've got another thought. I may stay at the office tonight."

"The office?" She sounded hysterical again.

"Listen, if I can't get a cab, if I can't hitch a ride, I'm going to walk across the street and stay in the office where it is warm and safe. In the morning the snow will be melted, and I'll get up there then. So I may be there tonight, but if I'm not, don't worry. I'll be at the office. I'll call and let you know."

"Okay. I'm going to go now. I have to get Chip. I have to get out of here."

"Dolores, make sure you lock the house. Set the alarm, leave lights on." He paused. Then: "Good luck."

She gulped. She wanted something more, any words but those. Couldn't he miss her a little? Couldn't he be worried about her?

Couldn't he even say . . . just for once, maybe for old times' sake . . . that he loved her? "Thanks," she said, and hung up.

Harry placed the receiver in the cradle, and almost immediately thoughts of his wife went out of his head; the glassy stare returned. He looked strange, almost giddy in a sinister kind of way, maybe even possessed. He glanced at the curator's manuscript. He ran his hand over it, over the title page. He looked at the clock on the wall. Almost midnight. His mind reeled, and he suddenly had a big grin on his face, and then he shook his head, as though someone were there with him and they were having a sight argument. No, it was too crazy; it was utterly preposterous. And yet the book said it was the simplest of things in the world, given the right circumstances, but the right circumstances had never really come to pass, not anywhere in the world, not at any time. Then Harry looked at the window and saw the snow and wondered if this weren't the only time, ever, that the circumstances were right. Could he count on it to last, at least long enough? It would mean leaving everything behind, changing his life, making a break, becoming a new person. But what a person, what wealth, what a position. Just to have them as his own. *His.* In his villa on an island somewhere. He wasn't thinking rationally any longer; a spark of insane daring filled his mind. He'd been in a mold all his life, more so than his brother. He'd worked for this, worked for that, and he'd go on working for more till the day he died, and what would he have to show for it? More of what he already had. But could he ever in his lifetime have what was down the very stairs outside the office? Could he ever attain such beauty, such fortune, such satisfaction in the life he'd been living?

He paced the office. He had to give up a lot if it were to work. But what did any of it mean? The house? He could have a hundred houses, one million houses. His marriage? What marriage. There were women all over the world. Dolores had ceased being his wife long ago. She was a drunk, and she was boring, and he felt sorry for her. No, he pitied her. Should he stick around her just to make himself miserable? She was tough; she'd survive. She had her bottle. The business? He hated it anyhow. The same thing every month, every year. More money, more prestige, more bullshit. He didn't even *like* public relations, advertising. He liked art. And downstairs was the richest art the world had ever seen.

He stopped himself and shook his head. *What the fuck's the matter with you? You really crazy?* He turned to leave. But he didn't move another muscle. His eyes seemed to fall back into the other world again, a world of dreams and wild ambition and magic reality. He told himself he'd try. Just for the hell of it. Just to see if it could be done. If it couldn't, who would believe he, Harry Sheppard, patron of fine art, who'd ever in the world believe that he'd tried to do it? It had suddenly become a challenge. It was real all right, but the only way he could deal with it—the only way he could even hope to pull it off—would be to tell himself the challenge was a kind of game, just to see if it could be done. If it could, he'd have to make yet another decision, whether or not to take it all the way, to carry it through.

He turned out the light in the office and waited until his eyes adjusted to the darkness. The outdoor lights surrounding the building seemed to fill the room. The snow blew outside the window. Then he opened the door leading into the hall and saw that the place was already dark; only a faint light came from the bottom of the stairs. He walked—softly, slowly—to the railing and looked down. The lobby was empty except for two men, both in uniform, both with guns at their sides. "Night, Jack. Good luck to ya gettin' home."

"You sure about this, Parker?"

"Yeah, who the hell'd come around here on a night like this? No one's gonna be movin' anywheres in this city tonight. You go home, and the boss'll never know you weren't here. I'll tell the guy that comes on in the mornin' you left just a few minutes ago."

The departing man slapped the other guard on the back. "You're sure a pal, Parker."

"Snow," the guard said after his partner had left. "Who the

hell would believe it? Never thought I'd live to see the day." Then he lit a cigarette and sat down on one of the benches. In front of him was the punch bowl from the reception, still half full. He dipped a glass into the bowl and took a drink. And then another. And yet another.

Harry smiled. The man was doing just what he wanted him to do. Harry sat down, on the floor, looking down. Anticipation filled his bloodstream, anxious anticipation, although he knew he had all the time in the world. The guard had been right: No one was going to come around the museum in the snow, Van Gogh or no Van Gogh. The man drank for about twenty minutes and finally curled up on the bench and nodded off to sleep. Harry waited another ten minutes to be sure the man was fast asleep, and then he made his first move.

He took off his shoes and crept down the stairs. He made his way through the lobby with the precision and quiet of a cat. He ran his fingers over the corner of "The Church at Auvers," which he knew Van Gogh had done in 1890, the famous painting he remembered seeing on his first trip to Europe, when he was in his twenties. He walked past it, past the others, to the gift shop. He'd seen them earlier, and they had caught his eye because they were so real. Prints. Prints of the priceless paintings behind him. Usually they were of inferior quality and looked like travel posters. But these were different, of good quality, and quite expensive. They just might fool somebody for some time.

He tried the lock on the gift shop door. It wouldn't move. He pulled his wallet from his tuxedo coat and found the little pocketknife hidden in it. That knife had come in handy many times, but never this handy. He slipped it into the lock as he'd remembered doing in the Army, and the door sprang open with only a little click. He went inside.

He selected six of the prints. They all were original size, matching the paintings as exactly as possible, and they had a border of white around the sides, about an inch wide. Which would be perfect. Then he looked into the lobby again and heard the guard snoring. Was it luck? Fate? Coincidence? Whatever, he was going to make the most of it. Even if the man woke up, he'd have the upper hand. Yes, the man had a gun, but Harry was younger, stronger, alert, and fast, and it was dark. He'd overpower the old coot before he had a chance to reach for his gun, before he could even realize what was going on. He had the upper hand. It was something he'd always wanted in life, and never quite thought he'd gained.

The adrenaline was surging through his body. He went up the steps again and into the office. He tried one door, and it turned out to be a closet. Then another, but that was a small workroom of a sort. Then the third door in the office, and it was what he wanted, the curator's private bathroom. He opened the medicine chest and saw the razor and the blades sitting next to it. His biggest fear was that the man used an electric shaver. He had to smile at that. To think one of the greatest crimes in the history of the world could be decided by the presence or lack of a razor blade, by whether or not a man's wife bought him a Norelco last Christmas, by whether or not a guy had sensitive skin and got shaving burn when he used a blade.... Harry almost laughed out loud. It was absurd, and that somehow made it even more exciting.

He stepped back into the office, took off his coat, and started for the door, which he'd shut tight, but silently. He stopped himself when he put his hand on the knob. He turned back and grabbed the phone and dialed his brother. "Bob? Yeah, isn't this something? Listen, I'm just calling to say I'm at the office ... yeah, the office. Dee's on her way to your place. I'll come up in the morning. I'm sacking out here, the hell with the streets...." He held the receiver to his face with his shoulder; he was rolling up his shirt sleeves as he talked softly. "Okay, I'll be there in the morning. Bob, take care of Dolores, she's ... well, her nerves are a little shot from this whole thing. Thanks." Just before he hung up he asked, "Have you heard anything more from DeSimone about it? What's the immediate future look like?" He listened as Bob told him he'd talked to Carter just an hour before and that the scientist had told him the duration of the snow could not be predicted. It was a massive arctic storm, and it had every intention of sticking around. "Jesus," Harry said, and then said good-bye. After he hung up, he smiled.

He was perhaps the only person in the whole sprawling city who was pleased that it looked as though it were going to get worse. He picked up the razor blade and went back downstairs. The further he committed himself, the more determined his next move became. He was onto his next move.

Dolores had called Mr. Robbins next door and explained she had to get to the other side of town. He'd told her Chip had already gone to bed, but he was happy to help a neighbor. He'd wake his son, and they both would see that they got her off safely.

And they did. Finding the tire chains was the hard part. Dolores had no idea what was even in the garage in the first place, much less where something specific may have been. Chip finally found them under a stack of newspapers. He and his father got them on the tires and checked the antifreeze in the radiator. But the man who'd come out to service the Gremlin had given it enough to keep it from freezing at even -30°. The car started right away, and Dolores thanked the man and his teenage son, and then she ran through the house, turning out the lights. Then back on, and finally jumped into the packed car, in her mink coat, her hair all bound up in a warm turban. "Good luck, Mrs. Sheppard," Chip said as the garage door shut behind them automatically. "Drive carefully."

When she backed out into the street and put the car into gear and slid to the corner, the boy's father said, "She's out of her mind going out in this weather." Then they went back to their house.

Had Dolores heard what the man said, she would have agreed with him. The car slid. It didn't stop; it slid. It didn't move; it slid. Even with the chains. But when she turned onto Sunset, the street was fairly wet, not as slippery. The chains dug into the mushy snow, and she seemed to be in control. She sat far forward on the seat, her neck strained forward to see out the messy windshield. The air was so cold the snow seemed to freeze on the windshield in little bumps, little patches, everywhere but the two spots where the blowers hit the glass. She had the heat up all the way and was nearly dying, sweating. The back window was still steamed up. She rolled her window down a little. It helped.

It was slow going, about 20 mph at the most, and stop and go, stop and go. She saw snow on palm trees, snow covering the UCLA buildings. On the Sunset Strip she saw people coming out of bars and restaurants, trying to get their cars out of snowed-in parking lots, some of them not even bothering. She saw a young man with long hair hitchhiking. He looked so cold, so helpless. She wanted to pick him up, but there was no room, the car was filled. For the first time ever she wished she were driving the Great White Boat. Well, no, not really . . . Chip had said she was lucky she had a little car with a six-cylinder engine, whatever the hell that meant.

She made it to the corner of Sunset and Crescent Heights by 2 A.M. and then turned into a gas station that was, for some reason, open. She jumped out of the car and ran inside. "Oh, do you have coffee?"

"Lady, that's all anybody wants here tonight; no one needs gas." The man poured her a cup of thick, strong coffee, and she gulped it down. She stretched her legs and moved her head around, getting the tension out. "Lady, where you going?"

She told him. And he told her there was a big accident just up the street on Sunset, at LaBrea. "You won't get through for days. Go up to Hollywood Boulevard, up the next street here. You got chains, you'll make it okay. I'm waiting for my truck to come back in, so I can get home. I'm the only truck that's got chains in the whole town, I think. Last time I seen anything like this was the hills of New Mexico, in '72 I think it was."

"I . . . I don't believe so much snow has fallen in such a short time," Dolores said, wrapping her mink around her again, ready to brave the cold once more.

"I swear it's the end of the world. Sodom and that other place, Gan-ore-ah? Same thing."

She couldn't listen to that. She ran out to the car and started up the next street, but it was treacherous now, going uphill on a street where few cars had driven. One car had obviously tried to make it and had ended up slammed into a tree, sideways to the street. Another was parked in the middle of the road, and she had a rough time getting around it. She lightly bumped a parked car at the curb, but what did it matter? At least she wasn't sliding back down to Sunset.

She turned onto Hollywood Boulevard and the going was the same. Snow had seemed to melt in patches and build up in other spots, making it difficult to maneuver. And the worst thing was everything was white; she couldn't tell where the road was divided. If it hadn't been for the cars parked along each side, she wouldn't have known where the curbs were either.

Her eyes watered. She'd smoked two packs of cigarettes by the time she reached LaBrea. She'd guzzled some of the scotch lying on the floor in the front seat. She'd opened the window all the way just to stay awake—the warm air seemed to be putting her to sleep. Finally, she reached the section of the street which most people referred to as Hollywood Boulevard, the gaudy stretch of land between LaBrea and Vine streets which most tourists thought to be the Hollywood they heard about back home. It was nothing but a cheap sideshow, Harry had once said, full of hustlers and hookers and every conceivable misfit in the world. He wouldn't go near the street, but Dolores found it exciting, sad and crazy maybe, but it provided her with an alternative to her Bel Air existence. And she never forgot the fact that she'd been on that street at one time in her life, broke and unhappy, looking for work, almost any kind of work. . . . She thought about the time she finally had the nerve to get into a car which had stopped near her. The man was old, but gentle, kind. He told her he could get her a singing job when she told him she was a singer. She knew what he really wanted; she'd not had to do anything like that yet, but it was now or never, now or get out of her apartment, now or starve. But it turned out he wasn't after her body; he was legit. He did give her a job. A lousy one, but a job. Hollywood Boulevard had been good to her, and she often went back, just to walk, sometimes even to chat with the hippies and the hustlers, the derelicts and the tourists, the gay boys and the motorcycle crowd and the girls with fat behinds walking hand in hand in blue jeans. It was one of her secret pleasures, and she hated the fact that she could never share it with her husband.

She glanced up at the marquee of Grauman's Chinese Theater. It was dark. Even the name had been changed. It was Mann's Chinese now, but for her it still remained Grauman's. It was the place she'd seen her first Hollywood movie. . . .

Suddenly the car stopped moving. She could barely see through the windshield. She stepped on the gas, but nothing happened; the car just seemed to rock back and forth. She thought she felt it going a little sideways. She gunned it again and again, swearing. She heard a man yell, "Give up, lady! You're stuck!"

She got out of the car. She stepped into a snowdrift, and the icy stuff went up to her knee. She made her way around to the front of the car and looked at the pile of snow. Why it had come to drift there like that, she didn't know. It was probably the big buildings on either side of the street; the wind was increasing and creating little whirlpools of snow. On some parts of the street there was patches of ground, no snow at all; then three feet away would be drifts almost four feet high. The wet, thick snow that Michael and Lorna had played in wasn't falling now. This was fine and dry.

She looked at the back of the car. One tire chain was gone. The other tire seemed to have been digging a hole in the street. The man who'd yelled to her came up and asked what he could do. He seemed prepared, wearing a parka, gloves, looking as though he knew what snow was all about. "I'm helping the police," he said. "I'm a ski instructor. Get in, put it in low gear, and hit the gas real slow. I'll try and rock you out."

She did as she was told; but the wheels spun, and the tire chain dug deeper. Under the hard thin layer of frozen earth was wet, soggy, muddy soil. It was no use.

The man told Dolores she'd have to go it on foot; she had no choice. He told her patrols were moving up and down the major streets, trucks with chains, and maybe she'd get a ride that way. He suggested she get to the nearest hotel or motel or house that would take her in. She thanked him.

Then she knelt on the front seat and chose what was going to go with her. It was a difficult process. She stuffed the jewelry into her pockets, into her purse. She put the important papers into the big bag she'd brought, along with more jewelry, and the bottles of liquor. Then she locked the car doors and the back tailgate. She told herself not to panic, that there was absolutely nothing she could do. Harry would have to make arrangements for someone to get the car in the morning. And if it had been broken into, so what? The food and the extra clothes, well, maybe they would help some of the poor kids who hung out on the Boulevard.

Then she turned and headed toward the sidewalk, where the snow wasn't so deep. The bag was heavy, and her feet felt frozen. She held her mink closed tight in front of her. And then she looked at the footprints in the famous area in front of the Chinese Theater. Only the footprints weren't in cement now; they were in snow. She thought she was dreaming, hallucinating. Oh, why didn't somebody wake her up from this nightmare?

She felt the tears on her cheeks turning to ice. She plodded on, heading east on the street, determined as she had never been determined in her life.

And the snow continued to fall.

At the Los Angeles International Airport air traffic controllers got the final word. *Closed.* Some were amazed that the airport had held on so long, that they'd taken so long finally to shut the place up. They were used to closing down at the slightest notice when thick ground fog lolled onto the runways from the adjacent coastline, making arrival and takeoff impossible.

One older controller was shocked into awareness of the situation outside when he stood up from his radar screen and experienced a feeling of *déjà vu.* He'd worked in the tower first at the Minneapolis-St. Paul airport and then at Chicago's huge

O'Hare Field. What he was looking at now was equal to the worst storm he'd seen in those other cities. But this was L.A.! Jesus.

The bustling airport had become a ghost town of the West; even the hookers who hung around the baggage arrival doors were nowhere to be seen. A pack of seagulls huddled together near the mouth of a huge hangar that serviced 747s, their backs to the gaping hole at the front of the building. On the roof of one of the terminals a lone figure made its way out to a small platform where numerous odd-shaped instruments sat. The unprotected man made his way quickly around the platform, making notes on a pad as he looked at the dials and scales before him. He paused a second before making a swift retreat back to shelter. In that second his mind seemed stunned into reality as he looked at the numbers he'd just written down. It couldn't be, but it was. Already eighteen inches of snow had fallen, and the storm was only six hours old and holding strong.

Flora Reynauld sat up in bed, startled. "Daddy, you hear that?" she said. Her father was sleeping with her, in her bed. It was closest to the small heater, and the body warmth was helpful too. The loud, creaking sound filled the room again. Flora looked at the clock. It read 2:28. "Daddy, what's happening?"

Before the man had time to answer, they heard it again, only louder this time. "The sky's fallin'!" he said, and got out of bed. He turned on the light and looked up at the ceiling. There was a crease down the center, a crack. "Holy Jesus, the roof's comin' down!"

From outside a voice shouted, "Flora! Harve! Get out! Get out of the building!" It was Michael. He was up on the roof with Greg, Tom, and a man who lived on the first floor. The snow had been piling up, wet and heavy. They'd been shoveling it off, or doing the best they could with a garden shovel, pieces of plywood, garbage-can lids, anything that would scoop it up. Lorna had helped for a time but felt chilled and went down to Marguerita's when Dawn started to cry for food.

Flora and her father put on their robes, and their coats over them, and ran to the front door. "Wait, child," Harve suddenly said, remembering. He went back into the bedroom and took her piggy bank from her dresser, the one he'd given her when she was only four years old. Then he grabbed his wallet and an old cigar box from his bureau and ran to the balcony. They looked up at the ceiling again—plasterboard was cracking, specks of paint falling. Water had already started to come through the middle of the living room. "We ain't gonna see this apartment no more," Flora said, pulling her dad with her as she stepped through the deep snow in her bare feet.

Michael shouted again, from the side of the roof. "Flora, rap on the Matthews' door, get them out!" They lived in the last apartment on the second floor—if the roof did collapse, they might have to jump from the second floor to get out. The other apartments on that side of the building were empty. Michael saw Marguerita open the door of her apartment. "Marguerita, call the Matthews, get them out!" She went inside to dial the phone as Flora hopped through the snow on the balcony. Her father walked down the steps, which had been salted and swept free of snow. He went into Marguerita's apartment.

Flora pounded on the door. "Christ Almighty," she said, "I hear 'em screwin' through the walls most nights, and the one time *they* should hear through the walls they're sleepin' sound." She kicked the door and pounded on their bathroom window. Finally a light turned on. The window slid open, and as it did, Flora heard a phone ringing inside. With Mr. Matthews on the phone and his wife looking out the window, they got the message. They said they'd come right down, even though their ceiling didn't look as bad as the Reynaulds'.

Michael came down the ladder first. "There's nothing more we can do," he said. Greg and Tom and the man from the first floor followed him. They were dead tired, their muscles aching. "I'm going to go up and get what I can out of there," Michael said. He bounded up the steps and into the apartment. In a minute he was throwing things over the side of the balcony. Lorna put on her coat and ran out and picked up the clothing, the blankets, the pillowcases he'd filled with things–she wondered what all he was taking, because there was the sound of crashing glass when one of the bags hit the coping around the pool.

Then the people in the end apartment, the Matthews, came down the steps, carrying suitcases. "Come in, you're welcome to stay in with us," Marguerita said. Her apartment was large, and the small recreation room off it would serve as a kind of communal crash pad. But Mr. Matthews told her they had relatives in Culver City, and they were going to do their best to drive over there. They'd gone to sleep early and had absolutely no idea the flurries of snow had turned into what looked like tons of it. The drains on the flat roof had already stopped up, and four inches of water lay on the roof, besides the great amount of snow.

Marguerita wished them well and said a prayer for them. Then she turned–they all turned–as a creaking sound seemed to squeal in the night. Michael ran down the stairs and hugged Lorna as they all stood there and watched the roof of that side of the building collapse. First, the heavy snow poured through the ceiling of Michael and Lorna's apartment. Windows broke, and the lights went out. Then they saw the same thing happen to Harve and Flora's living room. "Daddy!" Flora screamed as a chunk of plasterboard and planks of wood fell into their bedroom. They could see it clearly through the window, which seemed to blow out at the same time. Part of the end apartment's ceiling had fallen in, but the damage was not nearly as bad as the two middle ones, where most of the heavy wet snow had gathered. The apartment at the other end–the one on the opposite side of Michael and Lorna's–suffered the same kind of damage; luckily it was empty.

The four upstairs apartments were completely ruined, and the astonished people standing there watching most everything they owned being destroyed knew it wouldn't be long before the floor would give out and the same thing would happen to the four ground-level apartments. The middle ones were empty; they'd coincidentally been vacated at the same time, and they'd just been painted. Marguerita had planned to hang out the "For

Rent" sign that day, in fact. The apartment at the end nearest the street belonged to a man who hadn't been around in days, and the one on the far end, in back, was occupied by a young guy named Kenny Rupp, only in his 20s, who worked for a recording studio. His girlfriend was usually there with him, too.

The rest of the building was safe; the roof was peaked. The building called Genesee Gardens had been built in two pieces. The first section was L-shaped, with Marguerita's apartment taking up one side of the L and above her two apartments. On the other side of the L were four apartments, two on the second floor, and two on the first, which now belonged to Greg and Tom and the other to Mr. Rosenberg. The building had stood like that for three years, just the manager's apartment and six other units, and then the other piece had been added, the 8-unit section that turned the L shape into a U shape. When the new addition went on, the pool went in the middle. The style of the buildings was the same, except for the roofs. The original was tile, in the Spanish tradition, but the new one was flat, just tar and paper, which was cheaper. The walls were stucco, and the ornamentation was Spanish wrought iron.

So now the newest section of the building had been evacuated. Mr. Rosenberg invited Harvard and Flora to use his bedroom because he preferred to sleep on the couch in any case. Michael and Lorna would stay with Marguerita. Kenny Rupp and his girlfriend finally gave up the idea of sticking it out because water started to come through the ceiling. Greg and Tom invited them to bunk in their living room, and they eagerly took them up on it.

But no one rested well; no one slept well. Michael made a feeble attempt to get back up to the second floor to get some pills Flora had forgotten were in the medicine chest. But the still-falling snow prevented him from getting a good grip on anything, and he lost his footing trying to get through the rubble of what had been their homes. Beams had fallen through windows and stuck out of the cracked walls. It was far too dangerous. Greg found the breaker for the electricity to the entire newer section of building and tripped it; there were no fires, and it seemed the building would just sit there and freeze.

Flora couldn't sleep at all. She got up and walked around in the snow. She was so numb—not from the cold, from what had happened in such a fast period of time. She thought she couldn't feel anything at all; she couldn't laugh, she couldn't cry, she couldn't even be worried. She thought she had no feelings left anymore; the hell with everything. What could anyone do about it?

Flora looked at the water in the pool. A thin sheet of ice was beginning to form at the top. She shivered and went back to Mr. Rosenberg's apartment. The pills she'd left in the apartment were Valium, blue ones, ten grains. She needed one now. Even though she felt numb, she knew she wouldn't be able to sleep. They'd always helped her sleep before. So she sat there staring at the window, at the snow blowing against the pane, wondering if she could get her doctor on the phone in the morning and get over to a pharmacy.

On Marguerita's soft bed, Lorna curled up in Michael's arms after Dawn had finally fallen asleep. "It's incredible," she said.

"Yeah." He was obviously not in a joking mood. She had expected some wisecrack from him. "Jesus," he muttered.

"You think ... do you want to go to your parents' house?"

"I don't know. Go to sleep."

She didn't say another word. She shut her eyes and dropped off from sheer exhaustion.

But Michael lay awake, just like Flora, looking at the window and the white stuff in the air outside it.

Harry Sheppard carefully slit the inside edge of "A Starry Night." The canvas dropped into his hands with only a slight flapping sound. He carefully, almost reverently, laid it on top of the other four canvases he'd cut from their frames. Then he went to work on this last one, just as he'd done with the other five, replacing the priceless painting—Van Gogh's beautiful "The Sower"—with a poster which looked much like it in the darkened room. He didn't know what time it was—he didn't even know what day it was anymore; years could have gone by; time meant nothing—but he knew he'd completed the first stage of the most ingenious, outrageous, and courageous art heist in history. He lifted the canvases in his arms, his babies, his little loves, and carried them up the stairs to the curator's office.

By the time he got up there he realized how heavy old oil paintings could be. He set them down on the desk and ran his fingers through his hair. *God, I've done it! I don't believe it, but I've done it!* He looked out the window at the still-falling snow. Good. It was almost as beautiful as the paintings. He loved it. All he had to do now was get out of the building....

But how? How in the hell was he going to get the six canvases out of the museum? He hadn't thought about that. How would he get them outside? Just carry them? Walk through the wet snow with them in his hands? He doubted that anyone would really notice, but what about the snow? He couldn't let that happen to them. He looked around the room, his eyes frantic, racing, trying to find something plastic, something rubber, something to resist the wet. *I've come too far, it can't stop now.* He had a crazed expression on his face ... and then he dropped into the chair. He put his head in his hands.

He seriously contemplated giving up the whole scheme at that moment, walking out and pretending ignorance when questioned, as he would surely be. But then there was that villa on some island of his dreams, the money he had in his Swiss bank account. The airport was just a taxi ride away. He shook his head and told himself to calm down, to do it in a businesslike way and methodically. He had to make a choice. Stay in your rotten stinking nowhere life, or make a break with the biggest booty of all time. Was there really a choice to be made?

No. He knew he was going to go all the way. What did he have to lose—happiness, love, a good and fulfilling existence? Even if they caught him, if they hanged him for God's sake, so what? It would be the greatest thrill of his life, walking out those doors with those works of art under his belt; anything and everything was worth it. He had a vision of himself in a Western, the townsfolk gathered at the oak tree on the hill to watch him swing. And he laughed at them, spit at them, because he had the last laugh. He was the one who'd had the guts, the nerve to do something totally and completely outrageous. He'd done it; he'd had the nerve, the guts, the daring, the manhood to take a stab at it, and he'd gotten far. No man could match that. No thrills on earth could match the feeling of electricity which had raced through his bones as he carried those paintings out of the museum doors. No fuck he'd ever thrown into a woman could equal the orgasmic feeling he'd had at that instant. So the townspeople watched, and he laughed loud and hard....

Harry got up and walked around slowly. His eyes found some possibilities—a garbage can, but that would mean folding the canvases, and he couldn't crease them; they were too old even to be rolled, but if he had to do that he would and could, but to fold them was out. He found a raincoat in the curator's closet, but it was a child's size (probably the man's daughter's), and it would never cover the large canvases. No, there was nothing in the office which would work.

He went out into the upstairs hall. He stopped at the drinking fountain on his way to the storage room, where he figured there might be some wrapping materials, crating materials which were waterproof. As he bent over, he realized what was hanging on the wall next to him: a fire hose. He saw it, but nothing registered. He just stared. Then he became conscious of the possibility ... then....

A fire hose. Waterproof. Thick enough to slide a rolled canvas into. Easy enough to carry over one's shoulder. Something no one would question, a man carrying a fire hose. A goddamn *fire hose.* Harry felt his blood rush with excitement again. He unfastened the hose from inside the glass box and dragged it into the office.

Then he went about rolling the precious paintings, three to a pile on the floor, as carefully as he could so as not to damage them any more than he had to, and slide them, the two rolled piles, into the fire hose. Then, when all six were safely in the thick tubing, he took the knife from his wallet and sawed the stuffed piece from the rest of it. He stuffed the end with a chunk of the child's raincoat, rolled the unused part of the hose up, and put it back in the hall. He slung the six-foot section over his shoulder and looked at himself in the mirror in the bathroom. All he needed was a fireman's helmet.

He walked back into the office and put the hose down on the couch. At the desk he turned to the page of the manuscript which described the slitting of the paintings from their frames and replacing them with forgeries—his using cheap prints was his own sarcastic addition—and he grabbed a pen and after the line which read "But how ever to get them out under the guard's nose, no one could figure out!" Harry wrote, "Someone did!"

Then he dressed, putting on his tuxedo again, and bent over to put the fire hose with its precious treasure over his shoulder. He descended the stairs in his stockinged feet, carrying his shoes in one hand. He walked past the guard as if the man were not there. Then he opened the door slowly, silently, and slipped out into the icy air. He bent over and put his shoes on his feet. He looked back. The guard was out like a light. Out like most lights, he realized looking around; the buildings were exceptionally dark. He figured most cleaning women had not come to work that night.

And he hoped no cleaning women were working in the building that housed his office. Because that's where this man, in tails and black tie with a fire hose on one shoulder, was headed.

He looked up and thought that, in all his life, he'd never seen so much snow falling so fast.

"Lorna, wake up." She didn't move. "Honey, wake up. I think it's morning."

"What?" She opened her eyes. It was still pitch black outside. "Michael, we need sleep, we all need sleep."

"Lorna, I've been thinking. We ought to go to Dad's. If it gets worse, we're never going to be able to make it. There's such protection there, and I feel . . . well, I feel as though I should help protect them."

Lorna was wide awake suddenly. "Our allegiance lies first to each other and our child."

"That's what I'm saying. We belong in the safest possible place. That's Dad's."

"Michael," she said severely, raising her voice, "we have a duty to ourselves, and this is our home, and we can't abandon it."

"For God's sake, look at it!" He glanced at the window. "See it over there, that orange crate filled with snow and plaster and mush? That's home. Wonderful."

"You don't understand."

"I understand. You're doing social work again; you're going to save everyone here."

She jumped up to her knees. "Michael, listen to me! These people are our friends, and we're in this together. This is a crisis, and we need each other! Harry and Dee are going to your dad's—they're probably there already—and the neighbors may well be there. They're okay. A lot better off than these people. The Reynaulds don't have anything left! Did you—"

"Neither do we."

"But your parents are in a much more secure position than any of our friends here. We're staying, Michael. I love these people, and we're staying." She stopped and turned her head. "No, I have no right to say that. *I'm* staying. I can't force you, nor can I force you to keep Dawn here if you want to go. But *I'm* not going until I'm forced out."

Michael got up, put on his coat and pants and shoes, and walked out.

But he forgot all about the argument in less than five minutes. Outside he smelled the distinct odor of gas. It overwhelmed him. Then he remembered the electricity had been shut off, but not the gas. He shouted, banged on doors, cried out. "Evacuate the place until we can shut it off!" he screamed. Within fifteen minutes they all had dressed and were across the street. For another ten minutes he searched for the main valve with a man from the apartment house next door, who knew more than Michael did about gas pipes.

They watched in the snow from across the street, braving the second major crisis of the night. Lorna held Dawn close to her body, the girl covered with three blankets. Marguerita rubbed her hands together. Tom leaned against his lover, his head on his shoulder, worrying, praying, weary. Kenny Rupp and his girlfriend and others walked in circles and waited. Someone finally brought coffee out, and another woman opened her door to anyone who wanted to warm up. But no one did; they were all too concerned about their home, their building. They wanted to watch, as if their watchful vigil would save it from destruction.

Michael finally came running across the street. "He ... he found the valve ... he's getting the tools to do it. . . ." He was out of breath, his nose red, his lips purple. "He says all we can do is wait until he shuts it off and hope ... hope that the winds blow the gas away, not near a match. . . ."

Then they all went inside the woman's apartment and accepted the welcome of the warmth of her heater and the open oven which was heating the apartment more than the wall fixture.

Just twenty minutes later it was all over. They could go back home.

And they went, cold, afraid, hoping that this was the end of it. But inside each one of them lay the suspicion that there was more yet to come; a few of them—Michael especially—felt that what had already happened was nothing compared to what was in store for them in the future.

Marguerita said, "All we can do is have faith."

No one answered. There was nothing more to say.

A U.S. Army jeep stopped in front of the gates of a house at the top of a winding street in the Los Feliz area of Los Angeles. The woman who'd been riding in it with the national guardsmen picked up her bag and purse and pushed the turban down farther on her head. She thanked them, but the words were stilted. She was in shock, and they knew it; but she was surviving. A soldier pushed the buzzer after he brushed the snow from it. When a voice asked who it was, he told them he was a soldier and he had a Mrs. Sheppard there. Could someone come down the driveway and help her in? The voice said yes, thanked him, and the gates opened only a little, being stopped by the thick snow.

Dolores, without shoes, her feet nearly frostbitten, her legs cut, her face red and dry, windblown, began trekking up the driveway or what she thought was the driveway. As with the streets, she couldn't tell where the cement ended and the grass began. But what did it matter? As long as she got to the house. . . .

In a moment Bob was beside her. "I tried . . . I lost the car . . . I walked for so long . . . then the jeep and they . . . oh, God!" She broke down, falling to the ground, but he grabbed her and picked her up and held her. She sobbed against his heavy coat. "Harry . . . did Harry come?"

"No, he's staying at the office. Dolores, come on, we've got to get you in the house." He picked up her bag. She was still clutching her purse. He braced his arm under her shoulders, and together they staggered up the driveway.

Once inside, out of the wet clothes, wrapped in blankets in the living room near the fire, Dolores seemed to make a miraculous recovery. She was in control, strong. Julie marveled at her—what she had been through! Dolores described it in detail, and they listened with compassion. But she was there, alive and well but for a few cuts on her legs—walking in the snow was difficult and she had fallen a few times, hurting herself on rocks and a cactus and curbs—and a severe headache. Julie gave her aspirin and poured her a drink. "Oh, you don't know how relieved I am."

"You must have thought you wouldn't make it," Julie said.

"Never. I had no choice. I knew I'd get here. But to have done it, to actually have it behind me, that's the accomplishment."

Bob took her hand. "You're amazing, Dee. First everyone finds out you're the new Beverly Sills, and today you prove you're a mountain climber."

"I'll never set foot into snow again as long as I live," she said with an air of finality. "How about the kids?"

Julie told her they'd decided to stick it out at the apartment house as long as they could.

"It's the right thing, Julie," Dolores said.

"But I'm so frightened for them!"

"Honey," Bob said comfortingly.

Dolores grabbed Julie's hand and said, "They're better off where they are, don't you understand? To try to make it through that snow in a car with a baby, they'd have to be out of their minds. The safest place for them is where they are."

Julie nodded. She understood; she even agreed. But her heart wanted them with her.

Just as Bob was explaining to Dolores that Harry had called and told him to tell her he'd be up in the morning after spending the night at the office, Harry was entering his plush office. And when he was getting out of his wet tuxedo, the phone rang. He picked it up and seemed surprised at first that it was his wife. He had almost expected his secretary to be telling him who was calling....

"Honey, I've been asleep for the past four hours. It's almost daylight, for God's sake. After what you've been through, get some sleep, take a pill and sleep all day."

"Harry...."

"Dolores, I have to tell you. I'm ... I'm proud of you."

"Oh, Harry!" He could tell that she had tears in her eyes. "Harry, I—" *Bzzzzzzz.* Then a click. Then nothing.

The phones went dead.

Harry dropped the receiver to the cradle and let himself curl up on the couch near the window. He was naked and exhausted. He fell asleep on his side, one hand on the afghan, the one Julie had crocheted for his office when they first moved in there, and one hand on the floor, on the fire hose. One hand on the obsession. A hand on the reality, keeping warm, getting sleep to regain strength, and the other on the dream.

As his eyes closed, he remembered the other time, the time he'd gotten caught, busted, kicked out. Nothing like that would happen this time, no it wouldn't. He smiled as he remembered how good it had gone, for a hell of a long time. He was one of the few people on earth who had appreciated World War II. He'd done well in it, and not in combat. He smuggled goods and became one of the leaders in a black-market ring that was operating throughout the European theater. Eventually he was caught, though no one ever linked him to the massive operation he was so much involved in; he'd been busted because of petty thievery when one of his couriers had quit on him. No one had bothered to investigate just how deep the corruption went or how much Sergeant Harry Sheppard knew. And he knew a lot. After his dishonorable discharge—which no one but Dolores knew about—he sent word to certain officers that he would talk unless he was sent some reward in return for keeping quiet. It was pure blackmail, and he delighted in it—he was getting back at the Army for what it had done to him. The dishonorable discharge didn't mean much anyhow, especially since he had his own business; no one checked up on him.

But as he lay in the office with the paintings at his feet, he remembered that rush of excitement the first night he'd broken into the supply house with two other soldiers and discovered the guns which were to "disappear" without a trace. He remembered the gold and the diamonds which had crossed his palm in Italy. He remembered, recalled, for the first time in many many years, the incredible excitement of stealing, taking something that wasn't his. Now he'd done it again. And now they were his.

He fell into a sleep that would better be described as a coma.

In the first half of the twentieth century the cities of America were forested with the ever-present telephone poles and power lines that fed communication and energy to everyone. Progress, and Los Angeles was no exception—that is, until the last half of the century.

While other cities sent their lines underground, L.A. took its time about it, wondering about it. California was earthquake country, and past experience told the powers that be that putting too many power lines beneath the street where they would be most vulnerable was a dangerous and foolish thing to do. Even though modern technology had solved most of the problems of construction in the area, for some curious reason Los Angeles was in no rush to beautify itself by removing the eyesores of telephone poles and the like.

Why spare unnecessary expense when an earthquake would screw it all up anyway? That was the general feeling of the city planners. Only gradually were old lines being placed underground. Along Santa Monica Boulevard, Century Boulevard, and most other major arteries in the city, the poles had been kept. The artificial trees carried the life force that ran the metropolis.

They should never have been kept.

Telephone service was already out in most of the city. And the power would be next to go.

In the twilight Carter DeSimone got into a tractorlike truck with General Granville and headed toward the destination which would become home for however long this siege was to last: the disaster center set up above the observatory in Griffith Park. "It's letting up a bit," Carter said, seeing the snow was falling softly now, almost gently.

"The wind died down."

"They should have the machinery up there by afternoon," Alex said, referring to the computers and communications equipment necessary for the disaster center. The small building was being put together at that very moment, prefabricated walls and roof being taken up by trucks with huge snow tires and chains. The Army knew what it was doing, Carter had to admit.

They saw a truck stop at an intersection. From it came some fifty national guardsmen, armed with shovels and first-aid equipment. They were running through the snow to aid anyone in the area who needed help. "I've ordered the teams full force," Granville said, the ever-present cigar filling the air in the truck. "The whole fuckin' Army's gonna be here if we need it. I've got the President's promise."

Carter closed his eyes. *If only I could sleep,* he thought, just for a few hours. Granville continued talking, but his voice seemed to be slowing down, drifting. The truth was, he was bellowing. It was Carter who was fading. He fell asleep in the truck.

The general looked at him and smirked. "Some soldier you'd

make." He flicked his cigar ash on the floor and said, "Come on, get this buggy up the hill."

"Yes, sir," the driver said.

Dolores fell asleep on the couch, curled up there as her husband was curled up across town. Bob and Julie went upstairs and slept in the warmth of each other's arms in their big bed. Downstairs in her room, Susan felt Samantha bite her nose. She opened her eyes and hugged the cat to her breast. The little animal purred as Susan watched the flakes outside the window. There were few of them now, and she felt sad. It was all over. If only she had been well enough to go out and play in it.

The snow finally stopped.

As the light of early morning crept over the city, Carter looked down at the sight he'd seen so many times, the sprawling City of the Angels. Only now it looked different from any way he'd ever seen it. It was blanketed with white, as if someone had wiped a huge paintbrush over the scene.

What astonished him was the purity of it, the incredible soft beauty of the scene. It was ... it was pastoral. That was the word he felt best described it.

And yet he knew that under that pastoral, heavenly beauty lay nothing but pure hell.

THE FOURTH DAY

SUNDAY, JANUARY 18
HIGH TEMPERATURE 23°; LOW 14°

ON TELEVISION IN NEW YORK CITY, TOM BROKAW, EVEN though it wasn't Monday and time for the *Today Show* as yet, was giving a special early-morning broadcast. He couldn't help seeming a bit stunned by what he was reading: "The President has conferred with General Alex Granville, director of operations in the Los Angeles area, and has promised federal assistance immediately; it is expected that much of the city will be formally designated a disaster area in a few hours. The mayor of Los Angeles has said he is 'completely helpless' in the situation and has asked the military to begin the evacuation of hard-stricken areas—especially poverty areas—and to air-drop badly needed supplies to the city. The governor of California has concurred.

"Power has been lost in many parts of the huge city, and hospitals and other institutions are functioning on auxiliary generators. The telephone company has asked us to request those of you who have family and friends in the Los Angeles area not to try calling; phone lines have been down since early morning. There is no report yet on the death toll the snowstorm has accumulated, but sources estimate that as many as a thousand people in the area from Santa Barbara, California, down through San Diego may have died."

Brokaw set his paper aside. "I talked with a friend on the Coast late last night while the phones were still working," he said, not reading the news any longer, telling a personal side of the story, "and he said everyone seemed in good spirits, assuming this was a freak phenomenon of nature and that by morning the warm temperatures would melt the snow and life would go on. But the hope of snow melting did not come to pass this morning, and as long as the temperature stays well beneath freezing, it isn't going to melt. In fact, scientists report Los Angeles is due for a good deal more of the arctic storm, a good deal more snow."

He shook his head. "... all the much harder to believe when we realize the temperature here in New York on this January morning is seventy-six degrees. This is Tom Brokaw, and we'll have some tape of the Los Angeles snowstorm within the hour. Stay tuned, as important bulletins will be broadcast as soon as they come in."

"My God! Michael, look!" Lorna was peering out Marguerita's window as Michael jumped from the sofa bed. He stood next to her, naked, rubbing his eyes, watching the incredible sight. Greg was crawling through a window to get out to the patio area. "I don't believe it," Lorna said.

"I'm gonna help," Michael replied, and started getting into his clothes.

What Lorna didn't believe was not Greg's leap from the window to the ground. It was the amount of snow that was out there on the patio, the reason he had to crawl out of the window in the first place. It had built up; it had stayed. No longer was it mushy and wet as it had been in the night; no longer was it the kind of snow which had caused the roof of the building to fall in. It was thick and it was mounting instead of melting.

Greg and Tom had tried to open the door without any luck. It moved just two inches, and that was it. The water on the patio had frozen solid, and on top of that had piled some six inches of snow. It was impossible to move it. So the window seemed the next best bet. And they had a good reason for getting out: The heater had stopped working.

Michael dressed and got outside in time to help Greg and Tom dig the snow away from the door with a garden shovel. Kenny Rupp and his girlfriend, looking sleepy, walked out into the cold morning air. Everyone had the same expression on his face; they had thought by morning it would all be gone. Where were the warm temperatures they'd been having every morning? Wasn't the snow going to melt?

"Let's dig out Mr. Rosenberg and the Reynaulds," Michael said, seeing that Mr. Rosenberg's door was in the same condition. Whenever it rained, puddles always formed at the doorsteps to the apartments at the back of the building complex. Marguerita had mentioned it several times to the owners, and nothing had ever been done about it. Several tenants had complained. But since Mr. Rosenberg moved in, not a word had been said. He put on his rubbers and stepped over it; it was nothing to him. And Greg and Tom didn't seem to mind. This was the first time it really caused a problem.

Just as they freed the Rosenberg door, Tom said, "Look at the pool." They all turned their attention to the swimming pool, which now looked like an ice-skating rink. "It's frozen solid!" And with that, Tom danced on the ice, sliding across the ice where only three months before he'd been swimming. He twisted and turned and called out, "Hey, this is terrific!" And then he fell flat on his ass.

Everyone laughed, but it was strained laughter at best. Harvard and his daughter walked out into the daylight. Marguerita, wrapped in a blanket, came out to join her friends. They talked of heat and no heat, of staying in town or leaving, of what they felt they should do. And then, all at once it seemed, there wasn't a sound. Everyone was looking up, astonished again.

More snow was falling.

They gathered in Marguerita's apartment. She and Lorna made eggs and warmed up tortillas and mixed the last cans of frozen orange juice Marguerita had in her freezer. They discussed their plight, their problems. The heat had already gone out in Tom and Greg's apartment. Michael and Lorna and Harvard and Flora didn't even have apartments left. Kenny Rupp and his girlfriend had little to say; they seemed to agree with anything the others suggested. Marguerita felt Mr. Rosenberg was too old to be left alone, and his apartment too small and not warm enough for three people. The man and woman who lived directly above Marguerita's apartment stopped in and told the others they were going to go back east. They didn't know how they were going to get to the airport or train station; they just knew they had to go. They said they'd turned out the gas and shut off all the electricity in the apartment, and they gave Marguerita a big bag full of groceries from the refrigerator. She thanked them and wished them a safe and successful journey.

"Well, that leaves us, gang," Lorna said.

"How about the man in number two?" Michael asked. No one had seen him, and no one had mentioned him.

Marguerita shrugged. He had never come back to the apartment since the freezing rain had started.

"Well, what's the answer?" Greg asked. "I'm for sticking together, sticking it out together."

"Me too," his lover said.

"This is home," old Mr. Rosenberg said. "We stay home, all together, yes? It is like life in the *shtetl.*"

"Yes," Michael said.

"Yes," Lorna said.

Harvard Reynauld nodded.

Flora said, not very enthusiastically, "Right on."

"We've got friends in—" Kenny Rupp's girlfriend cut him off. She wanted a private conference. They talked in whispers in the corner of the room for a few moments. Then he said, "We've decided to stay for now."

"Good," Michael announced. "Then this is survival center, and we're the Genesee Gorillas, nothing'll get us down!"

"I think the best thing to do is pool everything we have and set up a communal shelter. . . ." "How will we stay warm?" "Where will we–" Everyone was talking at once.

"Here," Marguerita said staunchly. "You all come stay here."

It was the only logical place, the large apartment and the recreation room which was connected to it. It would hold the mattresses, the clothing and other supplies the tenants would want to bring, the food and whatever else they felt was necessary.

"What about heat? Will it be warm enough?" Greg was concerned because of what had happened in their apartment just a few hours before.

"Listen," Michael said, "I remember a thing from Boy Scouts about making your own fireplace, a makeshift fireplace. It can be done if we need it. All you need is brick or metal–we could use the metal linings from the ovens in the apartments."

"Tom's got some bricks," Greg said.

"Yeah, I've got a bookshelf made of them, quite a few. They're loose."

Michael said, "Great. Well, I guess the first thing we should do is get everything over here. Whatever you have in your places to keep warm, anything to eat. Maybe even a Monopoly game to keep the hours passing."

"I have some chickens in the icebox," Mr. Rosenberg offered.

"I cook up good arroz con pollo," Marguerita said. "Go get the chickens, old man. Someone collect food from all the apartments."

"I'll do it," Flora volunteered.

"We'll get blankets and things like that," Kenny Rupp said.

"I'm gonna try to shovel more snow away from the building," Michael said.

"And I start cooking," Marguerita said. "Food will give us strength."

And they went to work. There was a sense of family, a sense of togetherness, of adventure. They all realized for the first time in their lives–because this was the first time they'd ever really been faced with it—that there was a certain amount of excitement in survival. Perhaps it was what life was all about, but it was usually done on such easy terms. Now was the test.

As Michael shoveled the packed snow from Marguerita's door, he noticed what he thought was a crack leading from the pool. Sure enough, the coping had split and the concrete of the patio had a thin crack in it. The pool won't be good for shit, he thought, after it warms up. He tossed a shovelful of snow onto the ice, but it didn't matter, because the ice was already covered with the new falling snow.

And it was falling hard.

If the first storm front had caused chaos, it was nothing compared to what was following it. The second storm which was approaching Los Angeles was different in an important respect: It was producing dry snow. Being so close to the first storm, there was little chance for the air to settle and warm before the next attack.

Upon hitting the coast, the water molecules were thrown up faster into colder air than the ones the day before. They froze instantly into small crystals and began to fall. It was not the snowman kind of snow. It was drifting snow, dangerous snow, because all that was needed now was wind, and the situation would be ripe for a classic blizzard. A blizzard worse than the one raging in the San Bernardino Mountains. A blizzard more lethal than the one which had cut Palmdale off from the rest of the world.

Perhaps one of the most devastating blizzards in the *history* of the world.

Dolores woke up on the couch with a start. At first she didn't know where she was, what was happening? But in a moment it all came back to her. She felt the swelling in her feet, the aching of her bones, and the warmth of the roaring fire. She realized Bob must have been up several times during the night, tossing wood on the fire. She sat up and ran her fingers through her hair. *Oh, what a mess!* It felt thick and dirty and twisted and knotted. Her face felt puffy from the icy wind of the night, but she didn't dare look into a mirror, not yet. It would have been too difficult. What she didn't know for sure wouldn't hurt her.

She got up, holding the blanket she'd been sleeping under around her shoulders, and walked to one of the living-room windows. She looked out on the white lawn, an untouched blanket of snow. It was still falling from the skies. For as far as she could see, snow filled the air, sat on the tree branches, on the top of the wall surrounding the house. She couldn't see the footprints she and Bob had made getting up to the house early in the morning. It was as if it hadn't happened at all. It had been erased by the white.

But she remembered. The car sliding. The trek down the Boulevard, falling, slipping, the harsh wind blowing in her face, the snow blinding her eyes at times, her ears freezing at the bottom of her turban. The nightmare came back in full color—a color that was mostly black and white—and seemed to haunt her. She leaned against the window and saw it turn wet with her breathing. It steamed up, and she held back tears. "Harry," she moaned. "Oh, Harry, come soon. Maybe it will be all right."

She stared out at the sight she'd seen on so many Christmas cards, in art shows, in books. Winter in Wisconsin. Currier and Ives. "Dashing through the snow, in a one-horse open sleigh. . . ." It was supposed to be so heartwarming, so beautiful, so stimulating to the romantic imagination.

All Dolores could find for it was contempt.

And absolute fright.

The first helicopter landed at the disaster center landing pad, which had been known as the Griffith Observatory parking lot. Two government experts jumped out of the whirlybird, two men sent from Washington to help deal with the disaster. It was Granville's plan to utilize the parking lot as much as possible, even for evacuation purposes if necessary. It was doubtful that the Los Angeles International Airport was going to reopen. It had closed at 3 A.M. because of the mounting snow on the runways. Every effort was being made to get plows to the field, to clear at least two or three of the best runways, to at least utilize some of the equipment sitting in the snow for much-needed purposes—getting the sick and elderly out of the city, evacuating those who had lost their homes, for bringing in much-needed medical supplies, as well as clothing and food for the areas which had been hit the hardest, the most central part of the city and the houses near the ocean.

"They're gonna blame me, Carter," Alex Granville said, his cigar resting limply in his mouth. They stood on the landing pad, looking down at the city. It was snowing again, evenly, coming down everywhere. There was little wind. It just dropped from the skies. "They're gonna blame me 'cause it's on my shoulders now. Save the city, they tell me. Save the motherfucking city."

"We've been blamed before," Carter reminded him. "No matter how many lives you save, they only seem to remember the ones you lost."

"Yeah, well, this is different. It's so . . . so huge, so massive. You know how many people are down there?"

"About seven million."

"How we gonna get them out? Buffalo was chickenshit next to this."

Carter shook his head. "I don't know. All I know is no one's getting out until the snow stops. Choppers can't fly through this stuff."

"Then we gotta stop thinking about getting them out. We gotta know we have to stay put and find ways to live with it. You still got that list of buildings and such that'll serve as shelters, that plan you had drawn up months ago?"

"How'd you hear about that? As far as I knew, everyone who got one of those filed it away under DeSimone/Insanity."

"Let's just say I pulled one outta the trash. We've got the National Guard on their way in from every surrounding state. We've gotta give them someplace to stay, something to do."

Just then a soldier called down to the general. "Sir, a private plane, someone tried to take off from the Santa Monica Airport. Crashed into a building and killed fifty-six people."

"Got some men over there?"

"They're on their way, sir," the soldier said, lifting his collar against his neck in the cold air. "Sir, the casualties, they were gathered in the terminal building there, waiting to get out. There are a lot of survivors who have no homes. . . ."

"Carter, time to get your list out."

"Santa Monica Civic Auditorium. Get them moved there, and get the first medical supply truck over there. Come on."

They walked to the jeep and drove up the hill.

About half an hour later Bob Sheppard got a call on his shortwave radio. It was Carter. "We've put the first step of what they call Operation Snow into effect. It only means we're setting up shelters in strategic areas of the city, hospitals, government buildings, halls, stadiums. More and more apartments are without the capability to withstand this cold. The heaters just don't work. Fires are breaking out everywhere. How's Susan?"

Bob told him of her need for surgery soon.

"Jesus," Carter muttered. "Bob, the hospitals are panicking themselves. No one's going to do a delicate surgery like that—"

"No one *can* do this surgery except only a few experienced specialists. The one our doctor wanted isn't even in town. We have to wait till he gets in."

"Robert, no one's going to get in. Getting *out* is impossible, too. I know the mayor promised evacuation of every last person if necessary, but there's no way to do it as long as the snow continues."

"What's going to happen? How long do you think it will last?" Julie and Dolores were crouched over Bob's shoulder in the kitchen, listening to Carter.

"Maybe a day or two. Maybe as long as a week."

"Susan can't last a week, Carter! We've got to get her to a hospital."

"Bob, there's no assuring she'll get in. I'm told people are standing out in the snow waiting to get in. Heart attacks, falls, broken bones . . . and only half staffed. Bob, we'll—"

"Carter! How much more of this stuff do you think we're in for?"

There was no answer.

"Carter, you there? Carter?"

"Yeah, Bob. Listen, we're all pretty sure it could get up to six feet."

"Oh, God!" Dolores cried. Julie bit her lip, thinking it absolutely preposterous.

"Carter, you're not kidding, are you?"

"The San Joaquin Valley's got over a foot already, and it's only been hit by the fringe. Almost nine feet fell up in the Sierras!"

"But this is Los Angeles," Bob said, "not the high Sierras."

"There's not much difference anymore," Carter responded.

Bob took a deep breath. "All right, what's going to happen? What do you recommend we do?"

"Nothing. Keep your family and friends together, stay inside, and stay warm. Conserve food and fuel. Keep water running slowly so pipes won't freeze. I'll see what I can arrange about getting help to Susan."

"Carter, can you get her out?"

"I don't know, Bob. I just don't know. Nothing's flying in this. The orders are to bring aid *to* the city, not to attempt taking people out. There's so much snow falling, it's almost impossible for helicopters to maneuver. And if we get winds on top of it, this will turn into a full-scale blizzard, and then we're really sunk."

"Carter, thanks."

"I've gotta go, Bob. I'll keep in touch. I'm right above you. We set up shop above the observatory, and we're using it, too. If I get bored up here, I'll slide down the hill for coffee."

"You do that," Bob said.

Carter clicked off, and Bob turned to the women. "Never thought I'd live to the day I'd hear something like that."

Dolores asked, "He said it could become a blizzard. I thought it was—is. What the hell was that I was trudging through last night?"

Bob explained something Carter had explained to him. "There's a difference. What we had last night and what's happening right now is technically a snowstorm. A blizzard is extremely high winds blowing the already-fallen snow around; it's far worse."

"Nothing could be worse," Dolores muttered. She went to the liquor cabinet and poured herself another glass of scotch. It was her third this morning. It warmed her.

"I've gotta try draining the pool," Bob said.

"Oh, Bob, leave it. It doesn't matter. I don't want you going out in that!"

"Julie, the whole patio will crack. You want thirty-four thousand gallons of water spilling into the family room, washing half the yard away?"

Julie was silent. He was right.

He put on his mackinaw and went out into the yard. He brought in more firewood from the back of the patio. It was damp but not wet; it had been protected by the eaves of the house. The supply in the family room was just about gone. But there was still plenty outside.

Then he went to the far end of the yard and brushed the snow from the pool equipment, from the heater and pump and filter. He tripped the switch which turned off all power to the system, so it wouldn't be accidentally turned on and try to pump solid ice through the filters. Then he opened a valve down near the garage, a valve which acted as a siphon, which drained the pool slowly into a little gully, and then down the side of the road into the sewers. At first he couldn't turn the valve, but when he hit it with a hammer, it gave, and water gushed out. Steam rose from the warmer water hitting the ice and snow. He watched for a moment and then went up to the pool and stepped on the ice. It was very thick; it supported his full weight. He went down to the garage, found an ax, went back up to the patio, and started to chop the ice at the top of the water into little pieces. Already he could see a large crack at the side of the pool, in the plaster. He chopped at the ice until it gave and water splashed up through the splits. He remembered driving onto a lake in

Minnesota with the car, when he was just a boy, when his father and grandfather had taken him ice fishing in the middle of winter. They cracked a hole in the ice in just the same way he was doing now. As he chopped, he felt warm, sweaty. He opened his jacket and wiped the sweat on his chest with his long underwear under his shirt. He watched the chunks of ice mix with the water. It would drain out, and then the pieces of ice would be left on the bottom. The pool would be saved.

He put the ax away and grabbed a garden shovel and started to clear the steps leading to the patio from the garage, just in case they had to use them, to take Susan out, for Michael and Lorna and Dawn to get in, should they come. He looked up at the wall at the east side of the house and wondered how the nuns were doing. He figured they didn't have much to worry about; God was on their side.

Finally, his hands felt as though they wouldn't move anymore. He looked at his watch. It was nearly 2 P.M. already. He wondered if Harry had got through—if the phones were working yet. If not, where was his brother? He set the shovel down and went inside.

Just in time to hear the confrontation:

"You just can't let her *lie* there! At least let me hold her, let me. . . ." It was Dolores' voice. Bob knew what was happening. Dolores was objecting to Julie's attitude toward Susan. He walked into the hall outside the den and saw the women standing in the laundry room, just outside Susan's door.

"No," Julie stated firmly. "I know my daughter, and I know what is best for her."

"But some *comfort,* that's all I'm saying, for Christ's sake," Dolores answered. "I want to *do* something for the poor thing."

Julie tried to remain in control, but her words were definite, filled with a sense of pride and resentment. "She is not *the poor thing.* I know what's best for my daughter. Leaving her alone is the only thing we can do."

"But—"

"Dolores, I don't want to hear another word about it," Julie said, tossing the empty syringe into the trash pail in the laundry room.

Susan screamed in pain. They could hear it through the wall. Bob cringed.

Her eyes wide, Julie looked at Dolores and said, "You think it isn't hard, you think it doesn't hurt to hear that?"

Dolores said nothing.

"But there's nothing anyone can do but give her those"—referring to the syringe in the garbage—"and let her be."

Dolores walked away, looking helpless and lonely.

Bob walked into the laundry room. "I'm sorry," Julie said, "but I know Susan doesn't want someone in there hugging her and cooing over her. She doesn't want to have people looking at her curled up in pain."

"Darling, understand Dee's never had a child, and she's always wanted one. She's worried about Harry; she's got a motherly instinct; she just wants to love someone."

"I know what's best for my girl."

Bob just nodded. It was true; they both were right in their emotions. But it was Julie's child, it was Julie's home, and Julie's rules would be abided by. He cursed his brother for never giving Dolores the child she wanted, needed. Maybe then things would have turned out differently. Maybe then they'd have had a marriage instead of a cold war.

Bob took off his wet clothes and jumped into a warm bath.

Genesee Gardens was beginning to look like a refugee camp in the midst of some war. The recreation room off Marguerita's apartment was filled with broken furniture which would be burned in the makeshift fireplace Michael and Greg were building. They'd taken a trash can and cut big rectangular holes in the sides and punched round holes in the bottom for the ashes to fall through. Then they'd ripped out the range hoods from Kenny Rupp's apartment and hooked it up over the garbage can. The chimney was made from coffee cans taped together, which provided an exhaust. They'd knocked out one of the tall windows and replaced it with plywood with a round hole cut in it, just the size of the cans, and they taped around that too, to keep out the cold air.

Greg and Tom had brought in their mattress and set it in the corner of Marguerita's living room, next to the sofa bed Michael and Lorna were using, near the heater. Marguerita and little Dawn would sleep in Marguerita's bedroom, where there was another heater. In the recreation room, they'd set up an old Army cot for Mr. Rosenberg, and Harvard and Flora had his mattress on the floor near the new fireplace. Kenny Rupp and his girlfriend, a shy girl who rarely spoke, had brought their sleeping bags and placed them near the fireplace also. Each person's valuables, from carved mahogany boxes (Mr. Rosenberg's) to old Superman comic books (Kenny's), were stacked up in the corners. The kitchen was filled with food, cans and boxes and bottles, everything they could get from the apartments. Tom and Kenny had climbed up to the second-story balcony of the collapsed part of the building and had raided the Matthews' kitchen pantry—they were sure they wouldn't mind. They had enough food to last a while, a good two weeks if they had to.

They gathered in the recreation room, which they'd dubbed Snow City, and threw the first bit of wood onto the fire, the leg of a living room cocktail table from Mr. Rosenberg's apartment. It flared up after Michael squirted some charcoal lighter fluid on it. Then they added the pieces of the rest of the table and they had a crisp roaring fire in front of them, filling and warming the room. It was going to work.

Marguerita mothered them all, and her influence was good for their spirits. She told them a story about snow, a huge snowstorm which had been raging for days in the mountains of Mexico. She was living in a little village with her parents, and just as the snow had begun, bandits had taken over the town and forced all the people out. "We have to march over the hills in two feet of snow with all our possessions on our backs, an old mule, march for days until we find shelter." They had found an old abandoned mine and had holed up in it for five days while a blizzard had raged outside. "We make a fire too, burning timber from the mineshaft, not once worrying it should come falling down on our heads because we're taking the support away." She told them it was an incredible experience, and with prayer and faith it had strengthened them, it had made them better people. "It was as if it did not matter, we knew it would stand. God would protect us. He could not give us a fire like a miracle suddenly there in the cave, but he would see the roof would not come down." She looked out the window and smiled. "But God did not love Genesee Gardens as much as he loved that cave."

Everyone laughed.

"It was an incredible experience, and even though I am only so young when it happens, I learn from it. We had faith. That is the way we survive. I saw the children so cold you wanted to kill them just to stop their suffering."

Lorna squirmed.

"Oh, yes," Marguerita said, "you have so much to learn about life. This is the way we learn. You think, the poor children, they should not suffer. We should suffer, yes, maybe we deserve to suffer for our sins, but the children? They have not sinned. It is not fair that they should suffer. One niño lost his hand from the frostbite. An old woman was never found in the snow. One of the men of the village, a strong man, a man full of zest and life, and sometimes too much of the tequila, he changed into a person we could not recognize. The fear built up in him, and his heart stopped. He had no fight in his soul. He did not have faith. Perhaps hope, but no faith."

"How did you finally get rescued?" Kenny Rupp asked, all eyes.

"The snow finally stops; the wind settles. We cannot go on, we have to return to the village, and we find the bandits are gone, they have taken their treasures—what treasures did we have, some gold perhaps?—and gone. We gather in the church and thank the Lord Almighty, the Blessed Virgin. Marguerita learned then always to believe it will be better. We must all believe that."

"I was in Chicago for the big blizzard of 1967," Kenny Rupp said. "I was pretty young then, but I sure remember it. We were living on the North Side, on a place called Dover Street, and it was apartments a lot like these, with no inside hall, just outside balconies. There aren't many buildings like that in Chicago, but we had the bad luck to be living in one."

"What was it like?" Lorna asked.

"Well, there wasn't any prediction of snow. It was warm out. We went to bed at night, and when we woke up in the morning, we couldn't get out the door. We had slept late, and the phone woke us up, my grandmother calling us to ask how we were. Well, Dad went out the window just like Greg did. Then he shoveled the door open, and we were able to come and go. The first thing Mom did was go to the grocery store, the A&P over by Clark Street, but nothing was left. It was wiped out. She came back in tears and told us how a bread truck had pulled up and the people had attacked the driver and robbed the truck."

"People will do anything to feed their children," Marguerita said.

"I remember a lot about it because my brother is a writer for the Chicago *Tribune*. He did an article about the blizzard eight years later. It was amazing. In five hours twenty-three inches of snow fell, and then some storms in the next nine days added another foot to it. The worst thing was the winds—"

"Oh, Chicago's winds," Flora said. "Brrr. I heard all about that city."

"The winds were fifty miles an hour, and they blew the snow into twelve-foot drifts. Kids spent nights in schools, and people took refuge in tollway plazas, in restaurants and gas stations. I think there were over three thousand buses stranded on the streets. My brother wrote that seven hundred of them couldn't even be located."

Harvard asked, "How'd the mailmen do?"

"They stayed home. Everyone did. When people started going out, they lost their bearings. I remember we couldn't find the car. My old man had parked it on the street, and we couldn't find it! We dug for three days until we finally located it, and even then it was dumb 'cause no one could go anywhere. I remember a weatherman, Harry Volkman, he'd predicted four inches. Well, there was already four inches on the ground when he left for the station that morning. And he never got there to do his noon show. They said it was the snowstorm of the century."

"I wonder about that statement," Tom said, looking out the window.

As Kenny was still talking, Greg got up and walked over to the window and looked outside, pulling the drape aside a little. He turned nearly as white as the snow. He interrupted Kenny. "Holy fuck! Look at this!"

They all rushed to the windows and looked outside. They couldn't even see across the pool. The wind was howling, blowing snow everywhere, in every direction. The air was a white blanket.

"Is that . . . is that a blizzard?" Flora asked.

"Looks like Chicago did," Kenny said.

"God forgive us," Marguerita whispered.

Rob Wynters was reading from a book Carter had given him, and a particular page interested him:

> It is hard to think of a snowstorm in terms of sheer horror. Yet that is a term that can be aptly applied to the emotion a blizzard can produce. It is rare that an urban area experiences a true blizzard, and so few people have actually truly lived through one. Most powerful snowstorms are mistaken for blizzards.
>
> Out on the northern prairies of the Midwest, the terror of a blizzard is something everyone lives with in the back of his mind. It is something always to be prepared for. Every farmer knows to keep a healthy supply of canned foods and fuel in the cellar. Poles with clotheslines strung between them run from farmhouse to barns and other buildings; they act as guides when the visibility gets so bad that you cannot literally see your hand in front of your face.
>
> Disorientation is perhaps the worst aspect of a blizzard. With snow blowing everywhere and no visibility, a man can

walk only a few feet and be lost—completely lost—until the storm passes, and by that time he would most likely be dead. People caught on the road in a big storm know to stay with their cars; to leave them in search of help is to commit suicide.

On top of the disorientation, it is almost impossible to insulate the body against the attack of snow crystals. Fine particles of snow driven by gale-force winds can seep into any thickness of clothing. Caught out in the open, a person could not survive more than a few hours before the subfreezing wetness enveloped their body and they froze to death. It is not an easy way to die, and most people in the United States cannot—nor do they have reason to—imagine what it is like. Usually only the Midwest and Plains states and some regions of the Rocky Mountains have any reason to be concerned with it.

Rob looked outside. He wondered if the people of Los Angeles should now have reason to be concerned with it?

Harry awakened to find the afghan on the floor, one leg up over the top of the couch and an erection between his legs. He'd been dreaming about a girl, a specific girl, one he'd met at a cocktail party a few weeks ago, a girl he'd been determined to lay. She was just going down on him when he opened his eyes. The room was hot, but dark. He'd gone to bed with the lights on. What had happened to them?

He got up and tried the switch. Then he turned on the calculator on his desk, but it didn't light up. The power was off. But the heat was on, coming up through the vent at the side of the room, against the window. He opened the drape and looked out at a sight he didn't expect. The snow was worse than the night before, blowing through the air the way it had in Minnesota when he was a kid. Thoughts of the airport floated out of his head. Bus? Train? How the hell to get out of the city? He picked up the phone, and it was still dead. "Shit," he muttered, looking out the window again. "A fucking goddamn blizzard." It wasn't that he didn't believe it; he resented it for ruining his plans. He'd come this far; he couldn't turn back now. He walked over the fire hose to the couch and dressed. *I gotta think this out. I gotta figure what to do. There's gotta be a way.*

First on his list of priorities was food. He was starving. The last thing he'd eaten was some caviar on a Ritz cracker. He looked at the clock on the wall, but it read 8:00. It had stopped in the early morning. He went into the outer office. Bob's secretary, Ethel, had a windup clock on her desk, a little antique thing that bonged on the hour and drove him half out of his mind. Now he loved it. It told him the time was 4:35 P.M.

He opened the little office refrigerator, but all that was in it were melted ice cubes and a diet soda. So he went into the hall—it seemed deserted—and started down the stairwell, which he'd never used before. It was the only way to the first floor, where the Greenhouse restaurant was, where there was bound to be food. Not that he expected the place to be open; he would break in if he had to.

But it had already been broken into; a familiar man sat in the deserted restaurant, eating a variety of foods. "Harry Sheppard, I thought I heard someone coming! Want to join me in a feast? The Last Supper, maybe."

"What are you doing here?" Harry was surprised to see someone working in this weather. The man was the building's security guard.

"Been here all night."

"I didn't see you. I came in here and spent the night myself."

The guard took a bite of a sandwich. "I sacked out early, the hell with this place, and I don't give a damn what happens to it. I crawled back into an office and slept. Got up and thought I'd try getting home, but it's more comfortable here, more food, warmth."

"Where do you live?"

"Inglewood. Near the airport. I heard on the news buildings in that area are burning, from gas explosions. I'm staying here."

Harry sat himself down and started digging into a big casserole the guard had sitting on the table. "It's cold, but it's good," he said. "Listen, you got a wife?"

The guard nodded. "But she's up in a hospital up north. I never thought she'd be the lucky one, being up there. None of the storm hit the San Francisco area."

"I . . . my wife's up at my brother's house."

"Where's that?"

"Los Feliz."

"Where's that?"

"Up near Griffith Park, just past Hollywood, before Silverlake."

The guard nodded.

"I've got to get up there." And he did. Harry had thought about it on the way down the twelve flights of steps. Going to Bob's would be the best way to survive and probably the best way out of the city. With Bob's connections—Carter DeSimone, for example—he would surely be on top of things, one of the first people to be evacuated. Harry couldn't risk taking a chance on the airport or a truck someplace. He had to go with the safety, and safety meant his brother. He'd get out with them, and then he'd split. With the complete lack of communications, he knew the theft at the museum wouldn't be reported for a long time—who would even care, when human lives were most important? He even doubted that the theft would be discovered for a very long time.

"You got warm clothes?" the guard asked.

"Nothing. I came here in a tuxedo." Harry pointed to his satin-striped pants.

"Me neither. I need me a jacket. I think we should bust into the ski shop in the lobby."

Harry's eyes flashed at first, at the blatant suggestion that they steal. It was an automatic reaction—stealing was wrong.

"Hey, nobody's gonna care in this situation," the guard said, seeing Harry's eyes, reading him.

"Yeah, well, okay," he said. "I . . . it's just that I've never done anything like that before." *You should see what I've got upstairs.* His pulse began to race.

"Eat up and we'll get ourselves some good warm jackets." The guard drank milk from a carton. "The refrigerator's off, so it's all gonna spoil anyhow."

"Christ, I'm famished," Harry said, digging in.

"We interrupt this program to bring you a special update on the crisis in Southern California." One moment the residents of Washington, D.C., were watching a movie on NBC's *Big Event,* and the next they were looking at something they were used to, snow-covered houses and buildings, but these were somehow different, they looked wrong–palm trees bending in a blizzard? It didn't seem real. "The situation in Los Angeles continues to worsen as snow pounds on the city. Already the winds have reached blizzardlike force, and most of the city is at a complete standstill. San Diego seems to be hit less hard, with the temperatures warmer and snow melting slowly as it hits the ground.

"In Los Angeles it is mounting. It is reported that thirty-two inches lie on the ground at this time. Fires are beginning to plague the city, and deaths are being attributed to fires and the cold. The winds are dry, making it worse, and the temperature is, at this hour, a very cold sixteen degrees–with the windchill factor that puts it below zero. Many elderly people, attempting to leave the city or to shovel snow or to get supplies, have died of heart attacks. In some parts of the San Fernando Valley, residents are completely snowed into their houses, and the National Guard is working hard to get them out.

"Power failures now extend from Santa Barbara in the north to the bottom of Orange County, and east to and including San Bernardino and Riverside counties. The famous Disneyland Hotel has been gutted by a fire–no report yet on casualties in that inferno–and homes along the coast have been collapsing under the strain of the ever-mounting ice as the freezing sea spray adds to the weight of the snow. Food and clothing is being dropped near designated shelters, although General Alex Granville, who is directing rescue operations in the city, is apprehensive about the continuance of such measures. Helicopters will be grounded if the blizzardlike proportions of the storm continue.

"Another report tells us that polar bears have escaped from the Los Angeles Zoo, but we have no official word on this."

Harry Sheppard and the guard smashed the glass in the door of the ski shop in the lobby of the building. They opened the door easily and selected full outfits, insulated pants and jackets, good warm weatherproof boots, sweaters, even goggles if the blizzard continued. "I don't know where I'm going to go," the guard said, "but I guess I can't stay here forever."

"I know exactly where I'm going," Harry answered. "Up to sleep the night, then out in the morning, snow or no snow."

"Oh, there'll be snow all right. Ain't never going to stop. I'm getting out of here now."

"Good luck," Harry said, wishing him well, as he started back up the stairs. *Good luck, you stupid bastard.*

He reached the office again and curled up on the couch, staring at the fire hose on the floor. Then he picked out a book on Van Gogh and started to read, but his curiosity got the best of him. It would be dark soon, and he didn't even have a candle. He pulled one of the paintings from the fire hose and unrolled the canvas. Even in the dim gray light, the colors were radiant. They were cracked and chipped in places, but not enough to cause any great concern. The beauty was still there.

And they were his.

Bob Sheppard went out again, just before it got dark, and took pictures of the incredible scene. It was harder than he'd figured—snow constantly covered the lens, and he finally gave up. He snapped some shots from the windows of the house. As the sun—what sun?—set somewhere behind the snow clouds, the house took on a warmth and beauty he thought he'd never seen there before. The fireplace lit the living room with its orange glow. The pine logs popped and crackled. The lights were on in the den, and the white wicker was a match for the scene out the windows, the snow piling up on the patio. The ice level was going down in the pool, and a huge formation of solid ice was forming where the drainpipe flowed out into the street. Bob could smell something baking in the oven, cookies or a cake. Dolores sat in the corner of the living room, listening to original cast albums of Broadway shows on the stereo, a drink in one hand, sullen since her confrontation with Julie over Susan.

Bob went down to the family room, which was cold now. He went into the furnace room and counted 4 large bottles of Sparklettes water. He knew all supplies would go, including the water sooner or later. He wasn't sure why, but he always kept extra bottles of water downstairs; maybe this was the reason he'd never known. He carried a bottle upstairs and told Julie he was going to take it over to the Kuppermans'.

"You can't carry that heavy thing in the snow!" Julie said.

"Well, let's put it in pitchers or something."

Julie thought for a moment. "How about empty soda bottles? Or this." He pointed to the bottle of Ballantine that was nearly empty. He dumped it into a glass for Dolores, rinsed the bottle in the sink, and filled it with water. Julie took her cookies out of the oven and helped Bob fill the Coke bottles. They packed them in a cardboard box and Bob left to take them next door, along with a dozen of the hot cookies.

It wasn't easy, getting through the snow in the backyard, through the gate, to the Kuppermans' door. But once there, he was glad he'd come. The old man and woman appreciated the fresh water, and little Billy started downing the cookies with the last quart of milk that was left. They gave Bob some jars of fruit and vegetables Minnie had put up the year before, and he told them in case anything went wrong, to signal them by flashing a light from their upstairs windows at night or tossing something like a pillow over the fence into the yard during the day. "No sense in either of you trying to walk through that stuff," Bob said. He thanked them and went back to the house in the darkness.

The darkness came, and with it more snow. The storm raged all through the night, letting up at times to drop nothing but flurries, working up to blizzardlike winds every so often. In the apartment house on Genesee, the friends/tenants/roommates all sat around the fire burning in the homemade fireplace. Flora strummed her guitar, singing soft songs. Marguerita knelt in silent prayer in front of her little shrine, a rosary wound around her old fingers. Mr. Rosenberg put his yarmulke on his head and sat alone in meditation in the living room. Harry Sheppard slept soundly on his office couch, while up in the hills his wife bit her nails worrying about him, wondering when he would come.

And from the Griffith Observatory you could see fires dotting the city below, flames and smoke shooting up through the white falling snow. Carter DeSimone, getting into his bunk up at the observatory, looked over at the general, who stood puffing his cigar in his long underwear, pacing the floor. "You'd better get some sleep, Alex," Carter advised.

"Yeah, yeah."

Rob Wynters was snoring in the corner of the room. He'd finally turned in when he got a message from Washington which read PSYCHIC JEANE DIXON HAS PREDICTED THE SNOWSTORM IN LOS ANGELES WILL BE THE GREATEST SINGLE NATURAL DISASTER AMERICA HAS EVER KNOWN. He couldn't take it any longer; he needed some respite, some sleep.

Alex Granville had laughed at Rob, laughed at the report, calling Ms. Dixon a variety of obscenities, and finally said it really wasn't a "disaster" at all. It was an unfortunate quirk of nature. "We're here to stop it from *becoming* a disaster, for Christ's sake."

No one had replied.

Carter finally gave up. If Alex didn't want to sleep, the hell with him. He pulled the Army blanket up to his chin and closed his eyes. Then he heard the general mumble, "Damn broad's probably right."

Carter didn't say anything, but for the first time he was scared.

Most disasters last only a few brief moments. An earthquake can level a city in one minute, a hurricane can do its damage in just as short a time, sweeping from city to city. A tornado can carry off a house faster than you can see it coming. But a blizzard can go on for three, four, even five days, continually battering the land with snow and cold.

In Los Angeles, the second massive storm had nothing immediately behind it to push it out of the way. The storm it nudged was caught over the Rockies between the L.A. Basin and mountains higher to the east. Out off the coast another storm front prevented movement of air to the west. So the storm stayed put, dumping inch after inch of snow on the city. The fate of Los Angeles was now hinging on the air mass that lay hundreds of miles away on the other side of the mountains, and there was nothing that could be done about it.

The snow fell through the night, Sunday turning to Monday. It had been—for all its uniqueness—one of the dullest days the city of Los Angeles had ever experienced. There was nothing to do, nothing anyone could do. The people had little choice other than sit inside and wait, hope, pray. Before anything happened, before people started to do something about it, it had to get worse, or it had to get better. It was still too new, too stunning. People went to bed Sunday night hoping that when they woke up the next morning, the scene outside would have made a decision for them.

THE FIFTH DAY

MONDAY, JANUARY 19
HIGH TEMPERATURE 19°; LOW 10°

MONDAY MADE A DIFFERENCE. IT HAD SNOWED ALL NIGHT, AND the morning showed no sign of its letting up. People began to make decisions, right ones and wrong ones, but decisions nonetheless. People thought about what they had to do. People had to survive, and they were going to do it. No matter what it took, they would survive. People in Los Angeles began to *move.*

Harry Sheppard awoke in his office to see the snow still falling outside the window. He knew it was day, the next day, because it was fairly bright outside; other than that, it looked just like the night before, snow, snow, and more snow. He got up and felt the chill in the room. He walked to the windows and felt the heating vents. They were cold. The heat was off in the building. Well, he was leaving anyway.

He went into his private bathroom and splashed water on his face. The cold liquid woke him up completely. He pulled his electric shaver from the cabinet and plugged it in. Nothing happened. "Oh, damn," he said, remembering the electricity. He felt his stubble, ran his fingers over it. Well, he'd secretly desired to grow a beard for years now; this was his chance; he was being forced into it.

Harry dressed carefully, getting into the tight ski pants, the heavy sweater, tightening the boots, pulling the hood over his head, putting the gloves on. He was sweating by the time he was ready to leave. And then he bent over and picked up the fire hose, slinging it over his shoulder. He stood there for a moment, looking out the window at the forbidding sight. He couldn't see anything but snow blowing in the air, not even the museum across the street. It was going to be a long, hard climb to his brother's house, but he had to get there. He had to get there before they left without him. He was positive Bob was planning to get out. Fast.

Harry left the office and started down the twelve flights of steps to the lobby.

Dolores was worried sick about her husband. She'd had a nearly sleepless night, getting up from the sofa to peer out the window in the hope of seeing Harry making his way up the front lawn. But she'd seen only shadows. The fire danced on the ceiling, and she didn't have her sleeping pills—she'd left them in the Gremlin. She wondered what had happened to her car. But she didn't really care about the car, about anything. She cared about Harry. Why? She couldn't understand it. She couldn't stand him; they did nothing but argue or ignore one another; their marriage was something less than the word implied. What was it she was clinging to? Dependency? It shocked her, but she felt that maybe she couldn't live without him. It made no sense, it was nearly laughable, but it's how she felt. She hadn't been without Harry, in happiness or in pain, for thirty-five years. She doubted that she *ever* could be without him.

She had walked down to the family room about 4 A.M., to check what was in the bar down there. She found half a bottle of Jack Daniel's, a third of a bottle of Cutty Sark, and some vodka. She lugged them upstairs; they'd have to fill in for the Ballantine when it was gone, and it was going fast.

She'd just fallen asleep when she heard a call. She opened her eyes and heard it again. Susan was calling for help. Dolores jumped up, pulled her sleep mask from her eyes, and got into the robe Julie had given her. But by the time she reached Susan's door so had Julie. There was a silent confrontation, and Dolores backed off. She lay awake another hour, wishing she could go in and just sit by her niece, just hold her hand, wipe her forehead, help in some way. Tears fell down her cheeks as she felt unwanted, helpless. Harry may have been killed. He might have started out and something might have happened to him. Or maybe he hadn't started out at all; maybe he had gone the other way, out of town. Maybe he didn't want to see her again. *Oh, God, I need someone to need me. It's that simple, that clichéd. If only someone would need me....*

She drifted to sleep again, and when she awoke the next time, Bob was on his knees in front of the fire, filling it with fresh wood. "You awake?" he whispered.

"Yes."

"Sleep well?"

"You kidding?"

He sat at the foot of the couch as the fire roared. "Dee, he'll come, don't worry." He put his hand on her knee and patted it.

She shook her head. "I sat here all day yesterday, just like I always do on Sundays, sit home alone, while Harry's out somewhere, golfing, to a garden party, sailing. I sat here waiting for him, as though it were sunny and we would go to dinner when he got here. But he never came. He's never coming."

"Dolores, you can't think like that!" Bob got up and looked out the window. "I didn't sleep well either. I'm worried about the kids. With the phones out, we have no idea if they're coming or not, if they've changed their minds. We don't even know if we should be ready for them. I mean, they could be out there in that mess, with a six-month-old baby. Or they could be home, snug in their apartment, playing gin rummy. I don't know what to think."

Dolores reached for the bottle of scotch near the couch. "You really think he's coming?"

Bob bit his lip and turned to her. "I don't know. I just don't know. We can only go on what he said, and that was he was going to come here. It's rough moving through that stuff out there, Dolores. But he's a strong guy."

She drank from the bottle. "I wish to hell I were strong."

"You can be."

She turned sharply to him. "I have to drink, Bob," she said softly, desperately. "You must understand, I have no choice. I know I'm doing it, I know what it's doing to me, and yet I have no choice. After all, what else is there? What else do I have?"

"Us?"

She began to cry again. "Oh, I'm sorry," she said. He came to her and put his arms around her. "I'm so sorry," she sobbed.

"That's okay, okay," he said, letting her cry it out. "I'm just telling you, for what it's worth, we care about you. I do; Susan does; even Julie in her way."

"Oh, God, how I needed to hear that. And if only my husband could tell me that."

Bob held her until she stopped crying. "Listen, I was just going to stop in and say hi to Susan. Would you like to do it? If she's sleeping, don't wake her. But if she's up, she probably wouldn't mind seeing a face. She's due for another shot in about an hour, so now's the time she'd want to see someone."

Dolores' eyes lit up. She got up and walked through the den toward Susan's room. She smiled for the first time since she'd arrived at the house.

Never before in this century had California been so much at the mercy of its weather, and certainly never so quickly. There had been rainstorms and massive mud slides, the lingering drought of 1977 and many before it, mountain snowstorms, desert flash floods, even such thick fog in the San Joaquin Valley that residents could not venture from their homes for weeks at a time because visibility was zero.

And now man, animal, and machine were immobilized under a heavy blanket of snow and ice. In the Los Angeles Basin. The northern part of the state, up through Oregon and Washington, was wet with continuing rain and a depressing lack of any sunshine, but that was heaven next to what was happening in Southern California. The mountain regions in the north–Tahoe, Yosemite–were experiencing normal amounts of snowfall, but temperatures colder than usual by more than 40°. But the mountains surrounding the Los Angeles area were cut off from civilization, buried under a blanket of white that, at some points, reached up to the tips of the giant evergreens. The blizzard winds howled and drifted snow over man, houses, and trees alike.

The dire shortage of natural gas—a subject of great debate in recent years—forced people from homes and office and schools where they'd gone to seek respite from the unbelievable storm. They moved from one place to another, seeking warmth, a trek which left more dead with each hour. "It's the revenge of every jerk who wanted to be a Hollywood star and didn't make it," a noted film director muttered as he watched his Holmby Hills mansion burn to the ground because firemen were unable to fight it as their hoses froze. People tried their best to laugh at it, but it was becoming increasingly hard to do.

The balance—or unbalance—of the high- and low-pressure systems was not letting up and showed no signs of doing so. Thus, the flakes continued to fall and stick. And the winds blew the falling and fallen snow around and over again, recycling it in a sense, adding to the already-mounting disaster the horrors of a seemingly endless blizzard. There were no warm ocean currents to heat the destructive Arctic air rushing down the coast, and the Los Angeles Basin was the perfect target, the perfect spot for those winds and cold to end. The L.A. Basin embraced the wintry air, just as it embraced and held on to smog or fog when it rolled in off the Pacific. The cruel weather stayed locked in position over Los Angeles by that settled mass of freezing air and showed no signs of moving on.

In human terms, the cruelty was already defying reason. In a small hotel in downtown Los Angeles, an elderly man who had once been a movie extra and now sat around the lobby mostly, telling tales of Mae West and Garbo, lay under a paper-thin blanket, shivering. The heat had gone out hours before. Icicles had formed on the water pipes in the dingy room so quickly the man didn't even have time to think of moving somewhere else. All he thought about was staying in his little bed, away from the icicles, and when the manager of the building came later, to check to see if everyone had gone to the lobby where it was warmer, he heard the feeble voice moan, "I'm so cold. Oh, God, I'm so very cold." And then the old man went into a spasm—and died of overexposure. In his own bed.

Two little girls, venturing onto the ice of their backyard swimming pool, drowned in seconds as the ice broke. The pool was a huge one, and the ice in the center had not yet frozen enough to support them. Their father had to pull their bodies from the water. When he got his older daughter out, into the snow at the side of the pool where they'd had so many wonderful summers, he saw her hands were frozen to the chunk of ice she'd clung to in an attempt to save her life.

Simply venturing out of doors was risky. Many elderly people slipped and fell into the snow and died of suffocation when they could not pull their bodies up from the drifts. Thousands slipped on icy snow-covered stairs and driveways, and those with broken limbs, unable to move, either had to hope for someone to come along and help them or risk dying there—sometimes on their front steps—of overexposure.

The National Weather Service reported to the nation that the list of cities that set new low-level temperature records in the past weeks—and especially the past few days—was the longest ever recorded in Southern California.

One test of the horror of the weather was communicated to people by their pets. Animals sought shelter and warmth, as humans did. But owners of dogs had to push them bodily out the doors to get them to spend only a few minutes in the yard, a walk they had gladly taken every day for as long as they'd been living. Many households gave up and merely put down newspapers for their pets. And an even worse horror—one many people could not deal with—was the lack of food for animals. They were beginning to starve as supplies ran out and supermarkets were abandoned and stripped and people had no means to travel anywhere to get anything edible. It wasn't so bad to know you yourself had to starve, but to see the children hungry, to see the animals lifeless without food, it was almost too much to bear.

In churches all over the city, people had gathered in silent masses, rituals of hope and prayer and a search for the answer to just that question, *Why must we bear this?*

"Soup's on," Lorna said, as she helped Marguerita fill the bowls. Breakfast consisted of a big pot of soup, which had been put together by the blending of almost 20 individual cans of soup. Any flavor that would mix well was added—beef, chunky burger, vegetable, tomato—and the result was a tasty and healthy meal.

Greg got a bowl and some crackers and sat near the window, next to Tom. "I want to do it, Tom. I'm worried about them."

"Maybe the day before last, or—better yet—last week, but not now; we'd never make it." Greg had been talking about going to Malibu, where his parents had a small house. "Think how far away it is. And they're probably not even there. I think all the beach houses were evacuated days ago. At the office when I turned in a limo, Streisand and Dylan and—"

"My parents aren't Streisand and Dylan."

"Those houses are probably washed away," Tom said, not wanting to worry him, but to make him see things clearly. "They're probably in a place like this, huddled around a stove, waiting things out."

"Or they're dead."

"Greg, I didn't say that."

Greg put his soup on the floor and put his head on his knees. "Isn't it silly? I'm saying I want my mommy."

Then he shook, and Tom put his arm around him and held him. "Hey, it's not silly at all. I envy you. I don't even have a mommy to want."

"I'm scared. Like I was scared of the dark when I was a kid."

Tom just said, "I'm . . . I'm here. I guess I can't . . ."

Greg ran his fingers through his lover's hair. "I'm a big boy now. I need you more than I need my mommy."

Tom nodded. "That's all there is right now, all we can count on. Each other."

"Is it enough to get you through?"

Tom smiled. "You know it is. The question is for you to answer, not me. Can you brave it alone, just with me? I know you don't really have much of a choice, but I want to know what you're thinking, how you really feel."

"Yes," Greg finally said, "it's enough. Mom and Dad also have each other, so I shouldn't worry that much."

"Now you're making sense," Tom said, rustling his hair. "Now drink your breakfast."

Greg smiled. "It's delicious. And I don't even like soup."

"Get used to it. I think there's 50 more cans in there."

"Hey," Michael yelled, "firewood's getting low. Who's gonna brave the next expedition to the wilderness to get more? I think the dog sled leaves in about ten minutes."

"I'll help this time," Tom replied.

Michael came over to him and sat down. "Let's try to dig into the collapsed building. Under the snow, like on the first floor, in those apartments, there must be some timbers, some two-by-fours which will burn beautifully."

"Won't they be too wet?" Tom asked.

"Wet? Everything out there's frozen solid, not wet."

"Hey, everybody!" Kenny Rupp was talking, standing by the window. "Look at this."

They gathered around the window, peering out into the courtyard. The palm tree which was closest to the pool seemed to be tilting, falling. "The Leaning Palm Tree of Freeza," Michael joked. But it wasn't so funny. The pool wall had cracked wide open, the ice pushing the cement and plaster apart, and the palm tree had fallen sideways, its roots stopping it from collapsing completely onto the ice.

"Wish I had Dad's camera," Michael said as he sat down by the fire again. Flora had her Instamatic and was taking pictures of the group and the courtyard. She'd found it in the rubble. It had been on her dresser, but she'd forgotten to grab it as they ran from the apartment. But when the ceiling had fallen, the camera fell to the first floor, and it was easy to reach it. It seemed to be working fine. But she was almost out of film, and she felt sad. She knew there were more things to take pictures of. She wanted to go outside, down the street, but she didn't have any good warm shoes or boots. And yet she was glad she didn't; she didn't want to see any more tragedy, any more disaster. She couldn't deal with it; she couldn't handle it. This was bad enough, her father in pain still from his fall, the others worried, cranky, unhappy, their homes ruined forever, her teeth chattering. Suddenly she burst into tears and screamed, "Goddammit! Goddamn all of this!"

"Daughter!" Harvard exclaimed.

Lorna went to her and said, "Hey, it's okay, let it out. Don't stop her, anyone, it's understandable. Don't we all want to do it?"

There was no answer.

"Well, don't we?"

Finally, Greg said, "Yes, oh, yes."

"Well, go ahead. Come on, let's all do it." Lorna walked to the middle of the room. She heard Dawn cry from the bedroom. "Even better, the baby's awake. Let's do it now, scream, yell, make some noise. Let's protest what's happening here!" And she let out a whooping yell.

The others joined in, screaming, shouting, cursing. And then they were laughing, bending over, on hands and knees, laughing at the silliness of it, at the release of tension. Finally, they calmed down, and Lorna went to feed Dawn. Everyone went back to reading or playing chess (Mr. Rosenberg and Kenny Rupp's girlfriend) or just sitting, thinking. But everyone, without exception, felt better.

They were aware of one basic truth: Things could be worse.

Minnie Kupperman heard the knock on the back door. It would have frightened her if it had been at the front door, but since it was the back, she knew it had to be Bob. She opened the door and blinked. There stood a woman in a black mink coat, her hair stuffed into a turban. "Come in, come in," the old woman said, ushering Dolores into the kitchen. "Sit down, have coffee." Her husband and grandson walked into the room and said hello. "I'll bet you've come to sing us a song!" Minnie said.

"No, I . . . no thank you, I don't drink coffee . . . I came to ask if you have any scotch in the house."

Minnie flashed an eye at her husband. "Scotch?"

"Liquor. You see, Susan needs it desperately. Medicinal purposes. There are no pain drugs left–"

Minnie squinted. "Here, here. Worse thing there is for the pancreas is liquor."

Dolores looked embarrassed, and Mr. Kupperman ushered little Billy out of the kitchen. "I'm sorry," Dolores said, and got up and went to the door. But she couldn't turn the handle. She looked back at Minnie and said, "Oh, please! Please, if you have it, won't you give it to me? I beg you." She held back tears, leaning against the door.

Minnie felt sorry for the poor woman. She knew what it must have cost her–her dignity–in coming over to her house in the snow, to have to beg for a drink. "There's nothing," Minnie said softly.

"Here," Dolores said, "take it." She pulled off her wristwatch. "There are two diamonds in the band. Please."

"Oh, stop, don't do that!" Minnie exclaimed. "I'm not lying to you. We never have scotch in the house. There's a little brandy."

"Yes! Oh, please, anything!"

The woman's mad, Minnie thought to herself. She went into the dining room and fetched the nearly empty bottle of brandy. "The only thing we got."

Dolores took it and clutched it inside her coat. "My . . . my husband, you met him . . . he's out there . . . he's out there and I . . . I . . . oh, God. . . ." She sobbed and beat her fist against the door.

Minnie felt helpless. She reached out, touched Dolores' hand, trying to soothe her. So that was it; her husband was lost in the storm. She understood that kind of desperation, that kind of love.

But before Minnie could say anything, Dolores turned. "I must get back; they don't know I'm gone." She opened the door, and the snow fell on their heads. She started across the thick snow, following her own tracks. "I do thank you," she called back, trying to hold back still more tears.

"I do ... I do understand, I really do!" Minnie Kupperman called to her, but she wasn't sure the woman heard her.

She closed the door and walked into the living room. "It worries me, Sam," she said.

"What does?"

"The desperation in her eyes. What'll people be doing tomorrow, the day after that? The people who have nothing left, no food left, no houses? What will they do, what will stop them from getting what they want?"

Sam shook his head. "I don't know what you're getting at."

"I don't know myself. I just know it's not a fair trade to give diamonds for brandy. Diamonds don't mean much all of a sudden. What's going to happen to everyone?"

Sam shook his head. "I don't know, Minnie. I don't know."

Then Minnie, who was an avid reader, thought about a book she'd read a few years back. It was called *Alive,* and it was the story of a plane crash in the Andes where the survivors ate the dead passengers to stay alive. She cringed and sat down in her favorite chair. What would happen when the food ran out, when there was no more liquor, when people were on the brink of death? She closed her eyes and tried to get the thought out of her mind.

Harry Sheppard rested on the sixth-floor landing and then continued down. When he got to the lobby, he heard voices, and he stopped himself and looked through the door. In the lobby was a group of boys, teenagers, a gang, and they'd smashed the windows of all the stores in the arcade. They were pocketing jewels, clothes, taking cigars and cigarettes, everything they could get into their pockets. He hid behind the door, waiting for them to leave. It figured, he thought. Half the city must be looted by now. Good. Makes the heist at the museum look all the more natural.

Harry had counted on the boys going out the front way, but

they had another plan. Then came bursting through the door which led out the back, the door to the stairwell, and they confronted Harry. "Hey, what's this?" the leader said, smiling.

"I . . . my office is upstairs," Harry said, trying to act natural. But how natural can a man in a ski outfit with a fire hose over his shoulder look? "I was just leaving." He tried to walk into the lobby, but they stopped him.

"Wait, pops, what you doin', goin' to a fire?" A couple of the boys chuckled.

"What's in the fuckin' hose?" a voice asked.

"Nothing," Harry said. He wasn't very convincing. A boy pulled it off his shoulder, and the leader yanked the rolled-up plastic raincoat out of the end of it. "It's nothing you'd want, really," Harry said. "Look, I'll give you money . . ."

"Shut up, pops," the kid said. He pulled out one of the canvases and unrolled it a bit. "What's this shit?"

"I . . . I'm an artist. They're my finest works. I'm going to get them home." Harry was thinking fast, going on the premise that these kids knew nothing about art and/or couldn't care less.

"Shit, man, I figured you were getting outta here with ten grand in the hose." The kid stood up and dropped the canvas.

You should only know, Harry thought, as his heart started to work again. "My paintings, my life's work. . . ."

"Shit, man, keep your crummy pictures. Lotsa luck." The leader ran out the back door, and the others followed.

"Fuck you!" one of the kids yelled as he left.

"No, fuck *you,*" Harry said after they'd left. He sat down and slid the canvas back into the hose. Then he walked through the lobby and out into the real world again. The snow hit his face, but he didn't mind. He was going to make it and he knew it. Assured, he started across the street, taking secret pride and exhilaration in walking right past the County Museum of Art.

The place looked dead.

If the average citizen of Los Angeles felt helpless in the face of the crisis, the prisoners in the city jail felt completely vulnerable. One jail in particular was more conducive to the prisoners' terror, the one in downtown Los Angeles where the cells were on top floor, above a large municipal building. It was the jail in which Charles Manson had spent much time while he was being tried. The wind and snow howled fiercely 100 feet up, more incessantly than at ground level.

From the beginning the situation inside the cells was bad. Heating was inadequate, and tension so high that the prisoners were being confined to their cells for fear of a riot. There was no way to avoid the cold in the cellblock areas. Clothing was at a premium. Getting suitable clothing was impossible for free citizens, much less confined men and women. A thought always prominent in a prisoner's mind is freedom, but now, with the crisis of the weather and the sense of doom, freedom meant staying alive. The prisoners felt they were locked in concentration camps.

The problem was a difficult one. Officials felt that they could risk moving the prisoners—from all the jails—to another location only in the best weather, with the best of protection. Half the police force in the city couldn't even be located. There was trouble enough on the streets already, without the possibility of a large prison break which would come with the moving of the incarcerated men and women from one institution to another. The outlook was bleak. Food and supplies were already going to the poor and needy in the outside world. Behind the bars, each man was truly paying his debt to society; each man felt a loneliness far beyond that which he experienced in normal prison life. "Prisoners are people too," one man wrote in his diary, "but in a crisis such as this they are the last to be remembered."

Below on the street an occasional relative passed by, hoping to get some candy or bread to someone inside, but it was impossible. The doors were shut; the places were understaffed, and the few officials present feared visitors would attempt to get their loved ones out. A woman stood under the small window at the Sybil Brand Institute, the Los Angeles detention center for women. Her daughter was in there, and she had come with a thick coat, some food, some hot soup in a thermos. But she could not get in. So she stood there, in the terrible weather, chilled, crying, praying.

Her daughter in a sense had it easier. Whereas her mother had to deal with the realities of the storm, had to stand out there freezing, the girl only had to sit and wait. And hope for the end of it all.

Unusual numbers of recent episodes of abnormal weather–which included the Midwestern droughts of 1976 and the long hot summer of the same year in Western Europe, the stupefying blizzard which brought Chicago to its knees in '67, the terrible drought in California at the same time the "Big Freeze of '77" was choking the country east of the Rockies–had touched off concern that the earth's climate may be changing . . . drastically. The fact that while snow was piling up on the streets of Pasadena and the sands of Laguna Beach, New Yorkers were walking around in shorts and Ohioans were picnicking in the hot sunshine only intensified the suggestions that weather was not what it used to be, nor would it ever be again.

Most meteorologists were in agreement that the real freak of the current winter was the weather in the eastern section of the United States. The warming trend was more an offshoot of the fact that the arctic winds had gone straight down from the polar air mass and not so much in the counterclockwise fashion these westerlies usually traveled. It was the upper-level westerlies which caused big freezes. These winds–including one known as the jet stream–blow eternally around the Northern Hemisphere at altitudes of 30,000 to 45,000 feet. The problem is that though their overall course is steady, the westerlies may also veer sharply to the north or dip deeply into the south, as they were doing in California at this time. In past winters, the normal winters before 1977, these veerings brought the familiar pattern of cold snaps and thaws over much of the Northern Hemisphere. But this year the westerlies veered more sharply than ever before, moving down the globe, with no warm air moving off the Pacific to counter them and force them into the Midwest and eastern seaboard.

The northern and southern limits these chilling winds may reach are determined mainly by seasonal differences in temperatures at the North Pole and at the equator. These differences produce a climatic tug-of-war that pulls the westerlies far to the north in the summer and then sends them back down, much farther down south, in the winter. This year it was different. The westerlies were not reaching the territory east of the Rockies, and thus, most of the continental U.S. was experiencing summerlike temperatures in January, while the brunt of the extremely cold polar winds was striking the Pacific coast. The biting winds dropped down far into California and thus drew a heavy flow of warm winds over the Plains states. How long the situation would go on was anybody's guess–and they all were guessing.

Experts disagree strongly on the nature of such a drastic change in weather. Thus, the intense and heated discussion of an impending ice age after the numbing winter of 1977. Two different substances seem to be increasing in the atmosphere, predominantly as a result of human activities. Carter DeSimone was one person who felt *man* had a great deal to do with what was destroying man in Los Angeles this winter. He'd always been of the school that tampering with the weather–with the natural balance of weather–was wrong and dangerous.

One of the problems is what scientists call particulate matter–grit, dust–which is released by industry, volcanoes, and agriculture. The other is carbon dioxide, which is released whenever fossil fuels such as coal or oil are burned. Dust particles can cool down the atmosphere, because they reflect away from the earth before it can reach the surface. Carbon dioxide, by contrast, presents minimal hindrance to sunlight, but does prevent the long-wavelength heat radiation produced by the earth from escaping into outer space; carbon dioxide therefore tends to warm the atmosphere.

There were many–Carter among them–who thought that particulate matter–all that crap in the air–had already screened out enough sunlight to reduce the temperature of the Northern Hemisphere by almost 3° since 1970. The finest meteorological minds generally agree that a 6° drop would produce a full-scale ice age. The few winters since 1977 had not been as disastrous, but they had not been what they had been. It was not unusual for most of the Midwest and East to be in sub-zero temperatures for the months of January and February. Winters now lasted many weeks longer. People were becoming accustomed to it already; that is perhaps why they were taking such joy in the warm temperatures this winter, while they left California to battle the elements in the style to which they'd grown accustomed.

Around the globe things were no better. Russia's winter had begun in August and seemed to be the worst in memory, but Russians are used to harsh winters; perhaps they even love them. All Western Europe was experiencing a colder-than-usual winter, while, oddly enough, parts of Scandinavia basked in warm temperatures. Hurricanes and never-ending rains battered China, and earthquakes seemed almost a weekly occurrence around the globe. What was happening made little sense; but it frightened everyone.

Another matter of concern, perhaps partly to blame for the vengeful weather in Southern California this winter, was the seeding of clouds with artificial precipitation-inducing elements. Carter knew what could happen if such measures were carried to the extreme—it was just more particulate matter, after all—and they had been; after the lingering drought, California's farmers, businessmen, and private citizens alike put pressure on the governor and the President to do everything possible—everything—to soothe the parched and arid land with water. One way was to spike the clouds.

And now those same clouds hung like a pall over the cities near and in the Los Angeles Basin. They rained and rained, but the temperature was well below the freezing point, so the rain turned to snow, and it snowed and it snowed....

And it snowed.

Lorna ran into the apartment and brushed the snow from her shoulders. "Listen," she said anxiously, "they're really getting things together. There's a shelter set up—well, they're all over the city—but there's one set up at the gym of Hollywood High." She got a barrage of questions about what was happening outside, and she told them everything she'd found out. She had gone out to see what she could find out. The National Guard had a big truck down on Santa Monica Boulevard, and she talked to the soldiers there. They told her about the shelters, the food drops, the hope to evacuate people as soon as the snow stopped, and that fires and heart attacks had been the biggest problem so far.

"What's happening with businesses?" Flora asked. "Is anyone working? Any stores open?"

"They said the looting is getting terrible, but they're not doing anything to stop it because people are mostly looting for things like clothes and food."

"Do you think we should go to the high school?" Kenny asked.

Lorna shook her head. "No, not yet. Only the people who don't have any other place to go—or the sick—should go up there. It's really a shelter, a drastic measure. We're much better off here." She took the cup of hot cocoa from Marguerita.

"I make it with water instead of milk, but it just as good," the kind old woman said.

Lorna thanked her and tasted it. Yes, it was just as good. She sat down and told the others that everything looked quiet on their street, but several buildings had burned down on Santa Monica. "People are camped out in the Pussycat Theater," she said.

"The porno palace?" Greg asked.

Lorna nodded. "I'll bet theaters all over the city are being used for shelters. It's logical. I hope the Quesana family got to a warm place," she said directly to Michael.

He nodded. "Hey, guess what we've been doing since you've been gone? Playing charades."

"You're kidding."

"Nope. These people are terrific. Natural talent. You should have seen Flora do *Mother, Jugs and Speed.*"

"What's that?"

"A movie. Few years ago. Rotten movie with Raquel Welch running around town in an ambulance. But Flora was terrific."

"We niggers got rhythm," Flora kidded. "And jugs." She looked down at her breasts and smiled.

"Girl, hush!" her father snorted.

"Oh, Daddy," she said, giggling, hugging him.

A man pounded on the door. Michael opened it. He was a soldier, and he looked in and nodded. "Can we have help? A building down the street, we've got to evacuate it. The roof's giving. We need to get them to the theater on the Boulevard. Lots of kids–"

"We're coming!" Michael said, and they all got up. "Look, we all can't go. Marguerita and Mr. Rosenberg, you hold down the fort. Flora, if you want to go, you've gotta wear that pair of boots Mr. Rosenberg has there. Come on, let's go."

And they went, but just before they did, Kenny Rupp put more wood on the fire and doused it with charcoal lighter. He set the can down on the table near the makeshift fireplace, near where Harve was lying down, put on his stocking cap, and left, holding his girlfriend's hand.

Harvard soon drifted off to sleep. Marguerita and Mr. Rosenberg were left alone in the room. "All right, old man, let's have a good argument," she said with a smile. "Keep us in practice."

"Always glad to oblige you, Mrs. Alvarez. I've been meaning to tell you, the rent is too high. And the heat. You call this heat?" He pointed to the garbage can with the wooden breadbox from one of the apartments burning inside it.

"What do you call it, garbage?"

They could go on like that forever.

Carter was talking to Bob on the shortwave radio. "We got a call up here from a mobile unit, and they said some girl named Lorna Sheppard told a soldier to tell Carter DeSimone that everything was okay. I guess you've got a smart daughter-in-law; she knew how to get word to you in the midst of all this."

Bob breathed easy. "Thank God."

"But, Christ, Bob, you should see it from here, when you can see through the falling snow. Buildings are burning everywhere, and there's no fire department left, all the water mains are bursting."

"I know, my pool drain valve just froze up like some ice sculpture."

"And the worst is the center of the city; the people are moving toward higher ground."

"Makes sense," Bob said.

"They're looting like crazy. The Guard's doing nothing about them because what's there to do? If it means saving a life, they'll step in, but the looting seems to be to do just that, save lives. Supermarkets are being cleared out, food supply trucks, even ships in Long Beach. We're going to talk to the President and some top aides later today, and I want to know what to do to help contain riots, to get to the people, to stop panic. This sense of doom. . . ."

"Okay," Bob said, "more soldiers are needed, or will be to keep some kind of stability. Airlifts are out, but there's an alternative, Carter. The Marines. Camp Pendleton sits halfway between here and San Diego. The camp sprawls the coastline—why can't they be brought in by sea then? They're trained in amphibious assault. They can board ships south of San Clemente and land on the beaches at Venice, Manhattan, Redondo, maybe even up to Santa Monica, even Will Rogers. We're going to need a sense of strength, authority. Only soldiers and men in some kind of uniform can provide that. It's partly psychological. Get the Marines in here. It's the only chance I can think of."

"Sure," Carter said, his eyes lighting up. "Heck, I never thought of it, the water out there isn't frozen, it's warmer than the air! We'll get Granville to do it."

"I think it'll help. I'll bet the Marines are already helping out in San Diego," Bob said.

"Probably."

"Authority. Uniforms. People need leaders in situations like this; they cry out for someone to tell them what to do."

"Bob, thanks. It'll help. How's Susan?"

"Bad."

"Can she hold out a few days at least?"

"She's going to have to, right?"

"Yeah, well, I'm working on something. I promise you, Bob, I'll do something for her. Promise."

"I believe you, Carter. Thanks."

Bob got up from the table and told Julie and Dolores what he'd heard. They had been in the living room, not even aware that he'd been on the radio. Julie was knitting, and Dolores was trying to read a book, but she kept looking out the window. All the scotch was gone now. She was holding back on the other, the brandy, the vodka, the whiskey. She knew that was the last of it; there was no other source short of going over and stealing the holy wine from the good sisters. She was going to be in control. Harry would come, she believed it again. He would come, and then she wouldn't have to drink anymore.

Bob went down to the family room and unlocked his gun cabinet. He hadn't held one of those things in years, but it was time to do so again. He pulled out a shotgun and found the ammunition in the locked door beneath. He didn't know quite why he was doing it, but after Carter's words about looters and the people moving to higher ground, he just wanted to be sure. He took the gun upstairs and sneaked it into the broom closet off the laundry room, so as not to alarm the women. But it was nearby, and he knew it, and that's what counted.

In the living room Julie saw Dolores had no interest in the novel. "You know, the gas is still on," she said.

"What?"

"The gas is still on. It'll go, just like the electricity will go. It's gone in most places, Carter told Bob. Let's bake up everything we can while the stove is still working. Come on, it'll give us something constructive to do." Julie got up.

"Oh, shit, you just want to get me away from the bottle," Dolores snapped.

"That isn't it at all!" Julie retorted.

"Don't patronize me."

"How dare you? I was just thinking of something we could do to help!"

Dolores turned away and muttered, "Sure. I want to help your daughter, but you won't let me touch the precious child. You sit here staring at me like I'm diseased or something, drinking in your precious living room. Let's bake goodies, Dee! You don't want a drunk messing up your precious kitchen, do you?"

Julie screamed, "You said it, not me! Drunk! Yes, that's what you are! A drunk, and it isn't helping any of us! You embarrass me in front of my neighbors, asking for liquor as though it were plasma, and then you sit here on your big butt staring out the window in some lost hope, and what are you going to do when you realize he's not going to show up and the bottles all are empty?"

Bob ran into the room and stopped, frozen, stunned by the speech his wife had just given. Dolores jumped to her feet and ran upstairs, crying. Julie slumped into her chair and put her head in her hands. Bob went to her. "Jesus, she didn't deserve—"

"I said it, and I'm not sorry."

He stared at her. Waiting.

In a minute she looked up at him. "Oh, Bob, I don't know . . . I didn't know what I was saying. I'm so frightened, so on edge, and everything's getting to me. I can't stand it! A message from Lorna. Why aren't they *here?* We should have them here. And why doesn't that woman *do* something instead of just sit and guzzle?" She stopped herself. She was doing it again. She asked him to leave her alone for a while. She needed time to think, to relax, to get herself together. She needed time to go upstairs and find a way to apologize to Dolores.

Harry trudged along Wilshire Boulevard. No one seemed to be paying much attention to anyone, much less him and his fire hose. He felt hungry and searched for a place to get food. He saw a big restaurant across the street, but of course it was deserted. But it had to have. . . .

When he got across the street, he saw the outlines of a few people inside, behind the counter. He opened the doors, and a man said, "Nothing left."

"Just a piece of bread, anything," Harry said.

A woman turned to him and offered a stale danish. He took it and thanked her. And then there was the sound of gunfire and the plate glass window shattering. Everyone ducked, fell to the floor, the woman screaming, another man running out the back way.

An overzealous young national guardsman poked his head—and his rifle—in the open window. "We've got orders to shoot to kill looters. Get the hell outta there!"

No one argued, but once in the alley the woman, who had made off with a basket full of supplies like flour and sugar, said, "No one's ordered to shoot. He's out of his mind. I live right down the street here. Got seven kids to feed and my mother. No one's killing people for stealing food. People've got to eat."

Just at that second, another shot rang out and Harry pushed the woman down into the snow. The fire hose dropped to the ground. A bunch of young people ran out of the back of a clothing store in the alley, dragging coats and articles of clothing with them. The same soldier jumped from the building, firing shots into the snow. Harry jumped up, knocked the man to the ground, and wrestled with him until more guardsmen showed up. They pulled them apart and held the young guy who'd done the shooting on the ground. "He tried to kill those kids, for a goddamn coat!" Harry shouted.

"He's . . . he's not well," one of the soldiers said. "We've been looking for him." And they pulled him away, kicking.

Harry helped the woman to her feet. "You all right?" he asked.

"Sure, but you're not," she said. "Look, your arm!" Harry saw blood on his bright yellow jacket. He had been shot and didn't even feel it, didn't know it. Now it started to hurt. "Come on in the house," the woman ordered, picking up her flour and supplies. "I'll get you bandaged up."

Once inside, the woman and her oldest son cleaned up the wound. It was minor, just a scratch. They bandaged it and asked Harry to have dinner with them. It was the least they could do, because he'd pushed the woman out of the line of the crazed soldier's fire. Harry said he'd be happy to. He left the hose on the porch where he'd set it when they came in. No one asked about it. He ate dinner with them and then saw that it was nearly dark outside. They offered a warm place to spend the night, and he said he would take them up on it. A good night's sleep, he thought, and then up early to begin the trek again.

He fell asleep almost immediately, with the kids talking around him, the woman banging pans in the kitchen. The snow had exhausted him.

There was a section of the San Diego Freeway between the top of the Santa Monica Mountains–Mulholland Drive–and the San Fernando Valley where the gently rising roadway bent down into a 30° incline that was a challenge for almost any car or truck. It was ideal for skiing and sledding, a vision only realized in this crisis.

The young and the daring came out from their homes in nearby Encino, Sherman Oaks, and Van Nuys and made their way slowly to the top for the thrill of a lifetime. Many would live their entire lives with the memories of this day. For some it would be their last memory on earth.

Two young boys had struggled for an hour to reach the top of the hill with the sleds their parents had gotten them for the mountains. Standing at the top, their hearts racing, one yelled to the other, "Race ya!" and they began a familiar childhood experience.

Both boys flew down the steep incline, 20 mph, 30 mph, faster, faster. In their exhilaration they used no caution, no forethought. They just experienced. They couldn't see more than 100 feet in front of them, but what did that matter? All the way they never realized that they were slowly losing control of their sleds.

The end came quickly, quietly. No one ever saw what happened. It just happened. The lead boy began to tilt on his sled. He tried to adjust himself, but this threw him farther off-balance. In the few seconds of panic that followed he never saw the sharp-edged sign post directly in his path. He hit it square on with his head, and it split him clear down to his heart.

The other boy saw nothing. A few seconds later he realized his buddy was no longer in front of him. His mind diverted an instant too long. Going too fast to turn, he looked up to see the wall of a huge snowdrift in his way. He could only close his eyes as he entered into it, deep into. It swallowed him whole like some great shark. Just two minutes later, unable to move, he was dead from suffocation ... and no one knew where he had disappeared.

Harvard Reynauld woke up because he heard a crackling sound, and he felt unnaturally warm. He opened his eyes and saw the entire wall next to him covered with flames. The can of charcoal lighter on the table had fallen over, and the liquid had ignited once it made its way to the floor and the fire. The wall was one sheet of flames. His first thought was whether or not there were people upstairs. No, they were gone, he remembered. Then where were the others? He remembered Flora kissing him, telling him they'd be back soon–where had they all gone? It didn't matter; he had to get out of there. He got up and went to the door and opened it, and then he realized everyone couldn't be gone; the baby must still be there.

He ran to the bedroom and found Marguerita sound asleep near the little girl on the bed. Mr. Rosenberg was snoozing in the chair next to them, near the heater. "Mrs. Alvarez! Mr. Rosenberg! There's a fire ... *FIRE! Out, come on, out!*" He shook them. The apartment was already beginning to fill with smoke. They both understood.

"I get the baby," Marguerita cried, picking up Dawn. Harve turned and walked into the hall, and they followed him. But just as they were about to step into the living room, there was a tremendous explosion. Harvard heard Marguerita scream, *"Oh, dear God!"* as the whole building seemed to come down on them.

Down the street, everyone stopped in his tracks at the loud sound, the roar of a building falling, of fire roaring. Michael saw it first, sensed it first. "No," he said softly, dropping the little boy he was carrying into the snow. *"No ... no ... NO NO NO!"* He screamed and ran. He fell, twisting his leg, but he got up and somehow leaped over the snow, almost running on top of it.

Lorna followed him. *"Dawn, oh, my baby, my baby...."* Her voice seemed to cut through the roar of the fire.

They all saw it now, they saw it, but they wouldn't believe it; their minds wouldn't allow it. It wasn't happening. It was unthinkable, unbelievable. And yet they all ran toward the building or what had been their building. Flora squealed, *"Dad-deeeeeeee!"* as she crawled through the snow. Greg and Tom caught up with Michael. They rubbed snow on their faces and went in through the door. The living room was somewhat intact. Tom saw Harvard lying on the floor near the door, and he pulled the man out immediately. Michael pushed plaster and furniture aside, determined to get to the bedroom, but he didn't have to go that far. He found Marguerita's body at his feet, a beam lying on her head, a pool of blood under her. He heard the sound, the cry of a baby. Dawn. *"Where is she?"* he screamed, his eyes flooded with tears of desperation. He heard the muffled cry again, and he looked toward the bedroom. The whole hall seemed to be on fire. *"Dawn!"* he shouted, as if the girl would respond to her daddy's call.

Then heard the sound again, and he looked down. He fell to his knees, rolled the big woman's body over, and found the baby lying there on the floor. She was alive. She was crying loudly. Marguerita's body had protected her. He took her into his arms and ran from the doorway, colliding with Lorna, knocking her to the ground, he himself falling back into the snow, still holding the little baby up above him.

Lorna recovered and hugged him and Dawn. They crawled away from the burning building. The others were dragging Mr. Rosenberg from the rubble. Greg and Tom had found him still gasping for breath near Marguerita's body. They pulled him into the snow, into the street, away from the danger, and they tried to revive him. Greg gave him mouth to mouth, even pounded his fist into the man's chest, but nothing worked. He was dead, of a heart attack; there hadn't even been a bruise on his body.

They all gathered around Harvard as the building burned in the background. Tom had wanted to go back for Marguerita, but it was too dangerous, and Michael knew she was dead. The baby hadn't been hurt either, just startled and bruised a bit. "She saved her; the old woman saved her; I seen it with my own eyes," Harvard said. "She threw herself on top of the baby." He choked back tears and then let them out. "Oh, sweet Jesus, help us all." He cried as his daughter held him to her breast. She told him it was going to be all right. He wasn't hurt. That's what counted. Sweet Jesus had helped him.

The truth was they all were crying, even Kenny Rupp's girlfriend, who didn't know any of them well at all. They'd been together, a kind of family, and now they were out on the street, split up, the woman who had been the mother of them all lying in a pool of blood in the burning building, the kind old man dead in the snow. Now they had no place to go, no shelter, no food, perhaps not even each other any longer. The icy wind froze the tears on their faces. Greg fell to the ground, pounding his fist into the snow. "She didn't deserve it!" he cried. *"We* don't deserve it. What's with this dirty trick? What did we do that's so *bad,* huh?" He pounded the snow with both fists. *"I hate it! I hate it so fucking much!"* Tom knelt down next to him and grabbed his hands. Then Greg fell over, against him, and cried like a baby.

They stayed across the street, in the same woman's apartment who had given them coffee the first time they'd waited out the gas explosion threat. No one had ever thought about checking the upstairs apartments at Genesee Gardens, and it was apparent that there had been a leak in the gas heater, in the stove, in something in the apartment above Marguerita's. Harvard explained—shaken, but coherent—how he'd awakened to see the flames already hitting the ceiling. "The fire touched off the gas upstairs, and that's what blew," he said.

Kenny Rupp stood up. "What did you say?"

"The gas upstairs, the fire—"

"Fire? You mean the fire in the fireplace?"

"It had spread, all over the walls. I don't know how."

Kenny turned pale. "It's my fault," he said. "I left the can of lighter fluid on the table right there. I didn't even bother to close it. I remembered it when we were walking through the snow. Oh, Christ." His girlfriend put her arms around him.

"You can't blame yourself," Lorna said. "No one is to blame. There's no blame involved. It just happened, and we have to somehow go on."

"Where?" Flora asked.

"Hollywood High School," Lorna said. "The theater down here on the Boulevard is already full. We don't have a choice."

"You're welcome to stay here if you like," the woman who owned the apartment said, but that was impossible. It was small and not very warm, and she had little food left. Harvard was now complaining of pains in his neck and head, and Greg knew he should be examined by a doctor. Greg also felt he could be of some use there at the shelter. Tom agreed; he wanted to go where people were. Harvard said he was up to making the trip. The baby seemed to be fine, and Lorna knew she was strong enough to make the trip if they were, perhaps stronger.

So it was agreed. They would begin the long hard trip to the shelter set up at Hollywood High School. But before they did, they stood silently in the snow, watching the soldiers remove the body of the warm and wonderful woman they'd loved so much. They took her out and put her into a plastic bag and zipped it up. Michael felt something give in his stomach, and he retched. They did the same with the body of old Mr. Rosenberg.

Michael leaned up against a tree and turned away. Lorna put her hand on his. "Toss them into a garbage bag," he said, trying not to cry, feeling as though he were going to throw up. "Into a goddamn garbage bag."

"Come on," Lorna said, "we've got a long way to go."

And together, they took each other's hands and braved the wind and the snow as they went toward yet another home.

Dolores finished showering in the master bathroom. She blew her hair dry, or at least started to. In the middle of it the power went out. Bob called up, telling her not to worry; he'd be up with a candle. And he was, in a minute, and Dolores brushed her teeth by candlelight.

They'd had all the candles ready, but it was something else again to have to use them. The house took on an eerie glow, not nearly as romantic as it was when they dined by candlelight. Bob lit the camping lantern he'd had in the garage and set it up in the living room, but when Dolores came downstairs, she told them she wanted to sleep, and Bob put it out. There was no sense wasting the kerosene.

The wind howled through the fir trees. It seemed to be getting even colder, if that was possible. Dolores stretched out on the couch with her fur coat over the blanket. She'd accepted Julie's apology halfheartedly, and now she sat on the other sofa, across from her, still knitting. "I hope Harry's somewhere safe for the night," she said.

"Yes," Julie replied. "I wonder how the children are doing in that awful apartment house. The message from Lorna said they were all right, but I worry. I don't know how such a place can withstand this cold."

"They'll be all right. They'll all be all right." Dolores closed her eyes.

Julie worried about the children, about Harry, and about Dee too. Her dependency on alcohol had tripled since the storm had begun. She was down to the last of it now, the vodka—what would she do when it ran out? Julie understood how much she needed Harry, and she prayed her brother-in-law would come. Maybe the drinking was Dolores' way out, her way of getting away from all this....

And yet why wasn't she ripsnorting drunk? Julie just realized that. She wasn't really drunk. Oh, she tottered a little, like when she was going up to shower—Julie was afraid she'd fall in the shower stall, but she made it through fine—and when she was setting her mink on the couch. A few of her words were slurred, and she didn't talk as much as usual, signals that she'd had a lot to drink. Booze usually made people more talkative; it had the opposite effect on Dolores. She was usually quite gregarious, especially in the months before the rain had started, but now she was almost silent, as though the weather and the liquor had told her not to bother talking. She was as depressed—depressing?—as the bleak weather outside, Julie thought, and she felt sorry for her.

Julie set her knitting in her lap and looked at the now-sleeping woman. Oh, she'd been so beautiful. She still was, in a way. Everyone blamed Harry for what had happened to her, for what she'd become. Everyone but Julie—it wasn't just his fault. People had control over their lives and destinies, she believed, and one person could not completely change another, cause him to give up his spirit. Dolores had to have been willing to do it, perhaps in collusion with it, or it would never have happened at all. In those early years there were no great pressures to stay together; she was young and exciting and talented, and she could have found another man, a better and richer man than Harry any day. There was no fear of being alone—hadn't she lived alone for a long time before she met him? Julie wondered if Dolores had really had what it takes to make it in show business, if she'd ever really had that kind of guts and strength. She doubted it. If she had, she wouldn't have dropped it so easily, given it all up so quickly when Harry wanted to tie the knot. It wasn't as if Harry, for all his greed and arrogance and lack of consideration, had twisted her arm and pulled her off the nightclub stage. Julie felt Dolores really had not seen a future in it, a real future, whereas with Harry she saw a life that was good and wholesome and happy.

And that went sour. Julie did put a good deal of the blame on Harry, there. It was common knowledge he hated children, something he never told Dolores until after they were married. And she loved them and wanted one, two, three, so badly. Julie remembered how Dolores acted when Michael was born, as though he were part hers, fawning over him, sitting by his rocker for hours at a time, singing to him, baby-sitting every chance she could.

And then came the years of fighting, terrible fighting. Harry would stay at Bob's house more than one night a week, just to get away from "the shrew," as he called her. The arguments were over having a child. Dolores demanded it. She had a house, but not a home. She had a husband, but she wanted a family. And finally, after three years of knock-down drag-out, she was pregnant, and miraculously life seemed to be joyous again.

And then she suffered a miscarriage.

And Harry said never again. Julie was amazed at his attitude, as though he were the one lying in the hospital bed, the one who'd just lost the child and nearly bled to death. But Dolores could still have other children, the doctors said. It started again, but Harry put a quick stop to it. He told her you accept our life as it is–no kids–or you leave; there's the door.

Dolores took the door. She left him for nearly three months, during which time he was beside himself. He sent a detective out looking for her, had everyone in the country he knew who could possibly be in touch with her on the lookout, but no one found her. One day she called him. She told him she'd been traveling, she'd needed to do it, to get away from him; she was tired now, and she missed him. He broke down and cried on the phone–at least she always thought he really cried; she talked herself into believing he'd cried. When she came home, he was there, and he took her to bed almost immediately and promised her a baby.

What Dolores didn't know was that during the time Harry was home alone, when she was off sorting things out in her head, he'd gone into the hospital for a hernia operation. Not on the record was the fact that he'd also had a vasectomy. Now he could promise a baby with no fear that they'd ever really have one. Dolores kept believing she'd be pregnant again; she lived with the faith that it would happen. Then Susan was born, and she went into a severe depression and started to drink heavily for the first time in her life. One night, in Bob and Julie's living room, they had it out. Harry was drunk himself, and he told her he was unable to have children, that he'd had himself "fixed." He also told her it made it easier to screw any broads he wanted to screw.

The humiliation was too great. Dolores tried to kill herself that night, taking sleeping pills, but not enough and not secretly enough so no one would find her. She spent three weeks in the hospital, where doctors tried to cheer her up, and when she came out, she seemed to have accepted what was the fact of her life and marriage. Julie had hoped she'd get a divorce from Harry and find a man who really loved her, cared about her, treated her with some respect. But she didn't. She seemed not to care about anything anymore. She lived the façade of being the Bel Air housewife, spending a fortune on clothes, living in the beauty parlor, attending teas. She put Harry Sheppard into debt for the first time, and she liked doing it. But it still wasn't enough. He wasn't sleeping with her anymore; he often spent nights out. What she did to him wasn't coming close to what he was doing to her; she couldn't hurt him enough. So she found a friend named Ballantine, a label on a bottle.

And she'd been with him ever since.

Julie had seen her drunk, falling-down drunk, several times. It sickened her, but she tolerated it. Harry always apologized. Julie and Bob accepted. But never had Julie seen her put away what she'd put away in just one day and still remain coherent. It was as if her body were already saturated; more booze made no difference. Or was it the fright, the fear that was keeping her one foot into sobriety? Was it the worry about Harry and the panic over the weather that was keeping her from passing out cold from all the scotch? And the brandy. And now ... now the what? Julie reached over and turned the bottle around. The vodka.

"Honey," Bob said.

Julie turned and looked startled. "Oh, yes, I'm sorry, I was thinking."

"I'm closing up the den. There are too many windows; the air is coming in as though there's holes in the wall. Do you want anything out of here?"

Julie got up and went into the den with him. She took all the plants down and carried them into the living room. If she could save them, she would. Then she looked at the shelves and took down three or four books she hadn't read. "Maybe I'll get to them," she said.

That was it. Bob shut the heating vent and pulled the shades, blew out the candle, then he shut the doors leading to the living room and locked them. He went around in the hall and closed the other door leading to the den.

They blew out the candles in the living room. Dolores was already snoring. They stood in the dining room for a few minutes, looking out over the snow-covered yard. "Will it ever let up?" Julie ask.

Bob just shook his head. He didn't know. "Let's get some sleep," he said.

And they went upstairs.

Harry opened his eyes to see someone lying on the old battered sofa, just across the room from him. It was the woman's son, the oldest of the kids. The house was quiet now, and the candles were all out but for one on the top of the TV. "You've been sleeping real sound," the kid said.

"Yeah. Really tired."

"You really do public relations work?"

Harry nodded, stretching.

"I think that's exciting. I'm in college, and I want to get into industrial advertising. What do you think of that field?"

"I think it's shit. It's all shit. Get some sleep, kid."

"Gee." The boy was silent for a while. Then he got up, in his undershorts and a thick sweater, and went into the kitchen. He came back chomping on a cookie. "You feeling okay? I mean does your arm hurt? Ma asked me to tell you there's aspirin in the kitchen in case it hurts, in case you woke up."

"Listen, I'm fine, never felt better. Don't even feel the arm. I need some sleep."

The boy walked over to the window and looked out onto the glassed-in front porch. "Can I ask you a question? Why are you carrying that big hose with you?"

"It's my favorite keepsake," Harry said sarcastically.

"You don't like me, do you?"

Harry turned and looked up at him. "Hey, kid, sure I do. I'm just sleepy, that's all. I appreciate what you've done for me, but

I'd appreciate you even more if you didn't take this seriously and got some sleep yourself."

The boy sat down on the couch again. "What's in the hose?"

"Is that any of your business?"

"I'm curious by nature."

"Papers. Important papers."

"Wow," the kid said, and crawled back under the blanket. He looked at the ceiling. "Wow," he said again.

Harry felt paranoid. Had the kid looked in the hose when he was asleep? Did he know he was lying? Were the paintings safe? Maybe they weren't even there any longer. Harry jumped up and looked out onto the porch. The hose was right where he'd left it. "What's wrong?" the boy asked.

"Nothing," Harry mumbled and got back under the blankets.

"You sure are uptight about something. I'll tell you, no matter what the value of some papers, I wouldn't be set on dragging it through all that snow. I'd be more worried about just getting to where it was I had to go. I'd worry about my life."

"You worry about your life, and I'll worry about my business papers, okay?" Harry snorted.

"Sorry. Just making conversation."

Harry lay there awake for nearly an hour, listening to the wind rattle the screens on the windows. He made sure the boy was fast asleep before he even dared close his eyes. Several times he thought about getting up and leaving, but in the dark with the wind doing what it was, he knew he wouldn't get far. And besides, the kid was harmless. He was overreacting.

Overreacting or not, he didn't sleep well the rest of the night. He kept getting up and checking to see that the kid was there, that the fire hose was there. Neither the hose nor the kid had moved. The boy had a peaceful sleep; Harry had a sporadic, uncomfortable one. And he had no one to blame but himself.

Carter looked over the list of designated shelters in the city and surrounding areas. "They're not going to do it," Rob said. "I think we've got to use large private homes as well. All the public buildings and movie theaters and churches and sound stages in the city won't hold the people who've already lost homes and apartments."

"You're a pain in the ass, Wynters," Alex Granville said, "but you're right as usual. Right about the number of people. Wrong about private homes. How do we get Zsa Zsa Gabor to open her house to the masses? *Come in for coffee, dahlings?* Come on. You try and get past the dogs, past the electric gates of those rich bastard mansions in Bel Air. You can't just knock on the door and order the house open to the public."

"Then what's the answer?" Rob asked.

"I think there's gonna be a war down there. A class war. And the underdogs are gonna win, and we can't do a damn thing about it except treat people at the shelters we've got staffed and thank the Lord we can do that much."

Carter groaned. "I always wondered what 'bleak' meant. I mean I never found a situation where I felt the word was right to use. I think I have now."

Bob Sheppard went into the den and pushed one of the wicker chairs away from the closed cabinets under the bookshelves. Inside were piles of *Time* magazines, issues which he'd been saving for years, all the important ones. Julie had always kidded him, asking when he was going to toss out all those yellowing magazines he never seemed to go back and read. But they'd often come in handy, not only for business reference, but for personal revelation and memories as well.

He saved what he considered the issues with the big, important news. All the presidential elections, the assassinations of the Kennedy brothers, Dr. King, reports on important trends and fads, even issues which were important to him only for one or two pages of innovative advertising. He was fumbling with the stack marked "1977" when Julie came up to him. "What are you looking for?"

"It must be here in the Carter inauguration issue."

"What?"

"Stories about the winter that year."

"Oh. What for?"

"Just to see ... well, to read what they did back east ... oh, here, early February, here's something ... the *Roots* cover issue...."

Julie walked away. Bob took the magazine into the living room and sat by the fire. He flipped through the pages and read of the big freeze, the gas shortage, the icy grip the weather had over the land in 1977. He came to a specific story on Buffalo, the hardest hit city in the country, and he read with interest:

> The storm fostered a new spirit of camaraderie in the city. Bars were jammed with customers who could not get home. At the Rail Bar, bartender Casimer Kania ordered ten patrons to leave as each group of ten entered; he feared the floor would cave in under the crowd's weight.

"Julie, listen to this," Bob said. She came and sat by him. He read aloud, and even Dolores picked her head up and seemed attentive. " '... at Salvatore's Italian Gardens Restaurant in Lancaster, free sandwiches for everyone replaced costly Chateaubriand ...' "

"Oh, God, no!" Dolores moaned. "Harry would starve first."

Bob continued, " '... and fire departments set up soup and spaghetti lines. The Salvation Army served meals to 25,000 people, clothed 4,000 and gave medical supplies to 3,000. Citizens offered their snowmobiles for emergency rescue missions.' "

Julie remarked, "I'd like to see someone in Los Feliz with a snowmobile."

" 'Residents without electricity or gas found others willing to take them into their homes.' " Bob stopped and took a deep breath. "I think I'm reading about LA. They could print the same story and just change the location." He read on and then again, quoted aloud. " '... still, Buffalo also discovered its dark side during the siege. There was widespread looting of abandoned vehicles–' "

"My car!" Dolores cried out, and then bit the back of her hand, as if to tell them she was ashamed for worrying about her silly car.

" '—and vacant drug and jewelry stores. On a single night, 60 arrests were made by justifiably angry police.' " Julie said she couldn't imagine how there could be any police out on the streets of Los Angeles anymore. " 'Finally, Buffalo got help. President Carter first declared a regional state of emergency so that federal funds could be used to remove snow and restore health and safety services. The Army flew in 300 men from . . .' " Bob looked up. "That was General Granville. He's in charge *here*."

"Oh, damn," Dolores muttered. They looked at her. "Don't be so damned foolish to think some money from Congress is going to help us. They've been freezing their tails off in Boston—"

"Buffalo," Bob corrected her.

"Boston, Buffalo, what's the difference? They had it hard, sure, but they were ready for it. I mean, everyone there had some long johns in the closet, some nice woolly hats, and big pots of winter stew on the stoves. If someone chooses to live in such a godforsaken place as Bos . . . Buffalo, they deserve what they get. We don't. We don't deserve this one bit." She was getting worked up, running her hands through her hair, almost shouting. "We lose our husbands and our cars and our self-respect and our minds in this! No one's going to fly in here because you *can't* fly in this. No one's going to remove the goddamn snow because no one knows *how*. I sure as hell don't. Hah. Tell your general up on the hill to go back to Boston where he belongs. He can't do anything here. There's no hope. There's nothing anymore. . . ." Her voice drifted off, and then she jumped up and ran into the kitchen.

Bob looked at Julie. "I didn't mean to upset her. I was just fascinated how alike this situation is, reading about Buffalo."

"I know. Bob, she's so fragile; she's not well. Sometimes I want to hold her, comfort her, and other times I get . . . well, when she said no one knows how to remove snow, I wanted to tell her to breathe on it, with all that liquor in her. . . ."

"Julie," he cautioned, "she'll hear you."

Julie whispered. "I detest self-pity. I will not have self-pity and the feeling of giving up in my house." She rubbed her temples. The strain showed in her eyes. "Oh, Bob," she moaned, cuddling in his arms, "everyone has to remain positive. We *must.* Or . . . or I'll break down just like Dolores."

Bob just held her tight. It was the most positive thing he could do.

A moment later, more relaxed, Julie asked, "Do you think there will be a feeling of camaraderie? Or will it—" He stopped her by showing her the title of the article he'd been reading. She glared at it. "Buffalo: Camaraderie and Tragedy." Then he pointed to the last word and shook his head. "I thought so," she said. "I don't see how it can be any other way. This is so much—*so much*—worse."

"We'll make it, darling," Bob said. He kissed her gently and looked at the fire. Heat, he thought. It had never seemed precious before. "We have to make it. We have no choice."

The U.S. Army truck pulled up to the doors of Hollywood High School, to the doors leading to the gymnasium, and twenty-five cold but hopeful people got out, among them Lorna and Michael and Dawn, Flora and her father, Greg and Tom, and Kenny Rupp and his girlfriend. They walked inside, into the warm air, and their faces dropped. The place was a horror movie, hundreds upon hundreds of people on cots, on the floor, children crying, dogs barking, hopeless faces, doctors and nurses, the smell of medicine and sweat.

They settled together in a corner, but within half an hour Greg had begun to help the paramedics, and Lorna was comforting other families who'd just come in from out of the cold. Even Michael sat with a group of youngsters and told them jokes and made them laugh. Harvard and Flora marveled at their friends' energy and interest in helping others. Tom watched Greg moving near the examining tables in a white coat. He felt proud. Finally, they were doing something, not merely waiting it out. Tom asked what he could do to help, and he was told he could roll bandages in the morning, help with getting the medical and food supplies which would be dropped by helicopter when the weather allowed, any number of things. He felt useful, too.

Finally, Greg came and lay down next to him, and they slept. Lorna and Michael caught a few winks, too. Only Kenny Rupp couldn't sleep; he was too wracked with guilt over the fire. He sat up all night, his eyes red, his head pounding.

The picture of the bodies of Marguerita and the old man from the corner apartment would not leave his head.

Susan struggled to get out of bed. She staggered at first but caught herself on the windowsill. She looked outside, and the snow was blowing harder than ever. She opened her door, Samantha ran out to the kitty box, and Susan crept into the living room. She smiled. Auntie Dee was snoring.

Then she saw the den doors were closed, and she realized it must have been getting too cold. All the plants were on the piano in the corner of the room. She went back to the bedroom.

Pushing the curtains aside, she opened the window. It took all her strength, but she did it. She reached out and grabbed a handful of snow. She brought it to her lips and tasted it. It was cold and soothing. She tossed it back outside and rubbed her fingers over the flakes which were blowing against the glass. Oh, if she could only go outside for a while and play in it.

She cringed and fell forward a little. A sharp pain went through her stomach, and then she bent bent backward as it radiated around to her lower back. She reached up and pulled the window shut and eased herself down into bed again. She went as long as she could, biting on her thumb, holding her pillow tight with her fists, contorting her body into every conceivable position which would ease the pain. Then she could go on no longer.

She called her parents. Bob came down, gave her a hypo, and left. She closed her eyes, trying to relax, letting it work. She didn't even know what day it was anymore. She had lost track. She began to wish for the first time that she were in the hospital because whenever she left there, she was better. She wondered if they could go tomorrow. The pain wasn't getting better; it was getting worse each time. Something had to be done about it. Susan vowed she'd tell her mom and dad she wanted to go to the hospital. She knew she was supposed to have another operation. She even looked forward to it, for in her mind she thought it would cure her; it would make all the pain and suffering go away. She wanted that more than anything in the world.

Even more than the chance to play in the snow.

THE SIXTH DAY

TUESDAY, JANUARY 20
HIGH TEMPERATURE 19°; LOW 9°

JULIE GOT UP AND PUT ON HER ROBE. THE ROOM WAS WARM, but just the knowledge that there was snow outside seemed to chill her to the bone. She went into the bathroom, closing the door softly so as not to wake Bob. He'd gotten up twice during the night to give Susan hypos. She wanted him to get as much sleep as he could.

But she had to wake him when she came out of the bathroom because standing at the bedroom window, she saw someone moving through the snow, toward the front gate. "Bob! Bob, look!" He jumped up, alert, awake, and peered out of the window with her. They both were astonished to see Dolores trying to make her way through the snow to the road.

Bob opened the window. A pile of snow, which had gathered on the outer windowsill, fell into the room. *"Dee! Dee, come back! Dee!"* But she didn't hear, or if she did, she ignored him. He slammed the window shut. "Goddamn!" he muttered, and slipped into a pair of pants.

"What's she doing? Where's she going?" Julie asked, still at the window.

"Four feet of snow, and she's trying to walk in it," he said, putting on a shirt. Then he pulled a thick sweater over his head.

"She's probably delirious, out looking for Harry or some such thing." He stuffed his feet into his shoes.

"Bob, you're not going out there?"

"Of course, I'm going out there. Somebody's got to stop her." He jumped up and headed for the stairs. She followed. "Someone's got to talk some sense into her."

"Bob, just don't get lost—"

"Julie, come on, how am I going to get lost in my own front yard?" He put his mackinaw on.

"But you could . . . maybe you'll have to chase her far."

"You realize what you're saying? She can barely walk in the house, much less through four feet of snow. Julie, relax." He opened the front door and kicked the snow away from the outer screen door. Then he pushed it open and started down through the drifts of snow. Dolores had gone out the back door and down the steps by the garage. She evidently had not wanted them to hear her.

Julie ran back upstairs, to the master bedroom window, where she could see. Dolores had already reached the gates and had tried to get them to open by pulling the lever in the little box a few feet up the drive on the inside. But the snow stopped the gates from moving more than a few inches. She pulled on them, tugged them, and finally she slipped through. But Bob was fast, he knew what he was doing, and he caught up to her right outside the brick wall. Julie couldn't hear them, but she could see a confrontation. Dolores waved her arms through the air, and Bob kept trying to get her back inside the gates, pulling her arm, motioning to her, but she resisted. Finally, he seemed to give up, leaving her there. He turned and made his way back up the drive. Dolores watched him for a moment, and Julie thought—for a second—that she was going to follow him. But she abruptly turned and trudged through the snow in the street, going down the hill, disappearing into the trees.

Julie ran downstairs as Bob came to the door. She helped him off with his jacket. "What happened? I watched. What did she say? Where is she going?"

"To get liquor."

"What?"

"You heard it. She's going begging. She told me to tell you she's sorry if she's disgracing you to your neighbors, but anything's better than the DTs."

"She . . . she said that?"

Bob nodded, rubbing the snow off his hair. "It's coming down easier now, you notice?"

"Yes. What . . . what else did she say?"

"Nothing. I kept telling her to come back, but she kept saying there was nothing to drink and begged me to understand she needs something to drink. She'll be back when she finds some generous person down the street to give her a bottle."

"But the snow, after her ordeal the first night, how can she even stand to walk through it?"

"I don't know. Got some coffee on?"

"Right away." Julie walked into the kitchen, and Bob followed. She dumped some grounds into the Bunn and went to the sink to get cold water for the machine. "What am I doing?"

"Huh?"

"There's no electricity. We've got to have instant. Or pull out that old coffeepot that my mom used to have. I think it's in the closet in the hall somewhere."

"Instant's fine." Bob sat down and popped a cookie into his mouth. "I wonder when the gas will go?"

"Don't say that," she begged as she turned on the flame under the teakettle.

"Hey, look." She turned. He pointed to a bottle sitting on the counter. It hadn't been there the night before. "Cooking sherry. Do you think she was drinking it?"

Julie studied the bottle. "No, it's about where it was, the same level. But she was looking for more booze. Oh, I just don't understand that kind of dependency."

"It's a disease, honey. Come on, you've read enough about it. You know what it's like. Remember that kid in the hospital, little Tommy, addicted to Demerol? It's the same thing. He would have killed for a shot. A twelve-year-old kid! It's the same with Dolores. That's the force that made her go out there in her mink coat and a pair of my old boots, banging on people's doors, asking for a drink. She can't live without it, or so she thinks."

Julie stood near the warmth of the teakettle and put instant coffee into the mugs. "I wish to God this were over. I don't know how much longer we can take it, Bob."

"As long as we have to."

She turned to him questioningly.

"We have no other choice."

Harry had spent a sleepless night, but when morning came, he drifted into a deep sleep despite the noise of the children in the house. When he finally did wake up—at 11 A.M.—he jumped up with a start. The woman and her mother were in the kitchen cooking something, huddled around the stove. Two little kids were playing with dolls and building blocks on the floor. The oldest boy was nowhere to be seen. Harry looked out the window onto the front porch. "My paintings!" he shouted.

The women turned to him.

"Where is the hose? The fire hose? Your boy took it. I know he took it! Where is he?"

"Now, hush up, there's no cause for alarm," the woman said. "How's your arm this morning?"

"Where is he? Where'd he go with it?" The porch was covered with broken furniture, pieces of tables and chairs. The door opened, and he saw the boy who'd been sleeping across the room from him toss another busted chair onto the pile. "There he is! Goddammit! Get him!" Harry tried to push his way through the kitchen, to the back door. He knew he'd never be able to open the door leading to the porch with all that junk piled up there.

But the women stopped him. "Have you taken leave of your senses?" the older lady called to him, screaming in his ear.

The other one said, "Your silly hose is safe; it's just out back here. Jimmy Joe moved it so's we could put the wood on the porch for burning in the fireplace."

Harry opened the door and looked outside. Sure enough, the hose was there, hanging on a spoke of the fence which separated the yard from the alley. He went out into the snow and felt it with his bare fingers. It wouldn't give. He pressed harder. There was something in it. The paintings hadn't been touched. He let out a breath and realized he was standing in his stockinged feet. He ran back inside the house, just before Jimmy Joe was about to ask him what he was doing out there without a jacket or shoes.

"Ladies, I'm sorry ... it's just, well, important papers." He stomped the snow from his socks. "God, it's cold out there."

"Warmer'n last night," the old lady said.

The other woman said, "Jimmy Joe told us all about the chat you had last night. We know that there hose has meaning to you, but we had no choice but to put it on the fence. We're making off with the restaurant furniture as fast as we can. Figure on burning it. That there fire hose's waterproof, so I don't think you have to worry about your things getting wet. Mighty smart place to put valuables, I must say, Mr. Sheppard."

Harry smiled a little. "Yes, well, thank you. I'd best be getting on my way. I have to go up Western Avenue all the way to Griffith Park. Maybe I should take Vermont. Well, we'll see." He sat down and put his ski boots on.

"If what I says means anything," the old lady said with a cackle, "you won't be going anywheres. People are crazy to go out there for anything."

"I must join my family."

"You're gonna freeze doing it!" She slammed the oven door. "It's a curse on us all. A curse for our wicked ways."

"Oh, Mother, shut your mouth now," the woman said. "I wish you well, Mr. Sheppard. You'll make it. Care for some toast? I got some bread left from the restaurant before that crazy soldier started shooting."

"Yes, just a piece." Harry put his coat on and waited for the toast. The woman told him what she'd heard from her neighbor early that morning. That people from the central core of the city were taking to the mountains, killing if they had to, to reach higher ground. It wasn't as if there would be less snow up there. "Ah, but there are houses up there. Just the fact that there are houses up there, most of them big and warm ones." He thought of his beautiful home in Bel Air. God, what kinds of hippies were camping out in there? What had happened to his collection? The thought pained him, his paintings being stolen, perhaps burned to stay warm. He wondered if Dolores had packed everything into the car, the jewels, the mortgage papers, the insurance policies. Did she look at any of them? Jesus, if she did, she might have found out how little money they really had. How much he'd borrowed over the years to maintain their life-style. . . .

Jesus, what was he thinking about? How could that matter now? Was he forgetting about the fire hose, the paintings? The woman was talking to him, but he wasn't listening. He was telling himself what an ass he was.

". . . do you think that could be?"

"Pardon me?" Harry said.

"I asked if you think it could be."

"What?"

"That people are committing suicide, thinking it's the end of the world?"

Harry shook his head. "No, certainly not, unless they're depressive fanatics."

"My friend says so many people tried to get out of the city by car that every road, freeway and little mountain passes are full of abandoned cars. Buses are laying on their sides, every which way, snow blowing over them, deserted."

"Good God. How does she know all this?"

"Shortwave radio. One of those CB things, I think. Her boy's got one, got it for Christmas. People calling for help all over the place. Hear it's snowing all the way to Palm Springs. Frank Sinatra won't be doing any sunning at his pool today. Hah!"

"I must go," Harry said, looking out the window. "At least it's let up."

"But still falling a little. Over four feet by now. Can you believe it? I hope we live through it to tell our kids' kids."

"We will, we will." Harry bent over and kissed the woman on the cheek. "You've been wonderful. Listen, I hope I get back to thank you someday."

"You're crazy to go out there," the old lady said, looking into the oven.

"Oh, Ma, shut your mouth now. God bless, Mr. Sheppard." The woman waved him on and shut the door.

Outside, Harry picked up the heavy hose and met Jimmy Joe out front. "See ya around, kid."

"Sure, man. Hey, you want an old sack or something to put over that?"

Harry eyed him suspiciously. "Why?"

"So everybody don't look at you. It looks like you got something you want to hide in there."

Harry wondered if that was true or if the kid was only saying it because he'd been told something important was in it. "Have you got a sack?"

"Yeah, right here," the boy said. He opened the porch door and pulled out a big laundry bag. It was filled with eight-track tapes and cassettes, all of them unopened. He dumped them onto the porch floor.

"You've been doing a little scavenging yourself, I see," Harry said.

"Sure, why not? Trouble is I don't have anything to play them on. Someone got all the records in the place before we got there. Here." He handed Harry the sack, and he pulled it over the hose. Part of it stuck out, but he knew it might be easier to drag it along in the snow.

"Thanks, kid," Harry said as he walked away.

"See ya around."

There was quite a difference from the yard to the street, Harry realized very quickly. The woman had gotten her kids to keep shoveling the walk. The street was piled high with snow. Some big trucks–National Guard and city trucks equipped with snow tires and chains mostly–had packed the snow down in the middle of the street, but the sidewalks, or where he guessed the sidewalks to be, were just huge mounds of drifted snow. In some places it was at least six feet high, piled up. In other spots he could actually see pavement or grass.

He moved down Wilshire slowly. He saw cars which had been abandoned in the streets and a bus on its side. The woman's neighbor had been right. It was incredible. The only time he remembered seeing anything like it was the pictures of the big blizzard that wreaked havoc on Buffalo in '77 and paralyzed Chicago in the late '60s. He laughed. That would look like a tea party next to this.

He pushed on, determined to get to his brother's house by nightfall. Every time he felt tired, cold, he just thought about the paintings. Then his energy would rise; his feet seemed to plod on almost despite his weariness. He had to make it to Bob's before Bob got out of the city.

What he didn't know was Bob had no intention of getting out of the city, no inkling of it. There was no reason to—the house was secure; they had food and heat and water for two weeks. The only person who had to get out was Susan. Either get her to help or get the help to her.

Harry had visions of the whole family boarding a plane after an escorted ride in an Army truck to the airport. Bob had only a vision of a surgeon arriving by helicopter as they carried Susan into the hospital.

But the brothers were still miles apart, and no one knew if they would even see each other again. Bob, in fact, had pretty much given up on Harry. But Harry hadn't given up on Bob. He'd be there by night or he wasn't Harry Sheppard.

Whatever that meant.

Michael and Lorna and the others had slept from sheer exhaustion and sadness. The loss of Marguerita and Mr. Rosenberg, their apartment building, the aching in their bones from all they'd done in the past days, the emotional strain—everything was taking its toll. And now they had more responsibility. With morning upon them, Greg had started to help pets, mainly cats and dogs that people had brought with them, treating them as best he could without the proper medication and utensils. He thought about statistics. So many times he'd read that some 80,000 people had been killed in a flood in some country like China. But whoever thought of animals at a time like that? No one gave statistics on them. They were living things, more innocent than any human being. He knew there were 50 million pets in Los Angeles. What about them? They couldn't loot stores for food and clothing. They were completely dependent. Someone had to help them. He would do what he could.

Lorna attended a group meeting and was elected—she volunteered—as the director of her section. A council was formed to keep the place running smoothly, and Lorna was helping people adjust, helping calm them and assure them they were safe. Tom, Michael, and several other young men had made trips outside into the snow on the football field, to retrieve dropped parcels of food and water and medication, even magazines and candy. But there was bickering over the food and clothing once it was brought inside, and Michael said, "That's your division," to Lorna as she gave him an exasperated look. And it was her job. She tried to calm the people and divide the supplies evenly.

The only person of the group from Genesee Gardens who wasn't moving was Kenny Rupp. He sat alone on a cot. Even his girlfriend had gone to work, helping the doctors in the corner of the gym, holding people down while they were bandaged, holding the hand of someone who was frightened. But Kenny had withdrawn into himself. He sat there, nervously pulling at the frayed bottoms of his jeans, pulling on his long blond hair, looking lost. Lorna had tried to talk to him, but he snapped, "Just fuck off, huh?" So she let him alone, but not without a word about his being a baby to feel so guilty. He didn't respond.

Tom came in from the outside again and went over to the cot that he and Greg were sharing. He flopped back on it. Flora and her father had been helping a black woman and her children get settled—they'd gotten stuck in their car and the husband had tried to push it but slipped and hit his head on the bumper and died instantly—helping them in their grief. The doctor had given the woman a strong sedative, and Flora had rocked the youngest child to sleep. The others lay near the mother and finally fell asleep. "I thought *we* had it bad," Flora said to Tom.

"Yeah, we all did, until you meet your neighbors." Tom shut his eyes. "Jesus, what a lousy dream. And it's starting up again out there, the winds, snowing harder. I think that's the last of the drops today."

Harvard said, "Florabelle, I praise the Lord your mama didn't live to see this day." He lay back on his cot and coughed.

"You feelin' all right, Daddy?"

"Yup. Fine, just fine. Doctor says I got a *hundred* years in me yet."

Flora smiled and kissed him on the forehead. "I gotta get me something to drink." She got up and walked over to the food table. The woman gave her a glass of orange juice—a grocery warehouse nearby had been stocked with frozen orange juice, and most of it had been saved and brought to the gymnasium. Flora drank it and shook her head. It didn't taste like the orange juice she was used to.

As she was walking back to the cots, she noticed a young guy she'd seen when they first came in the night before. He smiled at her, and she walked up to him. "Hi," she said.

"Hi. Where you from?"

"Genesee, near Santa Monica. Place burned down. How about you?"

"I'm from back east. Just hanging around Hollywood for a few days. Now I guess I'll be here longer than I planned. Man, this is one fucking trip, ain't it?"

"Sure is," Flora said. She sized him up and wondered if she dare ask. . . .

"That your dad?"

She looked over to the corner. "Yes. He had a bad fall and then was in the building when it blew up. He's lucky to be alive. He's strong as an ox. Listen. . . ."

"Yeah?"

"You got—"

"Grass? No. Wish I did. Nobody here's got any. I've been asking. I'd sell my ass for a toke right now."

"No, man, a Valium. Even a Librium, I'd settle for a Librium."

He shook his head. "No, but see that chick over there?" He pointed.

"The big woman with the blue hair?"

"Yeah, she's dealing."

"You're kiddin' me! Her?"

"It's always the rich housewives that got more shit than you can believe. Her old man's probably a doctor. She's a walking pharmacy, I tell ya. She'll barter just about anything for it."

"Hey, thanks–what's your name?"

"Jake."

"Thanks, Jake." Flora offered her hand.

"Sure. . . ."

"Flora."

"Flora. Listen, I'll take you for a sleigh ride tomorrow, huh?"

She said coyly, "I'll have to check with my daddy first, see if he'll let me go out with you."

"Could I see ya when they turn out the lights tonight?"

Flora didn't answer him. She just smiled and left him hanging. Then she went up to the blue-haired woman, who was dressed in a flowered nightgown which looked like a shower curtain. It cost Flora her ring, the one her mother had given her. But she had ten little blue pills in her hand now.

She asked for another orange juice.

Dolores returned to the house. Bob and Julie gave her as much comfort and help as she would accept, but she seemed determined to keep her pride in front of them, keep some shred of dignity. She changed into a warm robe Julie had ready for her and soaked her cold feet in warm water with mineral salts. She told them she was glad she'd gone out. "I know why Harry's taking so long," she stated, still clinging to the hope that he was going to show up at the house. "The snow is so high, unbelievably high. Down the hill you can see silver things sticking out of the snow."

Julie asked, "Silver things? What?"

"Car antennas. I realized I was walking on top of a car. The drifts are over people's heads."

"Is there anyone out there?" Bob asked.

"No. Some people trying to shovel out. A woman who gave me a drink." She paused, feeling uncomfortable for a moment. Then she said, "A wonderful woman *understood,* and we shared a cocktail. She told me people have been seeking shelter anywhere they can find it. Buildings are collapsing from the snow on the roofs. I could see smoke, black smoke, from fires. She said there's fires everywhere. Her husband's a policeman."

Julie interrupted. "That's got to be Helen Morton. Her daughter's in Susan's class. In the stucco house, on the other side of the street, about a third of the way down the hill?"

"Yes, that's right."

"Are they okay?"

"They're fine."

"Did you tell them we're all right up here?"

Dolores gave her a strange look. "I didn't think you'd want anyone to know I was related to you."

"Oh, Dee." Julie turned her head away.

"I didn't say where I came from. She never asked. I just said I had friends in the area. Anyhow, they've estimated that over ten thousand people have died already, mostly older folk, senior citizens. She said her husband had been down on Hollywood Boulevard last night, right down near the corner at Western Avenue, and he said people had been huddled inside a laundromat, around a city trash can that they'd been burning anything that would burn inside. She said she's worried because of the looting and the fact that people have no place to go. The small apartment buildings have no heat. People are going to start attacking these houses, she said."

"Oh, Bob!"

He put his arms around his wife. "Julie, no one's going to hurt us. No one'll get in those gates."

Dolores lifted her feet from the pan and rubbed her toes with the towel. "They're still predicting more snow, a few more feet of it." Julie got up and walked out of the room, shaking. Dolores pulled slippers onto her feet and went to her coat. In the pocket was an unopened bottle of scotch. She held it up and looked at it. Bob just stared at her, a slight grin on his face. She looked at him, and her eyes were suddenly soft, apologetic, asking for his approval. "Please ... I'm sorry about this morning. Please try to understand. ..."

He put his hand up. "Not another word. It's okay."

She frowned, looking at the label, opening the bottle. "Never heard of the stuff, but it's better than drinking wood alcohol, huh?"

"Yeah."

She poured some into a glass and then walked to the window and forced it open. She reached out, scooped some snow off the sill, and dumped it into the glass. Then she closed the window and sat down and curled up on the couch. "I swear to you," she said to Bob, "if we get through this alive, I'm gonna go AA."

Bob said, "If we get through this, I'm gonna start to drink."

Across the country, the American people heard Walter Cronkite reporting on the phenomenon which was now being called the Great Los Angeles Blizzard. "The President, just out of a Cabinet meeting, issued a statement that everything will and is being done to help stricken Southern California. And what is the state of the snowbound city which at this time of the year should be having a little rain at most? Well, reports in say the reality of the situation staggers the imagination. Certainly the mounting damage reports in so far do. No American city has suffered so, ever. Only San Francisco perhaps could claim it had gone through worse hell, and there the residents were taken by surprise. What has happened and is happening in Los Angeles has been previewed by increasingly bad weather for months now. The death toll is near fifteen thousand at this time, and how many more are injured or missing is anyone's guess.

"The city is totally crippled. The port was closed after two freighters collided, blocking the right-of-way. The airports were closed; the railroads are not running. Nothing on wheels can move except for specially prepared military vehicles. The Army is trying to get snowmobiles, tractors, trucks with huge snow tires into the city as fast as they can, but most passages to the city are blocked. The automobile, the symbol of Los Angeles, is nowhere. They're all buried in the snow.

"The commercial outlook is just as poor. Industry halted when the cars did. There's no natural gas left and no way to get any supplies in. Steel mills closed their furnaces down, which means it will take weeks to get them back to temperature. Warehouses and mills are empty, silent. Out in the harbor in the Pacific, a pipeline that runs underwater to the shore from a point where supertankers unload their Alaskan oil has begun to leak, but nothing can be done now to stop it. By the time something can be done the damage may be overwhelming. Ships with precious heating oil sit frozen in Los Angeles Harbor."

Across the country people sat in front of their television sets with their mouths open, trying to comprehend such stories. It wasn't too difficult for those who lived in places where it did snow and where lousy weather was common. It wasn't difficult either for people who had visited California and knew the possibility of such a thing as snow was unthinkable, with all those beautiful ocean breezes, those palm trees, the pools, and the orange juice. To the people with no real fixed image of California in their minds, they felt it was too bad, of course, but they really didn't understand how unique and far-reaching the disaster had become. And they wouldn't understand until it affected them—economically—in the months to come. What would happen when there was almost no fruit left in the stores? No vegetables? Why were all the TV shows in rerun? Why were no new movies opening? Then they'd understand.

About the time Cronkite was talking about the stricken city, Carter DeSimone was talking to Bob Sheppard. "You've been a propaganda expert for the government, Bob. What way can we get word to people? Air-drop leaflets, what? The worse part of the situation is the panic in the streets. There's no communication of any kind except for shortwave radios. People have been wearing down their transistor radios."

"You've got to set up communications posts at all the shelters, even in trucks designated for such purposes, in the middle of the neighborhoods," Bob said. "People listen to the military, I said that before. It's important that the Army and Marines get posts set up where bulletins can be issued."

"We're getting loudspeaker trucks in. Seems the mayor and others had them lying around from their last campaign."

Bob laughed. "Last hurrah."

"No, seriously, there are some in the city, mainly at the movie studios. We're getting them set up. The city is taking on the air of a town under siege in World War Two."

"This is worse," Bob said. "Then we knew who the enemy was. Here we don't; it's intangible. How do you bomb raindrops? How do you combat snow? Shoot 't the dead?"

"Where's your brother?"

"We don't know."

"I'd like to pick his hardhearted brain. He's bound to have some ideas. That's what you two guys do so successfully together, don't you?" Carter asked sarcastically.

"Harry would come up with some devious scheme," Bob said. "I probably wouldn't agree with it, ethically, but it would work, by God. His ideas always do. They're just short of breaking the law, but they sure do work."

"There are no more laws to break, not in this. How's your girl?"

"Bad. She's got to get to a surgeon."

Carter DeSimone said to Bob, "No doctor's going to get in here. You say it's impossible to get her to a hospital?"

Bob shook his head. "You know what the streets are like."

Julie put her head near the radio. "Carter, can you get her out? Can you just get her out?"

"That's what I was going to say. We're going to have to get people out by helicopter. There's a chance. I'm working on it. She'll be the first on my list. I really think we can arrange it somehow. Damn," he said, "we're just going to *have* to arrange it, won't we?"

"If she can only get to a good surgeon—" Bob stopped when he heard Carter tell him he had to go. But Bob and Julie felt better; there was hope for their daughter.

Harry felt as though he were going to faint. He dropped to his knees. The stubble on his face had turned into a beard, and he felt it with his glove and it itched. He let himself fall backward into the snow, and he took a deep breath. The snow had stopped falling, but the wind was blowing. He knew he'd never make it to Bob's now, not tonight. He'd have to find another place to spend the night. He was on Western Avenue. He figured he was at the halfway mark. It wouldn't have been so bad if he hadn't had the fire hose to lug. It seemed to weigh a ton by now. It made walking difficult. Often he dropped the hose into the snow, and it took precious minutes and energy to lift it back to his shoulder. He'd given up the idea of pulling it in the sack. He could never quite get on top of the snow enough to drag it behind him.

He sat up again and looked at the buildings along the side of the street. It was uphill here, too, it would be all the way to his brother's house, and the thought of braving it at night was unthinkable. So he searched for a place to spend the night. He walked on a bit. There was a furniture store; but the windows had been boarded up, and there was no way to get in. He fantasized about spending the night on a soft bed inside or a big fluffy sofa.

Then he saw a dirty-book store. He looked inside the open door. Jesus, he thought, were they open for business? Inside, only a candle burned on the counter. Two teenage boys sat together on the floor, trying to stay warm under a blanket. In front of them was a loaf of bread. As soon as they saw Harry. they grabbed the bread and held it to their bodies, frightened. He looked around. The place was still filled with porno magazines, movies under the glass counter, "marital aids" and all kinds of sexual toys sitting in a display near the door. No one cared. The bread was the only thing of value in the place. Harry turned and left the boys alone.

Next door was a massage parlor, and a sign in the window said CLOSED. He tried to peer inside, putting his hands up to cup the glass. He saw a large black man sitting on a chair with a pistol in his hand. Harry jerked his face away and moved as fast as he could.

On the corner was a fried chicken place. There were some people inside. Harry walked up to the door, and a man opened it for him. "Come in, we're all in the same situation," the man said. Harry introduced himself. No one seemed much like talking. The people looked tired and numb. Harry was asked by an old man if he had any food. "I'm sorry," Harry said. He sat down. No one asked him about the fire hose. He snuggled his body up against it and fell into a deep sleep.

"I don't give a good goddamn what you did in a college test situation, this is real life, mister!" Lorna had been adamant but soft; now, however, she was letting go. She was shouting.

The fight was over two plans of rationing the food. Lorna had devised one, and so had a man who felt his credentials as a college professor in sociology certainly surpassed Lorna's work as a social worker. So they were having it out. Finally, it was put to a vote, by any of the people in the gym who wanted to voice their opinion. Many of them did. And Lorna's plan lost. She sat down, mumbling that she'd lost because he was a man and thus they believed he knew more, when the truth was her plan seemed the less logical. "Honey, his just sounded wiser," Michael said.

"Men," she said, as if it were a dirty word.

In a few minutes she was right up there, helping her opponent get the system going. But after another couple of hours, the wear and tear were getting to her, and she sat down. "I just want to rest for a while," she said. A woman ran up and asked her to help with some people who'd just come in. Lorna shrugged and got up. Then she saw who they were, and she called out, "Mrs. Quesana! Oh, my God, you're here!" She ran to them, and Michael turned to Greg and Tom and just shook his head.

Dawn was fine. Michael rocked her in the little crib someone had put together. A nurse had taken care of her ever since they'd come in the night before, and she was sure the little girl hadn't suffered anything but fright in the explosion of the apartment house. Now Michael was watching his baby sleep, and he envied her not knowing what was happening around her, envied the fact that she would never remember all this. "Her first words are probably gonna be Frosty the Snowman," Michael said.

"*I* feel like Frosty the Snowman," Tom said. "I froze my balls off out there today." He jabbed Greg with his elbow. "You're in here petting puppies while we're running around a football field in five feet of snow."

Greg laughed. "I never was much good at sports."

"Night, fellas," Michael said, pantomiming tipping a hat.

"Night, Mrs. Calabash, wherever in the snow you are," Tom said.

"Shut your mouth and sleep," Greg moaned.

They closed their eyes. The lights, which were being run by auxiliary generators, had been turned off now, leaving just a few small bulbs burning near the medical corner and the food tables. The gym was crowded, but quiet now. People would rather sleep, Lorna had said, than face it. Sleep was a wonderful escape.

About an hour later Lorna sat down on the cot next to Michael. "That the Quesana family you're always talking about?" he whispered. She nodded. "Hey, why so down?"

"That's *part* of the family. The oldest girl. . . ." She swallowed and brushed her hair back. "She froze to death going out for help. The soldiers found her, and she had a note in her pocket with the address, and they got the rest of them out."

"I'm sorry. I know you felt close to them."

Lorna suddenly began to cry. She turned to her husband and let him take her in his arms. "Michael, I'm beginning to change my mind . . . I want to get out of here."

He couldn't believe what he was hearing. "You're kidding?"

She shook her head and dug her fingers into his shoulders. "I swear. . . ." She turned her head and looked at the suffering humanity around her. "I swear people will start eating each other after a time."

"Lorna, come on."

She pulled back and stared into his eyes. "Michael, Beth Quesana didn't just fall over and die of the cold. She had a bag of cookies when she left. Her mother gave them to her so she would stay strong. Someone had beaten her for a bag of cookies and left her there to die." Lorna sobbed, and Michael held her close. "A bag of cookies," she repeated softly.

"My God," he whispered.

"In the morning let's go to your parents' house . . . just to get away from here, to get to civilized people. . . ."

"Honey, what makes you think things are any different up there? And the streets, how can we get to that side of town? It's coming down like gangbusters again."

Lorna didn't answer. She curled up on the cot and closed her eyes. "I want out," she moaned. "I just can't cut it."

Michael stood up. Well, surprise of surprises, the girl who was going to save the world. He looked down and wondered what to do. He wondered where his better judgment lay. From what he could see, staying where people were being cared for, where food was being dropped, was the correct decision. Sure, he'd love to be with his mom and dad and his uncle and aunt, but Jesus, if it meant risking their lives, forget it. Send a postcard. Wish you were here.

He was wandering around when he noticed something he wished he'd thought about before. A man was sitting by a shortwave radio. Michael ran up and asked if he could try to reach his father. The man told him he'd have to wait a few minutes; he was expecting a report on the helicopters, if they'd be making drops in the morning. The reply finally came through, and the outlook was negative; the winds were just too strong, and the snow showed signs of building. It was a full-fledged blizzard; nothing could fly in it, not even a strong eagle.

Then the man helped Michael. It took nearly twenty minutes, but they finally got through to Bob. "Dad! It's me, it's Michael."

"Oh, God. . . . Julie, it's our son! Michael, how are you, how's the baby, Lorna? Where are you?"

"Dad, we're at the high school, in Hollywood, on Highland. The building, there was an explosion, Mrs. Alvarez threw herself on Dawn to save her life. She was killed." He heard Julie stifle a scream in the background. "Mom, it's okay, we're fine, honest. Lorna wants to come to the house, but I don't think we should risk it."

"Son, Michael, listen to me. Dolores is here, and she's in bad shape. Harry is lost. Susan's not doing well at all. I'm having Carter try to get through to the doctor–"

"Dad, is it safe up there?"

The radio crackled with static. "Michael? You there, son?"

"Dad, is it *safe* up there? There's such stories of—"

"Everything is quiet and safe, Michael. We should be together. Can you get up here?"

"Dad. . . ." He didn't know how to say no, but he didn't know how to say yes either. "Do you think we should try?"

"Michael, listen to me. Closely." Bob's voice changed, and Michael read him. He was telling him more than the words said. "You must come. *Must.* Carter says it's going to be all right. *All right,* do you understand? Michael, it's worth any risk. Come to the house as soon as you can."

"I got ya, Dad."

"We'll wait for you."

Michael rubbed his nose and then lowered his voice. "Dad, Mom ... I ... I love you." He got up and walked away. He couldn't remember if he'd ever told them that so bluntly and simply before. He went back to Lorna and held her as she sniffed. "We're leaving in the morning," he said.

"Oh, Michael." She hugged him and drifted back to sleep.

A few minutes later Flora Reynauld got up and slipped another of the little blue pills in her mouth. She swallowed it with saliva. Then she tiptoed away from her friends and father.

On the other side of the room she slid into another cot. Jake said, "Hello there," and Flora just closed her eyes and felt his body against hers. For the first time in what seemed years, she was going to feel good—at least for an hour or so.

But that hour, in the midst of the worst experience of her life, seemed like an eternity. For an endless hour, at least, she was in heaven.

Right after Michael's call on the radio, Bob got one from Carter. "Bob, listen, I can talk now. We'll get you out by helicopter as soon as it's possible. They say no chopper's going to be in here tomorrow, and I agree, tomorrow's going to be the worst yet. But that's going to be the end of it, I'm sure. Bob, I've got to see you."

"See me?"

"Yes. Listen to me; others can hear us. What I have to tell you is private and important, and we need you up here for a few hours at least. We need your help; we need your mind. Can you climb up the hill?"

"I . . . sure, I can try." Julie stiffened at the thought of being in the house without him.

"Bob, it'll be a test, to see if you can get the family up the hill to the observatory. You've got to try it, in the morning, as soon as it's light. I'll expect you. You'll be back down by night."

"Carter. . . ." Bob paused and looked at his wife. "Okay, I'll take a stab at it."

He turned the radio off and said, "You must understand, it's our only chance of getting out. We've got to get to the top of the hill. I've got to see if we can do it, *how* we can do it. Is the rope still in the garage, with the backpacks we used up in the mountains?"

Julie nodded.

"Good. Listen, I've got to get some sleep. I've got to start out early. Julie, I must do this!" He shook her because tears were flooding her face.

"I know!" She took a deep breath. "Do you want me to be happy about it?"

"No, but I want you to tell me you understand."

Susan cried out from her room.

"I understand," Julie said softly. "I'll go to her." She pulled away and ran to Susan's room. Bob went upstairs. He didn't go into the living room to say good-night to Dolores. She had been drinking steadily for hours, and he figured she wanted to be left alone. He went upstairs and crawled into bed in his clothes.

Julie gave Susan yet another hypo. She cringed this time. It seemed there wasn't any unpunctured skin left on her thighs. She was a pincushion. Her skin was gray now; her eyes were dilated and glassy. "I'm not doing good, Mommy," she moaned.

Julie held the cotton on the place where she'd poked the needle, rubbing gently on the muscle. "We're going to get out, honey. A big helicopter is going to get us out."

"Just like in the beginning of *M*A*S*H*? "

Julie laughed. "Yes, just like the beginning of *M*A*S*H.*"

"Will Samantha be able to go, too? I don't want to leave without Samantha."

"Yes, of course, she'll go. We'll all go. Your brother and Lorna and Dawn are on their way. They'll be here tomorrow."

"Oh, oh, that's good," Susan said. "I worried that–" She stopped and doubled up in pain.

"Shhh, easy," Julie whispered. "Don't talk anymore."

"But I want to–"

"Honey, you need your strength. Get some sleep now. We may be leaving in another day."

Susan just curled up with the pillow against her stomach. Her mother kissed her and left the room.

A few moments later the door opened, and Susan turned to see who was there. "Auntie Dee, is that you?" she asked. She couldn't see very well in the candlelight.

"It's me. Mind if I sit down?" Dolores sat down on the floor and whispered, "I don't think your mother wants me visiting you this late."

"Oh, I'm glad you did. I wanted to talk to someone. I only have Samantha to talk to." At the sound of her name the kitten perked her head up, then dropped it right down again.

"How are you feeling, honey?"

"Mommy just gave me a shot. I get very groggy when I have a shot."

"We're in the same condition, honey."

"Auntie Dee, is Uncle Harry here?"

Dolores took a deep breath and shook her head. "No, darling, he's not here. We don't know where he is. I'm hoping he's in a nice warm place somewhere, eating a nice big hot meal."

"He's not lost in the snow, is he?"

"No, Susan, he's not lost in the snow. It's just that we're not sure where he is. He started to come here, but then the phones went out and more snow piled up and he was at your daddy's office, and that was the last we heard."

"He'll probably come with Michael tomorrow."

Dolores nodded. *Oh,* she thought, *the bliss of a young and simple mind. Susan thinks Michael and Lorna are coming, too. No, sweet thing, no one's coming. No one's coming, ever again.*

"Auntie Dee, will you do something for me?"

"Yes, honey, anything."

"Will you get an ice cube for me, for my lips? I get all dried up, and I can't talk. . . ."

"But there's no electricity . . . wait, I know." She went to the window and opened it and grabbed a handful of snow and set it in the empty water glass on the nightstand next to the bed. "Here, press some to your lips; it's nice and cold." She lifted some of the snow to Susan's mouth, and the girl licked at it, purring like her cat. "Here, a little more, I can't imagine it'll hurt you. . . ."

Susan turned on her back. The pain was obviously bad for a moment. Dolores grabbed her hand and let the girl squeeze it. *Oh, why didn't they let me do this in the first place? What harm is there in this?* "Auntie Dee, do you love Uncle Harry?"

The question startled her. "Ye . . . yes, I do. Very much."

"I do, too. He makes me laugh sometimes when he tells me jokes. I remember when I was little and he bought me that big stuffed lion."

Dolores remembered too. "Yes, how you loved that toy!" A thousand memories flashed in her mind. Good memories of the good gay times. "How a stuffed lion can make you remember so much," she said softly.

"I'm going to say a prayer that he gets here tomorrow. The sister in the hospital taught me a secret prayer that I only use at special times. It's for special people."

"Prayer," Dolores said. She once knew what the word meant. Not any longer.

"I said one for you today, too."

"Susan, what's the next song we're going to do? We haven't talked about one since we started working on 'Send in the Clowns.' "

"I don't know." She sounded sleepy now. "Can I have more ice? Snow."

Dolores rubbed more of the soft snow on her lips, soothing her.

"I've been thinking that there are a lot of old, old songs we've never done. Something like 'Can't Help Lovin' Dat Man of Mine.' "

"How does it go?"

"Oh, I'll sing it for you sometime."

"No, Auntie Dee, please sing it now. Please. I love it when you sing."

"Well. . . ." She made sure the door was closed tightly. They'd never hear her upstairs; the wind was howling too loudly. She started to sing. "Fish gotta swim, birds gotta fly, I've got to love one man till I die, Can't help lovin' dat man of mine." She looked at Susan and said, "It's from *Showboat;* you must know it."

Susan nodded. "But I've never heard it sung so nice. Do some more."

Dolores closed her eyes and softly sang, "Tell me he's lazy, Tell me he's slow, Tell me I'm crazy, maybe I know. Can't help lovin' dat man of mine." She hummed a little and looked at the window and beyond it. "When he goes away, dat's a rainy day, and when he comes back, dat day is fine, the sun will shine. . . ."

"Oh, it's beautiful," Susan whispered.

"He can come home just as late as can be, home without him ain't no home to me, can't help lovin dat man of mine." Dolores closed her eyes and tried to smile.

"I'll learn to play it for you. I promise I will. I . . . oh, I'm feeling so dizzy now."

"Honey, get some sleep. Go ahead, I'll leave you alone." She started to get up.

"No. Please don't go. Hold my hand. Please, hold my hand just for a little while."

Dolores choked up. "Oh, oh, yes, of course." She took Susan's small warm hand and grasped it in both of hers. She felt wanted, needed, cared for. She felt . . . she felt beautiful. She felt something she couldn't even explain to herself, a feeling she thought she once would have had with a child of her own. Susan closed her eyes, and soon her breathing became slower, softer. She was asleep.

Dolores sat there for nearly an hour, just holding Susan's hand, her mind alternating between the dismal future and the wonderful moments of years gone by. She wished for a while that she could be twelve again. She wished she could go off and work up an act together. She wished for so many things, but the reality, she knew, was that she wasn't even going to get what she deserved. Life was unfair. Proof of that statement was this little girl, lying in pain, somewhere close to death.

Dolores gently pulled her hands away and stood up. The kitten watched her as she turned the door handle. She opened it slowly, so as not to make a sound. But she heard a voice behind her: "Auntie Dee, I love you very much."

She didn't look back. She stood there, unable to move. She began to cry, her whole body shaking. She opened her mouth to tell Susan she loved her, too, but no words would come. She ran from the room and fell onto the couch in the living room.

Susan could hear her crying all the way in her room.

THE SEVENTH DAY

WEDNESDAY, JANUARY 21
HIGH TEMPERATURE 14°; LOW 0°

BOB AND JULIE GOT UP AT THE TIME THE SUN WAS SUPPOSED TO rise, but there was no sun, just a white haze in the sky and the strong wind and still more snow. But that wasn't the main concern. The bedroom felt cold. Bob breathed hard. He could just make out his breath in the air. "The furnace gave out."

He went down the stairs, through the kitchen, and down to the furnace room. Sure enough, the pilot on the master bedroom furnace was out. He tried relighting it, but it wouldn't start. He shut off the gas valve and left it. The hot-water heater and the main furnace were still on. Thank God for gravity heat which did not need electricity for power, and a very new water heater.

Julie was in the kitchen. "That's it for the bedroom, for the upstairs," Bob said as he sat down at the table. "It's okay, we'll all bunk in the living room."

"Is Dolores ... was she down there with you?"

"What? Of course not."

Julie leaned against the stove, near the flame under the kettle. "She's not in the living room."

Bob remembered the day before. "The bathroom?"

Julie went into the hall and checked. It was empty. She poked her head into Susan's room, but Dolores wasn't there. Bob called upstairs, but there was no answer. Julie checked the den. They met in the living room. Dolores' coat was gone, the boots, the turban she wore on her head. Next to the couch lay a pile of used Kleenex. And the empty bottle. "It was half full when we went to bed," Bob said. "I remember seeing her pouring from it just before I talked to Carter the last time."

"Bob, she's gone. This time–"

Bob ran to the front door and opened it. Yes, she was gone, and this time she'd gone out the front way. He walked out onto the porch. Her tracks were barely visible.

"Bob, you're not going after her! You can't!"

"Jesus Christ, Julie, of course I'm not. She's got a couple of hours on me. Look, you can barely see the footprints." He walked back inside and slammed the door. Julie just stood there, silent. Bob paced in the hall. "Oh, God, why?"

"Bob, there's nothing we can do. She'll be back. She'll see Helen Morton and get another drink, and she'll be back."

The teakettle whistled. They went into the kitchen and had coffee together. Bob made a list of important things Julie should know, where the gas valves were, what to do in case of fire, how to handle the gun. She cringed, but she listened, mainly so she wouldn't upset him. She'd never have to use a gun, and she'd never be able to do it in any case. But it pleased him to think it would make Susan and her safer.

Then Bob went out the back door and shoveled some of the snow off the patio, near the door. All the plants hanging over the outdoor table and chairs were frozen stiff. The pool was nearly filled with snow, the side nearest the house drifting up over the coping. He couldn't see any of the red brick of the patio. Everything was white.

He slid down the back steps or where the back steps had been. Getting into the garage was no easy task. He had to shovel five feet of snow from in front of the door. When he finally got inside, he had to sit and rest. Next to the station wagon was the big cabinet, right next to his workbench. He opened it and found the five backpacks and pulled them out and spread them on the floor. Then he dug for the hiking boots, the ones with the big spikes in them, and finally the coil of rope. He and Michael—at Michael's insistence—had done a little "mountain climbing" two years back, up near Mount Baldy. The backpacks had come in handy many times, but he never thought he'd have to use the boots and rope again. He was glad he hadn't sold them in the garage sale they'd had early in the summer.

He took one of the backpacks, the rope and the boots, and made his way back up to the house. His nose was red when he got inside; his ears felt like ice. "It's colder than it's been, much colder," he told Julie. She told him he had to wear his hood up, even put a scarf over his nose and mouth. She ran up to the bedroom to find one for him.

When she came back down, he was ready to leave. The boots were on his feet, the rope already attached to his belt, the backpack on his back. He'd put some papers in it, a notebook with thoughts he'd written down that he figured Carter would want, and some cookies and Hershey bars and a few cans of soda pop. He handed Julie a key.

"What's this to?" she asked.

"The gun cabinet. Just in case."

She started to protest but stopped herself and put the key on the windowsill near the sink. "Tell Michael where it is," Bob ordered. She nodded. "And say a prayer for me, huh?"

At the door, she kissed him. "I don't want to be alone! I'm scared for you! Oh, Bob. . . ."

"Julie, if I don't make it up there, then I know none of us can make it up. Better one person tries and finds out than all of us attempt it and not be able to. I've got to find out what Carter was trying to tell me on the radio. There's something he knows that he doesn't want anyone else to know. At least not yet. Julie, I'll be back by night. I'll call you on the radio. You know how to work it?"

She said she did.

He told her he loved her, and he went off into the snow. She watched him until he'd gone around the pool and into the trees. Then she went into the living room and threw another log on the fire. She sat down, and her teeth began to chatter.

* * *

The satellite picture was the first in days to show a break in the weather. Finally, the huge storm was weakening. It could not hold up its force much longer. Arms of air reached out of its center, searching for a way east. The arms were beginning to find holes in the air close to the mountains.

Though the storm would linger, it would have no more clout. Now the only worry was over the cold. From the north-central plains, cold air was finding its way across the northern Rockies and down to Los Angeles. It would mix with the weakened storm and cause wind—harsh, cruel wind—and cold. The storm would be over soon, but not before the wind had had its fun with all the snow that lay on the ground.

"We have nowhere to go. We're going to stay here where we can at least be of some help." Greg was talking. Tom sat next to him on the cot. "Are you sure about leaving?"

Michael and Lorna both said yes.

"I feel ... I'm going to miss you two," Tom said, looking sad. "We've been through so much together."

Lorna said, "Someday we'll meet and write a book on it."

"Make it a movie, too," Harvard added. "I get to play myself, yessirree! "

"Daddy, hush up." Flora looked tired. She hadn't slept much. "I've been talking to some people here; they're thinking of trying to get down to Watts when the snow lifts. Daddy's got a brother there. We may try it."

"Not on my mother's grave," Harvard said. "You ain't movin' this old man to save your soul."

"Old fart," Flora muttered.

"Watch your tongue, girl, hear?"

"Hey, you two, cut it out." Michael lifted Dawn and wrapped her in a pink blanket. He looked around. "Hey, where's Kenny? " They all looked around. His girlfriend was lying down a few feet away from them. "Do you know where he is? " Michael asked.

"He's gone," the girl said, talking in a monotone, as if in shock.

"Gone?" Lorna asked.

"He disappeared during the night."

They all gasped. "Oh, my God, what next?" Greg said. And there was nothing they could do. It hurt to see a young, gregarious boy turn into a shattered shell of what he had been. No one could even say *Oh, well, he'll be back* or *Don't worry, he probably just went out for a Coke.* It wasn't real. He was gone, and no one would ever see him again, and that was the fact they all understood. Their perception of life had changed drastically. There was nothing even to say to Kenny's girlfriend. Nothing at all.

Greg, Tom, and Flora walked to the door with the Sheppards. "Listen," Michael said, "we're gonna form a club, you know, like people who've been on a cruise together do, meet every year to commemorate the occasion. We're gonna meet every January, now don't forget. The Snow City Survivors!"

"Hopefully on a desert island," Tom said.

"Right on," Flora chimed in. She smiled. "God bless you, hear? And God help you." She turned and walked back into the mass of people.

Greg hugged Lorna and kissed her good-bye; then Tom did the same. Michael handed her the baby and put another blanket around her. Then he wrapped his arms around Greg and held him tight for a moment, and then Tom pressed his head against his, kissing him lightly on his ear. He whispered, "Good luck." Then Tom felt himself choking up, and he stood with his lover, their arms around each other, as Michael and Lorna and the little baby set out into the blizzard for yet another destination.

Harry was making his way up Western Avenue. His eyes burned, and his skin felt raw, and he thought his shoulder was going to fall off. But he was obsessed with getting out. He dreamed of the future. The living room of the villa lined with Van Goghs. It would all be worth it. His brother would get him out. He knew they'd wait for him. He was sure of it. He plodded on as fast as he could. At Sunset Boulevard he got a ride on a jeep that somehow was making it up the steep incline. He rode all the way up to Los Feliz Boulevard. The jeep was turning around and going back down. It had dropped off medical supplies at Immaculate Heart College, at the top of the hill just under the park, where hundreds of people from the Hollywood area had gathered. Harry would have to go it on foot again, but he was in Los Feliz now. It wasn't all that far. He would be there by late afternoon. This time it was certain.

As Harry was working his way up the long mountain slope which made up the Los Feliz area, his wife was making her way down. Julie had been right; Dolores had stopped at Helen Morton's house, but Helen had no liquor left, no water, no beverage of any kind. She explained that the water pipes had burst during the night. She didn't know what they were going to do. "I think we're going to go up to the convent, see if the sisters will take us in. We can't stay here. The house next door, it was empty, looters broke in during the night. We're very scared. Would you like to go up to the convent with us?"

Dolores had refused the offer. She said she had business down the hill, but the truth was she didn't know where she was going or why. She'd been up all night, crying. Drinking. Half a bottle, a quart, in three hours. She'd thrown up once. Then she'd dressed and left. She had thought of Susan and cried again. She'd thought of Harry. He'd let her down. He wasn't coming. She had to go out, go and find him. . . .

She made it down to the big street, Los Feliz Boulevard. She didn't know which way to turn, right or left. She saw a house on fire to her right. She didn't want to go near that. She turned left and fell. She got up and pulled herself along, holding her coat closed in front of her. She fell again, but she was determined. She looked over her shoulder and saw the flames rising in the sky. She was glad she hadn't gone that way. She couldn't stand to see more suffering.

But had she turned right instead of left, she might have run into the one person who could have got her back to the house. Harry Sheppard could see the same burning house in the distance in front of him.

Bob gritted his teeth and held onto the tree. He pulled himself around it and fell back against it. He took off one glove and reached over his shoulder into the backpack and pulled out a

Hershey bar. He chomped it down and put the scarf over his face again. He was halfway up the hill. But now it got steeper. This would be the rough part. He tossed the rope up and snagged another tall pine tree. It held. He started to work his way up, his spiked shoes digging into the thick snow. He slipped a bit but retained his balance. He was going to make it. He had to make it.

Up at the observatory, Alex Granville was barking orders into an Army radio. "Get them in there, get the guns in there, and shoot until they understand." He listened for a minute. "Bullshit! Look at it as war down there. That's an order." He walked away and smashed his cigar into an ashtray.

Rob Wynters had heard enough. "General, that's a ghetto down there near USC, and that's not some race riot or uprising to overthrow the government. People are fighting to survive down there; that's what's going on. They're attacking hospitals because they want medicine. They're raiding houses because they want food and blankets. Shooting them won't do any good, it won't stop their ... it won't fulfill their needs! They need provisions, not guns in their backs! "

"Fuck you." Granville left the room.

Rob fell into a chair and ran his fingers through his hair. Carter looked at him, but said nothing. "Oh, shit," Rob muttered, and closed his eyes.

Michael hollered to Lorna through the falling snow. "I never thought I'd relate to those lines of refugees you see in movies on the late show, you know, the village burning behind them." It was an awesome sight, what they could see. Buildings gutted by fire, others ransacked, others completely razed by explosions. And people, everywhere, going every which way. Homeless, helpless people searching for a warm place, some food, more clothing. Everyone was incredibly self-protective; no one even talked to each other. Lorna had said hello to a woman huddled inside the door of what had been the Hamburger Hamlet on Hollywood Boulevard. *"Don't come near me!"* the woman had screamed at her. *"Don't take another step!"* She pressed a big purse to her chest. Lorna moved on, stunned.

Michael had thought he was going to find the people "animals," but it wasn't so. Everyone had one major purpose in life at this unique time and in this unique situation: self-preservation. Together, and separately, single people, families, lovers. But not collectively. There were no marauding bands of looters on the streets anymore, no groups moving with a leader at the front to take over the rich homes, none of the silly stories Michael had heard in the high school gym. People were moving, that was certain, and it seemed that most of the traffic was to the hills, toward higher ground. He wasn't sure why—was it any better up there? Maybe it was just instinct, survival. The empty pool fills, and you go to the top or you'll drown. Los Angeles was one big pool, and it was filled; people were moving to the top.

Dawn cried a great deal, which worried Michael, but not Lorna. She said she'd be worried if the baby didn't cry. They took turns carrying her, Michael more than Lorna, for her legs were shorter and it was more difficult for her to move through the snow. But the street was a major artery; it had been traveled constantly since the snow had begun. Cars were buried all along it, but the snow was so high now that the paths went right over little cars and around the bigger ones. Houses seemed to have sunk into the earth because the snow, in some cases, reached the rooftops or at least the windows. Most apartment houses looked like Genesee Gardens—abandoned, stripped, some burned out, some collapsed. The thing that looked the strangest was the snow on the palm trees. It was too much to accept; it was mind-boggling. Michael had to laugh at the sight. It just made absolutely no sense.

They passed the Broadway department store on the corner of Hollywood and Vine. The windows were all missing, the mannequins standing there looking cold because the clothing had been stripped from them. Michael and Lorna went inside and sat down. It was a place to rest, to get out of the snow. It was full of people, but again, no one spoke to anyone else. They all eyed one another suspiciously.

The interesting thing was what had been cleaned out of the place and what remained. Michael walked around and couldn't believe his eyes, and yet it made good sense, and it said something about the basics of life. Jewelry sat on the counters, untouched. Cosmetics and perfumes, free for the taking, but no one was taking. What was gone? The clothing, every garment with any kind of warmth. Bras and girdles and thin blouses sat on the shelves, on the countertops. Sweaters, coats, pants—they all were gone. Not a sock left in the store. Michael went downstairs to the men's department and found the same to be true. T-shirts and bikini shorts sat there. The Cardin cologne sat there, as did the umbrellas and shoeshine kits and cameras and projectors and pocket calculators. Gone were the gloves and the shoes and the robes and suits. Values changed; priorities switched around.

Upstairs, Lorna had the same secretive, untrusting look as all the others, as if she were concealing something and she were going to be found out at any moment. The same look she'd had when she was seventeen and had been caught shoplifting; the look which had got her caught. "Hey, you rob a bank?" Michael asked.

"Shhh. Come here."

He bent forward. "What?"

"I found a box of candy. Right here, under the counter. The last one. They overlooked it."

"Who?" he whispered.

"I don't know who, whoever took the rest." He looked around. The candy counter was bare. "Anyhow, sit down, and let's eat them before someone sees us. It'll be good energy."

He said down. "I feel like Bonnie and Clyde."

"Shhh. Here, slip them into your mouth without looking like you're feasting."

He popped a chocolate into his mouth and noticed the quick flash of a man's eyes. He was standing about five feet away, looking very hungry. Michael suddenly turned red. He didn't dare chew the damned thing. And it was a caramel. He slid it to the back of his mouth and swallowed it whole. Then he turned his head away. "I think you're right about this, Bonnie, darling," he said.

Lorna turned around and faced the counter, holding the baby in her lap. She stuffed her face full of candy. She thought she'd never tasted anything so delicious. The man who'd been watching them finally sat down and closed his eyes. "I think we'd better get going. Don't want to overstay our welcome," Michael said.

They got up and started their journey again.

The knock at the door startled Julie. She let out a shout and then cupped her hand over her mouth. At first she started to walk to the door, and then she stopped herself. She turned and looked at the gun standing there in the hall. She'd taken it out of the closet the minute Bob had left, just to be safe. She knew she'd never be able to fire it, but she could hold it and pretend she had the courage to do it. She went into the kitchen, deciding to sneak into the dining room, where the windows looked out on the porch, to see who was at the door. Just as she started to round the corner of the kitchen, it dawned on her–it had to be Dolores.

She walked into the dining room and screamed. She saw nothing but two hooded figures in black. She caught her breath as one of them turned to her and pulled the black scarf from its face. It was a woman. She had a veil over her head. It was a nun.

Julie quickly opened the door. "Oh, sisters, forgive me," she said, "come in, come in." They moved inside quickly and slammed the door. "Come by the fire and warm yourselves. You're both so wet."

"No, thank you, dear woman," the older of the two said. "We are from a convent on a street not too far from here. There are only five of us, and we had no heat, nothing left. We are up at the motherhouse here, Saint Theresa's next door."

"Yes," Julie said, "I've never seen the nuns here with full habits on."

"We still wear them. Not many do." The younger sister had a

soft, pleasant voice. And Julie detected a great deal of fear in it.

"Sister Benedicta and I are going from house to house. There are a few priests and some other sisters gathered next door. And a rabbi, too." She smiled. "We have room, and there is much food and water. Early this morning a family came to us from down a few blocks. Their home had been taken by men wanting food and shelter. They had refused to let them in, and they forced themselves in. We had a discussion and came to the conclusion that we would all be best served if we gathered together at the Motherhouse here and let the people coming from the central area of the city have these houses."

"It is the Christian thing to do," the younger nun, Sister Benedicta, said. "We do not condemn the people for wanting a respite from the cold. But there should be no force, no violence. We are in a bad enough condition as it is."

"Come with us then," the older nun said. "Gather your family and come join us. We are all neighbors, we will be able to live for the next few days or weeks in harmony, God providing. The sisters who live here asked of your daughter. They said she is ill."

"Yes," Julie said. "I've sometimes talked over the fence with the sisters when I'm out gardening."

"Please come."

Julie explained that she was in the house alone, that almost everyone in her family was out in the snow, or she supposed. She was waiting for her son and daughter-in-law and granddaughter to arrive, for Dolores to come back. "Oh, maybe she's up at the convent already?"

The nuns shook their heads. "I don't believe I remember seeing the woman you describe."

Julie said there was also the possibility that her brother-in-law would show up, though it was a remote hope. "Nothing is hopeless," the older nun said, and Julie wanted to remark that Harry was, but she didn't. She told them about her husband having to go to the observatory, but she didn't mention the possibility of their getting out by helicopter.

"Then join us when your family is together," Sister Benedicta said. "There is no immediate danger, but by tomorrow perhaps there will be many people coming up to this part of the city."

The other sister said, "Father Bertram told us that people have seen the helicopters landing at the observatory, and thus they think they can go up there and take one out of the city. Or word has been passed that it is a way out."

Julie felt they were reading her mind. "What about the others here on the street?" she asked.

"Your neighbors, the Kuppermans, prefer to stay in their house. The woman is quite spirited, I must say. She said she's going to defend her castle, and what's more, she says no one wants anything she's got there in any case. But I do hope they will join us because they have little firewood left and they're confined to the living room. I told them the rabbi was with us, and the husband seemed pleased at that."

"He's very religious," Julie said. "They're wonderful people. I hope they'll be all right."

Sister Benedicta said, "Well, the woman did say that when their wood ran out, they would be coming to you. She said you would take care of them."

"Oh, yes," Julie said, "I told them to come here the other day. Maybe we'll *all* be joining you, eventually."

The older nun put her hand on Julie's shoulder. "My dear girl, you must. The Motherhouse is as strong as a fortress. You are welcome; everyone is welcome."

Julie asked, "But what if . . . when you're full and can't take any more people?"

Sister Benedicta said, "Then the people who will want to come in will have these houses."

But the older nun was more to the point. "Then we will defend ourselves if it comes to that. We can do just so much. God will guide us."

"Can I offer you coffee, tea, anything?"

They shook their heads. "No, we've been to all the houses now; we're going back to rest." Sister Benedicta pulled her scarf up over her mouth again. "I will say a prayer for your family."

The older sister said, "We have some medical supplies at the

Motherhouse. We may be able to help if anyone is sick—your daughter—or injured. Every conceivable supply is there. We have our own power. The building was built and planned to be self-sufficient in case of any disaster." Then she smiled as she buttoned up. "But I'm sure they never thought of this one."

"Thank you, sisters. We will be seeing you shortly, I think. Thank you for your prayers." She opened the doors.

Sister Benedicta made her way out and started down the steps, holding her hand out for the older nun, helping her. The woman turned back to Julie and called, "Almost all the families on the street are joining us. Perhaps . . . if you must stay here, you won't be bothered by desperate characters. They will have the other houses."

Julie nodded and closed the door. She peered through the dining-room window until the black figures had disappeared into the white wind.

She sat in front of the fire. She thought about the building next door, the Motherhouse. It had been built to withstand anything, that was true—earthquakes, floods, fires. The millionaire who'd put it up had taken pains to make sure he'd outlive them all. She hadn't known, however, that they had their own medical supplies and power generator. She wondered what they would be doing tomorrow. Climbing the forbidding-looking hill at the back of the property or sitting comfortably in front of a fire in the Catholic mansion next door, behind the high walls? She wondered about the safety of her own house. Would people really try to break in? And how long would their supplies hold out? When Bob was back, and Michael and Lorna, and Dolores, the food that was left, the water, would go fast. And only one furnace was left operating. There was a lot of firewood, sure, but if the heat went, the firewood would go five times as fast as it was going. She began to worry.

She was pleased, however, that Minnie and Sam and little Billy would come to them. She thought it wasn't wise for them to refuse the sisters' offer, but Minnie could be stubborn. She had great pride and believed in the goodness of people. Julie was almost glad their firewood was low. She would feel better having them in the house; over the years they'd grown to be like part of the family.

The family. She looked up at the pictures, the photographs in the frames on the antique stand in the corner of the room. Her family. *Where are they now?* Out there, she thought, looking at the windows. *Out there.* It didn't make any sense.

Then Susan called and she went to her.

Bob was pulled up the last ten feet to the building by a strong pair of hands, a young soldier who'd been looking for him for hours. He helped him into the observatory, and Carter hugged him. "You made it!"

"Just barely." Bob collapsed into a chair and tried to breath normally. "God, what's the fire out there?"

"Fire?"

"I saw . . . I saw flames. I was dizzy, staggering up the steps. But I know I saw flames."

"Flamethrowers. Keeping the snow melted, so we can get the choppers in and out of here."

Bob's eyes opened wide. "So there's a chance?"

"Not in this wind. No one knows, but one crashed on the other side of the mountain just an hour ago. Tomorrow maybe, the next day." Carter turned to the soldier and said, "Leave us." The young man left immediately. Rob Wynters came into the room and said hello to Bob. Then Carter said, "The threat isn't snow anymore."

Bob sat up straight as Rob poured him a cup of coffee. "What are you telling me?"

"Brace yourself for this one," Rob cautioned. "I don't want you to have the same reaction as General Granville. Carter couldn't take another guy spitting in his face."

Bob looked at Carter. "You've got that look in your eyes that says it's too unbelievable for words but it's really gonna happen, right?"

"You ought to go into a new profession, reading people."

Bob smiled. "I've seen it before." He took off his jacket and unbuttoned his sweater. "Well, what?"

"I said, the snow isn't the danger."

"What are you getting at? Not the danger? It's almost the end of us all. . . ."

"Robert, yesterday I came to a new conclusion, how this would all end. I predicted it would begin today up north, above San Francisco. And it did."

"What did? Carter, quit playing guessing games."

"What's the biggest fear next to earthquakes in California?"

"Fire."

"And after a fire, what?"

"Huh? Well, rain . . . flooding. There's always floods, and the hills don't have grass to keep the mud back . . . *oh, Jesus!*" Bob jumped to his feet. "It's gonna *rain?*"

Carter nodded. Bob sat back down. "I know it, I'm sure of it. We're going to get a taste of what the East has been having. We're going to get it fast. Hot air, too, Robert."

"You mean Santa Anas are gonna blow in here and melt all this?"

"It's a good bet. But look, don't confuse the two. They come from different sources."

"So straighten me out, Carter."

"To start with, the weakening of the polar outbreak and our blizzard is causing the atmosphere to recoil back into a more normal winter condition. You might say that nature is taking a breather like in '77 after the Big Freeze when temperatures rose over 50° in some areas—"

"—and there was flooding then," Bob interrupted.

"That's right. But we're in a far more dangerous position. Santa Anas usually occur several times during a normal winter. When they do, temperatures may rise as high as 90° for days. All that is needed is for a high-pressure system to build over the Pacific Northwest or just east of the Rockies, and a low-pressure system to settle off the Southwest coast. Then winds will form and blow from the northeast over the mountains, and as they drop through the passes near L.A. they will warm from compression."

"Where is the rain?" Bob asked.

"Santa Anas are hot dry winds; they have no rain. That's just it—we're being threatened on two fronts. There's a mild Santa Ana condition building now, but it's not a strong force yet. Our big danger is out in the Pacific. A powerful tropical storm front is being held at bay by what's over us now. There's a lot of warm, moist air in that system, and if it ever hit this city, we'd have to worry about its freezing. The choice is rain, heat, or both, one at a time."

"Carter," Bob said, comprehending, but shocked, "you're saying the whole city of L.A. might wash into the ocean!"

Carter sat down across from Bob and took his glasses off and started to chew on them. "That's exactly what I'm saying. Warming winds have hit parts of the San Joaquin Valley and the northern desert areas. It's starting to happen and now they'll believe me."

"And what can we do about it? What can be done?"

"I wish I knew."

Bob sat there with his mouth open.

Dolores had sweet-talked a soldier into giving her a ride at the corner of Vermont. She didn't know what she was riding on. It seemed to be some kind of snowmobile, a small thing. He was a courier, he'd told her, but of what and for whom, she didn't know. She didn't care. At least he gave her a rest from moving through the snow.

She got off at Griffith Park Boulevard. She wasn't sure what she was doing there or even where she was. She'd never gotten to know the Los Feliz area very well. She turned right on Griffith Park Boulevard and walked to the first cross street, Rowena. She turned left, because ahead on Griffith Park were small groups of people heading uphill, carrying sacks on their backs. Poor devils, she thought. She searched the faces for Harry, but he wasn't among them. She moved from the intersection as fast as she could.

When she got to the corner, she stopped and sat in the snow. It was all over her now, in her dress, down her back, her turban ice cold. She didn't care. She'd tallen so many times, and it was still coming down ... or was it the wind blowing it all around? She saw double for a minute and then moaned. She needed a drink. Desperately. She got up and leaned against the top of a street sign. It said "Waverly Drive." *Waverly Drive, Waverly Drive.* She'd heard of it. Where? She looked around. *Christ, I've been here.* When? And then it came to her. Waverly Drive was the street of the LaBianca house. She'd read about it in *Helter Skelter.* Bob had once driven them past the house, shortly after Manson had put his mark on it for the rest of time. She couldn't even look. But she remembered the street. It looked deserted now, the big houses dark, forbidding.

She felt better. She walked all the way to Hyperion Avenue and saw a shopping center, both sides of the street, buildings and signs. As she got closer, she saw the big red and white Mayfair Market standing proudly in the wind. She crawled through the parking lot. It took her half an hour to get to the doors, and when she did, she found them locked. She pulled and cursed and beat her fists on them. *All I want is one bottle. No more. Just one.* She kicked the door and felt the glass giving way. It was already cracked; her kick had just finally done it in. She watched it fall, and then she went inside.

But once inside, she realized there were no windows at all in the front of the building; they'd all been shattered. She hadn't even noticed. Snow was blowing into the big empty building, covering the shelves. It was eerie, uncanny. She walked to the first shelves and saw the toothpaste and mouthwash lying under icicles. She turned an aisle and saw several boxes of Tide sticking out of a drift of snow. Then she walked up to the pile of deodorants and shampoos. She looked through them. She moved the eye drops aside. Then she picked up a tube of Chapstick. And she moved it over her lips. It felt good.

She walked to the sign that said LIQUOR. But there was no liquor but a few broken bottles. She pushed the snow aside with hands. Her gloves were soaked, her fingers hard to move. She found nothing but a wet copy of *Playboy.* She looked up and listened. The wind was creating a shrill, crying sound in the building. She cupped her hands over her ears. "Stop!" she screamed. But it seemed to get louder. *"Stop it! Stop it!"* She ran out one of the big frames that had held the windows and plowed through the snow to the street.

That's when she noticed it. It was almost impossible to see on a clear, sunny day, the place was so nondescript, nestled between two other buildings, no sign to announce itself, just a little plaque on the front which said THE HYPERION. But Dolores knew it was a bar. Some sense told her it had to be a bar. She pushed her way through the snow and made it to the front door. Sure enough, it was a bar. The door was open. Snow had fallen in, but not much. It was dark and damp and cold, but not nearly as cold as outside. And it was empty.

She stood there, here eyes getting used to the darkness. She saw the Remington prints on the wall, the pool table in the back. Light came from a back door, which was partially opened. All the liquor behind the bar had been cleaned out. She went back there and looked, breaking bottles, pushing doors to cabinets open. Nothing.

But then, in the back room, on a hunch in her obsessive search, she came across an unopened box. It said "Smirnoff" on the side. But inside was three bottles of Smirnoff, three of gin, and three of J&B scotch. Dolores started to cry. She hugged one of the bottles and fell to her knees. Then she opened it and put it to her trembling lips. Half of it seemed to spill down her neck, but she didn't care. There was enough to waste.

After she'd drunk half the bottle in record time, she leaned back and her head hit the wall. All of a sudden she let out a terrified scream. *"Harrrrrrrrry!"* And then she put her head in her hands and cried it out.

Harry had seen two nuns on the street, but he ignored them, mainly because they looked as though they wanted to be helpful. He'd had enough of helpful people; they asked too many questions. But today no one seemed particularly helpful. No one was smiling. No kindness-to-your-brother-man shit. Today it was every man for himself. Tomorrow it would be people shooting each other. He didn't care. He'd made it, and he was going to get out. Even if he had to do it without his brother. He'd gotten to Griffith Park alone with a fire hose over his arm; he could damn well get up another thousand feet to the landing pad where the helicopters were.

He could see the smoke coming from the chimney. That meant they were still there. That was good. He didn't think anyone had seen him make his way up the drive. He went to the back of the house and into the garage. He had to put the hose somewhere where no one would ask about it. He was surprised to find four backpacks littered on the floor, and sleeping bags, all the stuff Bob had kept for camping in the mountains. Well, maybe they'd need it. He sat down and caught his breath. As he relaxed for the first time in days, he realized that inside each backpack was a sleeping bag. A rolled-up sleeping bag. He had an idea. They'd have to use the backpacks, for sure. Well, he'd use them at least. He had to get the paintings out of the hose somehow—why not? Why not now, while no one realized he was there? It was perfect.

He unrolled the hose. It was difficult because it had frozen into a V, into the position it had been on his shoulder. He fought with it. He could see where the two rolls of paintings came together, where the crease was. He grabbed a garden shovel and tried to chop it in half between two of the canvases, but it didn't cut. He searched the garage and found an ax. That did it. He bent down and pulled one of the beautiful precious paintings from the hose and set it on an open sleeping bag. Then another and another, until they all were in the bag. He zipped it up, rolled it up. The bag barely fitted into the backpack, but he stuffed it. He'd done it. All he had to do now was strap it to his back and climb.

But first he needed food and rest. God, all his energy had left him, as though he'd been living on nerves alone, sheer willpower to get to the house, get the paintings ready for the last move. He felt sick to his stomach. He kicked the pieces of hose under the station wagon and set the backpack on the workbench, away from the others. Then he went outside, for the one last climb up the stairs to the house.

It was almost over.

In the parking lot of the Zody's discount store on Sunset and Western, a communications truck got a call from the field. A soldier said, "Listen, we've got a guy here, says he knows he can get authorization to have us drive him up under the observatory. He's a relative of someone named DeSimone. You wanna call up there? Got a wife and a baby here. God, people are fucking crazy, taking a baby out in this. They're in pretty bad shape."

"I'll get back to you."

"Okay. I'll tell them to hold on here. We're at the corner of Hollywood and Wilton."

"Right. What did you say the name was?"

"DeSimone."

"What about the guy's name, who is he?"

"Oh. Hold a second." There was noise in the background and the sound of wind hissing into the walkie-talkie. Then: "Mike Sheppard."

"Got ya. I'll be back as soon as I can."

Dolores felt warm now, almost hot. She thought maybe the weather had changed. She crawled to the door, the back door of the little bar, and saw the forbidding winds again. No, nothing had changed. But she was all right now. She was okay. She was warm inside. It was darker outside than it had been. They'd be waiting for her. She had to get back. Harry would be waiting for her, too. She was sure of it. At the office, he'd stayed at the office. Maybe she should go there instead of back to Bob's. The only person who really appreciated her there was Susan, and they wouldn't let her touch her. As if she were diseased. It was Susan who had the disease; she only wanted to help. . . .

Dolores closed her eyes. She asked her brain to stop working. If only she could just go on without having to think. To remember. If only she could just forget everything. She took another drink. The last bottle of scotch was nearly empty. She'd never drunk so much in such a short period of time. Her stomach hurt. Pains shot up through her chest. She felt good and warm and almost serene, but she was in pain. It seemed difficult to breathe. She needed air.

She went out the front way, the way she'd come in. She tried to remember what direction she'd come from, but couldn't. Then she turned and went back inside the bar. She stuffed a bottle of vodka into her pockets, one into each big pocket of her mink coat, and carried the other in her hands. It wasn't until she was out of the place and across the snow-covered street that she remembered she'd left her gloves in there. Oh, no matter, Bob's house was just up the street . . . wasn't it?

She stood near the supermarket again, wondering which way to go. She chose straight ahead, along the side of the building where it seemed easier to walk. It was uphill, and it was difficult. She thought, though, that she could see Bob's house in the distance. She would be there in no time. Julie would just have to put up with the embarrassment, with the humiliation. What humiliation? *I got this stuff from a bar! I didn't beg it off her neighbors. The hell with her.*

She saw an alley leading north, and she turned into it. It would be a shortcut. She realized soon, however, that it had been a mistake–no one had been walking in it, the snow was loose, and she sank into it too easily. But there was no turning back. She would have to make it. She pulled herself along, holding onto the top of a steel link fence, the side of a truck parked behind a building. She heard voices and looked up. She saw some faces peering out a window, looking down at her. She spoke with her eyes. *He's dead! Haven't you seen a woman in black before? Don't you have any respect?* Then she fell to her knees and admitted what she'd been keeping from admitting for a long time. "Harry's dead." She cried, and the tears fell into the snow. She'd known it when she'd sung to Susan the night before. She had that kind of intuition. He was gone. What was the point of going on? Why bother. . . ?

But she picked herself up again and moved ahead slowly, her body so cold now again. She would prove to him she could do it. Damn him anyway, for leaving her, abandoning her just as he'd abandoned his big white car so easily that day. Just to spite him, she'd live, she'd make it; she was stronger than he was. The house is just up the hill, at the end of the alley. . . .

With every last bit of energy she had in her body, she continued to climb up the alleyway.

She didn't see the figures moving in the snow behind her.

"We got you up here because Carter tells me you're the only damn person who knows how to stay calm and communicate with people. So then he lays his bullshit about rain on me, and that's the ball game. I don't know what the fuck to think." Granville puffed on his cigar, leaning back in a chair that didn't hold his large body very well. "You tell me what to do. Today I'm taking lessons from Mickey Mouse. Today I don't really give a good goddamn anymore."

"Look, General," Bob said, "I find that hard to believe. I mean, twenty-five thousand people have died down there already. You do give a good goddamn. You give a good goddamn about the rest of the lives that could be lost should everything start to reverse, should the snow melt." He turned to Carter. "Hey, wouldn't it take time? I mean, back home in Minnesota, we had five feet of snow, and it took weeks for it to melt. Sure some rivers flooded, but cities didn't wash away."

Carter said, "You're forgetting one important point. Back there the freezing temperatures come slowly, freezing the ground to a good depth. What happened in Los Angeles is that a foot of mud, wet mushy soil, was suddenly frozen over. That mud is still there. Under just a few inches of frozen earth is the makings of the biggest mud slide the world has ever seen. It's going to melt faster than the snow mounted."

Now Bob understood.

"What ideas did you have?" Carter asked Bob.

"Oh, a million. Ways to get word to the people, to calm them, lots of lies but sometimes lies save lives. The real danger always lies in panic, and if you can reduce panic you've got a chance to do something. But if the satellite says rain, what's the point in trying to bring the population—what's left of it—to coming to terms with its fate? The fate is no longer snow. It's really something else, something worse. Jesus. I never thought I'd hear myself admitting anything could be worse."

"Well, save your ideas for the next blizzard," Granville huffed. "Right now I got to figure out how we're going to deal with this when it happens. What a business, saving lives. I'd rather be selling insurance."

A woman put her head in the room. "General, there's a call from the mayor."

"Screw the mayor. Tell him I'm in a conference. Get me the President again; that's who I have to talk to." Granville got up and started to leave. "Sheppard, I understand you're a good man. Sorry you had to go through all the ordeal of getting up here, but that's weather for you. Good luck." He left.

Bob turned to Carter. "Jesus, Carter, it's not my fault he can't have a nice simple snow disaster to continue dealing with. I was promised a trip out of here—"

"Bob, you know I'll keep my word, if I have a hijack his helicopter. Go back down, get the others, and come up as soon as you can. We'll get you out. I'll get out with you. That's the only thing we can do, save ourselves."

"Is there any plan at all? Anything?"

"Every helicopter and short-run aircraft in America is positioned from here to Denver, ready to come in and take people out. Ships—aircraft carriers—are sitting out there in the water, waiting. Even Hawaii. There's planes there from all over the Pacific, waiting for the call that it's over, come and get 'em. But if it rains, it could be torrential. I don't know." He shook his head and looked despondent. "I just don't know. What bothers me most is I couldn't really do anything. I just couldn't help."

Bob said, "How do you fight fate, Carter? How do you fight, how do they say it, the hand of God?"

The same woman stuck her head in the room again. "Professor, I'm sorry to bother you again; but there's a call from the comm truck in Hollywood, and they said to tell you some cousin or something, a Mike Sheppard, is saying you'll authorize a ride in one of the trucks to . . . up here? How can a truck get—"

"Michael!" Bob shouted.

"God, yes, tell them yes. Not up here, that's not what they want, a house below us. Tell them to take him anywhere he wants to go."

"I'm sorry, sir, but only General Granville can give that kind of order."

Carter ran to the other door and swung it open. "Alex! Alex, tell this woman you've authorized the Guard to transport Bob's son up to his house."

"What the hell?"

"Damn it, Alex, just do it."

"Yeah, it's okay, I'm ordering it, official." He went back to the phone.

Carter shut the door. "You heard the general. Get on that phone."

"Yes, sir," the woman said, backing away.

"They're all right. They're going to make it." Bob sat down again and thanked God.

"You'd better spend the night here. The snow's going to get worse as the winds pick up to gale forces again. It's late. Get some sleep, and we'll help you get down early in the morning. Call your wife, and tell her about Michael coming. Come on, the radio's in the lobby here."

They went into the lobby of the observatory building. It took half an hour, but they finally got through to Julie.

Bob told her about Michael, and she was overjoyed. He said he would be home the next day, and that they were going to go on a journey, a hard one, but they'd get away. How was Susan? Julie didn't think she could last another three days. She was barely speaking and in constant pain. "Bob, I've got a surprise for you," she said. And then another voice came through the speaker.

"Harry? Harry! That's you!"

"My God, brother, did I hear you say we're getting out of this mess?"

"Harry, how long have you been there?"

"An hour at the most. I'm fine, Julie's fine. Don't worry about a thing, I'm taking good care of the place."

"I'll be down in the morning. Christ, I feel good." And with that, Bob signed off.

Harry had banged on the back door off the patio. "Julie, Dolores, it's me, it's Harry! Let me in!" He saw Julie standing next to a gun in the hall, peering through the sheer curtain on the door window to make sure it was indeed him. When she did realize it, she ran to the door and swung it open.

"Oh, God, thank God! Harry, get out of those clothes. I'll make tea ... the water just stopped running, but we've got bottled. Tell me where you've been. How are you? I've never seen you with a beard! We'd given you up for lost. Michael and Lorna are coming, you heard that. Oh, Bob's up at the observatory, that's where he was calling from. We–"

"Julie, where's Dolores?"

Her eyes answered him.

"What happened?"

"We don't exactly know. She went out early in the morning. That's all we know. We thought she went ... well, looking for some liquor. But she hasn't come back."

"Early in the morning?"

Julie nodded. "Harry, there's a chance–"

"And it's nearly dark now." He paused and reflected. "No, Julie, let's not give ourselves false illusions. I know what it's like out there. She's not strong. She's not coming back." He said it unemotionally, matter-of-factly. Julie hated him at that moment. She wanted to slap him, ask him to care at least a little, show some consideration, some loss. But he'd never shown Dolores consideration in life; why now when it was presumed she was dead?

Harry changed the subject. "We're going to get out by helicopter? I knew it, I told myself that all the way. We've got connections."

You pompous bastard. Bob has the connections, not you.

"I'm so happy! God, I feel like a new man!"

She poured his tea. She never hated anyone so much as she now hated this man. His wife was out there lost, the poor thing, lost in the snow, and he was drinking tea and talking about his connections which were going to save him. But then he said something which made her think she had perhaps misjudged him. "You know, Julie, it's all going to be beautiful. Oh, Dolores will show up. A couple of drinks, and she's as good as new. But the future with her, well, I don't know if anyone will ever be able to really control her drinking. She's on a path to self-destruction. But it'll work out, and we'll be saved, and life from the minute we fly out will be better than I'd ever possibly dreamed in all my life."

Julie took his statement on face value—some heart, some concern for his wife and the future, and belief that she was not lost. But he was pacifying her and disguising what he was really thinking about: the priceless treasure lying on the workbench in the garage. That's where the optimism—the near euphoria—came in about getting out and having a wonderful life. And the worry over Dolores and her drinking was not that at all; he'd written her off. His worry was still that something could slip up, go wrong, and his plan would be ruined.

Julie had tea with him, and they compared notes on the last few days.

Self-destruction? If that was so, why was Dolores working so hard, so desperately to get back to the house? Her hands were bleeding; her face was nearly completely frostbitten. Even her teeth were chilled to the nerves. She plodded along through the alley as the winds blew snow into her eyes. Her body was wracked with pain. Snot ran from her nose into her mouth, and she had to use the sleeve of her mink to wipe herself.

But then she fell again, and she didn't make an effort to move this time. She needed to rest, to warm herself. She yanked one of the bottles out of her purse—she'd dropped the one in her hand into the snow some yards back, without even realizing it. She opened it and drank from the bottle. She shut her eyes and felt the snow hitting her face. She drank some more. She felt it warming her. She could go on again. She got up.

But almost immediately, she fell again. And this time she

didn't move. She was lying facedown in the snow, but she didn't move.

The three figures behind her stopped moving, too, crouching. It was getting dark. That was good. She looked as though she'd had it. But they weren't sure. "Wait a few minutes," the oldest man said.

Carter said, "Come up to the building up at the top of the mountain. We've got the hot food there. Get a good supper, and then we'll drive you back here to sleep." In the background Bob could hear the general barking orders about mass burials, Rob disagreeing with him on some point. Bob was only too glad to get away from Granville; the man grated on his nerves.

They went outside and got into a big tractor which took them over the parking lot–landing pad–and up the hill to the makeshift building. Looking down over the stricken city, Bob thought he was in Alaska. It was a stupefying sight. White. Everything white.

Then Bob sat down to a warm dinner, and for nearly half an hour he forgot all his troubles.

"Okay, it's set. You're getting your taxi service." The soldier helped Lorna into the back of the truck. She looked pale, almost sick. Michael jumped in with her. "This may take some time," the young officer said, "but we'll get there. You just guide us up the right street when we're near there. Hold on, this ain't easy."

As the truck started to move–and slide–Lorna leaned her head to Michael's shoulder and said, "I take back any word I've ever said about your parents and their upper-middle-class ways. I suddenly want to be a housewife like Julie."

Michael smiled. He rocked Dawn in his arms. She was sleeping, but he knew she was hungry. "Honey, ten minutes after we get there, you'll be back into saving the world and arguing with Mom about dependence on men."

"No, I won't."

"Hey, I *want* you to. Why did you think I married you?"

She smiled and said, "God, you're so wonderful."

"I'll buy that."

Dolores lay there in the fresh, pure snow, a bottle clutched in her fist. *I have to lift my head up, but I can't.* Then she heard voices. "Do you think she's dead?" "Yeah, aw, hell, yes." "Well, it's dark, so let's get it. Mom needs it." Then Dolores felt hands all over her body, and she realized her coat was gone. She lay there in her dress and turban and Bob's boots. No, someone was pulling them off her feet. Well, maybe it was time for bed. Julie and Bob were helping her off with her clothes. If she just closed her eyes, she could sleep and then wake up fresh and warm. . . .

She turned her head to the side. She had no feeling left in her body. Her hair was spilling out from under her turban; she could feel it on her neck. Or was that snow? No, it was the blanket Julie'd put over her to keep her warm. Everything was all right now. She could sleep peacefully.

She closed her eyes for the last time and fell into a deep, deep sleep as the snow began to drift over her.

Within two hours she had frozen to death.

THE EIGHTH DAY

THURSDAY, JANUARY 22
HIGH TEMPERATURE 20°; LOW 7°

IT HAD BEEN SAID THAT FEW SECTIONS OF THE LOS ANGELES Basin had any real feeling of character, of identity, but Venice was certainly one. Even with the threat of extinction from the land developers who wanted to turn it into another "swinging singles" Marina Del Rey, Venice managed to attract the young, the talented, the aged, the dropouts, those people who wished to live in but separate themselves from the real Los Angeles. Hip movie producers like Tony Bill had taken over entire buildings in Venice, turned them into centers of creativity and excitement. And yet the hip and rich and creative sat next to bums in the same coffee shops, they walked the same boardwalk with the senior citizens, watched the same street musicians who were always playing somewhere in town.

But no one was playing anything on the streets now. Venice, in the snow crisis, was no different from any other part of the city, save for the fact that the snowfall along the immediate coast was half what it was a few miles inland; they could thank the Pacific Ocean for that. For the younger residents this was their first taste of danger, but for the older people, the hundreds of elderly men and women, this was yet another crisis in what had been lives filled with crisis and difficulty. The old people were dying off like flies, and little could be done.

But even more painful than the deaths—for death was final, it was immediate and over no matter how long it had taken actually to come—were the memories, the horrible, painful memories of the past. Many of these people were the Jewish refugees who came from Europe over the past fifty years to settle in some better place where they could live out their lives in peace, not persecution. They thought Venice was that place.

Many wore scars from the past, the tattoos of the concentration camps, the shrapnel wounds from the siege of Warsaw, the torture marks of the Stalin purge. The snow brought the return of old nightmares.

One old woman sat huddled in her one-room apartment along the boardwalk, remembering how it was. She could see those crumbling streets of her native Stalingrad, pounded to rubble by the relentless German siege. She remembered the day her son caught a rat in the basement of their bombed-out home. It had been their first meal in a week, all six of them. That was the last day of her son's life. It was snowing then. He had been shot, and she saw the blood flow red on the sooty snow. But there was no time to mourn. The German soldiers were near at hand, and they had to move to some other cellar on some other street. She remembered with painful eyes as she looked out on what had been a sandy beach, now looking like the fields outside her Russian home. The fields where so much blood had been shed, where so many had died for no reason at all.

To an old man with the number engraved on his wrist, the air outside seemed warm compared to the air he remembered in that winter of 1944, his first winter in Auschwitz. At least here he had a roof over his head and shoes on his feet. It was ironic that he had put so much effort into finding a spot like Venice to end his life, a place that never knew real cold. And now look.

For the past few days he had avoided standing up. His friend and roommate understood and got him what food they had at hand. Those many years ago he had seen the bone-bare bodies standing, no, hanging around him, everyone huddled so close together that it was impossible to fall down. It had been the only way to keep warm. The man beside him, pressing against his right shoulder, had died, but his body stood propped there against him for more than twenty-four hours. Now he lay down, but he felt he almost wanted the warmth of those other people, even the dead body. It was one of so many incidents attacking his mind.

He would soon be dead, he knew. Oh, yes, he was sure of it. He could not go out, and neither could his friend. And where was there to go? It was much like the camps on the other side of the world. He'd survived them, but not their memories. This time he would not survive, and he would be free of the nightmare, of remembering what it had been like in Los Angeles that year. He would soon be a statistic, but he knew too well it wasn't the blizzard alone that robbed him of a few more years. Maybe the blizzard was just a magnificent figment of his memory, his imagination playing tricks on him. He was old, and he would die, as most of the elderly had died in the camps. They had not been able to do anything about it, and neither could he now.

He accepted it peacefully.

Many did not. They fought for life, but the cold and the snow were too much for them, for their old weary hearts and bodies. They died in their homes, in retirement buildings, on the streets, in the snow. One old lady, dying in her daughter's arms, said, "You must promise me something." The daughter asked what. She was a screenwriter. The old woman said, "Harrison Salisbury wrote *The 900 Days.* The nine hundred days of Stalingrad. Promise me you will write *The Nine Days.* The nine days of Los Angeles. I cannot say which was the worst. . . ."

"Shhh, Mama," the girl whispered.

"No, you must promise. . . . I count the days since it is too cold even to go out the door . . . you must. . . ."

The girl's eyes promised as the old woman closed her heavy eyelids for the last time. The girl felt tears well up, and then she rested her head on her mother's silent and still breast. "Oh, Mama, for you it was nine days. Luckily for you it was only nine days. Who knows how long it will last for the rest of us? Oh, Mama, it may go on forever." The girl kissed her for the last time. Yes, she would write the story someday. If she lived to tell about it. She had little hope now that anyone would ever live to tell about it.

Julie and Harry were each curled up on a sofa in front of the fire. The room was dark but for the glowing embers. Julie awakened first—she knew something was wrong. She'd seen a flash of light. First she thought the fire had burst up, exploded; maybe one of the logs had somehow rolled out through the screen. But they were just coals now. She and Harry had been asleep, and no one had put fresh logs on the fire.

Then she saw the light again. A steady beam, flashing through the windows, over the walls. She thought of movies with prison break scenes and the searchlight seeking out the convicts as they crouched in the woods. She woke Harry and crouched on the floor. "What is it?"

Before he could answer, they heard something. A voice over a loudspeaker. It wasn't clear because the snow was great acoustical absorbing material, but someone was shouting to them over a loudspeaker. Julie and Harry went to the window, and the bright light was coming from the street, from the cul-de-sac. "What do they want?" Julie asked.

Harry opened the window. He could make out the words "... *we have your son and daughter here."*

Julie heard it too. "Oh, thank God!"

Then the loudspeaker asked, "Is there anyone there?"

"Get a flashlight," Harry ordered. Julie grabbed the big flashlight from the kitchen and shone it out the dining-room window. The spotlight caught Harry waving his hands in the living-room window, and it shut off.

Julie ran to the door, waiting. Harry closed the window and put some more logs on the fire. "Well, they made it. I knew they would."

"Mommy!" It was Susan calling.

Julie ran to her room. "Susan, Michael and Lorna are here!

They're here, darling. Now we can leave, as soon as Daddy gets back." Then she ran back to the hall and waited, anxious, her pulse racing.

It seemed like hours before they reached the house. The climb was difficult. The winds had died down a bit, but the snow was still falling, as difficult as that was to believe. "What time is it?" Harry asked. Julie looked at her watch in the dim candlelight. "Almost four A.M."

"Good Lord. What day is it?"

"Thursday."

"I'll be damned. Thought it was Wednesday."

And then they heard them. Julie opened the door as they came up the mountain of snow that had been the front steps. Michael was first, carrying Dawn, and Lorna followed him, holding onto the back of his heavy jacket. "Michael! Oh, God, I'm so glad to see you!"

Michael stepped inside and handed Dawn to his mother, gave her a kiss, and sat down on the steps leading upstairs. She'd never seen him looking so happy, so relieved, yet so worn out. And Lorna looked even worse. Her eyes were red and swollen, and her lips were cracked, broken. She looked ten years, maybe twenty years, older than she was. She just sat on the floor and breathed deeply. They'd made it. Each of them secretly wondered if the other had really believed they would. Maybe one day they would ask each other.

"Where the hell you two been?" Harry asked loudly, trying to put some levity into the homecoming. "Told you not to go out on a date in this weather!"

They smiled, but no one was up to laughing. Not even Michael, who, in any other situation, would have come back with a fast and funny line. "That thing . . . that tractor, truck, tank, whatever it was, we never thought it would make it up the hill." Michael took his jacket off and dropped it on the beautiful natural oak floor, but no one seemed to mind. What did floors and houses mean any longer? The important thing was being alive. And they were.

"Is Dawn all right?" Lorna asked. "I have no milk left in me."

Julie had been holding her close to her warm body, soothing the shocked little girl. "I think she's fine. We've got some powdered milk in the kitchen. It'll have to do."

"She needs to be changed," Lorna said. "I would, but I'm—"

"Hush," Julie said. "That's what a grandma is for." She put the baby on the couch and went to get a Pampers. "Michael, Susan's very ill. Don't be alarmed when you see her, I mean don't let her see you look alarmed. Go in and tell her you're okay. She's been very worried. She doesn't really realize what's happening, I don't think, but she knows you were in danger."

Michael got up. "Lorna, come by the fire. I'll get you some warm clothes," Julie said, putting her coat on. Lorna and Michael looked at her quizzically. "Oh, they'll be warm when we get them by the fire. There's no heat upstairs."

Michael went to Susan's room.

Lorna walked to the living room and sprawled on her back on the floor. Her feet still felt as though they were walking through the snow. Harry offered her something to drink. "I'd love a shot of anything!" she said.

"I hate to tell you this, but Dolores got it all."

"Then anything, anything warm."

"Julie has tea in there. I've never made tea in my whole damn life, but I'm going to try right now. You stay put." He started toward the kitchen.

"Harry, how ... well ... Dolores, is she—"

Harry shook his head. "She's gone," Harry said. "She's gone. We're never going to see her again." And then he disappeared into the kitchen.

Lorna stretched and looked up at the beautiful baby lying there so quiet on the couch. "After all you've been through," Lorna said, "you're the strongest of us all."

"Hey, sis, how're ya doing?" Michael sat down on the floor next to her.

She opened her eyes, and it took her a moment to focus. "Oh, where were you?"

"Out there, in winter wonderland." He saw that his mother

had been right. He'd seen Susan sick over the years, in and out of hospitals, but he'd never seen her like this. It frightened him and made him forget his own aches and pains.

"You don't look so hot," she said.

Man, he thought, *you should talk!* He just smiled. "You like the beard? We've all got them now, Uncle Harry, me, Lorna."

"Lorna?"

"Well, she wears the pants in the family." Susan giggled. Then she closed her eyes and seemed to be drifting off. "Hey, you still with me?"

Softly she said, "I want Auntie Dee to come back in and sing to me."

Michael held her feeble hand. "Sure, pumpkin, later. Get some sleep."

She was already somewhere else.

"Mom, Jesus, she's dying!" Michael screamed up in the master bedroom. Julie was standing there with her arms full of clothes. She turned away, pained by his words. "Ma, what can we do—something's gotta be done fast!"

"Michael, don't say that! It's bad enough with Dolores disappeared out there someplace, not knowing if your father's going to get down that mountain slope this morning; not knowing if any of us are going to survive this. . . ."

"Mom, I just, man, I just never expected to see her like that. It's like she's almost in a coma. She wants Dolores to come in and sing to her—doesn't she know?"

Julie shook her head. Then she handed him the clothes. "Here, this stuff should fit Lorna, and there's an old pair of jeans you left here last time you did your laundry, you should get out of those wet clothes. Do you want a pair of your father's undershorts?"

"I don't wear any. Ma, listen to me, have you talked to the doctors? What can they do? I mean, she was supposed to have surgery by now. . . ."

"Michael, all we can do is hope to God we can leave here

tomorrow. Today. I don't know. Your father's trying to get a hold of Doctor Sherman somehow. You think it doesn't pain me to see her like this? I would trade places this minute if I could. But the fact is we can't do anything. We can only go on and pray."

"You know what, Mom?" Michael asked, lowering his voice. "The good guys always lose. The creeps win. And they're out there, we saw them. They're breaking into houses. They're stopping at nothing to stay alive."

"That's what the nuns said."

"Nuns?"

"Come down stairs, I'll tell you about it. Harry hasn't heard the story yet either."

Out of the frying pan and into the fire. People fled their flimsy buildings and packed themselves into larger flimsy buildings. On the east side of the city, several hundred people were waiting out the snow in an old high school auditorium. Everyone was nervous, hungry, tired, but they all shared a sense of relief from the hell of what they'd already been through. It was becoming bearable, then....

It started with a sound. A loud moan, as if Paul Bunyan had gotten a stomachache and were crying out for relief. But the relief never came. The giant was the roof, and the weight of the ice and snow was too much to bear. This was no small apartment building; the people couldn't believe it. This was an auditorium! It was strong and....

One moment there were several hundred innocent faces staring up at the ceiling. And in the next that ceiling was upon them.

Across town, the ceiling on the huge Los Angeles Forum began to give. The thousands of people taking shelter below looked up and let out a scream which rocked the hall, as so many concerts had done in recent years. But this time there was no applause for Paul McCartney, no cheers for David Bowie. This time no one stuck around to demand an encore. This time people shoved for the doors, trampling their friends, running, clawing at each other to get out.

No building with a flat roof was safe. The trouble was, so many of the buildings had flat roofs.

A building with a *sloping tile roof* was the Sisters of Saint Theresa Motherhouse. In the Sheppard living room, drinking tea, they were talking about it. Julie told them of the nuns' visit, of the invitation to move in there.

"Sounds like a palace," Michael said to his mom.

"Absolutely not," Harry said. "What bullshit. They're as much in danger as we are, as anybody in this godforsaken place. We're getting out. Out." Harry was adamant.

"The sun's coming up," Lorna said. They looked at the windows. It was lighter outside. But the winds still were blowing the snow around.

"What was it like for you, Harry?" Julie asked.

"What was it like on the streets?" Harry said. "At first everyone was helpful, all in the same goddamn boat, ya know? Then, like snap, everyone is distrusting; everyone is paranoid the other guy's gonna rip off his boots. Jesus, people are out of their minds." This from a man who had lugged a fire hose through the worst blizzard in America.

"Uncle Harry's right, it was like that," Michael said. "Oh, the nuts are still around, people singing and playing in the stuff, some of them not even knowing what the hell is coming down. But you should have seen it tonight. More people are out of their apartments and houses than ever. Carrying possessions on their backs, one man with a stupid rocking chair."

"Yes," Lorna added, "and the look in their eyes. That's what frightens me. People crying, people looking stunned and sick. But people looking crazed, like animals. The soldiers we came up here with said the blacks down in Watts are singing their praises to the Lord. We heard the mayor cracked up."

"Cracked up?" Harry bellowed. "Truth is, he should have been committed years ago. What do you mean, cracked up?"

"They said a news broadcast in Phoenix said he put his hand

through a window, as if trying to stop the snow, and the rest of him went through it, too."

"My Lord," Julie said. It was her first contact with the realities of what was happening in her city in a long time. "What else?"

"Well, half the city is burned to the ground, I think," Michael said. "Even the Hollywood studios stopped working, and when they stop, you *know* something's wrong. And, yeah, you know the traveling exhibit of the Van Gogh paintings?"

Harry's every muscle tightened. "Hey, I was there at the opening, the night it started snowing."

"Well," Michael continued, "someone stole all the paintings."

"*All*?" Harry asked.

"That's what I heard."

"How could they ever have done that?" Harry asked.

"I guess they just walked out with them. I don't know. It's probably just a blown-up rumor."

Julie shook her head. "But what good is it? They have no meaning, no value in a situation like this."

"It's like the jewelry in the Broadway, just sitting there," Lorna said. "People would choose a saltine cracker over a diamond necklace."

And they talked like that for hours. Julie told them about Dolores, but not to so great an extent as to upset Harry, that she wondered if he wasn't really somewhat relieved by her disappearance. She told them about Carter's assurance of getting them out by helicopter, and though Lorna and Michael didn't relish another climb, they knew it was their only hope. She told them how glad she was that her family was together again.

Harry told them snatches of his ordeal, making himself the hero in every case. But they were interested in hearing what he'd seen on the streets. And Lorna and Michael told them their story, which topped all. Both Harry and Julie listened with horror as they heard the tale of their fight to survive with their friends. Julie had met Marguerita several times and cried when she heard the woman had died to save her granddaughter. She was proud of Michael, thinking of demanding that a soldier get through to Carter to help them. "If I hadn't, we would never have made it. Not with the baby," he said.

Julie shuddered to think what they would have done.

Finally, everyone went to sleep. Everyone but Julie. She sat by Susan, watching her, trying to read but the light wasn't strong enough. She gave her another hypo—there were only four left—and wiped her body down with alcohol, because she felt the fever rising again. She waited until the girl had fallen into a deep sleep before she went into the kitchen to prepare whatever kind of meal she could put together.

Standing at the counter in her sweater, she suddenly saw Harry standing in the dining room. What startled her so—she dropped the dish she was holding—was the gun he had raised to his shoulder. As the dish broke, so did the window. He had shoved the barrel through one of the panels of beveled glass. "Don't move another foot, or I'll shoot!" he shouted.

"Harry!" Julie screamed.

Michael and Lorna came running from the living room. But Michael was too late to stop him. *Pow.* The shot rang out. It echoed in the stillness of the morning. Julie and Michael and Lorna got to the window in time to see the figure of a man trying to get out of the yard as fast as possible. "Just a warning shot to scare him off, the bastard!" He yanked the shotgun back in and set it on the floor. "That'll teach 'em."

"I think we've got to watch the yard, the gate," Michael said. "There were a lot of people on the street in the night, Mom."

"Oh," Julie moaned, "I wish the Kuppermans would come over. I hate thinking of them all alone."

"They'll be okay. That woman's a tough character," Harry said. "The old man, too."

Julie shook her head. "They're gentle and kind."

"But they're still tough." No one answered him.

There was reason to worry, reason to watch the gates. Down on the street people were huddled in small groups, forming gangs to break into houses. Good people, nice people, turning vicious, wanting to survive. Surprisingly, they found most of the big warm homes empty. But some had moved clear up to the cul-de-sac and were eyeing the houses up there, the Kuppermans' red-brick house, the Sheppards' stucco one, and the magnificent castle the nuns lived in. The people were not killers, not madmen, not lunatics. They were refugees from the central part of Los Angeles. They had been burned out, frightened; they were starving; they wanted to live. They would stop at nothing to get what they wanted.

An hour later Michael was at the window. It was his "watch." They were each taking about an hour, sitting in the dining room. The window had been covered with the Monopoly board and taped with masking tape, but still the wind came through. Michael had his coat on. It had dried quickly near the big fire.

Suddenly he shouted, "Uncle Harry, come here!"

Harry got up from the piano bench, where he'd been sitting tapping his fingers nervously, and ran into the dining room. "Look," Michael pointed, "see that woman down there?"

Harry squinted and looked again from another window. "God, I think it's *her*. The coat . . . it looks like her hair."

Julie was watching too now. "She was always wearing her turban, but it could have been lost. Oh, I do think so. It looks like her."

"Well, whether it is or not, I'm going down there," Michael said.

"No, let me," Harry offered.

"Uncle Harry, you're better with the gun. Just cover me. Maybe they won't let her up here. There's people all around her. Maybe they want us to come out. You stay here and be on guard. I'll get her." He put his boots on, slipped his hands into his gloves, ran out the front door, and made his way down through the snow to the driveway.

They all watched from the window.

By the time Michael made it to three feet within the gates he realized the woman had come inside. "Dolores?" he shouted. "Auntie Dee?" He couldn't see her face. He rushed to her.

And then she turned and slipped through the open gates. And

Michael saw it wasn't Dolores at all. The same kind of coat, the same hair and body, but a different face. "Get out of this yard!" he shouted. The woman moved back among six or seven others.

"Rich boy, we only want some place to warm up in. You got a whole house in there."

"I'm warning you, stay away. The house is full. There's no room. Go somewhere else. Go back home."

There were shouts and cries. A man ran up and grabbed Michael by the neck and pulled him through the gates. Michael tried up pull away, to wrestle himself out of the grasp, but he couldn't. The woman spit in his face. Michael kicked the man in the groin and rushed to the gates again, but another man, a guy his own age, pulled his legs, tackling him. But Michael hung onto the gate with his hands, and as the man pulled on him, the gates moved through the snow, little by little, until they snapped shut. Then Michael fell into the snow again and the man started to beat him.

"Should I open the gates?" Julie shouted.

"No! He'll handle it," Harry said. Lorna was holding her breath, biting her lip as she watched the incredible scene. To have gotten this far without a mishap, and now....

Michael found power in his bones where he didn't know he had any left. He slugged the man in the jaw and knocked the old woman into the snow. Then he jumped as high as he could and kicked the younger guy down in front of him. He turned and ran, as fast as he could, through the evergreens in front of the Kupperman house. He knew he could get through the back gate easily, the one between the lots, and he doubted if the people would follow him. He ran, ran as fast as he could. He fell once but got up as fast as he'd hit the snow.

When he reached the gate, he turned around for the first time. The younger man was following him. "You son of a bitch," he screamed, "I'll kill you!"

Michael tugged on the gate and it finally opened, though not far because the snow was so thick. He entered his dad's yard. And a man leaped out at him from the side of the garage.

Michael had barely seen his shadow when he was down in the

snow, being pummeled. *Jesus,* he thought, *I've never really been in a fight in my life.* Now was obviously the time to learn basic training. He got up and kicked the man in the balls—it was the only real defense he could think of—and the fellow rolled over in pain. Then he grabbed the young guy who'd been chasing him, grabbed him by the neck of his thin jacket, and rapped his head up against the brick wall, knocking him out.

Michael stood back. Blood poured from his lip. He felt his lungs hyperventilating. He shook. But he'd won. The bastard who was rolling around with his hands between his legs finally begged, "Don't, don't hurt us. Please. We'll go. We'll go." He got up, still in great pain, and dragged his unconscious friend through the gate.

Michael turned to the house, looked up, and saw Harry there with the gun, on the patio, looking down over the fence. "Good show, Mike. Come on up. I'll cover you."

Michael fainted.

He was bruised, and his lip was double the normal size; but he was all right. A little proud of himself, in fact. If he hadn't gone around the back, they all might have been killed by the man who had got into the backyard. Michael was a hero, and he was taking a hero's welcome on the floor by the fire, sipping camomile tea and liking the fact he was being fawned over. Lorna, who despised violence, said she was proud of him and took his hand.

But the atomosphere was gloomy. It was already afternoon. Where was Bob? Why hadn't they heard from him?

Bob was on his way down. He'd got a later start than he'd figured on. They'd all happened to have breakfast together—coffee and bread—and then started talking, Carter and Alex and Rob and Bob. Alex Granville had talked with Washington, San Francisco, some of the major universities that had been working on the problem, and all agreed with Carter—rain would come, and flooding of such magnitude that nowhere on earth had been recorded before. "How do you tell seven million people to move to high ground, through seven feet of snow?" Bob asked.

"It would take weeks," Rob said.

"I think the first thing to do," Bob said, "is to suspend all airdrops, stop the lifts, and concentrate on using those choppers, the first moment they can fly, for mass evacuation."

"We'd need every copter in the whole entire world," Granville said.

"So get them," Bob answered.

"Even then," Rob added, "we're talking about going from twenty degrees to eighty degrees in a matter of some twenty-four hours. That's like turning a faucet on an ant colony."

Carter made it clearer: "That's like opening Hoover Dam on them."

"Well," the general summed it up, "we've done everything we could do. The rescue teams are ready just as soon as we give the word it's safe to fly in here. How's the wind?"

Rob shook his head.

"I don't think we'll get safe winds until the rain starts," Carter said.

"Then we fly in when the rain comes. It's all we can do."

And they adjourned their "meeting."

Bob dressed for the journey down the hill. "You've got to start up tomorrow, Bob," Carter said. "Rain or snow, you've got to. I don't know which would make the climb worse. You've got to brave it."

"We will. We have to. Carter, thanks, I appreciate it, taking us first."

"First?" He shook his head. "I'm going, and I'm taking you along. I don't know about anyone else. I'm getting out, and that's all. If we're first, that's fine, but I'm not coming back for more. That's other people's department."

"I don't think your general is well."

"The pressure's getting to him. He's depressed. The old man has been through a lot, always the hero, on top. This time he's coming out a loser. He can't take it."

"But he's fighting the elements, not the Chinese Army! He hasn't got a chance, no man does."

"Alex Granville considers himself above the elements."

"Okay, Carter, I'm off. We'll be here tomorrow. Don't give up on us, hey?"

"Bob, you're my best friend. I've never given up on you yet."

They shook hands, and Bob went outside. The same strong young soldier was there to help him again. He tied a rope around a big pine tree, and slowly the soldier let out the rope as Bob descended the hill. Bob hooked the rope from tree to tree, to guide their journey back up.

It was a hell of a lot easier going down than it had been coming up.

Rain was a frightening word to most people of Los Angeles. It meant inconvenience, problems, annoyance, sure, but it also meant possible flooding, always a threat in that part of the country. Few residents ever thought about it, but the Los Angeles Basin was a web of riverbeds that came down from the surrounding hills and mountains and spread out over the flatlands. For many decades those riverbeds had been camouflaged by civilization. The main arteries of the city running north and south from the hills were, in reality, viaducts for water runoff. The city engineers knew it, and that's why sewers, large sewers, had been built under the broad boulevards. But they learned from experience that they weren't big enough to handle the rainwaters that came with the big storms. The place flooded every now and then.

In the winter of 1955 a heavy rain produced enough water to cause a flood all along LaCienega Boulevard, L.A.'s "Restaurant Row." Near the base of the street a large department store ended up with four feet of water on its first floor. Hundreds of buildings had been damaged; hundreds of people injured.

From that incident, from that time on, engineers respected the power of these natural beds. They realized all the famous canyons, Benedict and Coldwater and Nichols, had been cut from the earth by water at one time, and they too were perfect natural waterways in the case of a torrential rain lasting several days. But nothing had or was being done to alleviate the problem which would occur with the heavy rains, mainly because Los Angeles hadn't had that strong a rainfall in many years. Time tends to make things better. Not only the city fathers, but also the residents tended to forget. It was a typical reaction of people who lived in L.A. When it happened, it was terrible. After it had passed, it seemed, well, annoying. But it wasn't so bad. Wait till the next time. It will go away. Life goes on.

But life was coming to a halt, and the problem of what to do with lots of water in Los Angeles had not been solved.

Julie and Lorna gathered around the radio. Someone was trying to get through to them. Michael watched the front yard, and Harry the back, but nothing was happening that they could see. It was deserted out there. Only some smoke came from the street, and Michael figured the people were huddled around a fire in the middle of the cul-de-sac.

Finally, Carter got through. "Julie, this is Carter DeSimone. Do you hear me?" She pressed the button and told him she did. "Bob is on his way down. You're all coming up tomorrow, before the rains start. I don't mind saying it now; everyone's going to know soon." Julie looked at Lorna. *Rains?* "It's going to get warm—even hot—and we're going to have rain. It's all going to be over. You've got to get out fast. Is everyone there, your son and daughter-in-law?" Julie told him they were all there, but Susan was in poor condition; how could she make it up the hill when she couldn't even walk? "You have to find a way of carrying her." Michael was listening. "I know, we'll make a sled of some kind," he said. The radio went dead.

"Rain!" Julie exclaimed. "Oh, just think of it." She smiled. "What a blessing."

"Are you out of your mind?" Lorna asked. "What happens when all this melts?"

Julie thought about it. "Oh. Oh, dear. Oh, my God." Her face seemed to tighten in horror. "Oh, we've got to do something for Susan."

Michael was already looking around the house for something to turn into a sled. He thought of a garbage can cover because he'd heard of kids back in the Midwest sliding down snowbanks on them. But theirs were plastic, and they weren't big enough for a twelve-year-old girl to lie on. He went into the family room—God, it was freezing down there—but found nothing. Then, back upstairs, in the living room, he noticed the coffee table. It was oval, a thick oak table that would be sturdy and rigid. All he had to do was pull the top off from the legs and fashion some kind of blades on it, maybe pieces of wood.

"How about skis?" Julie asked.

"Skis?"

"Susan's skis. They're in the garage."

"I didn't know she had skis."

"Last year, for Christmas. She's never used them, but they're there. Can't you hook them under the tabletop somehow?"

"Sure. I'll get them."

Harry butted in. "No, let me. You're in no condition to go back out there yet, Mike." He put on his coat and went down to the garage.

There they were. In the backpack. He could feel them. He hugged them. Then he grabbed the skis from the rafters and carried them back up to the house, along with a hammer and nails.

Harry and Michael ripped the beautiful table apart in front of the fireplace. Julie groaned, "I remember the day I found that at Sloan's. It was over four hundred dollars. God, but it hurts to see you whack it apart." Hurt it did, but it was the only way of getting her little girl out, and if she'd had to, she'd have swung the hammer at it herself.

Michael nailed the skis to it. A sled had been born. "No Cadillac," he said, but it would have to do. They agreed.

The beast poked its nose out of the water near a piling beneath the Santa Monica amusement pier and sniffed the air. It was strange territory for the mammal, but the feeding in the bay had more than calmed its doubts that this was an unfriendly territory. In the distance it could see movement. That was a sight it didn't like. Was it one of those two-legged creatures? It paused, then decided to swim out to the islands thirty miles away. The feeding would be just as good, and it wouldn't have to fear the beasts.

Thus, the sea lion, which usually spent its winters off the coast of Vancouver, found itself driven with the cold waters south to places it had never been nor would have ever seen if it hadn't been for the storm. It had no idea what it was looking at when it popped out of the water in Los Angeles. But it smelled death in the air, and it did not want to be part of it.

Another hour passed. A sound began to echo in the air. The sound of people, many people. A chanting. It got stronger in the next hour as the day began to fade. "There must be a lot of them out there by now," Julie said. And there were. They all had their eyes on the big house with the smoke coming out the chimney. They were making plans to get into that very house.

Lorna was the first to see Bob. At first he startled her. She thought it was one of the people who were still chanting out front. But he called her name. She opened the back door. He seemed to be in good shape. "I made it. We're getting out! Rains are coming." Then he hugged Julie and kissed her. "Michael, Lorna, you don't know how I worried. Michael, what the hell happened to your lip?"

"Lorna got mad. I made a pass at her when she wanted to do nothing but freeze in the snow. She slugged me."

Bob laughed. "Harry, my brother, by God. Where the hell have you been, golfing? Lunch at Perino's?"

"What the hell you doing climbing mountains these days?" Then, seriously: "When do we leave?"

"Tomorrow. We've got to plan this well. It isn't easy. And it could be raining in the morning."

"But it's freezing now," Julie said. "It can't change that fast."

"Don't you realize by now anything can happen?"

She thought about it. "I guess if you said pink fog was going to come, I'd believe it. I'd believe anything."

"Hey, I'm tired. And what's that noise?"

They told him about the people camped out front, about the nuns and their offer, about the houses being deserted. Again, Julie expressed her worry about the Kuppermans. Bob said, "If they're not here by morning, I'll go over and make them come. We can't leave them behind. There's got to be room."

"Do you think they can take the climb?"

He thought about it. "No, actually I don't. We'll get them to go to the Motherhouse. How's that?"

"Anything but staying there alone in that big house," Julie answered.

"Okay, in the morning then. Listen, Michael, go down and get two more guns. Get a rifle for me. I don't want to take any chances. I'm going to get some sleep. You and Harry keep an eye out, and I'll take over in a few hours. Then we've got to decide what we're taking up the hill with us. And we've got to get the backpacks from the garage. It's the only way to carry things. The sled will work perfectly. How is she?"

Julie just shook her head.

"Dolores?"

No one answered. Just sad looks. Bob shook his head, lay down, and was asleep when his head hit the pillow.

No one said much of anything; what was there to say anymore? Lorna held the baby in her arms. She was worried about her. She didn't look good. She was crying often. She wasn't eating well, spitting up too much. She only hoped she'd be all right till they got out, till they got to a warm climate, to a good hospital.

Michael went down and got the guns and ammunition. The house was now an arsenal. Julie tried to ignore it, but she knew where every gun was; she'd memorized it. She still felt she was capable of faking it, holding one to warn an intruder. She went into the kitchen to see what food was left for the journey, what was left for them to eat still that night.

Harry and Michael stood guard as the chanting continued.

Susan cried out in pain again. "I'm coming, darling," Julie called to her. But she was on a little ladder in the kitchen, getting preserves out of a cupboard. Lorna was near the door to

Susan's room, and she went in. The girl was off the mattress, on the floor next to the box spring, squirming in pain. She was making a sound that Lorna had never heard before. "Susan, Susan, darling, come back in bed, here, get back up. . . ." She tried to help her up, but it only caused more pain.

Susan screamed, "Don't touch meeeeeeeee!"

Julie rushed into the room. "Stop! Leave her alone!" Lorna turned and tried to explain. "Get out of here!" Julie ordered. Lorna rushed out.

After Julie had given Susan the shot—now there were only three left—she found Lorna waiting for her in the hall. "I want to talk to you." Julie walked past her, into the kitchen, ignoring her. "I said I want to talk to you!"

Julie turned around and snapped, "Sure, talk to me. You want to deride me and tell me I'm a lousy mother, just like everyone who thinks they know best what's right for my daughter, the girl I gave birth to, the girl I've been living pancreatitis with since before you were even in our life! She was on the floor, Lorna. Yes, she was on the floor and you wanted to move her because a sick person is supposed to be in bed, right? Well, let me tell you, I've found her on the stairway. I've found her outside on the grass. I've seen her literally crawling the walls in pain. I saw her tied down—yes, strapped down—once in an emergency room because she was in so much violent pain she had actually *pulled hair* from her head!" Julie was fighting back tears, but she was fighting mad, too. "And so I know how to help her. She was on the floor, and I left her there because in such pain she can't be moved. The shot will help; then she can get back into bed. Don't you know that I know what I'm doing, for God's sake? I'm her *mother*. Do you know what that *means?*"

Softly, Lorna said. "I couldn't live with it if that were Dawn in there."

Julie looked at her and shook her head. "Oh, Lorna, you're so young." She hugged her. "I'm sorry. Listen, you could live with it. You could, and you would. You'd be surprised the things a mother can cope with."

"I had you pegged wrong, Julie. You've got more strength in you than anyone I've ever seen."

Julie smiled. "Oh, the illusions we give. As I said the other day, I'm terrified. But I can't be less strong than she. And that, that girl in there suffering, that's strength. I've learned from her. She's fighting for her life."

"And so are you." Lorna kissed Julie. "I'm sorry. I really am."

"Shhh. Let's get some food up for our men."

But the men were calling from the living room.

"Look out there!" Harry said. "The bastards are trying to break in the gate again!" He pointed. They seemed to be carrying torches, and they were chanting, "Let us in! Let us in!"

In the background there was the sound of an explosion. Michael and Lorna stiffened; it was all too familiar. Then the sky burst red, and they could see the flames. "Oh, God, I wonder whose house it is," Julie said.

Bob just shook his head and returned to the couch. "It doesn't matter anymore. It just doesn't."

"They're still trying to get in," Harry said. He thought of his knapsack, and he would defend it to the death. "Michael, let's go scare them ... *look! They're coming over the fence!"* He saw the torches going up and coming down. Three people had already dropped over the fence.

"Let's go, Uncle Harry!" Michael yelled.

"Be careful!" Lorna screamed.

In a minute Harry and Michael had descended half the steps, confronting the marauders in the yard. They were unarmed, against the powerful guns Harry and Michael wielded. "Off this property or we'll shoot! Back up!"

Finally, the men started backing up. One of them shouted, "We'll be back! We'll be back! There'll be more of us!"

Michael and Harry stood there until they were well past the gate. Then Harry said, "Let's have a look around the yard as long as we're out here. You never know."

"Right."

They made their way around the house, slowly. Harry especially wanted to check the garage. Most especially.

And while they were outside, Bob drifted off to sleep again. He was completely worn out, and he knew he'd need his strength for the big climb. Julie was in the kitchen. Lorna was feeding Dawn in the living room. Susan was sleeping soundly in her room, on the floor next to her bed. Julie stuck her head in the room for a moment and considered moving her, but she seemed peaceful. She let her be; the room was warm. Then she walked into the living room and felt her sleeping husband's head. He didn't have a fever; he was just tired. She smiled at him, put another log into the fire, and went back to the kitchen. She looked at the shotgun standing near the refrigerator, loaded, forbidding, and she shivered. Had she ever dreamed she'd be standing in her kitchen next to a gun, they'd have told her she should seek professional help. To think this place, this wonderful house, would have to be abandoned. To think it had become an armed camp. To think it had become snowbound, where the beautiful turquoise water of the pool had glimmered with the azaleas around it. The house which had been so filled with love and laughter and Michael's blasting Pink Floyd albums. Oh, how could she leave it? This was her home. The first new house she'd ever had. She and Bob had done so much to it. Now she would probably never see it again. Or at least not for a long time. Would it even be standing when they got back? She leaned against the counter. She wondered what was taking Michael and Harry so long.

She went to the window in the living room, the one behind the piano, and looked down onto the driveway. She saw the door to the garage open. They were in there. Well, at least they were safe. She should have told them to go get the Kuppermans. She went back to the kitchen, to continue taking inventory of the few supplies left.

Down in the garage, Harry and Michael were pulling a pair of hiking boots from a box in the rafters. Michael had remembered them, and sure enough, they were still there. They would come in handy. Their voices could be heard up on the patio.

What they didn't know was there was someone up there listening to them.

The figure peered into the den. It was dark, and the windows were locked tight. Then the shabbily dressed man crept to the window where he saw light. He looked in. A girl was sleeping on the floor. Was she dead, for God's sake, sprawled out like that? He looked closely. Maybe there was no one else in the house. But then the girl moved a little, and he knew he'd have to be careful, silent. He touched the window. It moved. It was open. He slid it as far open as he would need to get in. Then he lifted his leg and carefully put one foot on the floor of the warm room. Then he lifted his body inside and set his other foot down. But it didn't hit the floor. It struck something hard, yet mushy. It moved. It squealed. He'd stepped on a cat.

Julie jerked back as she heard the screech of the animal. She'd heard that sound only once before, when she was closing a drawer and hadn't realized Samantha had her paw in it. She turned to go to Susan's room, to see what had happened. Had Susan rolled over on the little kitten? Or had she tried to get up and fallen?

In the hall she heard a more terrifying sound. Everyone in the house heard it, everyone outside. Susan screamed at the top of her lungs. *"Eeeeeeeeeeeeeee!"* Julie had never heard anything like it before. Without even thinking–automatically–she grabbed the gun in the kitchen and got to the door of Susan's room before Bob did. She opened it. He stood there, facing her, standing in front of the window, glaring at her, daring her.

Without blinking she pulled the trigger. The blast of the gun rocked the house. The force of it knocked the man back against the window, and his torso fell backward, his head and shoulders hanging out in the snow, his feet still on the carpet. The blood seemed to spurt from the gaping hole in his abdomen. Julie stood there, silent, frozen, the gun shaking in her arms. Her eyes were glassy. She stared at the knife that had fallen from between the teeth of the man. Bob stood behind her. Susan sat with her mouth open in terror, against the wall. The little kitten had run out of the room as soon as Julie had opened the door.

In the hall Harry and Michael were calling to them, asking what happened. They pushed into the room. "My God Almighty!" Harry muttered. Lorna wrapped her arms around Michael, thinking she would fall over; her knees felt as though they were giving out.

Bob pulled Julie away and took the gun from her hands. He led her to the living room and put her in the wing chair. She was in a state of shock. He pulled a blanket over her. Lorna sat near her. "It's going to be all right, Julie. You saved us; you saved your daughter. You did what you had to."

"I . . . I took a man's life. Dear God, I killed a man." She put her head back and closed her eyes and said nothing more.

Bob and Harry pushed the body out the window and closed it. Michael had taken his sister—carried her—to the living room and put her on one of the sofas. She was in shock, too, not really comprehending what she'd seen, thinking perhaps she'd dreamed it. Samantha jumped up and curled up at her feet. She meowed. Michael changed the subject, trying to forget the horror and forge ahead. "Poor little thing," Michael said, "there's no cat food left."

"There's one can of tuna fish," Lorna said. "I saw it on the counter with the other things."

"It's protein," Michael said. The cat meowed again. "Hungry?" he asked her. She moaned, understanding that word. He said, "Well, come on, tuna it is. You're as important as the rest of us."

Michael fed the cat while Harry and Bob closed off the heater vent in Susan's room, wiped up some of the blood, tossed the knife into the trash, and collected some warm clothes for Susan, and her favorite picture from the wall, one of the family Bob had taken with an automatic timer the year before. Funny. It had been taken up at Big Bear Lake. There was snow in the background.

And so they had the living room, dining room, and kitchen left. The firewood was nearly gone, but there was furniture to burn. Julie lay in the chair, silent, her eyes closed, but she was not asleep. The two little girls lay on the sofas, the baby and Susan, both ill, but both, because of their youth, strong. Harry paced the room, gun in hand, watching the drive, thinking of nothing but his booty in the garage. Michael, weak, skinnier than ever, tired, his ebullient nature almost nonexistent now, watching the backyard through the door leading to the patio. And the leader of the family, Bob, sitting there in the kitchen, trying without luck to get Carter on the shortwave, making a list of what would be needed the next day.

And outside, a body crumpled up, freezing there on the patio. In front, hundreds of people, camping there, waiting, planning an attack. Down the hill across the street, a magnificent house burning because someone had fought over the place and had spilled kerosene in a scuffle, kerosene which had ignited quickly when it trickled near the fireplace. And next door, smoke still came from the chimney, which meant somehow the Kuppermans were making it through. Bob would go get them when the sun came up–if it did. He knew he couldn't count on sun, but he could certainly count on rain. Of that he was positive.

At midnight he went outside. There wasn't a flurry in the air. For the first time in days, the snow had stopped completely. And the temperature–it had to be well above zero now. It was warmer; he was sure of it.

Earlier that night Barbara Walters had summed it up for the rest of the country, a country whose eyes focused only on Southern California now. "There is an unearthly silence in the city," she had said, "punctuated only by explosions and the cries of the homeless, the hungry, the cold. No one knows the death toll. Thousands upon thousands of people have frozen to death, some in their tracks as they searched for a way out. Officials say when–and if–the snow melts, the bodies will cover the streets. There have been reports in the past two days of desperate acts, murders for chocolate bars, killings for a winter coat. Now that seems to have changed. People are numb, losing energy, perhaps even the instinct, to survive."

Harry Reasoner added, "Even with the fate of the city still unknown at this time, what is now and will always be known as the Great Los Angeles Blizzard will go down in history as one of the most awesome and gruesome tragedies mankind has ever known."

At the end of his list of things to do for the journey up to the observatory, Bob Sheppard printed the words "We will survive!" Then he dropped the pencil and put his head into his hands.

Michael walked in and put his hand on his father's shoulder. "Is Mom going to be all right?" he asked.

"Yes, Michael, she will be." Then Bob pulled his hair. He was in obvious pain, holding himself back from smashing his fists into the table, from breaking down.

Michael bent over and kissed his father on his head and left the room.

Bob sat straight up and looked determined. He grabbed the pencil again and underlined what he'd written. Underlined it twice.

THE NINTH DAY

FRIDAY, JANUARY 23

HIGH TEMPERATURE OF 60° IS REACHED BY MIDNIGHT

THE WEATHER PATTERN WHICH HAD BEEN FORMING IN THE PAST twenty-four hours was as frightening now as the blizzard itself, though normally, without the blizzard, without the snow, it would have been cause for little concern. The warmer tropical-low storm systems from the Pacific south of California were flexing their muscles and eyeing the gap in the atmosphere over Los Angeles. The massive storm was dissolving, pushing eastward. Cold remained from the north, but that too had little power behind it. It meant that it was an ideal time for a strong storm like the one off the coast of Baja to work its way into the area of Los Angeles, with its tropical rains ready to drench everything underneath it.

On the other side of the city, to the east of the Rockies, where the high had held the blizzard at bay, conditions were brewing for something quite the opposite from rain; it was perfect weather for the hot, dry Santa Ana winds to pour through the mountain passes, the air warming, heating, as it condensed in those narrow spaces. These were the winds that brought the 90° weather to Los Angeles every fall and sometimes in the winter months.

The tropical rainstorm and the Santa Ana winds. Two encores to the blizzard, but they couldn't happen at once. Which would take stage first? Would one cancel out the other? Both meant havoc. But which would come first?

The answer was that it didn't really matter. Both were perfect conditions to cause that other Los Angeles phenomenon—flooding.

Both, in this situation, were equally as lethal.

They all could feel the change: it was warmer.

The temperature had risen during the night, steadily. It was still below freezing, but no snow was falling. The morning seemed somewhat majestic, the towering fir tree in front of the house covered with white, the front yard one rolling mound of snow. Even the sky seemed clearer than it had been for weeks.

Julie opened her eyes and looked out the window from the same chair she'd fallen asleep in. It was light already. How long had she been there? What happened? She remembered; it all came back so vividly. She closed her eyes again and wished it had never happened, told herself it had never happened, and then, almost miraculously, she was asleep again.

But this time she had a dream; she relived the whole experience. She saw the man's eyes, the cold steel blue eyes in the candlelight. She saw the knife in his teeth shine like quicksilver. She felt her finger pulling, pressing the hard metal thing. She felt the gun push her body back. She saw him, that look on his face, that look of stunned surprise, as if he had time to say, "Why are you doing this?" And then the way he fell backward, his whole body, both feet actually lifting from the floor. She did something in her dream which hadn't actually happened the night before, however. She screamed.

Lorna sat up on the couch. *What was that sound?* Michael lifted his head from the floor. Harry came into the room from the hall where he'd been guarding the house, holding the same gun which Julie had shot. Bob ran up to his wife, trying to wake her. But she screamed again and again. He finally slapped her across the face, hard.

Her eyes opened. There wasn't a sound in the room. "Oh, Bob!" she cried. "Bob, don't let it happen again, don't let me do it." She hugged him to her.

"Honey, it's all right, you were just dreaming, that's all. It's morning, and everything is fine. We're going to be leaving today. It's warmer."

"Warmer?"

"Much."

She got up and looked out the window. It was clear. No snow was falling. She could see houses in the distance. Michael and Lorna joined them. "Hey, where'd the campers go?" Michael asked.

"You're right," Bob said, "I don't see anyone out there."

"Probably to the nuns. I'll bet they took them in." Michael had figured that's what would eventually happened. The Kuppermans and the Sheppards would resist, but the church would take in the lost souls. Let the church have them, he thought. "The hell with them. We're safe."

"We've got a lot to do." They all turned to look at Bob. He was right, and they knew it. For although no snow was falling—the blizzard was over—there was still just a little more than six feet of it on the ground; some of the drifts were a whopping twelve and thirteen feet high. But Bob had told them the hill leading up to the observatory wasn't as difficult as it could have been because of all the trees. They provided support, something to grab onto, something to lean against and rest, something to break your fall.

They went into the kitchen and had what they called breakfast. They cleaned up all the food left, and each person chose the thing that interested him most. Lorna gave the cat the second half of the can of tuna fish, and she herself had a seafood breakfast—canned oysters and New England clam chowder. Michael ate stale Triscuit crackers with peanut butter and pickles. Harry opened a can of eggplant appetizer and cooked himself some noodles. Miraculously, the gas was still working. He dumped half a tin of Parmesan cheese on the noodles, but the lack of butter or margarine made them taste dry. He added some olive oil. It helped. Bob and Julie shared a can of stewed tomatoes—Bob drank the juice—and a can of peas and one of french fried onion rings.

As they were eating, the radio crackled. Carter was calling. "We're going to have a copter waiting," he assured them, giving them strength for the climb. Bob asked if there were any change in the predictions. None. Then he asked why they couldn't evacuate people now while it was clear? "There's torrential rain in the mountains and off the coast. No planes can get in, not even choppers. Oh, a few, but not enough for any mass evacuation. We are sending some whirlybirds to hospitals to take out the emergency cases. We're doing everything we can, until the rain starts. Are you ready?"

"We're getting things together. We're going to pack and get dressed for it, and we should be leaving in a few hours." Carter said that was fine. Perhaps they could beat the rain. Bob told them about his neighbors, and Carter too felt they were too old, and he couldn't promise them room. "I'm not even supposed to be doing this for you," he reminded Bob. But he suggested they get them to the convent. "I know that building. You realize they even have a reservoir up there behind the main building? And a retaining wall that will probably offer good protection when the mud starts to slide. I'd get them out of the house next door. The mud could wash it away."

Julie cringed. She got up and put on her coat. "Where are you going?" Lorna asked.

"Next door."

Bob told Carter to wish them luck and stay in touch. Then he stopped his wife. "You're not going anywhere." He could see she was not fit for anything; she was still in shock. Her mind was on her friends, but she wasn't going out in the snow until she absolutely had to. "Michael and I will go."

Lorna jabbed Michael with her elbow. "Yeah, right."

"Well, all right," Julie said feebly. She sat back down and suddenly burst into tears. "I didn't mean to kill him. I saw the knife, and it was the only thing I could do." Michael put his arm around her. Bob took her hand.

Lorna said, "If you hadn't done it to him, he'd have done it to you. Or Susan. Or maybe all of us."

That got through to Julie; she needed to hear it. She managed a smile. "Okay, now, you two, go next door. Tell Minnie we're ordering her out of that house. Drag her over here if you have to. Perhaps she'll let Billy go with us. After all, there's one of us missing. He could take Dolores'—" She stopped and looked at Harry, ready to tell him she was sorry. But she changed her mind. What was was. "He could take Dolores' place."

"Come on, Dad." Michael got up.

They dressed in their warm clothing. When they went out onto the patio, they really felt the change in the weather. Bob put his hood down. "It's not that warm," Michael said.

"This is hot compared to what we've been having."

They both turned and looked at the body lying under Susan's window. He was frozen stiff, his head buried in the snow. Bloody splotches were all around him, on the wall of the house, on the windowsill. Michael turned away. He felt sick to his stomach. Not so much for what his mother had done—actually, he was proud of her courage—but for what the crazed maniac could have done to them.

They made their way down the steps leading to the driveway and the garage. Then they went through the gate where Michael had defended himself and the house. He still couldn't believe he had done it, the weakling, the pacifist. A lot of things he'd done lately had amazed him. A lot of the things everyone had done lately had amazed him. A crisis always brought the best and worst out in people; it really laid everything on the line, values, attitudes, the way you looked at life. Without believing in it, he thought, he would have slit his wrists long ago.

The Kuppermans' back door was locked. They pounded, and still no one came to the door. "Figures," Bob said. "They're probably holed up in the living room like we are."

Michael looked in the kitchen window and saw nothing but a lot of cans and bottles strewn around. "Jesus, Minnie sure gave up on the kitchen. Look."

Bob cupped his hands to the window and looked inside. It was his first inkling that something was wrong. He'd known Sam and Minnie for years, and nothing could make either one of them mess up the kitchen like that. "Michael, we should have brought the gun."

"What? Why?"

Bob didn't answer. He led Michael around to the front of the house. And then he got his second clue that something was amiss: footprints. Hundreds of them, it seemed. Leading from the street to the front door. The snow was trampled down deep. The front door was ajar.

"Dad, I'll bet they went to the convent days ago. Mom hasn't talked to Minnie in days. No one's seen them. You think we should go in there?"

"Let's have a look." Bob stepped on the porch and opened the door all the way. The first thing he saw was the leg of a man in the vestibule. He took a step inside and saw the rest of him. It was Sam Kupperman. A knife stuck out of his back. He'd been dead only a few hours. "No," he whispered. "Oh, God, no."

Michael seemed to be in a trance. "So ... that's ... so that's where all the derelicts in the street went."

They both looked up now, looking inside. They became aware of the noises, the sounds, the smells. People, lots of them. Sitting in every corner of the room, around the fire. A young man and woman were making love right there on the floor, their pants down to their knees, big jackets still on their bodies. The place smelled of urine and burning food which they couldn't recognize. A woman was holding a frying pan over the fire.

No one talked. The noises were sniffles, moans, cries. The sighs of the couple making love. No one seemed even to notice them. Everyone was dazed. Michael thought they looked stoned. Their faces were red, hardened from the cold, from the wind. In the corner of the room sat a little boy, shivering with fear, his face white, his eyes red from crying. It was little Billy.

"I'm going to get him, Michael," Bob said. He walked through the big living room and bent down in front of the boy. "Billy, it's Bob Sheppard from next door. You remember me, don't you?"

The boy nodded. "They killed Grandma and Grandpa." His voice was a monotone. "They killed Grandma and Grandpa."

"Come on, Billy. We're going to get you out of here." Bob picked him up and slung him over his shoulder. No one made a move to stop him. No one was even watching.

They walked out the front door. Bob carried the boy past the body of his grandfather as fast as he could, but as soon as they got out on the porch, they saw something they were surprised they'd missed on the way in. The body of Minnie Kupperman lay in the snow, to the left of the porch, in the snow between two tall evergreens. A pillow lay near her; she'd been trying to signal for help. She too had been stabbed to death. Michael winced and wondered if it had been the same guy who'd climbed in Susan's window. Christ, he hoped so!

And so they carried little Billy—in his shirt sleeves—through the snow to the house. They asked him where his jacket had gone, but he didn't answer. He didn't respond to anything. Bob figured someone had just taken the jacket off him for his own child. The only words the boy uttered, again and again, were, "They killed Grandma and Grandpa."

When they got into the house, Julie ran and hugged Billy. She looked behind the boy for his grandparents, and then he said the words, and she gasped and covered her mouth with her hands. She looked at Bob—their eyes met in sorrow and shock—and turned and ran into the living room. Bob caught up with her and put his arm around her. "Honey, you've got to get through this. He needs us. There's nothing we can do about what's happened."

"I can't," she cried, "I can't. After last night . . . oh, Bob, I can't even think anymore. With Susan lying there so close to death . . . death, it's all around us—"

"Julie, stop it!" He grabbed her and shook her. "Listen to me, we've got to save our lives, the lives of our children. You did that yesterday, in an extreme form. You had to. Now we have to do our damnedest to climb to safety, and the only way we're going to do that is to be strong, unemotional. Let it all out when we get the hell away from here. Julie, do you understand me? Susan needs you. Little Billy needs you; he needs us now more than ever. Even Michael and Lorna need you."

Softly she reflected, "I wonder if Dolores didn't need me too. I wonder if I could have done something, something more."

"You want to take the blame for the whole thing? Do it, Julie. Put it all on your shoulders, all the guilt. Do it because I won't. I won't accept the guilt for anything. You go ahead. Good luck." He turned to walk away.

"Bob!"

"Yes?" He stopped without turning back.

"Bob, I'm sorry. I'll . . . I'll be strong."

"You always were. Now's a hell of a time to quit."

She looked down at Susan, curled up on the sofa. "I won't quit. I can't quit." She sat down and ran her hand through her daughter's hair. It was hot, greasy, stringy. She remembered how soft it usually was, how bright. *It would be again,* she promised. She bent forward and kissed her. *It's almost time to leave. We're going to go away, and you're going to get well.*

Bob shouted, "Michael, come with me, let's get the backpacks."

"I'll go," Harry said, volunteering.

"Okay. They're in the garage."

"I know. Michael and I were in there last night when we went down to the gate. They're on the floor."

"I used one. It's just outside the back door. There should be four in the garage."

"Let's go." Harry put his jacket and gloves on.

"Where's the boy?" Bob asked.

"Michael and Lorna are with him in the kitchen, giving him something to eat."

"They'll take care of him. What a traumatic experience. Both the kids have to see that, Susan with the maniac who came through the window, Billy with Minnie and Sam. The world stinks."

Harry opened the back door. "Amazing to finally hear you say that, Robert, my brother. You're the one always defending the radicals and the young crazy fuckers who screw up society. Now the whole world stinks, huh? Well, I always said it did."

"I'm just a late bloomer when it comes to cynicism," Bob said.

"Jesus Christ!" Harry said, stopping outside the door.

"What?"

"It's starting to melt."

Sure enough, the snow was feeling wet. The sky was brighter than it had been. There were already icicles hanging from the roof. There was a little puddle under the window, near the last of the firewood. "It's gonna happen faster than we realize."

"I want outta here."

They started down the steps. "That's precisely why we're getting the backpacks."

Once in the garage, Harry quickly moved over to the workbench and grabbed the backpack in which he'd put the paintings. Bob picked two others up from the floor, and Harry grabbed the other one. "I think there are more hiking boots somewhere." He looked in a small cabinet. Nothing. But there was some more rope. "This will come in handy."

"The boots are in the house."

"Could be. I checked the rafters yesterday. Only mine were up there. Damn, I know Michael left his here, and Julie had a pair, too. They could be in the storage box in the attic."

They climbed the steps again and went into the house. Bob dragged the backpack he'd used to climb the hill into the house and set it near the door. "I still have a few candy bars in it. What else should we take?"

"Does anyone have anything valuable?" Lorna asked. "We lost everything in the building. We got what we could save when the roof collapsed, but then it all burned up when the explosion came."

"I even lost my wallet," Michael said. "Oh, well, I never liked the picture on my driver's license anyway."

"There are some things," Julie said. "Some things we could save."

"Get them, Ma," Michael told her. "We've got these. You might as well take as much as you can fit into them. Better than leaving it if you can take it."

"Throw the sleeping bags out," Bob said. "Each pack has a sleeping bag. We won't need them."

Michael picked up a pack. So did Lorna. So did Julie. Bob's was by the back door. Harry already held one. He said, "Listen, don't you think we should take at least one sleeping bag? Just in case we need it?"

"What for?" Michael asked.

"Warmth. If someone gets hurt–" He was trying to think of a damn good reason.

"Well," Lorna said, "if someone got hurt, we could conceivably put them into a sleeping bag and tie a rope to it and pull them through the snow, right?"

"Yes, yes," Julie said. "Let's take two. They'll fit in one pack."

Harry thanked God. "Listen, I'll carry the sleeping bags. I don't have anything personal either. Dolores had all the money, the papers and stuff. Give me one of the bags, and I'll put it in on top of the one already in here." Michael handed him the sleeping bag from his backpack. Harry turned around, pretending to put it in his bag. While they talked and concentrated on packing their own packs, he stuffed it in the dishwasher.

"I'll take the food," Michael said, " 'cause it's pretty heavy." His father warned him not to take too much. Just enough to give them some energy if they needed it or if they had to wait a long time up at the observatory. "Carter had a pretty good feast up there, huh, Dad?" Michael asked.

"Well, there was food, let's just put it that way. But there's no telling if they have enough for five adults and two kids and a baby."

Michael started packing anything with sugar and protein.

Lorna and Julie collected valuables from around the house. Not only valuables, but mementos that Julie cherished. They had the packs; why not use them? If they had to, they could discard them, but if they could take things, why not? Julie took a photograph album, her favorite, with pictures of her wedding,

Michael's wedding, Dawn's first photograph, happy pictures of their vacations, even a photograph of the same group, minus Harry, standing with the same backpacks on up near Ojai, when they'd gone camping for a weekend. Marvelous memories, and that's all that was left now.

Julie went up into the cold bedrooms and made sure there was nothing she wanted to take. Oh, she wanted everything, absolutely everything! She wanted her clothes and her framed drawings that Michael and Susan had done when they were only little kids. She wanted her furniture and her house. She didn't want to leave.

Bob went through his office. It felt as though it were 20° below zero in there; he could see his breath. He opened a window, and that actually felt better. He went through the file cabinets, taking out papers he felt were important, but everything of any real value was in the safe-deposit box of Wells Fargo Bank, and he was sure the bank wasn't going to be open that morning. He took some money he always kept for emergency use and put it into his backpack, as well as some papers which would come in handy for identification, in the future.

Julie brought down her hand-carved jewelry box. She didn't have the kind of jewels Dolores had, but what she did have had meaning to her, a pearl ring that Bob had bought her on their twentieth anniversary, a gold necklace she'd fallen in love with when they were in Rome, an antique brooch which had been her mother's, and various trinkets of sentimental value. She also stuffed some of the children's report cards from school into her pack, cards which she'd saved and often went back to look at. Bob gave her a strange look. "I'm carrying the thing," she said, almost embarrassed, "so I can put anything into it that I please."

He just smiled.

He felt the jewelry box was too heavy for her to carry, so he put it into his backpack. Lorna stuffed hers with diapers for Dawn, warm clothes for the baby (old baby clothes Julie had saved in the attic, from Susan) in case they were soaked when they got to the top of the hill, which was likely. In the attic they found some old clothes from when Michael was a boy, and they would have to fit little Billy. Michael packed them in his pack. They found a coat of Susan's and decided the boy would have to wear that up the hill; there was nothing else small enough for him. "How is he?" Lorna asked Michael. She'd been up going through the attic boxes with Julie.

"He's asleep in the living room. I think he's really in a bad way, in shock. He doesn't realize what's happening at all. When he gets back to his parents, he'll be fine."

"What parents? They're getting a divorce."

"Whichever has custody."

Finally, the packs were filled. They set them in the hall. Everyone but Harry—he put his close to the chair in which he was sitting in the living room.

"My God," Michael said. Everyone turned to him, wondering what was wrong now? "The cat."

"The cat?" Harry asked.

"Oh, my goodness," Julie moaned. "We can't leave Samantha behind. We can't!"

Bob agreed. "She'd never forgive us." The sleeping girl moaned and turned over, nearly falling off the couch. "Do you think we should put her on the floor?"

Julie shook her head. "No, we'll put her on the sled soon. She'll be all right."

Michael said, "Ma, you got a straw purse?"

"Yes, of course."

"Big enough for Samantha to fit into?"

"Samantha's pretty small. Sure, she'll fit."

"Get it. And get some thread and a needle. We're going to make a cat carrier."

"But she'll claw her way out. Straw isn't all that strong, and she's liable to panic being tossed around out there on the snow."

Michael thought about it. But Lorna came up with something. "Does anyone have a tranquilizer?"

They looked around. Who would be carrying tranquilizers? "I wish Flora were here," Lorna said. "She used to down Valium like popcorn."

"Valium?" Julie asked. "That's what the doctor gave Susan a few years ago, when she was having a hard time sleeping because of the pain and worrying. I think there are some left—"

"Get them," Michael ordered.

"But what for? You feeling upset, Michael?" Julie asked.

"No, for the cat."

"For the cat?" Harry bellowed. "You're gonna give the goddamn cat tranquilizers? You crazy?"

"Greg told me once that they give dogs and cats tranquilizers just like humans, the same thing, and he mentioned Valium. I'm going to give one to Samantha and see if it calms her down. It can't hurt. I know it's safe."

"But I don't know where they are," Julie said, thinking. "It's been so long since she'd needed them."

"Think, Ma."

She did. But Bob came up with the answer. "Hey, I know. There's a bottle of pills in my dresser drawer. No, in the armoire, in my drawer in the armoire. I think they're in there. We took them with us on a vacation, and they're all mixed in with aspirin and stuff like that."

"You're right!" Julie said.

Bob ran upstairs to get them. Harry muttered, "Giving a goddamn cat a tranquilizer, you people *are* crazy."

"I think *you* need one, Uncle Harry," Michael said.

"Shit, I need a good stiff drink, that's what I need."

Bob came down with the bottle of pills. He opened them and spilled them into his hand. "That's it, the little yellow tablet," Lorna said. Michael agreed. "It's five grains," Lorna said. "I think we'll try that."

Michael picked the kitten up in his arms and opened her mouth. "Here, sweet little cat, now you're gonna take what all the grown-up downer freaks take." He pushed the pill to the back of the cat's throat, forcing her to swallow it. She jumped out of his arms and licked her nose. "Done," he said.

"Honey," Lorna said, "take them along. We may all need one before the day's done."

Michael dropped the pills into his jeans pocket.

"I think we should heat up another bottle for Dawn. I'm still very dry," Lorna said.

"Come on." Julie and Lorna went into the kitchen.

Susan moaned and then opened her eyes. "Daddy," she said, softly. "I need some water." Bob grabbed the glass from the lamp table and put it to her lips. "Just enough to wet them," he said. "We can't put anything in that stomach of yours now. Tomorrow you'll be in a good hospital, all well."

"It's hurting again. It's starting–"

"Can you go a little while longer?" he asked.

"No, I don't want to," she said. "I . . . I don't want to have it hurt bad again. I can't . . . can't stand it anymore."

Bob nodded. Why not? They were leaving. The two shots would get her up the hill. He prepared one for her. Harry watched, wincing when Bob jabbed the needle into the girl's buttocks. Jesus, he was glad he'd be getting away from all this.

Susan drifted off again. Bob woke little Billy and told him they were going to go on an adventure. He pulled a sweater over the boy's head, cutting off the all-too-long sleeves. Then he gave him a pair of Susan's gloves and her old coat. "I know they won't fit well, but they'll keep you warm. You just wait here until we're ready to leave. Do you need anything? Are you thirsty? Have to go to the bathroom?"

The boy said nothing.

Lorna fed Dawn. Julie said, "We'll warm some milk, what's left, just before we start out. That way she'll have some on the way. You may be able to breast-feed her tomorrow, since you've had food and you're not so tired anymore."

"I hope so," Lorna said.

And then they turned their heads. A sound was coming from the other room, the dining room. No, they heard it outside the kitchen window too. It was coming from everywhere. Julie recognized it immediately; it had been one of her favorite sounds in the winters when she was baking and the fireplaces were lit. But this year it had become a sound she despised, for it had never let up, not until the snow had begun.

It was raining.

Harry ran to the front window. "I'll be goddamned!" He saw the rain, and his mouth fell open.

Michael opened the patio door and ran out in it. "Just singin' in the rain," he sang, dancing around. His father told him to get in the house before he caught pneumonia. Michael came in. "It'll make the climb easier, with the snow being melted."

"I'm not so sure," Bob said. He looked out at it. It was coming down faster now, the usual way it rained in Los Angeles, the tropical rains that just dumped inches on the city within an hour or so.

And Bob was right. They were prepared to leave. Everyone had backpack loaded, ropes ready, hiking boots on (Bob and Julie and Lorna, who had squeezed into Susan's), except Harry, who had his ski boots. They were set for the climb, the climb to safety. Then the radio crackled, and Carter warned them they had to hurry. It was going to be coming down by the bucketfuls soon; they had to beat it. If they didn't, they'd never make it in the night, not with torrential rain hindering them in the darkness.

Bob was telling Carter they were leaving that moment, when he heard his brother call out from the den. Harry had gone in there to get a better look at the hill they were going to have to climb, to see what the rain was doing to the snow. And instead of an empty yard and trees behind it, he saw people. Men, women, children. People coming around the back of the big red-brick fence, people coming in from the Kuppermans' yard.

They all ran to the back windows. "Holy shit!" Michael said. "They're coming this way!"

"Get the guns," Bob ordered. "Michael, into Susan's window, Harry, you stay here. Julie, you and Lorna, get to the front of the house, see if they're coming up that way, too. Jesus, they took the Kuppermans' house, wasn't that enough?"

"Enough for some of them," Michael yelled as he grabbed the gun in the hall and dashed into Susan's cold room. He opened the window. Blood was dried on the sill. He aimed the shotgun and heard his dad yell to the people, warning them back. They kept coming. Michael shot into the trees above their heads. They ducked and scrambled back to the trees, to the hill, to the point where the fence ended.

"No one's out front," Lorna reported to Bob. "With the rain, you'd think they'd go back down the hill. The snow will be gone—"

"They're not that dumb," Bob said, shaking his head, watching to see if anyone was coming up around the garage, if anyone had come through the gate which led to the Kuppermans' backyard. "They're still the same . . . they're still hungry, Lorna; they're still cold and wet; they still need shelter. Now more than ever. They're not dumb enough to believe the rain is good for us. Anyone with half a brain knows we're going to have floods."

Then Michael shouted another warning as more people entered the backyard. "Get out of here or we'll blow your heads off!" A man started running for the house, and Bob shot into the snow in front of him. The man wasn't hurt, but he was frightened. He turned back and huddled in the group. Soon it was hard to see them in the rain, and they took turns guarding their posts, their eyes straining to see what was happening.

And it went on. A standoff. Neither side giving. "But we have to leave!" Julie cried. "Can't we just tell them to take the house? Can't we tell them we're leaving?" Bob's mind flashed the scene in the house next door. Perhaps Minnie and Sam Kupperman had also invited the squatters in, had told them they were leaving. What did they get for it? Knives in their bodies. He told Julie they just couldn't take the chance.

Julie stood guard. She thought she'd never be able to put her hands on a gun again, but she did it; she had to do it. She shook with terror, with the diminishing hope of getting out, past those terrible faces camped out on the back lawn, in the rain, in the snow, in the slush. Why was everything going wrong? Now, when they were just about to have something go right for a change?

Bob called Carter while Julie guarded the yard. He told him their plight, and the man understood. "Listen, Bob, you can only afford to stick out your neck once, and that's going to have to be morning, because if you don't start climbing by then, there won't be any hill left to climb. If you have to make a run for it through them in the morning, do it. You can't stay there and hold them off until the house floats down the hill."

"How long's the rain going to last, Carter?"

"Listen, by night you won't be able to stand up in it. It's the same thing that's happened north. In Santa Barbara, half the city seemed to crack under the force of the rain. Ventura's washed out. Even if you make a run for it now, Bob, there's little chance of getting up before dark, if you get through those monsters out there. Maybe it is best if you wait until morning. The rain should diminish then. But even if it doesn't, that's the time to give it a try. Do you get me? The landing pad up here's going to turn to mud, and that'll be it for helicopters getting anyone out, at least from here." There was a pause. Then Carter said, "I'm looking out the window. A chopper can't fly in this. We can't see three feet in front of our noses up here. Stay there for the night, and make a break for it in the morning. Maybe they'll be gone."

"Where are they going to go?" Bob asked. No, they would be there. He would just have to get through them, let them have the house. Maybe they could sneak out the front way and down around the Motherhouse—but what about the street; were there more of them still there? And the Motherhouse was too big to climb around, the land was almost three acres large. Around the Kuppermans'? Perhaps, but that was going out of the way, too, and risking the unknown. No, the best way up was straight up the hill, dead center in the yard. They would just have to make it. Even if they had to get through the people with the use of their shotguns. Bob knew he could kill for his family's safety if he had to. After all, his wife had.

Carter was right, the rain was torrential. It was as though someone were standing above the kitchen window with a garden hose on full blast. Michael yelled from Susan's room. "Looks like the great fire hose in the sky is aimed on this yard!"

Harry almost choked on Michael's choice of words.

And so, slowly, quietly, they accepted the fact that their flight to freedom was going to be delayed. They held the gang of people off with guns in the windows as the rain pounded on the roof and hit the snow on the patio. Julie worried about Susan, with only one hypo left, and now another full afternoon, another dreadful night in this house. They took turns, as the hours passed, warming themselves in front of the fire. They took turns eating whatever hadn't been put into the backpacks. They took turns going to the bathroom, and they took turns sleeping. They all slept on the floor in front of the fire, everyone but Harry. When he slept, it was in the wing chair in the corner of the living room, right next to his backpack.

It was the longest night any one of them had ever experienced. They could see nothing outside the windows. They had to rely on their ears, and the rain drowned out any sound of humans approaching, if there were any. Now and then they noticed a fire in the trees at the bottom of the hill, but they could not make out what the people were doing. But they were still there, that was for sure.

Go away, Julie prayed as she knelt in the chilly den with the gun in her hands. *Just go away and leave us alone.*

Nerves were shattered everywhere.

Up at the observatory Rob Wynters was making his last plea for mass evacuation. Alex Granville, who hadn't had sleep for many days, snapped at him again. "I'll get back to you in an hour." Rob and Carter stood there. "Get the hell out of here, both of you." They left.

And so he sat there, the great general who'd been a hero in every situation he'd encountered. Every situation but this one. He looked out the little window of the makeshift building that sat up above the observatory. He couldn't see anything but rain hitting the glass. It was incomprehensible. And he'd be blamed; yes, he'd be blamed. They'd been out to get him for years, the guys who were jealous, the ones who wanted his position, who thought they knew more than he did. Now was their chance.

He let the dam burst. He smashed his fists on the desk and threw the walkie-talkie through the plastic window. It fell out from the force of the throw, and water rushed in. He got up and looked at the rain hitting the snow, the white stuff lower by a foot already, looking heavy and forbidding now. He'd been wrong. Carter had been right about the rain. He was right, too, about the impossibility of saving everyone. But even though it was a fact, he couldn't accept that. He couldn't accept failure, even if anyone else in his position would have done nothing but fail also. He pulled a cigar out of his pocket and lit it. He wiped his eyes and took a deep breath. He looked as he'd never looked before, unsure, unsteady, even afraid. He was old, and it showed. He'd had it.

He walked through the computer room, where Carter and the young punk, Rob, sat talking on phones. He ignored them, ignored the others milling about, the guys in Army uniforms, the women who seemed to giggle more than talk. He looked at Carter finally and said, "Do what you can do. Get your ass out. That's all anyone can do now." Then he opened the door.

"Where are you going?" Carter asked. He figured he was going down to the observatory, but he wanted to tell him no one was there, everyone was up at the disaster center. Carter had ordered the observatory to be vacated because he was afraid the water rushing down the mountainside would cut a hole in the grass in front of it, in the parking lot, and they'd be trapped there. They were safer up high. All they had to do from there was get down to the parking lot, the landing pad. *If* that too didn't crack under the melting snows.

But the general just said, "I'm going out for a walk."

"A walk?" Carter asked.

"A walk." No one stopped him. No one knew what he meant, but he was the general, still in charge, and who was to tell him he could not go out for a walk in any weather?

Alex Granville puffed on his cigar and looked around. The rain hit his bald head and soaked through his uniform in a matter of minutes. He saw the helicopter sitting down on the landing pad. He could barely see the big observatory building just behind it. He turned and walked up the hill, up Mount Hollywood. He thought about his past triumphs, his medals, his commendations.

He thought about when he was young and the honor and prestige and applause he'd received. That was enough; that was satisfactory. He didn't need this last hurrah which would be a final humiliation. Better he should be remembered for what he'd done in the past and what he tried to do in Los Angeles in the incredible blizzard. There would be a lot of famous casualties, famous movie stars, politicians, people in business. But there would only be one great military man who'd been lost in the storm. And he'd be remembered, if not for anything else, for that alone. That was plenty.

He continued to climb. He was wet. His cigar had fallen in a soggy clump at his feet. The snow was melting. The day was almost gone; it was getting dark. He never looked back.

Never.

THE TENTH DAY

SATURDAY, JANUARY 24

HIGH TEMPERATURE OF 80° IS REACHED BY NOON

THE SUNRISE CAME, SOMEWHERE OVER THE RAIN CLOUDS, BUT the backyard came into view, into focus. It was still raining, but not quite as hard. At least they could see what was happening.

Nothing.

Harry and Michael were on watch in the back windows, Bob in front. Julie and Lorna were both sleeping. Michael called everyone to see what he and his uncle were seeing. A yard, still, quiet, no one out there anywhere. But there had been one change, and a big one. At the right side of the yard was a pile of just about everything that had been outside in the yard when it had started snowing. The gang of people had found the lounge chairs, the picnic table, the old wheelbarrow behind the garage; they'd even ripped whole boards out of the back of the garage. What they'd done was made a bridge, a little mountain to climb, right up and over the fence into the nuns' yard. They'd gone over the wall to the Motherhouse.

"I heard movement out there all night long," Harry said. Michael was tempted to tell him he'd slept most of the night, that he'd been in the chair more than anyone. But he kept his mouth shut. "I knew something was going on."

"I never heard a sound except for the rain," Bob said. "But, they're gone." He said it as if he didn't believe it, as though the people were going to jump out from behind the trees and bushes and attack. But there were no more people. They were gone over the high wall. Now someone else had to deal with them. No one pondered what the sisters had done, what kind of confrontation had taken place, if any. No one cared. It was time to go, time to climb.

They dressed all at once. Then they strapped Susan onto the makeshift sled and tied her securely with three of Bob's belts. They watched as Bob gave her the last hypo. Michael gave the kitten another Valium, because she'd slept all night and was frisky now, and put her into the straw bag; Julie quickly stitched it shut with heavy thread. The cat cried but finally quieted down when she realized no one was hurting her. They fastened the straw bag to the sled, at Susan's feet. They each put their packs on their backs.

And that was it. They left the house. Julie turned back only once, her eyes brimming with tears, leaving the house she loved so much, knowing she would never see it again. She looked over at the house next door and said a silent prayer for Minnie and Sam. And then she looked up at the forbidding hill in front of them, the trees and the patches of snow and the mud and begged God's help.

They needed it. It was still raining, but not as hard as it had been coming down all night. In some spots the snow had melted down to the soil. In others it was still three or four feet high, drifts of wet, mushy, dirty snow. They reminded Michael of sno-cones, the kind you got at Santa Monica Pier. What he wouldn't have given to have been basking in the heat on the beach at that moment. Then it dawned on him. Christ, it's *warm!*

Bob led the group. Michael followed him, then Lorna, Julie and Harry. They took turns pulling Susan on the sled, and little Billy, though he was not saying anything, moved as briskly as the rest of them, most often holding onto Bob's belt.

Bob would get to a tree and hold onto it, and then the others would pull themselves up, holding onto the ropes that locked them together, until they were near him, and then he'd move again. Often the snow gave way and they slid in the mud underneath. Carter had been right; the ground thawed rapidly because it had never frozen to any depth. The whole hillside seemed to be a pile of mud.

The hardest thing of all was pulling the sled. The skis moved rather easily over the snow that was left but had a hard time getting over the dirt and leaves and roots from the trees. And the water from far above on the mountain was causing a small river—many small rivers actually—to flow down the side of the hill, cutting deep crevices into the earth. When they'd walked out of the house, they all noticed that the pool was filling with water and mud which was rushing in a kind of stream down the side of the steep hill.

Susan groaned. Bob had given her the last hypo just before they set out, although she'd been in terrible pain since midnight. He knew it was better to make her suffer in the house than on the sled. But if only she didn't have to suffer at all. *She's going to live,* he told himself. *She's going to live through this.* He was making the climb as much for her as he was for himself.

Maybe more so.

Only three months before, Southern California had experienced its annual fire season when the Santa Ana winds blew hot dry air into the basin, dropping the humidity down to nothing. The result had always been numerous brush fires which burned thousands of acres of land in the canyons and mountains. But this year had not been the worst for fires; however, the fact remained that from preceding years a lot of plant life which held the soft earth together was gone, leaving the ground open to the effects of heavy rain and mud slides. The city had made sure that the burned-out areas were reseeded with fast-growing shrubs to lock the soil back up. But the fires had been a few weeks late this past year, and in many a canyon area there was little strong growth to prevent the ground from moving wherever rains took it. While it was frozen and snow lay upon it, it was okay, it was stationary. But as soon as it got wet, as soon as it unfroze and the snow began turning to water, it would become a force bigger and more powerful than anything man had developed to fight it off with.

All he could do was flee.

A small search party went out early in the morning when it was realized that General Granville was neither at the disaster center nor at the observatory building, but the rain set them back. They tried again and found no trace of the man. Rob Wynters took charge of operations, whatever operations there were to take charge of, and it was a role he relished. "Remember once when I said you reminded me of young Gary Hart, who managed the McGovern presidential campaign?" Carter said to him, putting his raincoat on.

"Yes."

"Well, you remind me of him now more than ever."

"How so, Carter?"

"Gary Hart is now a senator in his own right. Good luck." He left the building to go down to the observatory to await Bob and his family.

But he began to have his doubts about the family making the trip up the hill. He saw the snow was nearly gone up on the mountaintop, and little was left around the observatory building. Water was rushing from the hills above, water with the force of cutting steel. There were chunks of the parking lot already torn away. He could see one major stream—it looked like a stampeding river—already beginning to take trees with it as it dug a deep canyon down the side of the hill, directly toward a group of Los Feliz homes. He figured the situation was the same in the other areas, the other canyons especially. Funny, that's where the people had been going—up. And now up would be the worst place to be, at least at the start. The homes in Benedict Canyon, Beverly Glen, Coldwater, and Laurel would no doubt come sliding down into the middle of the city. He remembered that LaCienega Boulevard had once been a major runoff from the water in the mountains, years and years before Los Angeles was even half the city it now was.

Carter remembered the flash flood in Colorado's Big Thompson River Canyon in 1976. Communities had disappeared in minutes, streets and homes and stores wiped off the map with a splash of water. And it happened because of a bad rainstorm up in the mountains. There had been no warnings of such a flood, only of thunderstorms up at the top of the canyon. And what had the thunderstorms caused? They had caused 40,000 cubic feet of water per second to flow through a section called the Narrows, which had been only 12 feet deep and was, by the time it was over, 30 feet deep. Carter did some math in his head and realized that was 320,000 gallons per second. Not that the same would happen to Los Angeles, but the water was going to be amazingly plentiful, amazingly strong. He looked over the city from the side of the observatory building and thought it wasn't wrong to assume the entire city could be, in the end, washed right out into the ocean. This arid place, where in past years droughts had done so much damage.

He turned and started up around the building, but something caught his eye. He moved close to study it. He looked around, seeing the water had dug deep holes, trenches, all around the base of the building. It was as though someone were scraping the earth away from it and all it was perched on was earth. What would happen when that earth was no longer there?

What had caught Carter's eye was a deep and wide crack in the foundation of the observatory building. The building was cracking. There was no doubt in his mind that part of it could conceivably crumble and go rolling down the hill.

Right into Bob Sheppard's backyard.

Carter went inside the building. Yes, one of the shortwave radios was still there. He wanted to call and see if they'd left yet. He would warn them against the water, the deep trenches, the gullies. He would tell them to go off to the side, to climb the hill more behind the Motherhouse than Bob's own place, since it looked to him that if part of the observatory wall were to go, it would be the side closest to Bob's land. The other side seemed strong, intact.

But there was no answer. The Sheppards had already started

out. Well, he was glad of that, because every minute wasted was a minute against them. He wondered what more he could do to help? Nothing, there was nothing else he could do. Just make sure there was a helicopter waiting, and be ready to go when they got there.

If they ever did.

Already, incredibly, the rains of the night and the rising temperatures had taken their toll on Los Angeles. Dodger Stadium had cracked open and collapsed because it had been built on a land-filled base, which eroded faster than the rain seemed to fall. The Pacific Coast Highway from Santa Monica north to Point Dume above Malibu—what had been Malibu—was completely wiped out by massive mud slides. On that highway, the famous J. Paul Getty Museum had crumbled into the Pacific, the countless art treasures floating out to sea in the cold water. The Pacific Palisades literally disappeared; Palisades Park was now one slope of mud and twisted underground telephone lines and chunks of what had been Ocean Avenue. The same was true of the rich canyons. Houses had oozed down the sides of the hills, stranding the residents who were lucky, in trees, up telephone poles or streetlight poles which hadn't fallen, killing those who were not so lucky. The rain was leaving now, allowing the northeasterly dry winds to invade the L.A. Basin. The Santa Anas had let the rains slip into Southern California first, so now they wanted their turn. Their turn to ravage the city.

But there wasn't much left to ravage.

The Sheppards knew they needed luck.

It was an immense struggle. They were doing fine for the first hour, but then they had a major setback. The rope around Michael had slipped off, and he lost his footing, sliding down into the snow and mud, and he took everyone with him. Susan's little makeshift sled had hit a tree and been stopped. But everyone had fallen, and they were shaken by it. Lorna had twisted her arm and found it very painful to use in climbing.

The rain had soaked through their clothing quickly, soaked them to the bone. And it was getting hotter and hotter. Bob finally discarded his heavy jacket and went on in his sweater. Lorna followed suit, and so did Michael. And each time one of them took off a piece of clothing, they all had to stop and wait while the person took off his backpack, got the jacket off, retied the rope around his waist, and then put the backpack on again. It was time-consuming.

There were other problems. The women, especially Julie, could not move as fast as the men. Thus, everyone's pace was slower than it should have been. They took turns pulling the sled. It was dead weight, difficult. Sometimes two of them had to lift it. Susan was delirious, crying out at times, looking as though she'd passed out at others. They stopped constantly to make sure she was all right, breathing all right. Her head burned of fever, and her lips looked parched and broken even though a steady stream of water was hitting them.

Little Billy did his best; but his legs were short, and he had difficulty climbing. Lorna had a terrible time with the shoes she was wearing. The others had shoes that fit, her hiking boots didn't, and they were wet, muddy, and nearly falling apart. All of them felt their pants being snagged on branches and bushes that miraculously appeared out of the snow. They cut their legs and scratched their hands; they had long since discarded their gloves because it was so warm.

And Michael asked everyone to stop at a time when there seemed no reason to. "What is it?" Bob asked. Michael looked embarrassed. "Michael, what's wrong?"

"I have to take a leak."

So he went behind a tree.

And Dawn cried incessantly. Lorna finally asked the group to stop so she could feed the baby. They sheltered under a big tree, and she put a bottle in the girl's mouth, which stopped her tears for a few minutes, but not much longer than that. Once they started moving again, the baby squealed. "God, I can't stand it!" Lorna screamed. But she knew she would have to.

They were about one-third of the way up the hill when Bob

tossed the rope around a small tree. "Dad," Michael called through the downpour, "I swear it doesn't look strong enough. It'll break."

Bob tested it. "No, it's gonna do it." He pulled himself up a few feet and looked back. "Okay. Come on." They started to move, and then they heard Bob shout. He fell backward, and Michael caught him. The tree had simply come out of the ground, uprooted. Water had been hitting it, hitting the base of it, and when the tree pulled out, the whole hillside seemed to go with it. A stream of water carried the snow and ice out from under Bob, and he hurt his back as Michael braced himself and stopped his fall.

"Dad, you okay?"

Bob nodded. "I'm sorry, I thought—"

"It's okay, you didn't know. Listen, I'll lead for a while."

"Yeah, Michael. I don't have any strength left."

So Michael braved the rain and the slush and the mud and led the party. Bob and Julie together pulled the sled, and Lorna held Dawn, with Billy at her side. Harry brought up the rear as usual, never looking back for fear he'd lose his balance. He was breathing hard, his chest hurting, his legs feeling as they had when he was making the long trek from the office to Bob's house. But he had something on his back which would make it all worth it. Hell, they could amputate his legs, and it would still be worth it. He had the world on his back.

They shed more clothing as they went. Everyone was down to sweaters, and even that seemed oppressive in the heat. It had to be 70°, Julie thought. Finally, she could stand it no longer. She asked them to stop a minute. She pulled her sweater up over her head and tossed it aside, standing there in the rain in her white blouse. Lorna did the same, but she was wearing no sweater. She'd had on a sweat shirt and only a bra underneath. So now she made the climb only in her bra. Michael took his shirt off and wore only his jeans now, with his backpack against his skin.

Everyone stripped down as much as they could except Harry. He was still in his ski outfit. He didn't want to set the precious backpack on the ground for fear the water would push it down the hill.

Carter walked around the building again. As the hours passed, the situation became more critical. The building was cracking in many places. The back wall over the hillside was nearly suspended in air, the earth having washed out from under it. There were large cracks in the plaster everywhere, even inside. He went up to one of the telescopes and searched in his pocket for a dime. Surprisingly it worked. He looked through it. The entire basin still seemed to be filled with snow, but he could once again see the red-tile rooftops and the flat roofs of buildings. But he also saw a house collapse and slide down a hill, right in front of his eyes. He happened to pan in on it, seeing it on stilts on a hillside in the Silverlake area. He watched as the stilts seemed to slide out from under it. The building just fell in. He thought he saw people falling in the rubble, but he wasn't sure. The thing he knew was it was happening all over the city. The earth was nothing but water mixed with soil. Six plus feet of snow would turn to water. It would wash away even the biggest and strongest buildings in the downtown area. He pictured the Atlantic Richfield Towers toppling, the Bonaventure Hotel with its glass walls, the place someone had called "the world's largest capuccino maker," falling into the lake in its lobby. He knew the sewers would overflow and the streets would become seaways, carrying lives out into the ocean. He already doubted that many people were alive in the beach cities. If only the rain would stop, he thought. Then there would be a chance to get some people out. He didn't want another Santa Barbara. There was no Santa Barbara left; it had, incredibly enough, washed into the ocean.

And Carter was right. At that very moment, all across the country, newscasts were reporting the change in the weather in Southern California. The temperature in Los Angeles was 72° and still rising, and it wasn't even noon. The mud slides already reported by military command posts were the worst in the history of the state where there had been terrible mud slides.

California's famous scenic Highway One did not exist any longer. No city was being spared the rain. San Francisco had missed the snow, but now some six inches of rain had fallen in less than twenty-four hours. The entire San Joaquin Valley was a kind of lake now; no city had been spared flooding, and some towns were completely wiped out. There were virtually no crops left in the state of California, which would cause an economic shock that would affect the entire world. The total snowfall had been six feet and seven inches in only eight days' time. And it was melting faster than it had piled up. It was science fiction, a horror story.

Horror story, yes, but it was very real.

The downtown section of Los Angeles was by no means spared. With the snowstorm, the railroad yards had ceased to be of importance, the trains freezing where they'd stopped. Now the rains knocked the tracks from their holdings, and whole trains fell over. The concrete aqueduct which was the Los Angeles River, where kids usually rode their bicycles, filled with flash floods and overflowed its banks. It was built on a natural riverbed, however, and the water had begun to undermine the tall buildings of the L.A. Civic Center. The Dorothy Chandler Pavilion in Los Angeles' Music Center seemed to move, as though a slight earth tremor had hit. Its huge windows fell out, the crystal chandeliers smashing to the marble floors. The building was ruined forever. Just down the hill, Bunker Hill, almost 2,000 people had been sheltered in the underground shopping center in the Atlantic Richfield building. The flooding hit them at once, filling the underground levels. Very few could get out as the waters rushed down staircases, escalators, even through cracks in the walls. Olvera Street, the birthplace of the mission which had become the city of Los Angeles, the chapel, the shops, the pueblo hotel, gone. An explosion in the Hilton Hotel rocked the nearby area, and the building crashed down onto the snow-covered Harbor Freeway and burned. The L.A. Coliseum had become a large swimming pool.

Power lines arced and snapped and electrocuted people all

over the city, literally frying them in the streets. One of the tall LaBrea Towers caught fire and went up like a torch, the orange glow lighting the wet skies. Roofs continued to cave in everywhere in the city, and walls followed them. People who had managed to stay in their homes during the blizzard were forced out now, and they tried to take refuge in cars which had been buried in the snow. But the water took them like rubber ducks in a bathtub, tossing them around as they moved with the force of the newly created rivers. All the major streets leading down from the hills, streets like Vermont and Western avenues, LaCienega Boulevard, Doheny Drive, streets which had been full of life, became pathways of destruction; they were now rushing rivers, and anything in their path was destroyed. The Arboretum near Pasadena was desolate, devoid now of any living plant. Pickfair, the famous home of Mary Pickford, already seized by hungry, homeless victims, burned to the ground; the panic-stricken people inside had tossed priceless antiques into the fire to stay warm, and the flames had been too powerful and had spread in a matter of minutes. The Harold Lloyd estate burned down, as did the homes of Lucille Ball, Cher, Danny Thomas, and other celebrities; other famous people such as Ronald Reagan and Dinah Shore and Vicki Carr lost their houses to the the mud. Most of the San Fernando Valley looked like the Pacific Ocean.

Almost everything was being destroyed, but people still fought for life, clinging to survive.

In the winter of 1846-47, a group of emigrants known as the Donner Party met with what was to become one of the most infamous tragedies in western history. The California-bound group, led by two families named Donner, were mostly from Illinois and Iowa, and in going west they took a little-used route after leaving Fort Bridger, and thus were delayed. By the time they reached the Sierra Nevada in October, dissension and ill-feelings had taken an emotional toll in addition to the rigors of the journey. And so they paused to recover their strength.

But an early snow caught them, snow falling deep into the

mountain passes, trapping them. Their limited food supply quickly gave out, a blizzard raged for what seemed an eternity, and bitter cold paralyzed even the strongest members of the group. The suffering in the huts on Alder Creek and what would become known as Donner Lake grew intense. A party that attempted to make its way through the snow-choked passes in December suffered horribly; the surviving members of the Donner Party were driven to cannibalism.

Finally, expeditions from the Sacramento Valley made their way through the snowdrifts to rescue the hunger-maddened migrants. Only about half of the original group of eighty-seven reached California. The survivors later disagreed violently as to the details of the disaster, blaming one another particularly on the topic of cannibalism. A monument to the group was later erected, and today Donner Lake is a popular mountain resort. Ironically, nearby Donner Pass has a U.S. weather observatory.

The saga of the Donner Party was well-remembered as bits and pieces of news filtered in from the Palmdale/Lancaster area. The reports shocked and astounded all those who heard them. The people—maddened by hunger, determined to survive at any cost—had been driven to cannibalism.

Besides the fact that the cities of Palmdale and Lancaster were the hardest hit, the most completely cut off, of any of the towns in the Los Angeles area, there had been a strike by the trucking union that brought food supplies to the area just a month before the snow began to fall. Pickets were still marching as the blizzard began. Supermarkets were cleaned out quickly and totally, and when the frenzied people broke into the grocery chains' warehouses, they found precious little supplies. With absolutely no way to get staples into the ravaged area, people killed others to get their food, and then, in final desperation, made food of the dead around them.

As the snow began to melt, the city unfroze and word trickled out. As with the Donner Party, the survivors violently disagreed. As with the Donner Party, the dissension and ill-feelings among the few groups that had banded together was intense. As with the Donner Party, only about half of the original number of residents of the Palmdale/Lancaster area would live to tell the horror story.

No one could say whether or not a monument of any kind would someday be erected.

The Sheppards were at the halfway point. Lorna's arm was terribly swollen, and she was in pain; but she gritted her teeth and tried to bear it. Complaining wouldn't help. Every last bit of energy and stamina was needed to make it the rest of the way. They could see the big observatory building looming above them. The destination seemed so far away and yet so close. Was it an illusion? They all felt they'd been climbing for days on end.

Michael jumped across a big stream of water which was cutting its way through the hillside. Then he reached out to help the others across, and his backpack got in the way. "What the hell am I carrying this silly thing for?" he asked out loud. He took it off and opened the straps. "Look," he called out, "this is the one with the food in it. Do you think we'll really need this stuff or should I get rid of it?"

"We won't need it," Bob said. "We probably only need the first-aid supplies. Harry's got them."

"No, I don't," Harry said. "I got the sleeping bags."

"No," Michael called. It was hard to hear through the steady downpour. He had to shout. "You've got first-aid stuff and a copy of Susan's medical file that Mom had at home." Julie had always kept copies of Susan's reports in case she should need emergency treatment where they didn't know her. It was quite thick, heavy. It felt as heavy as the sleeping bags—the paintings—had.

Harry propped himself against a tree and tore open the backpack. He pulled out a blanket, and inside it were bandages, bottles of antiseptic, pills, ointments, and a large, thick folder filled with medical records and hospital reports from over the years Susan had been sick. "Where . . . how?"

"Don't be upset, Harry," Julie said. "Michael put them in during the night. We were up talking, and I remembered the file and thought we should take it."

"Let's get moving," Bob said.

"Wait!" Harry yelled, his face showing panic. "Why *my* bag?"

"Well, because we thought we didn't need the sleeping bags as much as we needed medical supplies, and the food and what was already in the other bags."

Harry seemed crazed. "Pampers! You need diapers more than you need art. You need Xerox files of case histories. You need damn Bactine! Where are the sleeping bags? *Where?*" They'd never seen him look so out of control, never heard him shout so angrily, so loud.

"Jesus, Harry, settle down," his brother said.

"Shut up. Michael, where're the bags?"

"Uncle Harry, I just yanked them out of the backpack and left them right there on the floor. Actually, I think there was only one."

"Where on the floor? Answer me!" He slipped and started to fall. He caught himself. His fingers dug into the mud, and he clasped the roots of a tree. "Where, damn you, you son of a bitch?"

Julie gasped. What was wrong with him? "Uncle Harry, I think you're losing your mind, man, you know?" Michael snapped.

Harry got up and made a leap. He kicked the sled and nearly shoved it down the hill. Julie screamed and grabbed for it, and Bob did, too. He couldn't believe his brother was acting the way he was. Harry jumped on top of Michael, pinning him to the ground. "Where on the floor? Tell me, you little prick!"

Michael felt his head being pushed into the muddy soil. "On the floor in the hall. We walked right past them on the way out. Get the fuck off me!" He pushed the man up, but Harry jumped away on his own. He untied the rope from his waist.

"Harry!" Bob shouted. He was going down the hill, back down. "Harry, *don't!*"

"Bastards!" Harry called back. "You're all selfish bastards. You're all. . . ." His voice faded away. He slid and he fell and he got up and he ran, and soon he was gone, disappeared, in the snow, through the trees.

Bob started to move, but he stopped himself. "I can't go after him. I can't," he muttered.

Michael got up, covered with mud and slush. "Dad, he's lost his mind. Sleeping bags? I just pulled them out ... Mom saw me."

"There had to be something in them," Julie said. "That's the only explanation."

Lorna said, "He said art."

"Yeah," Michael said, "I heard it, too."

Bob shook his head. "It doesn't matter. We've got to climb. We can't think about it now. Come on."

"But he'll never–" Then Julie stopped. There was nothing that could be done.

Michael took the lead again, and they clawed their way up the hill. It was warm now, just like an average California summer day. The sky was brighter than before, and the clouds seemed less dark, less thick. The sun was trying to get through. The winds were Santa Anas, that was for sure, hot and dry. And the rain was finally stopping. The water dropping on them fell from tree leaves, from the pine needles which had survived the snow.

They pushed on, lifting the sled with its heavy weight, carrying the little boy over deep gullies the water had dug. Every so often the little kitten clawed at the straw purse she was in. Lorna clenched her teeth in pain as her arm throbbed. Michael caught the pocket of his jeans on a branch and ripped half the rear out of the pants. He climbed the hill with his bare ass sticking out. It gave them something to smile about. "You're going to be naked as a jaybird by the time we get up there," his father said.

Michael said, "I've been wanting to get a tan for weeks."

The rain had stopped, but the melting snow continued to push water down from the tops of the mountains. The observatory creaked, and parts of the west wall already had begun to collapse, chunks of cement stairs being carried down the hill with the little rivers. Carter stood on the east side of the building, where he knew Bob and his family would come up. If they would come up. He'd give them another hour at most. The building wouldn't last more than that. He stood there and hoped.

Harry rolled down the last few feet. He felt himself finally on flat ground and looked around. He was against the wall which surrounded the nuns' place. He looked to his side and saw water and mud rushing into Bob's swimming pool. He tried to get up, but he couldn't move; he seemed to be paralyzed. He rested for a minute, looking up at the bright sky. It hurt his eyes. He wasn't used to it. *By God, maybe the sun would be out yet today,* he thought.

Finally, he pulled himself to his feet and walked through the yard. In places the snow was still in drifts, and in other spots he could see the red brick of the patio. He heard a gushing sound and saw water pouring from the drainpipe, the open valve leading from the pool. Water was up to the back door by now, and when he opened it, he saw that it had trickled inside, over the oak floors, and was making its way to the carpeting in the living room.

There was the sleeping bag, just as the little bastard had said it was, lying right there. Shit, he'd just walked by it on the way out. It was still rolled up, tied. No one had even guessed anything was in it. He unrolled it and took out the canvases. He cried out in glee and hugged them to his body.

Carter thought he could see movement. Not water, not the trees, but skin, a human being, some slim man with no shirt. He called to him, but the guy obviously didn't hear him. So he eased himself down a bit, holding onto the trunk of a tree, and then found firm footing on a rock and started toward them. He finally could make out the figure. It was a young man, and he wasn't wearing anything but a pair of jeans and big boots. It was Michael Sheppard. "Michael! Mike!" he called.

Michael finally looked up. He saw Carter waving both his arms at him. *"Hot damn!"* Michael yelled. He turned to the rest of them, who were about fifteen feet behind him. "I see him! I see Carter! We made it!"

Not quite. There was still a way to go, and it was the most difficult of all, because the water was taking everything in its path. Julie remarked it was like trying to climb up Niagara Falls. Mud and rocks and bits of pavement from the parking lot came rushing at them as though someone were tossing them, trying to hit them. There was no snow left under their feet anymore. It was nearly impossible to pull the sled; they had to carry it. Susan moaned and turned her head deliriously.

Bob saw Carter and felt his heart quicken. This was it, the end of the line, and they *would* make it. He felt a new surge of energy. It was going to be over in a few minutes. He grabbed Julie's hand and squeezed it tight. His feelings rushed through her body without the need for words.

Carter reached out, and Michael grasped his hand. Carter helped him up onto the rock. "We have to move fast. I think the whole building is going to come down." Carter patted him on the back. "I knew you'd do it."

Michael had no voice left. Shouting all the way up the hill had taken its toll on his vocal cords. He sat down and pulled on the rope with Carter, pulling the sled up to the rock. Then they both grabbed it and carried Susan and Samantha up to a flat piece of cement next to the crumbling building. When they turned around, they saw Julie coming up the path with little Billy, who was walking by himself again now. Then Lorna with the baby, and then Bob, who looked the worst of all, as though he were going to collapse.

"Come on, we've got to get up to the building up there," Carter said, pointing.

"Hey, it's falling apart!" Bob exclaimed. And sure enough, the Griffith Observatory was beginning to collapse. They all looked up at it through red eyes. There was a loud crunching sound and they turned to see one of the upper pillars on the southern wall of the observatory fall out and crash to the ground below. Three large pine trees fell under the weight of the cement and plaster and steel bracing.

"Good God," Lorna said.

"Come on, we're taking the helicopter at the top there,"

Carter said. They had no choice. The chopper which had been sitting in the parking lot, on the landing pad, had fallen over as the parking lot had come apart.

"It's a long climb," Michael said, looking up at the muddy road leading to the little building.

"The tractor," Carter said, pointing to the big machine at the side of the road. "We're going to brave it in that."

And they all hurried to the big machine. They unstrapped Susan from the cocktail table sled, and Carter carried her. He still had strength. Julie pulled Billy alongside her. Lorna had the baby, but she felt her arm was going to fall off, so Michael took her from his wife. Bob walked along behind them, barely moving. He had never felt so weak in all his life.

They sloshed through the mud until they came to the big tractor. It looked like a cross between an Army tank and an earthmover. They began to climb on. Carter set the sick girl down, and Julie sat next to her with the straw bag between her legs. The others huddled around. Lorna and Michael clung to each other. The tractor started, and behind them they heard another loud crash. Another pillar had fallen off the building. The whole thing was tilting. It seemed to be hanging onto the edge of the cliff by only a thread.

Carter put the vehicle in gear, and the treads tore through the deep mud. But they moved. They started up the mushy road, slowly, getting closer and closer to the little building, closer to the helicopter, closer to freedom.

Harry tore through the kitchen. He looked in the cabinets under the counters, in the pantry. Nothing. Then he looked under the kitchen sink and found what he wanted: a box of heavy-duty trash bags. He opened one on the counter and slid the precious paintings into it and closed it with the plastic tie. Then he slung it over his shoulder and looked at the floor. An inch of water was already covering the floor of the kitchen.

He walked out into the yard. No rain anymore. That was good. He would have to make the climb again, but he could do it. He didn't need them. There would be many helicopters up there. He didn't have to worry. He ran to the trees and started up. He had a smile on his face. He'd been set back again, by that little bastard, but he had survived it. And survive he would. The dream of the villa and the sun and the beautiful paintings hanging on his walls filled his mind. He could think of nothing else.

The tractor came to a halt as close to the building as was possible. One helicopter was waiting. Rob Wynters came out of the building. "Almost everyone got out," he said to Carter. "I'm here with two others. We've called out everyone, every damn thing that'll fly. It's the best we can do now. I'll get out on the next chopper. You get going."

Carter led the others toward the large Army helicopter. But just as he was about to lift Susan up and set her inside the big machine, the ground seemed to rattle. At first they thought it was an earthquake, but they all turned in the direction of the earth-shattering sound coming from behind them. What they saw was the most astonishing sight yet.

The Griffith Park Observatory crumbled before their eyes. It vanished. It collapsed and slid down the hill with a mighty roar. All that was left was mud.

Harry Sheppard heard the sound and felt it in his feet, in his whole body. He had time only to look up once, to see the wall of concrete coming down on him, like an avalanche in a movie. He tried to cry out. His mouth opened but he couldn't make a sound. He fell backward onto the black garbage bag as a chunk of cement and tile and twisted steel bracing flattened him and ended his life with incredible force.

The sky seemed to be raining pieces of the building. Trees fell with the walls of the observatory. The wall behind the Motherhouse of the Sisters of Saint Theresa collapsed, the wall which had been built to withstand anything. The telescope which had stood in the dome of the building lay at the bottom of the Sheppards' pool, and where their house had been lay stone, plaster, tile, rubble.

And in the midst of it all, barely noticeable, chips of brightly colored pieces of canvas, little chips of oil paint floated through the still-rushing water, all the way down to the street, down the hill and into the sewers.

Michael gave Lorna his hand and lifted her into the helicopter. Then Carter lifted little Billy up into the waiting aircraft, and Bob and Julie pulled him inside. Then Carter himself got in and closed the door. They took their backpacks off, the mementos of what had been their lives. The pilot was ready. He started the engines. Lorna closed her eyes as she felt Michael's arm around her, as she felt the warmth of her little daughter pressed against her breast. Bob and Julie held hands. Susan opened her eyes and looked around. Bob ripped the straw bag open and set Samantha at Susan's side, and the girl was conscious enough to bring her arm up and wrap it around her dear kitty. Then they felt a jolt, and they were moving. Bob and Julie and Michael and Lorna got to their knees and looked out over the mountains, over the city, over the ocean as they rose far above it all, above the nightmare they'd lived through. No one said a word; no one even cried. The roar of the chopper's blade filled the compartment. The only feeling in their hearts at that moment was relief. Relief that it was finally over.

As their helicopter moved inland, away from the melting snow and rushing waters and death and destruction, a locust rain of rescue helicopters came over the mountaintops, filling the skies, bringing the one thing everyone in stricken Southern California had lost by this time. The sight of thousands of evacuation aircraft brought people *hope.*

And, for the first time in over a month, there wasn't a cloud in the sky.

The sun was shining.